'Relentlessly paced actio
with humour and the touc

Debbie Morton

'My anxiety, excitement, anticipation and my relief throughout the story kept me reading. The tongue in cheek style, the retro feel to the story and the humour which flowed throughout kept me laughing, even during adversity.'

Camilla Davis

'A story tough as granite, papered with razor sharp characters, all guns blazing, an awesome read!'

Laurie Brooks

'Always entertaining, full of action and humour, with a quirky vein of noir running through it.'

Laraissa Nevins

'Fast paced, if this was a film, you wouldn't have time to put the kettle on! Humour and credible characters!'

Mary Simon

I found this book was crying out to be read I couldn't put it down. I enjoyed the subtle sometimes in your face humour. The action was well written the retribution justly deserved. I enjoyed the creeping love story it was heart-warming.

Kelly Rodrigues

Rock Paper Scissors Bullet

G. R. Marks

A Requisite Read Book

First published in England
By Requisite Read Publications 2023
*Requisite Read Publications, created and
reserved for the publication of works by
G.R. Marks, only.*
ISBN 978 1 7393024 0 5
eBook ISBN 978 1 7393024 2 9
Rock, Paper, Scissors, Bullet
Copyright © 2023 G.R. MARKS
All rights reserved

THIS BOOK IS DEDICATED TO THE
MEMORY OF JOE AND CONNIE BROWN

Thank for your
Help Janet

PART ONE

Russia's president is nothing but an alpha male autocrat, a coward, a bully, and a murderer who disguises his criminality by pretending the west hates us, therefore we must be Sabre-rattlers to display how tough we are.

S.I.A. PALCHIKOVA

ONE

1989 is the year it happened, totally unexpected, it will go down in the annals of history, it had changed lives before it happened and will change lives forever after, it has been prayed for, dreamed of, it is a rite of passage.

Dick snapped his notebook shut, an hour and a half to write four-and-a-bit lines, he pondered before opening it again, he grabbed his pencil.......

The name's Chase, Dick Chase, I'm a one-time New York cop turned gumshoe, that doesn't make me Spiderman, he's some character in a kid's comic, I'm for real, very for real. I buy my suits at Larry's Welcome Mall, they cater for over 6 footers, I'm 5.10, I've got long arms, they come in handy if I've gotta punch the lights outta some low-life criminal trash. Oh yeah, I guess I must have struck lucky on the follicle front – I've got a full head of dark hair. This is my true story, I didn't change my name to protect my identity, why should I, if I did, I wouldn't get any credit.

'Hmm, not bad.'
He knew it was going to happen, where, when, the exact time and place, it's not the above, they're a random set of thoughts that popped into his head, they do that, random thoughts, dip into his brain. Dick fancies himself as a writer and keeps

threatening to jot things down, but for now, he's about to make some history, this will happen, it's not Dick's past, it's his present, he's got forty-five minutes. He's been studying the news of late, it's a Monday or Thursday, a prostitute is murdered, the time of death is always around midnight, the cause, strangulation by sheer nylon. So far it's five victims, all prostitutes, all soaked to the skin, the police think it's random, some aquatic obsessive on a quest. That's where they've been going wrong, Dick's analytical brain has sussed it, there's a pattern, he knows exactly how it plays out, he could write a book about it.

Down an inconsequential back street, the sort that doesn't appear in the brochure, depicting its ill-lit qualities, or the fact it's a druggie's nirvana, no one takes any notice of an unwashed, tobacco-stained, shiny suited bum, dozing on a nest of flat cardboard boxes in the doorway of a closed bookies, situated in this Manhattan trace-dystopian hangout. A half-drunk, giggling female stumbles out of a taxi, she leans in to pay her dues before draping herself, wantonly, against a billboard, one of many fronting a building site. It's nearly the witching hour, slowly making its way up the street is a municipal road cleaner labouring amid its jettisoned cloud, the mist diminishes before, a couple of yards further on, it pulls up in front of the girl, she laughs, falsely, unafraid, it goes with the territory. The bum sees beneath the dripping, grease-laden undercarriage her feet step up, she's in the cab, already he's across the street. The driver looks around as the girl plies her trade, the bum, let's be clear, it's Chase, is indifferent, it's expected, a diversion. Through a low window designed to spot undertaking cyclists, all he sees in the folds of the overalls, strung across the jerk's legs, is a pair of tights. Too soon to have relished the hedonic act, the jerk grabs the tights in each hand and quickly crosses his fists to pull them firmly around his victim's neck, she struggles, Dick slings the door wide open.

'I'm gonna blow your brains out jerk, got any last requests?' The driver swings around and glares at him.

'Screw you asshole, you must be….' Dick blows his brains out.

'Joking?' A single pigeon, flustered, frightened, scrambles from behind a billboard and flutters off into the black vacant night, Dick looks at the blood-splattered girl and smiles as he hands her a hundred dollars. 'Look at it this way Honey, you'll clean up, he won't, you've saved the lives of some of your co-workers, without you we wouldn't have caught him.' He looks about, content with himself, a warm tingle coursing through his veins, this is his kind of justice. 'The police will be here soon, tell them.' He grins at the girl. 'Tell them it was Super Bum.' He walks off, now a fitter-looking, larger-than-life bum than the girl remembered when he first approached her, and again, when she laid eyes on his pathetic shape in the bookie's doorway.

*

It was a hot July Saturday, the phone rang, 10 a.m. New York time, I remember because I'd been staring aimlessly at the clock wondering whether resigning from the New York police department had been one of my better moves.

'Dick Chase, private investigator, no felony too small.' The male caller presented badly with what a decade later will be termed a sexist remark.

'Put me through to Chase will you lovie?' I lower my voice.

'This is Chase speaking.'

'The name's Henry T. Broadmain, that's some smart chick you've got working your golf ball, I think my wife is seeing another man.' I know the name, he's a wealthy oil tycoon, but what it didn't say in last month's edition of Petroleum Probed was, Broadmain is a male chauvinist failed psychic. Broadbenzine, with its sister company Main Oil, runs about every third gas station throughout the northern States, I told the mogul we'd better talk in my office, he agreed and I gave him my address. It's a six-story brownstone with windows to match, it's a dump, but it's conveniently situated above a burger bar. It must be a far cry from the opulent elegance of his offices on the 46th floor of the Sky Spirit building down Central Avenue. The weather's a real scorcher, in New York the crime rate has fallen, have you tried wearing a stocking over your head through a heat wave?

Broadmain is in his late fifties, he's medium height and medium build, that's where mediocrity takes a back seat, he's immaculately manicured from his fingernails down to the welts of his crocodile skin shoes. His wife is on the board of Adheezyeasy, the famous glue company in Mineola, Long Island, they've recently had a new director, Leo Schoeman.

Guess what, ever since Mrs. Broadmain has been coming home at odd hours, staying out all night, and worst of all having too many headaches, yeah, she drives a pink Cadillac. Broadmain agreed my fee and as he disappeared into the clawing, saccharine atmosphere generated by grilling burgers and fries coming up from downstairs, I said I'll be in touch.

*

It's Monday afternoon, my garage didn't fix my wheels, I've been loaned a courtesy car, my plan is to hang around the glue factory till I spot the pink convertible, with a bit of luck I'll have this case sewn up by the end of the week leaving me free to enjoy a sunbaked, Bourbon-laced, body-hugging, beach lazin, thigh-parting weekend with Chantel the delight of my life, well, the last two weeks anyhow. It's just gone three and as I make my way to the glue factory I spot Joe's Café, a seedy, prefabricated place with bent Venetian blinds looking like ten people are peering out to see who's just rolled up. Inside it's a pine fest, rusting radiators, blinking fluorescent lights, there's an ominous dark patch on the ceiling, a large panoramic of old New York pasted to one wall is curling at the corners. Half a dozen lorry drivers pay me scant attention over their eggs and waffles.

'A steak sandwich and a coffee, Joe.'

'My name's not Joe it's Red.' The guy gave me short shrift.

'Hey Pal, I gave you a promotion, there's no need to get stuffy.'

'I'll stuff you in a minute *Pal,* Joe was killed on his own forecourt, run over by a glue tanker.' How about that, we're Pals already, I gave Red my disarming smile. Over my sandwich I ponder the link between Joe being run over by a glue tanker and my case, but I can't get Chantel and the prospect of some extracurricular fun time activity outta my head so I go over to the phone booth to firm things up, there's no answer, hmmmm.

As I park outside the factory, I can hear a hooter blasting off into the dusk, it's a grey concrete building with ironwork sticking out all over, two galvanized stacks like great Canadian red pines stripped of all their foliage eject swelling white steam that rises and melts into the blue-grey evening sky. I don't have long to admire the view, amid the mêlée of vehicles jostling for position on the home run is a pink convertible, driven by a lady, I bet my bottom dollar that's her.

By the time we hit the city, dusk is upon us, Mrs. Broadmain makes a beeline for the train station where her fancy man waives her down and gets in, I didn't see his face but I know it's not her husband. We head for the docks to a familiar restaurant, The Spaghetti Boat, as they enter between the alfresco tables and traditional potted olive trees, I tag along behind, once inside I make for the phone booth, still no answer Chantel's a busy girl. I take a table next to the fish tank, I've got one eye on the menu the other on Mrs. Broadmain, she's in her early forties has dark wavy hair, a big mouth and staring eyes, she's staring at the gigolo sitting opposite, she laughed out loud, maybe he told her a dirty story.

We're on coffee when she gets up to make a phone call, my luck's in, I've bugged the booth, I take out my receiver, attach the earpiece and tune in.

'I'm with Fields' partner now.'...'No Leo, he doesn't suspect a thing.' The trouble with these cheap bugs is I only get to hear half the conversation. 'I'm sure he's not interested.'...'Exactly as we planned.'...'Don't you trust me, listen, tell me about West Berlin?'...'The Spree-Havel hotel, got that.'... 'Wednesday, British Airways.'...'Flight BA 904, check in by 1300hrs. Ah ha, what about tonight?'... 'I'll make it worth your while.'...'Hmmm, I'll look forward to that, ciao.'

She hangs up, refreshes her lippy, and heads back to her fancy man, I wait a few moments before going to collect my bug.

'Excuse me buster.' King Kong appears from outta nowhere wanting to make a call.

'Sure thing, go right ahead, you were here first.' I never argue with gorillas after a meal, it upsets my stomach.

Broadmain drops Fields' partner opposite the train station, I'm parked up outside in a taxi rank-it's a dispensation. He stalls, looks up and down the street, then crosses over, oblivious he's walking towards me, for the first time I recognize him. Well I'll be, if it isn't my Pal, Red, a hunch says I follow her. I soon realize she's not heading home, instead we seem to be following the line. Eventually she veers down a side road marked "Railroad Marshalling Yard, No Through-Way", there's a line of garbage trucks parked up for the night, I leave my car on the end and continue on foot. As I reach the last one, I slide inside to view the scene through the windshield, I'm hot and beginning to sweat. To my front there's a sea of railroad lines, on the far side a slow suburban is meandering its way home, I can just make out the faces of the people inside, those conversing, reading, homeward-bound faces, strangely juxtaposed by the Neanderthal effect of the graffiti-daubed carriages. Soon it's gone and the panorama falls silent. The garbage truck stinks like hell, it's really hot now and I'm sweating like a pig. I smile, there she is, four wheels are visible between the bogies of a caboose, a concrete road has been laid across the tracks to allow access. A train leaving the city judders to a halt hijacking my view. A door opens and two bundles of early papers are dropped by the line, on the far side someone slips out, I see their feet scurry over to Broadmain's motor and climb in. The door slams, a bell sounds from somewhere up front, a distant ambulance screams shift and the train moves off. Before I can process the action on come her lights, she veers out of her hiding place and scattering today's headlines all over the tracks with her rear wheels she disappears up the road. I'm running to my car, someone got off the train and Mrs. B is the pickup, I dive into the driver's seat, start the engine and throw it into reverse, nothing happens, I rev harder, the engine's roaring but not budging an inch. 'What the hell?' I peer into the rear-view mirror and there, looming out of the blue-grey angry exhaust I see it. 'Augh Jesus.' A truck has parked behind me, we're fender to fender and I'm darn well locked in.

TWO

Click:

'Good morning New Yorkers this is your faaave disc spinner, Lue Walsh, saying a gigantic Hi! on day thirty-seven of this faaantastic heat wave. We'll be hearing from our eye in the sky, Fred Walters, he'll be keeping us up to date with the latest on the traffic situation out there in....er....er commuter land. And later, I'll be having breakfast with today's special guest, none other than....' Click:

'Mickey Mouse.' I scorned, switching off the radio, after last night I woke up like a bear with a sore head. I lay there piecing together my case, Mrs. B', Vanessa, I am a detective, and Leo Schoeman are setting up Field's partner, Red, the big question is do I have my cereals dry or borrow some milk from my neighbour across the hall? Ethel Rhynmould dotes over three scruffy poodles like she'd given birth to them herself, I can always depend on Ethel if I run short of supplies, I'm halfway through my bowl of Krunchies when the phone rings.

'Dick Chase, private investigator.' A match strikes the sandpaper strip of a book of matches.

'Hold it Chase.' The unmistakable, satisfied draw on a cigar puts my life on hold, I know it's Cainem, of Cainem Autos fame, I can hear the distant clout of hammers, the metallic clink of spanners and the shrill hiss of an air line. 'Chase, it's Cainem, tell me, on the level, are you in trouble with the law?' He knows about the car.

'Yeah, I'm wanted for bigamy in five States.'

'Listen Chase, I'm doing you a favour, have you heard the news, some poor guy, Red Heywood, was wasted last night, on a late train leaving the city, guess what, the cops found our car parked near the scene, some nosey passenger thought they saw the perpetrator get off at an unscheduled stop? They looked through my books, I kinda knew once they realized who you are they'd be off your case.'

'Off my case?' Cainem sobered up.

'Yeah, I don't have too many FBI agents on my books.' I like the sound of that, so I decide to play along.

'O.K. Cainem, just FYI, I'm on a secret mission right now, when will my car be fixed?'

'It's ready already, I had my men rush it through special.'

Jesus, did Broadmain and Schoeman waste Red Haywood last night, if it all adds up, Schoeman followed him onto the train, did him in and got off the same time the papers were dropped? It looks like my case just got some bigger shoes.

At around four, I decide to pay my client a visit, I park in the basement of the Sky Spirit Building and take the elevator to the 46th, the girl at reception is busy on the phone, I take a seat and pick up the late news, surprise, surprise, the body on the train *was* Red Haywood, curiously, the police are calling it suicide.

'Can I help you sir?' The blond, with rainbow talons and tight cashmere sweater is smart, so I lean on the desk for a better look at her intellect.

'Yes ma'am, if you tell your boss, it's Dick Chase, I'm sure he'll give you a raise.' She returns my smile and after a brief consultation over the intercom I'm shown in to Broadmain's office. We got over the niceties and charged with a very agreeable malt, I let him have it, except my theory, his wife's possible involvement in Red Haywood's "suicide", I decided to keep schtum about that, for the time being, I tell Broadmain all he needs to know.

'…they're the arrangements, it's the Spree Havel hotel.' As I finish off, he's scrabbling in a drawer while announcing his intention to send me to West Berlin, he wants the low-down on all the gritty details. 'Sure thing, but they're going tomorrow, I'll have to get my skates on.'

'Leave it with me Chase, I'll have my secretary arrange everything, I have a locker at the airport, my chauffeur will deposit all you'll need, the number's on the fob.' I catch a well-aimed key. We talk about the heatwave and its effects on the human body, his golf handicap has gone from seven to sixteen in a week, I sympathized, I haven't won on the dogs for over a month.

With the prospect of a night with Chantel I feel like a dog with two tails, I pick up a bottle of vino, that should get rid of any inhibitions on her part, while I need a downer. As I leave my car outside the neat, private apartment block where Chantel lives, my aftershave stings with the first cool breeze there's been in weeks. I ride the elevator to the ninth, Chantel's apartment is small but comfortable with a view from the lounge overlooking Central Park, grasping the wine and an orchid I press the bell... eagerly I press it again, this time I give it a long one. A shaft of light appears down the hall, with it I can just make out the dulcet tones of Caruso straining away on an old seventy-eight.

'You will be fortunate to receive a reply young man.' The voice belongs to a lady, it's slurred and she sounds English, I don't answer, impatiently my informant speaks again. 'If it is Chantel you are seeking she is on her honeymoon...**Did you hear me?**' Out of the blue I've lost all interest, so has the dame, who disappears taking the shaft of light with her. I'm alone, standing in front of Chantel's apartment, it's dark but illuminations from adjoining buildings are making coloured patterns that dance a mocking two-step as they flash on and off down the hall, I stuff the orchid through her letterbox and head for the nearest bar.

I don't remember much about last night, I drank a lot, I must have because as I lay in bed with my eyes closed it feels like I'm riding a roller coaster. I danced a lot too, with some broad...Helen. Ah yes, Helen, the divorcee from Jersey City, mmm, there's a nudge in my side.

'Do you want coffee?' I sit up, so quickly my roller coaster plunges as though on an endless dive, I fall back into the pillows where I struggle to regain my equilibrium.

'Helen?'

'Coffee?' It's Helen.

'Please, black, with plenty of sugar, tell me, am I in Jersey City?'

'If you open your eyes you'll see.' She left the room and slowly I opened my eyes, geez, I am.

'ARE YOU MARRIED, HELEN? No, you're divorced, I'M DIVORCED.

'I KNOW ALL ABOUT YOU, YOU'RE FBI, YOU'RE DIVORCED AND YOUR GIRLFRIEND STOOD YOU UP.'

'STOOD ME UP? SHE GOT DARN WELL MARRIED.' We're shouting at each other through the wall. 'D'YOU KNOW I DON'T REMEMBER ....what you look like.' As I'm speaking Helen returns, coffees in one hand, a paper in the other and a long cool menthol between her lips, clad only in panties and a bra she's the jackpot, a real stunner, a cropped blond about 5.7, intelligent, black glasses, spray tan, oh yeah, my guess is she swims a lot, I've got a concern. 'Did we make love last night?'

'Was I that good you remember, no, you fell asleep, just when things looked like they might be getting started?' She dragged on her menthol and passed it to me, I shook my head, she took one long look at the smouldering cylinder and put it out. 'Sorry about the glasses, I don't usually put the contacts in till nine.'

'There's no need to apologize, you look stunning, it's private eye by the way...not FBI...thought I'd better...for the record.'

Helen, turned out to be a real nice kid with a great sense of humour, she's just 30 and had been married six years to a real Casanova, he made curb crawling into an art. I banished any thoughts I had of congenial ravishment, now I'm sober I feel like I wanna make up for last night first. Over breakfast I break the news of my impending trip, Helen's disappointed but I promised to take her to dinner on Monday night, she's a secretary for some firm of attorneys in Manhattan, while she's making her face up, I try my hand at a jigsaw, the Grand Canyon, laying half-finished on her coffee table. Helen drives a gold Volkswagen Beetle she affectionately calls Goldie, as the three of us enter Holland tunnel I'm deep in thought, something is nagging me about the case, by the exit I'm fast asleep. As I sat dreaming the answer came to me, but as Helen tries to wake me with shouts and tugs on my arm, it disappeared back into my subconscious.

'Hey dreamboat, we're here, where did you park your wheels?' I opened my eyes to find we're outside the bar where we'd met the previous night, my car's across the street. A noisy garbage truck is descending on us from behind, it looks like all New York's trash has been dumped in this one street, getting out of the gold Beetle I speak to Helen.

'Don't forget our dinner date, I know the best Italian in town.'

'I'll be there, don't miss your return flight, or I'LL PUT YOUR OBITUARY IN THE NEW YORK TIMES.'

Helen is shouting as she drives off, I smile and raise an arm in a feeble attempt to wave, as I do, that nagging feeling returns. I look around, and there, across the street, singing out in vibrant blue neon, is the answer, Joe's Snack Bar, it's another Joe, in another place that concerns me, Joe's Café. Red Heywood was Joe Field's partner, he was run over

by a *glue tanker*, on his own forecourt, it looks like my case has just turned into a double homicide…..
Geez, is that cop serving me a parking fine?

'Hey Buddy, it's me, Dick Chase, ex-New York Cop.'

THREE

Back at my apartment I grab the phone book and look up Joe's Café, it all checks out his name is Fields, I decide to enlist the help of an old friend, I call the city police, I wanna speak to McDougall, fraud squad, McDougall is like the twin brother I never had, only I came out first, if you get my drift. While I'm being put through, my eye is caught by the movement of a squeegee operative in a cradle hanging from the building across the street, surplus water dropping from his wrung leather, like a necklace of diamonds, reflect the early sun as it creeps up behind us.

'NYPD, McDougall speaking.'

'Hi, Doogie, it's Dick, how's that gammy brain of yours?'

'Dick Chase, long time no see, what makes me think I'm about to break with police protocol?' McDougall is nobody's fool, I told him I want the lowdown on a couple jerks for a case I'm working on.

'O.K. ex-partner, I'll see what I can come up with, hey, why don't you give me the brief over dinner tonight, we can sink a couple of beers and talk about old times?'

'I'd like to Doogie, but I'm going away for a few days, on business, I'll call you at home, say around eight.' I gave him what I had on Fields and Haywood and bid my farewell, if I'm gonna make my flight I've gotta get my skates on.

I'm halfway across Brooklyn Bridge, heading for JFK, the day is beginning to warm up, I wind down the window and turn on the radio.

'......leaked out this morning about a security breakdown at NASA, for the latest news update we head straight there and join our man at the scene, Duke Nuke.'

'Thanks Bill, joining me now, is NASA's top press liaison officer, Commander Len Lewis. Commander, exactly what details can you give us on the breakdown?'

'The facts are classified, all I can say at this stage is during the past few weeks a person or persons has stolen data containing every conceivable scrap of information about the space shuttle program.'

'Can you elaborate commander?'

'Let me spell it out son, if this information was to fall into the wrong hands it would enable an enemy not only to build its own shuttle but to use it against us in the event of conflict. Apart from that we'd lose the lead in the space race.'

I switch off, espionage is a bit outside my league, I'm driving along minding my own business when something in the rear-view mirror grabs my attention, it's the pink convertible. As they cruise by I glimpse Schoeman, he's playing Parker to Vanessa's Lady Penelope, she's making her face up, or…I thought for a moment she was using her mirror to look at me, maybe they're onto me, I decide to ignore them till we arrive in Berlin, they can't escape midway across the Atlantic anyhow. At JFK I put my car in the multi-story and go collect the goods from Broadmain's locker, I'm now seated in the coffee lounge, I take a bite outta my raspberry croissant and begin to undo the package.

'Concorde'. I said it out loud, the man sitting next to me points in the direction of the departure lounge and mutters something about par excellence, I nod my head. 'We've come a long way since Orville and Dean.' Orville and Dean, geez who the hell are they, they're the Wright brothers aren't they? I look through the rest of the contents to see if there are any more surprises, there is, one big one, no hotel reservation, instead, there's a note from Broadmain.

Chase, your reservation isn't certain, they want cash. I left your card at home my wife may have seen it. I booked you in under the name Moody......Broadmain.

Great, now I'm Moody, broody Moody, I look inside the envelope, $600 in nice sealed new ones, right, that's it, now I'm money laundering, next I'll be passing secrets to the KGB.

*

The flight to London was a dream and the changeover at Heathrow went smoothly, Berlin's Tegel Airport was a textbook landing and pretty soon I'm in a taxi heading for the hotel, Vanessa and Shoeman are ahead of me, they can wait till the morning. We pull up at the Spree-Havel, as I cross the marble threshold, two smoked glass doors slide open, I shiver and go in. At the desk a small man who's busily fussing about like a gerbil making its bed reeled and almost keeled over at the mention of my name.

'Herr Moody, if you will please wait.' He scurried off out the back, what choice do I have? Keeping me company there's a big stag's head peering down, looking sorry for itself.

'Don't look at me like that, I didn't shoot you.'

'Herr Moody, I see you are admiring Tsar Nicholas, he is a beautiful specimen do you not agree?' Cold gunmetal eyes and a shock of steely grey hair, starting an inch above his eyebrows, owns the voice. 'We do have a last-minute cancellation, of course, you have the necessary payment.'

'How much is it?' My luck's in, here comes my spending money.

'Two hundred dollars a night for three nights, that is six hundred new American dollars, is your part of the bargain.' He leans forward. 'That includes breakfast.'

'Bargain, hm?' There goes my vacation sweater, I hand him the lucre.

'Thank you, Herr Moody.' He looked at me, or more like, he looked through me. 'I hope you will enjoy your stay in this "menial" city, while you are here you might like to take in some of the sights, I can recommend the Charlottenburg palace, I believe it is 17th century, then there is the imperial grandeur of the Reichstag, that is always a big one with the English, or if you are interested in space, as I am, you will find our Planetarium most illuminating. Now, if you will excuse me, I must deposit this in a safe place.' He disappears and right on cue the gerbil returns.

'You work a short shift here.' He gave me a look of distilled pity.

'If you will sign in Herr Moody the porter will show you to your room.' I sign in just below Mr. and Mrs. Smyth, they don't fool me one bit.

Once in my room I drop the latch and letting my holdall fall to the floor, I sling myself on the bed. Abruptly I'm jolted out of oblivion by someone knocking on my door, I look at my watch, it's time to make my call. I ask who's there, a male American accent seeps urgently through from the hallway.

'Let me in, I've got a message from McDougall.' I summon my inner gorilla and open the door, a smart Brylcreemed nine o'clock shadow, on a no-fuss square chin, entered, and made straight for the window on the other side of the room.

'Come in why don't you.' Slowly moving the curtain away from the wall, he peers out.

'I don't know what you're up to Moody but you'd better be good at it.' He is American, and he's armed, in my book, knowing it is halfway to owning it, I feel a match for him so I keep my cool, for the time being.

'This might come as a surprise to you Pal, but the only thing we've got in common so far is the name McDougall.' He lets go of the curtain and turns his face toward me.

'Well, Dick Chase, now we have something else don't we.' The wind whistles between the frames as the curtain breathes, and I stand down my gorilla.

'O.K. who are you and what's this all about?'

'My name's John Harris, I'm attached to the American Embassy, you're a New York cop turned gumshoe working for a man named Broadmain, ostensibly, it's a divorce job, about now,' He looks at his watch 'You're supposed to call a friend of yours, a cop, McDougall, he's gonna fill you in on a couple of wise guys, Joe Fields and some jerk named Haywood, is that enough to keep your curiosity satisfied?'

'What about the call, do I make it?'

'That depends on whether or not you want to blow your cover, I advise against it, we'll go and have something to eat in a nice safe restaurant and I'll tell you all about it.'

FOUR

Benjamin and Adrian Leven, father and son, are the unspoken, foremost experts in the diamond trade in Moscow, the whole of Russia, and the eastern hemisphere. Benjamin's grandfather, Morris Leven was a diamond mine manager at Kimberly, in the Northern Cape province of South Africa. At the tender age of nineteen, in 1872, Morris became known as the Kimberly Tsar, what was never known is by that time he was ferrying diamonds out of there at a rate of knots, neatly packed into hidden compartments in his luggage, and gifts that regularly made their way to the family back home in Moscow. To this day razor-sharp trading, a keen eye for the big one, and being in league with "certain" people and business associates across the world, especially in America, London and Brazil, has allowed the Leven Empire to flourish and bloom, boom is the better adjective. Of all its outlets nowhere has it asserted its authority as being the world's premier diamond supplier as it has in Moscow.

It's 1982, someone who is oblivious to all that is a stunning, nineteen-year-old woman fresh from a gruelling 6-month military training course, her name is Salinka. Amazonian by design, only she doesn't know it, she's 5.10 - out of heels, a cropped brunette that she's in the process of growing, she loves cherry gloss lips when she's not up to her knees in mud or halfway down a snow-driven mountain, she's got green eyes. For her security, that her inexperience does not allow her yet to realise, I will keep her full identity a secret. Salinka is back home in Moscow at the beginning of a well-earned 2-week period of leave. Travelling in a taxi, to visit friends on the outskirts of this Moscowtropolise, they pull up amid the busy lunchtime traffic. Salinka, looking around, settles her eye through the window of B. Leven and Son, where she witnesses a frightened old man shielding a younger man, the older man's face is so set with fear and horror, bleak and full of dread, she can't help but be moved by the scene. Her curiosity falls on two others, just a glimpse before the taxi pulls off reveals they are armed, it's like a snapshot has been taken in her brain. She cranes her head back towards the gone shop, but all she can see is the weapon, everywhere she looks, superimposed in her head, is the lethal black shape of a 9mm Makarov.

'Stop, pull over.' Salinka instructs the surprised driver who thought this lucrative fare was going to employ him for at least the next ten minutes. Preoccupied, his ride slaps into his open hand enough notes to tend his concern without complaint, in truth, at this stage in her career, Salinka has no clue what she is doing, or what she is going to do, but such is her sense of fair play she cannot stand by and let this obscenity go unchecked.

The adjoining premises is an old haberdasher's who, by happy coincidence, is another Jewish family-owned concern, their success owes a great deal to the Leven Empire whose friendship they have relished for over a century. Salinka's winning smile and quick thinking easily get her through the shop to the backyard, now niceties must be abandoned as she enters the rear of this diamond emporium. Without hesitation, but devoid of any plan, Salinka walks into the main shop where she immediately plays horror-struck and distressed.

'Oh my god, uncle, what is going on?' The Levens are confused, the gunmen are agitated, while Salinka, is on a roll, she puts herself in front of the old man, "her uncle". On the counter she spy's a wooden tray strewn with diamonds and some black velvet pouches loose at the neck, this "mystery niece" leans back and spills the tray on the floor. The enraged gunman forces his shooter at her, instantly his 9mm Makarov is in her hands, a little trick she has been practicing to perfection throughout her tough military training, as insurance she shoots the firearm out of the hand of the accomplice. The enraged gunman goes to grab her, Salinka strikes him hard across the face with his own weapon, the force of it makes him double up, she slugs him across the back of the head. At this point her peripheral vision is vital, Salinka shoots the accomplice in the temple, his Russian throwing knife hits the floor before he does, strange, her first killing, not what she had in mind for that day, she smiles at the father and son.

'The gunshots will bring the Militsiya running, I must go.' With straight fingers she strikes her brow in a salute and turns to leave.

'Miss, wait, just….' It's Leven junior. 'Take this, please, take it, this.' Salinka holds out her hand and Adrian places a small diamond in the middle of her palm, she smiles and nods her head in appreciation. 'I must go.'

Back in the present. As Chase follows Harris through the fire escape window in the gents on the third floor, Broadmain must be choking on his dinner, Dick is cursing him like hell. The escape led to a small courtyard at the back of the hotel, Harris has a smart Saab turbo parked outside, as they pull away Dick began asking questions....

'O.K. what's this all about, how do I know I can trust you?'

'Chase, why did you want a report on those jerks, did you know they were murdered?' I told him I'd read in the paper Haywood committed suicide, on board a late train, Harris shook his head. 'That story was put about by the cops because they were on to him, they didn't know you were involved till McDougall went waltzing into the records office asking for information on their two top suspects.'

'O.K. Harris, I believe you, now I'm not going any further till you tell me what the hell's going down.' Immediately he slammed his foot on the gas, the car lunged forward pinning me to my seat.

'From here it looks like you don't have much choice, the KGB will have you over the wall before you can say Edward Lee Howard, you've already met Streckovitch, the merciless head of the KGB, you'd better take this.' He took his foot off the pedal, leaned over, and opened the glove compartment, a small interior light came on, 'Happy birthday, take it, it's yours.' Inside there's a 9mm Smith & Wesson Chief Special, complete with ammo, it's cold, smooth, and slides nicely into my jacket pocket, I feel cock-a-hoop already. In fifteen minutes we've reached The China Wall, a poky Chinese hidden away in a West Berlin side street, we take a table at the back, Harris put a finger behind a bamboo curtain and raised his eyebrows, I get it.

'Don't tell me, a fire escape?' He clenched his fist letting the bamboo rattle back into place.

'How long have you known McDougall?'

'We met in '68, at police academy, a year there and we both got New York City, I went solo in 79.' While I'm speaking, I scrutinize his face, I'm a physiognomist, it comes with the territory, Harris is tough, loyal and holds his cards close to his chest. 'Why the interest in McDougall?' With a reassuring glance he offers me a cigarette.

'He put his neck on the line for you, that's why I've come out in the open, and why you're sitting there with that heater in your pocket.' A Chinese waiter hovered with a small pad and minute pencil, Harris made our order and watched the Chinaman disappear before returning to me. 'You've been set up, it's a red herring, the "Smyths" came down the stairs as you went up in the elevator, they're on their way to Paris as we speak. Broadmain and Fields go back a long way, it was Broadmain who arranged forged papers and references for Fields and Haywood, to secure them driving jobs with NASA, they were there a year when they upped sticks and vamoosed buying the freehold on a small roadside café.' I don't need it in Technicolor to see what's coming, it's the news broadcast on my way to the airport.

'Geez, don't tell me, they filched the space shuttle data.'

'Hey, you're good, and if I hadn't pulled you out so quickly Broadmain would have had you handing it over to the Russians, lock, stock and heat shield.' Before I can say anything, the waiter returned and began dishing out breakfast. Harris leans back and drags copiously on his cigarette while I sit fingering my left temple, and watching the steam come off the egg-fried rice, he continued. 'It stumped me at first but after I'd thought about it, it was obvious, it's in microfilm hidden in your return airline ticket, the KGB were simply going to lift it while you weren't looking.' I give him a long hard stare while shaking my head.

'How could anyone get all that information, even in microfilm, into an airline ticket? Broadmain gave me six hundred dollars in crisp bills, that's where the goods were stashed and I'll give you three guesses where they are now.' I catch the crumpled look of an agent who's just failed in his attempt to foil one of the biggest espionage coups this century, he jabs a thoughtful finger at the cuisine.

'Don't eat all the prawn balls, I'm going to the john.'

With Harris gone to powder his nose, I'm sitting here having my last cigarette and planning how best to gut a red herring, that's when I heard it, the merciless thud a silencer makes in the uncongenial, aqueous confines of a toilet cubicle, I knew Harris had bought it, I also knew it was no good trying to escape, before I can determine my next move, I'm joined at the table by Streckovitch.

'We meet again Herr Moody, or is it, Chase? I am not sure how you Americans pronounce fool.' He sat in Harris's chair and pushed his plate away. 'The Chinese are our allies, but their food, it is shit.' He glanced over my shoulder, the restaurant fell silent as my arms are grabbed from behind, another hand delves inside my jacket and withdraws clutching my birthday present. I'm released and the conversation picks up again like nothing had happened. A thin veneer of amusement turned into disdain. 'First things first, I think you know there are three men standing by the door.' Streckovitch parts the bamboo, as Harris had done, there are two more standing outside, he took a cigarette from a pack. 'Now you know the situation we can get down to business, this does not have to end badly for you, as it did for your friend, just as long as you, I think you Americans say, play ball.' He speaks holding the cigarette between his first two fingers while, in a practiced manner, he manipulates it, to and fro, along all his fingers, back and forth. 'What have you done with my microfilm, that is all I want to know then you will be free to go back to your United States, I do not think a "pack-mule" is such a threat to the Soviet Union?'

So that's it, Broadmain has double-crossed them leaving me to take the rap, not to mention Harris, that will account for the Smyth's disappearing act, I play for time, I pass him my card.

'I'm just a small-time private investigator with an office in New York, I do missing persons, divorce cases, a bit of collecting, here, take my card, you might need my services someday. A man named

Broadmain.....' Streckovitch stops me with a wave of his hand, he lights his cigarette and disperses the match smoke with his arm and a frown.

'Yes, Chase, yes, I know all that and I dare say you find missing cats. If you are, as you claim, small-time why would a man with Broadmain's resources hire you instead of Ralph Bliss Inc, Manhattan? They have twenty eyes on their books, I have their card too. Listen to me.' He leaned forward. 'I am, what is it in the English? A de-featherer of people's nests, to line my own pockets, I "worry" the opposition, I will be the next President of the USSR of that there is no doubt, this is my last assignment running the KGB before the top job will mysteriously become vacant.' Without taking his eyes off me he crushed the cigarette in his hand. 'Mr. Chase, I will personally go to great pains to extract the information I want from you.' Like a petulant child he crashed his fist on the table and shouted. *'Where is my micro-film?'*
I slammed my reply back with interest.

'Why don't you ask Broadmain? You toxic, chicken-livered, sadomasochist Red.'
Someone slugged me from behind, for a moment I couldn't move, then, the table came rushing towards me as I passed out.

FIVE

'Dick, Dick, is that you, you're home?'

'Hmm!?!' Half asleep I stretch my arms in the air lifting the handpiece, like a stunt dumbbell, toward the ceiling, quietly, more distant.

'Dick is that you?' As the cord fully extends the phone lifts off my bedside table, it swings over and hits the side of my face.

'Jesus!' I sit bolt upright only to find myself in bed in my own apartment, the sun is queuing up outside the blind. I drop the phone and before you can say road runner, I'm standing by the open window sampling the familiar aroma of Pedro's dish of the day wafting up from the extractor below. I know I'm good but not this good, how did I get here? A small voice in my head makes me think of Helen, it is Helen, shouting at me down the phone, I make a dive for the bed.

'Dick, where the hell have you been, you promised?'

'Yeah, I know Honey, something turned up, gee it's great to hear your voice.'

'Yeah well, some people have been hearing it all week, where have you been, why didn't you call?' Something Helen said focused my attention.

'What day is it Honey?'

'It's Friday 30th now why didn't you call meeee?' Helen's voice is a mixture of despair and concern, I threw the brake on my witty repartee and unleashed my nurturing parent, she adopted her natural child leaving the way clear for my gibbering idiot, I didn't know where the hell I'd been. Helen was as nice as pie, I told her I'm in a spot of trouble and need some time to sort things out, she accepted my invitation to dinner tonight and we hung up the best of friends. I worked out it had been two days since my tête-à-tête with Streckovitch, two days, where had I been all that time and why didn't I know about it? First, I'll have breakfast, then I'm gonna pay Broadmain a visit, the prospect of confronting Henry is burning a hole in my feet.

I'm halfway downstairs when I meet my neighbour Mrs. Rhynmould, with Arnie in tow, Arnie's one of her pet mutts. Conversation soon turned to what I had delivered last night, news that made me guess this is where I came in.

'What do you think it was Ethel?'

'Well let me see, it was heavy, it took four or five men to carry it, it's difficult to see through the key-hole…I mean.' Mrs. Rhynmould blushed.

'Don't worry Ethel, I always check out strange noises, especially at night.' She smiled confidently.

'Why, I'd put my money on a new closet.' I'm saved by the timely choking of Arnie's chorus craving the kinship of doggie kind, Ethel's face lit up. 'I'd better go, they miss him so much, they miss you don't they Arnie.' I smile, I wouldn't miss the smelly mutt if NASA put it into orbit. With their clinical precision and attention to detail I knew the KGB wouldn't let me down, as I approach my parking spot, there's my car, I also know I'm being followed as I edge my way through the smouldering traffic toward Broadmain's office, but I don't care, all I can think of is Harris and his attempt to get me out that cost him his life. I park in the executive bay next to Henry's Roller and take the elevator to the 46th floor.

I walk into Broadbenzine like Wyatt Earp walking into the O.K. Corral, there's an icy silence while his secretary, a new one, runs my features through her brain. The phone rings, she holds a hand up and answers it, I smile, hold my hand up and walk into Broadmain's office. Henry's on the blower, he looked surprised but I wasn't, I'd planned to rip his phone from its socket. He protested but that subsided when he saw the business end of my Colt 45 pointing at his head, he sat up and raised his hands in front of him displaying the instinctive passive-submissive role a primate adopts when confronted by a dominant male holding a Colt 45.

'Now look Chase, let's talk this thing through like civilised ....' Were Broadmain's last words, strangely I find myself pinned to the wall, he's been shot through the head, someone with a high-powered rifle, telescopic sight, and a grudge. The bullet travelled clean through his cranium and lodged in the wall opposite. A deformed crimson silhouette is being drawn by the blotter his head is lying on, while drifting in through the holed pane the distant hum of all Manhattan life, unmoved, unknowing, continues along the road towards its own unbidden but inevitable mortality.

Bizarrely the intercom on Broadmain's desk is giving me a course in Russian for beginners, as my concentration becomes attuned, I realise it's our friends from the KGB, I was expecting them to turn up but I wasn't ready for this, the voice belongs to a dame.

'Mr. Chase, I very much regret what has occurred, I was on my way to warn you, it is important we soon shall meet, I will be ringing at six to your apartment to arrange this, but for now your police will soon be here so I must not be, goodbye Mr. Chase.' The machine fell silent, that information was brought to you by your friendly KGB agent, visit your local branch for a quick chat and a bullet in the head, I think not, mind you if the dame is as sexy as she sounds, I might just risk it. I entered reception to see but I'm too late, like an elusive siren from some Greek myth, she'd vanished. I keep Rowena, talking till the police arrive, she's young, this is only her second week, Broadmain had given her a good package, private health care and three paid vacational flights a year, I didn't have the heart to tell her. Before long she's being led out by a policewoman who I happen to know is one of the best. Now it's my turn to be led out, it seems my story is so interesting they just have to hear it at the station.

I'm sitting in a squad car heading down fifth avenue, we keep passing the same dark blue limo with black tinted windows, either it's model of the year, or someone's playing hide and seek, I can't help thinking they've found me. I'm not cuffed so I'll make a run for it at the next set of lights, as we pull up the limo stops next to us, so close I can't open the door anyhow. The lights are on red and I just know something's gonna happen on green, quickly I scan the interior of the squad car for a means of escape, there's no trap door but there is the next best thing, I pull it up and lay it over my knees.

'A bulletproof jacket, this is an impressive bit of kit, are these on general release?' I'm looking at the driver as I speak, but I'm keeping an eye on the opposite set of lights, he mumbles something about it being on trial but I'm not listening, my concentration is on staying alive. The lights begin to change...amber, two three, red, I look at the limo simmering in drive, I see the window begin to creep down, I'm ready, two three amber, two three green, I thrust the jacket hard against the window next to me. 'Hey, made in Taiwan!' As I speak, I can feel the shock waves pound through my arms, I follow the incoming around as it cracks through the windshield, the limo speeds off, it was like being on the receiving end of a volley of punches from the Rock. I look at the two dumbstruck cops. 'Hey, I think this one has just passed the test.'

SIX

'Ah, Chase boy, sit down, sit down, here have a cigar.' The chief takes a Havana from an unvarnished plywood box then slides it in my direction, without taking his eyes off me he lights up snatching four or five quick puffs. 'One of our agents bites it in a toilet cubicle and my boy is still in the game, hm, you can tell me, son, shoot him yourself did you? Accidental discharge was it, eh?' What were you doing with him in a toilet cubicle in the first place, that's what I wanna know, don't answer that Chase, I know you're straight. The chief puffed matter-of-factly. 'Now listen to me son, on the record I don't wanna know what you're up to, I've got strict instructions from the top not to ask, off the record I wanna know every darn thing that happened, is happening and is about to happen right down to when you last changed your underpants, and listen up boy, if one of my men so much as catches a cold while you're on this case I'll have you kicked out the force.'

'I'm already out chief.'

'Well then I'll have your licence revoked.' The chief's phone rang, he holds a hand up like he's stopping traffic.

'The chief'…'Yep'…'That's right'…'He what?' … 'They what?' It must be his shrink, directly he calms down. 'He did, well I never.'…'Yeah, a copy in my office, pronto, thanks.' The chief hangs up, takes a moment and changes colour. 'You didn't tell me you'd just saved two of my young officers from having their heads blown off, very commendable, and it seems whoever it was is pretty desperate to hit you after missing once and getting that broad bean magnate.'

'It's oil magnate chief and I'm sure it was him they were after.'

'Well, oil magnate what the heck? You saved two of my men, hmmm, that's a good day's work in my book son, a good day's work. I've had it right from the top not to ask about this case, do you realise that's the first time in 30 years' service that's happened to me, right from the top?' Shaking his head in disbelief the chief went over to the door, paused, took a couple of puffs on his cigar and opened it. 'Go and get'em boy, and remember.' He pointed the soggy end in my face. 'We're all rooting for you son.' Darn it, as I said goodbye I saluted, it just slipped out, as I passed through the office the whole day shift, who are a bunch of comedians right down to the last cop stood up simultaneously and saluted.

First, I gotta square things with Helen, with possible threats on my life I thought we'd better stay in tonight. I catch a cab, Helen's office is on 79th street east, between 2nd and 3rd avenues, it's an impressive cream marble block divided like a chessboard with tinted green windows, according to Helen it's supposed to make for a stress-free working environment. I amble over to reception and ask the lady if I can speak to Helen McCluskie.

'She's gone to lunch with clients from the Soviet Union…Ah yes sir, I can see you're surprised, our company does have customers worldwide, mind you, we usually know in advance when they're due.'

'You mean Helen has gone to lunch with clients from Russia and you didn't know they were due, how did you know they were kosher?' The lady smiled.

'Well, it was easy, they were wearing fur hats.'

'Fur hats, in a heat wave lady?' As I left the building, I felt momentarily disoriented, I put it down to the sudden return of all that stress. Jumping into a cab I tell the driver it's the Sky Spirit building on Central, and pretty soon I'm in my car heading for the Spaghetti Boat, I'm gonna retrieve my bug and have a drink while I think things through. It's the usual waiter with the impeccable manners, I order myself a stiff one.

'Cheers, here's to Helen.'

'Helen, she's just been in?' The malt plummeted to the pit of my stomach.

'Say that again.'

'She called in for a working lunch with a couple of clients, after having a drink she became ill, her clients had to help her to the car, they left about ten minutes ago.' All of a sudden this isn't a game, the stakes have gone through the roof, they've got Helen and now they've got me, this time I've run out of miracles, I order another drink, the door clicked quietly behind me.

'You had better make that the double and I will have the double vodka.' I'd know that voice anywhere it belongs to the dame over the intercom in Broadmain's office. 'Do not look so worried Mr. Chase I am not going to eat you.' Now that's a disappointment, the lady's a real stunner, we shake hands. 'My name is Salinka, I was sorry to learn of your friend, and I am thinking, we had better meet sooner rather than later.' I'm blown away by this fit woman waltzing into my life, she's about 27, above average height, she's wearing a yellow long-sleeved top with a crimson leather skirt displaying a fair complexion as far as the eye can see, she has a small leather bag slung over her left shoulder, I know she's armed - we take a table.

'How come you knew where to find me?'

'When your police took you in this morning, I brushed past you in the lobby, I placed a small homing device in your pocket.' My fingers play with the bug.

'I'll leave it where it is you never know you might need to find me again someday.' I don't waste time. 'O.K. Salinka, tell your men to let Helen go and I'll try to help you in any way I can.'

'Mr. Chase if only it was that simple, there is a lot more at stake here.'

'Check this out lady, I don't wanna rain on your parade but there's only one thing at stake here and that's Helen's safety.' The Russian is piercing me with her wild green eyes.

'I am part of a small group of covert subversives who are going to alter history, an unofficial arm of the Civilise Russian Politics Party, we aim to extinguish the murdering element at the Kremlin and replace it with a more enlightened leader, if we succeed it will be the end of the cold war.'

'That's all very touching but will it be before or after you shoot Helen McCluskie?' A look of anger flashed across her face.

'What do you take me for, you jump into this conclusion before you let me finish, who do you think it was risked their neck to get you out of East Berlin?' Geez it was her, she got me out, she's got every right to be angry I'm seriously outta line here, I owe her my life. Wait a minute, she knew Harris, they were cohorts, more, lovers. The silence is disturbed by the waiter who thought he'd been summoned, I ordered coffee and the check, the waiter nodded politely and disappeared leaving me to make up with Salinka.

'Hey, look, I'm sorry, I didn't mean it, I'm having one of those days, I saw my client shot dead, my fee go out the window, my girlfriend gets abducted, I just wanna know what the hell's going on. Will you tell me the rest of your story especially the bit about getting this dummy private eye out of Berlin?' The Russian raised one eyebrow while I went weak at the knees.

'O.K. Mr. Dummy Chase, now you are prepared to listen I will tell you what the hell is going on.

SEVEN

The Russian's story is about as convincing as a poodle with a pink rinse, after practising communism since the revolution, the reds have finally realised the capitalists are right, the problem is the KGB hierarchy and a few diehard party members are calling the tune.

'The curse of Russia is to have to suffer endless dictators, bullies and murderers, you have already met Streckovitch, despot in waiting, if we remove him our man becomes next in line for president, you know John has already paid the price.' I thought Harris was an American agent but I was only halfway there, according to Salinka he was a double agent. The waiter appeared with coffee and placed it on the draped white linen in front of us, Miss Russia continued. 'What has this to do with your space shuttle? Streckovitch wants to commandeer your Star Wars deterrent, despite its advanced technology it is designed to utilize the same remote-control system, even you Americans must economize.' I lean back on my chair, the minutia is interesting but I can't help admiring the view, she knows it, of course she does, she understands. We sip our coffee from azure china cups with gilded cameo gondolas floating past St Mark's Basilica, could it happen, could the Russians intercept?

'So, the Russian military want to usurp our star-wars deterrent and use it against us.'

'With Russia a pariah State, the threat of war between the superpowers is always on the cards....' She leaned towards me and thought for a moment...

'Mr. Chase, Russia's president is nothing but an alpha male autocrat, a coward, a bully, and a murderer who disguises his criminality by pretending the west hates us, therefore we must be Sabre-rattlers to display how tough we are.' Salinka has wound herself up.

'Do you feel better now?' She sat back and smiled.

'Yes, I am sorry about that, anyway, something had to be done so we passed the information to your CIA, but it was too late you had already handed the microdots over.' She's grinning. 'I did manage to swap them with meaningless information about your rail network, when Streckovitch realized he had the wrong data it was hard not to burst with laughter.'

'Hey wait a minute, burst with laughter, you mean you were there?'

'But of course, I am a Russian agent what did you expect?' Before I can answer, two men burst in brandishing firearms, in an instant Salinka is behind me. 'It is me they are after they want you alive.' As if to confirm her statement two bullets neatly missed my head, she retreated under a table.

'My gun is in the glove compartment of my car I keep it there so it's handy.'

'What is that, handy to shoot the jaywalker, I am not so stupid?' Miss KGB pulled out a firearm, I held out my hand. 'You must be joking.' The men, one tall and heavily built the other shorter but with a matching set of biceps split and went either side of the restaurant, I decided if Salinka was gonna stand a chance I've gotta flex some muscle. Unexpectedly there's a gift from Neptune as a loose round smashed into the giant fish tank perched along one wall, the jerk passing close by let out an agonized scream, an angry piranha had slithered across the soaking tablecloth and buried its teeth into the fleshy part of his hand, I dived beneath the tables, grabbed his legs and pulled him to the floor. As we struggle on the damp, musty carpet I can hear shots ringing out from across the room, this guy's tough but I hung on - so did the piranha. As his head bobbed in the fray, I noticed the antiquated heating system, next time he's in line with that ninety-degree three-inch connector I'll have him. Like now, I crash into his head with my left shoulder, hard and fast, once, twice, three times and again until the only movement left in his body is a trickle of blood emitting from somewhere above his hairline.

From my vantage point I can see it's all over, his cohort is doing a kind of pastiche on the carpet with his body fluids, my new partner is sitting leaning against the wall one fit arm anchored to the floor by the weight of her smoking automatic, the other is raised and cutely waving at me. Curious I look across the tables and for the first time I see the smile that will one day come to mean more to me than anything I could possibly imagine. We tied Piranhaman firmly to the central heating with strips of tablecloth I'd hastily ripped apart with my bare hands. Salinka pours a bucket of ice water over his head, it's the perfect pick me up, she interrogates him throwing in the odd translation for my benefit. I can make out words like Helen and the Florence Hotel, her interrogation over she begins filling me in, the good news, Helen is safe, she's heavily sedated in room 612 at the hotel. I know it already, it's a small, jaded place on the east side of Central Park at the junction of 5th avenue and 73rd street east. Her babysitter is a new boy an ex-para who's recently spent time in the Afghan foothills causing havoc amongst the rebel insurgents, he doesn't know it but he's about to get some sick leave. I pick up a rubber band and stretching it between my first finger and thumb I flick it satisfyingly across the room. We found the waiter and an Italian chef huddled in the linen cupboard, they wouldn't come out so I gave them a bottle of house white and a couple of glasses and told them to drink to our success. The last thing I did was call the cops, we didn't hang about I can't face two of the chief's cigars in one day, now we're in my car making a beeline for the Florence.

'Mr. Chase, thank you for what you did back there if it had not been for you, I would be dead now.' I smiled I guess I did put on a good show.

'That's O.K. ma'am, it's what I do, it's my job, it's what pays the rent, hey, do me a favour will yer, the name's Dick let's knock this Mr. Chase bit on the head shall we?' I reach into the glove compartment for my gun, check it's loaded and slide it into my shoulder holster, while Salinka sits pondering.

'Hmmm Dick, I like Dick..................... 'So, that's really handy then.'

EIGHT

The Florence Hotel is where the French navvies, who were responsible for the installation and fitting out of the Statue of Liberty in 1886, were billeted.

It's because of the dogged determination and passion of the archaeological faculty at downtown Bronx University, graffiti, daubed on the walls by the navvies has been restored and preserved under glass, and can still be seen, today, in many of the rooms.

As I parked in a space opposite, a rumble of thunder made me look up, heavy clouds are moving in. I caught the cool whiff of change through the open window, briefly, before an invisible thermal whipped it away and brought back the heat of summer. The battle is neatly going on around us but I have a feeling the sun's reign is almost over.

My eyes fell on the building, it's a twelve-storey time capsule with a fire escape at one end and a 150-foot drop at the other, I know the joint has no basement it's been turned into a cellar bar called Satan's Pit, the stairs have been blocked off to stop non-members swanning down from the hotel and getting a free look at Satan's topless Vampettes. We're now standing along from the room on the 6th, floor discussing tactics, while pretending to admire an Andy Warhol print, we position ourselves either side of the door, one last check on the weapons and Geronimo, we burst in. It's all over in a second, Salinka hit his arm, a messy shot high into the shoulder, he fell to his knees holding his bicep while exploding into what I guess is a whole bunch of choice Russian expletives. Salinka's cool response is to sit back in a wicker chair with what I now know is her 9mm Makarov, trained on him. I check Helen over, she's out for the count, I phone down for an ambulance and the police and pretty soon it's a waiting game.

'Ma'am you didn't say how I wound up back in my apartment? She aimed her weapon at the kidnapper's head, but then changed her mind.

'It was John, he wanted to get you out, he had to try you were a fellow countryman, I don't know what happened.' There's a longing in her voice. 'Anyway, your fate fell to me, I was in charge of a small team of medics, our job was to keep people like you alive, to administer truth drugs and prime you up for the interrogation. Remarkably there was a complete power failure, some rats had chewed through the main cable, with the help of a trusted medic, I managed to smuggle you out.'

According to the Russian that's when my luck really changed, a contact in the French Embassy came up trumps, a man in the diplomatic corps, had suddenly died from a short illness, the staff duplicated the death certificate, passport, exit visa and made sure I was dispatched on a separate flight, from Paris I was in the hands of the CIA and the American air force. The door behind us burst opened.

'Heyyy! Chase you old bloodhound.' I turned around.

'Heyyy! McDougall you terminal malingerer, what the hell are you doing on this job?' We hugged, but just a quick one. 'I thought you were fraud squad.'

'Yeah, I am but…' He lowered his voice and pulled me away from the mêlée of cops and ambulance personnel who are beginning to fill this small hotel room. 'Well Dick, you know you implicated me in this little espionage case you're working on.' I cut in.

'I don't wanna disappoint you Doogie but at the time I didn't know it was espionage, hell, if I had I wouldn't have risked it for Lucy and the boy's sakes.'

'I appreciate that, hey, why don't you come to dinner tonight? Lucy would love to see you and I'll tell you about being interrogated by the FBI and the CIA for two days solid.' The idea sounded interesting but not as good as the prospect of a quiet night with Salinka and I might not have to sleep on the couch, politely I declined and changed the subject.

'Doogie there's someone I'd like you to meet.' Her charge gone my temporary cohort is standing by the window looking out of this world. 'This is Salinka, a friend of mine, Ma'am, Peter McDougall, we were in the force together.' She approached smiling and offering an outstretched hand.

'I am pleased to meet with you Peter, you have the same name as one of our great composers.'

'Gee, Salinka, it's great to meet you, do you mean Pete Seeger?' I pulled McDougall to ear level.

'I think she's talking about Tchaikovsky, listen, keep this under your hat, we're in the presence of a KGB agent.'

'No.'

'Yep.'

'You're kidding.'

'Nope.'

'How about that, and I thought Tchaikovsky was his first name.'

This is no run-of-the-mill job, it turns out the injured clown has to be hospitalised and heavily guarded till the CIA arrive and pick him up, then it's smoke and mirrors, the NYPD has no jurisdiction, it didn't happen. In the meantime, McDougall and Salinka are getting on like a house on fire, when two things surface, the conversation turns to dinner invitations, and, it occurs to me I'm in love with Salinka, I might be just infatuated but either way, no way is McDougall gonna persuade her to get me to agree to a foursome over dinner tonight.

'Dick, you did not mention we have to be somewhere in such a hurry, where are you taking me?' I've got something on my mind, Helen's fine and still my girlfriend, I'm holding on to the Russian's arm and feeling every vibe in her body, I'm heading for trouble here. We travelled in silence to the ground floor. 'Dick, you did not answer my question.' Suddenly it's too late, as we swept out of the hotel the heavens opened, I grab Salinka's wrist and pull her through the sheets of pounding rain to my car, I get in and throw open the passenger door, she falls in, breathless, saturated. 'God I am soaked to the skin and my clothes, look, they are clinging to me.' I daren't look, she's too beautiful, too tempting and besides I've got my reputation to think of. Again it's Salinka, now with soft tender tones. 'In Russia we have a saying, when two strangers shelter from the storm it is as if they have known each other for a lifetime.' She leans back and closes her eyes while running her fingers through her hair, letting beads of soft rain fall onto the rear mat. I notice the tiny hairs on her forearms standing to attention, daring me to stroke them flat, in response my arms shift a couple of inches but I control the urge to cascade her drying goosebumps with my hot hands. I thought about her Russian folklore "It is as if they have known each other for a lifetime". Is Salinka giving me the come-on, should I take a chance? What have I got to lose, after all, we are "Two strangers sheltering from the storm" Hey wait a minute, who the hell am I kidding, I've got no reputation, I reach across and kiss her red-hot lips, she reciprocates, and in that instant, that careless, crazy, unguarded moment, her Russian saying becomes flesh and blood.

A squall rocks the car and rattles the rain hard against it while we kiss as if passion is going out of style, as the rain eases off, so do we, we sit there in silence without looking at each other, there are too many miles in between, there'd be no future in it. Are we both being rational? I didn't ask and she didn't tell, instead I started the motor and we headed over to my place.

I wanted to go straight to the hospital but the paramedic turkey had given Helen a jab just before we burst in, according to Salinka it was enough to knock her out for another twelve hours, so it's back to my place to consummate our kisses. Afterwards we lay in each other's arms the pair of us, in different worlds, I'm feeling as guilty as sin, while she had been in Harris's arms, not mine, as I'd been kidding myself. She made to get dressed, I took her hand and stalled for a moment, as I look into those wild green eyes they narrow as she tries to read my mind, I knit my brow, I've got this smart idea to throw some jeopardy into the mix.

'Back at the hotel McDougall slipped me an airline ticket.' I'm playing sheepish like I'm auditioning for Broadway. 'It's one way to Moscow courtesy of the American Government, your flight leaves in two hours.' I can see the news slowly sink in.

'No, how can they do this? I risk my life to bring home their private investigator Mr. Dick Chase, if I go back now before the situation at home has changed, I will surely face the firing squad. No Dick, is there nothing you can do, please.' I look thoughtfully into space.

'Actually, I'm joking.' Almost before I can get the words out, she has me pinned to the bed.

'I hate you.' She's rubbing her hair in my face, up and down and side to side. 'I hate you, I hate you, you, you - you Dickie Yankee.'

'Dickie Yankee!!?'

Salinka collapsed next to Dick, laughing, really laughing it was as if a dam had burst, she laughed in a way she hadn't done for such a long time. In that brief moment she forgot the oppressive, suffocating regime of Russian autocracy that hacks away at freedom and self-esteem to ascend the unsalted, all-embracing crepidoma of democracy. And for that instant she found herself free, full of latent fun, she felt, for now, she could do anything.

NINE

'Voilà! cheese on al dente cauliflower florets.' The spy who came to dinner looked at my dish, then at me and burst out laughing, I ignore her and begin dishing up.

'Wait till you taste it.' I'm sampling the aroma wafting from the melted mozzarella, still in hysterics my KGB agent manages to spell it out.

'No, it is, it's the apron.' From then on she's unstoppable. I look at the apron I'd slung on, it was a birthday present from the McDougalls, one of those glossy numbers depicting a pair of skinny legs sporting some baggy Pink Panther boxer shorts, see the connection?

Over dinner Salinka filled in some of the gaps, I didn't know a lot of Broadmain's oil wealth was from the Soviet Union, he'd been advising and giving technical aid without a licence for years, hence the KGB had a hold over him. When Streckovitch wanted the shuttle information, part of the deal was a lucrative foothold in the Velikiye oil field, the rest was hush money.

'Who killed Fields and Haywood and why did the KGB top Broadmain before they had a chance to talk to him?'

'Make no mistake, Broadmain had the blood on his hands, he had the two stooges killed to keep them quiet, it was self-preservation. Streckovitch was convinced it was you who intercepted the shuttle data and when you escaped back here, he thought Broadmain would kill you too, before he could retrieve the information.'

'Where's the data now?'

'It's back in the hands of the CIA, it was your ticket home, to think I could have been rich, I know at least two regimes who would have paid a fortune for that information.' She beamed and carried on eating, that's it I'm not gonna get paid, two weeks work for zilch and nothing in the pipeline, I felt depressed, so depressed I allowed it to fog my brain.

'I'm just going to the car, I left my handbag and I want my lipstick.'

'Sure Honey, the keys are hanging on the plastic dog's nose by the door, take my jacket it might be raining out there.' I'm pouring a couple of whiskeys to accompany what I hope is gonna be a memorable evening, when a squeal of brakes halts my flow. That's funny, I thought I heard my name 'Diicckkk!' Jesus, it's Salinka, as I reach the window she shouts again, two men are bundling her, at gunpoint, into the back of that dark blue limo, a third stands looking up at my apartment, it's Streckovitch, he makes a gesture with his fingers that mimics shooting himself in the head, complete with recoil, he's indicating an execution. I'm pounding down the steps four at a time, as I burst onto the street, I know it's too late. A flash of lightning illuminates the night sky while a rumble of thunder echoes threateningly. I'm standing in the road looking down at the spot where she was seized, when swiftly from nothing rain is falling like bullets and bouncing three inches off the tarmac, off the back of my neck. Immediately I know what I've gotta do, drive around New York, Long Island and the whole of New Jersey looking for a sign saying Salinka is here, difficult, my only set of car keys are in the jacket she's wearing, I've gotta call Cainem.

'Joe Cainem here, watching the late-movie!'

'Yeah Joe, sorry about that, it's Dick Chase, I'm in trouble and I need some wheels.' Cainem listened while I précised my plight, it turns out he couldn't be more obliging and we arranged to meet at his garage in half an hour. His premises are across the street from the subway, he runs an all-night cab service so it's open when I arrive. The girl at the desk is smart, she offers me a smile, coffee and trivial conversation, but I'm only half listening I've got more important things on my mind. With a squeal of brakes and some high-octane revs Cainem pulls up on the zesty, virgin-mopped green and white tiles of his showroom and soon we're sitting in his office facing each other across a desk strewn with overflowing ashtrays, empty beer cans and the remains of dried-up pizzas, I run the relevant bits over him.

'My guess is Streckovitch is playing for the straight swap, Salinka for the microfilm, if I'm wrong, she's dead, if I'm right I don't have it anyway, I gotta find her and get her out, it's her only chance.'

'Seems to me Chase, you've got yourself a problem, sure I'll help, sure you can have a car, I'll even go looking myself, but what'll we do, drive around New York, Long Island and the whole of New Jersey looking for a sign saying Salinka is here?' Cainem stole my line. He removed the head from a carved wooden chicken to reveal two fat cigars sticking out at the neck and waved it in front of me, I declined, it's too early. Taking one himself he rolled it satisfyingly next to his ear, then, lighting up, he took two or three quick puffs before absentmindedly flicking his ash two feet into an ashtray, he zeroed in.

'Man, you know you can't trust a spy, I'd have bugged her right from the get-go, at least that way you'd have known where she was coming from.' Cainem's a genius, just an off-the-cuff remark but so full of verve and meaning.

'Wait a minute Joe, she is bugged she's wearing my jacket with a bug in the pocket, she planted it to follow me, the thing is it was made in the USSR.' With the deadly accuracy of a Cobra, Cainem flicked his ash into a dead pizza, before conducting a general pause with the Havana.

'I've got it, I've got a nephew who's a complete military memorabilia freak, he collects from all over the world, it's big business. He's got a warehouse down by the Docks, I'll call him up, hey, I'll call him up, that's a joke, d'ya get it?'

'Yeah, sure I do, but will he be there at this time?'

'Listen, he sleeps on the premises, he doesn't trust those Securihound people, and besides it cuts down on his overheads.'

For the first time I begin to feel positive about this rescue, Salinka's safety and subsequent freedom are beginning to look like a possibility, of course I've still got the hard bit to come, Dick Chase versus the KGB, but I'll cross that bridge when I get to it. I like Cainem, nothing is too much trouble, he's generous, helpful and he's got a nephew with a warehouse full of Red Army surplus.

TEN

My optimism is beginning to wilt, we got the gear O.K. Cainem has a neat KGBX2 sitting on the passenger seat of his Porsche, while I've got a 16-foot antenna sticking out of a condemned Buick Sedan with a trunk and rear seat crammed full of state-of-the-ark Ruskie receiver.

'Come in Chase, this is Cainem over.' One thing's f'sure, I'm not gonna fall asleep on the job.

'Yeah Joe, still here, how's it going?'

'I'm halfway down Central Park on the east side, not a tweak, how about you, over?'

'I'm travelling west about four blocks from the park and it's no show, I'll be at the rendezvous point in five.' I know she's not in Manhattan because I'm now turning east on my last stretch and so far neither of us have come up trumps. Cainem should be parked on my side of the street looking like a Christmas tree with full beams and flashers going, and if I'm not mistaken that's him there. I park close to his Porsche and wind down the window, Cainem's electric window purrs open simultaneously, shaking his head he shouts through the relentless pouring rain.

'No luck, what do we do now?'

'Queens, we'll take the bridge, follow me.' The plan is I'll take 21st up to Astoria Park and start working my way down, Cainem can shoot along Northern Boulevard to the Shea Stadium and work his way back, we'll meet at the junction of Jackson Ave and 21st Street. We stopped on the east side of the bridge where I gave Cainem the gen and pretty soon he's speeding off in a cloud of crimson mist and spray.

It's an hour later, my deputy reached the rendezvous point before me, he's fallen asleep at the wheel. I get out of the car and light a cigarette, looking up, the sky is full of stars and I'm five years old again standing in the backyard with Mom wondering at those same stars the night my cat was run over. "That's where all the cats go when they die, Richie, they lounge about up there in heaven nice and warm and cosy keeping watch over their folks to see that all shall be well" Mmm, Richie, it's been a long time.

'Hey Chase are you sleepwalking?' I turn to see Cainem homing in on me like a human hotdog stall, he buries his face in his hands eclipsing the flame from his lighter while he struggles with a cigar. 'Hey I've been calling you.' An orange sun appears like magic in front of his face. 'What's up, cat got your tongue? Listen, I've got an idea. There's an all-night diner just south of here, where we can get ourselves a coffee and they make a nice steak sandwich, how about it?' I take pity on him, he is helping me out after all, I concede but we monitor on route.

We'd gone about three miles when out of the blue the receiver bleeped, I looked over the bench seat as it went again, my glance fell on the thin green line that momentarily went haywire as it sounded a third time.

'Woweeee Chase, are you getting this, we've got her?'

'Yeah, thanks Joe, I wasn't sure.' I told him to pull over there're a couple of things I need to ram home, like this isn't gonna be a joyride, there's gonna be some shooting and I'm not talking pool, he said he guessed as much and patted the 9mm piece he's got sitting in his pocket.

'This little beauty is armed and dangerous and I'm not taking it on a picnic.' I looked at him, hard, it took me three seconds.

'O.K. Cainem, you're in, just don't go standing behind me. Tell me, this diner, is it Joe's Café, along Grand Street, right before you go over the creek?'

'Yeah, sure, d'you know it?'

'You betcha I do, only the steak's off, it's beef tonight, beef stroganoff, let's go.'

We'll pull off the road just before the café, stop there and skirt around the back on foot to see who's inside, that way I can size up the opposition and see how they're spread. By the time we reach the spot the bleep's one continuous tone, I lean over the bench seat and switch it off. Dim lights from the café are visible about fifty yards away, at the rear there's a bit of wasteland, a muddy minefield full of rabbit holes and empty drink cans where Fields and Haywood have used them for rifle practice. Soon we're standing some 10 yards behind the place, from the front it's that half-decent Café, from the back it's nothing but a crummy shack. Venetian blinds make it impossible to see inside, that's a setback but nothing compared to what's about to happen. I'm telling Cainem the plan when, in an explosion of transparent silence, we're floodlit like two boxers in a ring, a sharp euphoric voice heads towards us like an arrow on steroids.

'Chase, how convenient, you have saved me the trouble of having you brought in.' I can't see who's milking the spiel, I don't have to.

'If it's a ball game you want, Streckovitch, you're in the wrong park.'

'The lights, very good, just one small thing, the pair of you make excellent target practice, I wouldn't try anything if I were you, now, "gumshoe", my patience is running out, I will give you one last chance to tell me what you have done with the microfilm.'

'O.K. "Strecky" you win, it looks like I don't have much choice, this is what we're gonna do, you hand over the girl, in one piece, and I'll tell you where the goods are stashed.' Without warning a burst of automatic fire obliterates a pile of cans just to our front, Cainem's getting nervous.

'Listen Chase, why not let them have whatever it is they want, that way we can take the dame and get the hell outta here?' I reply softly, from the side of my mouth.

'Because I don't have it, I'm bluffing.'

'Geez you're joking me.'

'Chase, I see you do not realize Colonel Palchikova is one of our top agents who will receive great honours for her part in luring you into this trap, all you have to do is hand over the microfilm.'
My money's on the Russian being drugged and tied to some bed frame inside the shack, she won't make roll call, from the darkness comes the answer, clear and damning.

'Just say the word, Ivor, and I'll blow his brains out, the microfilm has to be in the apartment.'

'Salinka, are you O.K. what's going…?' I'm cut short as a couple of shots ring out, it's Cainem taking pot-shots at the lights, he missed but a burst of heavier calibre fire sent him crashing to the ground.

'Don't you try anything foolish, gumshoe, just do exactly as I tell you, beginning with discarding your weapon.'

For the first time I realise the floodlights have been set a couple of feet off the ground, Cainem, who's completely in the dark, is attempting to put his gun down my sock, I fiddle with my shoulder holster to give him more time. I feel the warm chamber against my ankle, he's done it, as I throw my gun away the orders are coming in thick and fast, I put my hands above my head and approach the shack. Out of the floodlights I can see a narrow wooden walkway with three steps leading up to it, Streckovitch, Salinka and two hit men are standing, waiting, I catch her glance, it's narrow, unyielding, she's giving nothing away.

I stand there, owning the top step, hard as steel, defiant, I pitch a careless observation.

'The cockroaches are out in force tonight.' Like lightning Streckovitch brings the butt of his weapon up to catch the underside of my jaw, the warm bitter taste of blood fills my mouth as my saliva begins to run profusely, I spit the slimy waste out, it's reluctant to go, against orders I bring my hand down and wipe my mouth with the back of it. At this point things aren't looking good, but it could be worse, Cainem could have blown my foot off.

ELEVEN

The shack turned out to be a store, a metal bay shelving labyrinth with an overriding whiff of cheese and cabbage, it led into an office with a window displaying that floodlit void. The walls are mostly covered with "centre pages" of graphic detail in shocking pink, the main café is next, we don't go that far. Someone pushed me from behind, it's an unexpected heavy blow, I slam into the office desk, shoving it against the wall, and finish up on the floor. I turn around only to receive a heavy kick just below my ribs followed by another to my head. Looking up at the spinning lights, I'm wondering how to dodge the rifle butt that's heading my way, I move sluggishly in some direction, but it connects hard between my neck and shoulder, Streckovitch intervenes.

'Welcome to our little hideout, I see you are warming to the place already.' Struggling to retain control I manage to swing myself up and lean against the desk, I'm sitting staring at my four legs trying to work out which one has the gun tucked down its sock, Streckovitch looks at his watch. 'I am not accustomed to boiling my potatoes twice, you have two minutes to remember the whereabouts of the microfilm, fail, and it will be the last thing you remember.' Time is running out, while short bursts of conversation are traded in Russian, gradually I bring my left leg up to see if I can locate the shooter, their exchange sounds heated, eager and I've located the wrong ankle, slowly I straighten my leg.

Streckovitch strides across the room where he takes a gun and magazine from a brown leather briefcase hanging from a cold, rusting radiator, he bangs the mag home and slings the whole caboodle to Salinka, who catches it comfortably with both hands, a satisfied glow seems to radiate through her whole body, Streckovitch spells it out.

'You know what to do, the microfilm first.' The room falls silent except for the click of the safety catch, she advances towards me stealing the limelight like a stripper in some seedy downtown strip joint. Holding the gun with both hands, her arms locked straight out in front of her, she aims it at my head, her voice is calm and collected.

'I am good do you not think? I had you going all this time.' With all eyes on her I manage a reassuring touch on the weapon, I know exactly how it's placed. This "enigma" wonders at me, and for a fleeting moment I thought I saw, I did see, a faint smile, she speaks, only to stun me with her insight. 'Should that not be in the glove compartment where it is handy?' Streckovitch intervenes.

'Get on with it Palchikova.' Still looking at me her lips curl and she winks, her attention has shifted and I've become a front row voyeur.

Like a twister erupting in a sudden squall, she spins around downing the three men in her wake, in an instant she had turned through 270 degrees, time enough for the last dude to react, he made the classic mistake, he aimed, she anticipated it and dropped like a stone blasting him twice as she fell, he collapsed against the wall his legs folded and he slumped to the floor. The whole massacre is over in a second, Salinka's speed and momentum roll her with a crash into a chair that tips over as she hits it. Silence saturates the room, a blue hue colours the light and the acrid resonance of cordite smacks. On her hands and knees, she crawls towards me and makes with a kiss, except it isn't a kiss, it's a whisper, it's intel.

'They were blanks.' Dick's face hardens, he stands and moves towards the window where the floodlights are still projecting into the night.

'I'm worried about Cainem, d'yer think he'll be alright?' He's bluffing.

'I would not worry about your comrade, we will finish him off.' Feigning surprise Dick turns around, his face a picture of shock and disbelief at the three dead men walking, their weapons already surgically trained. Streckovitch heads straight for his prize and stands heavily on her foot splaying it outwards, for good measure he forces the muzzle of his Kalashnikov hard against her breastbone, enough to draw blood. 'Palchikova, do you think you fooled me with your lies? I have known all along you are part of this civilise Russian Politics Brigade, and I am not so stupid I cannot tell when a traitor will hang herself if given a gun loaded with blanks.' They all sneer at her. Salinka knows what's coming, she had set the bar, it's over in a second, four shots in quick succession, they all go home, all in the head, it was easy, too easy. Dick grabs the Kalashnikov and pans it across their bodies, nothing, it's amazing the advantage live rounds have over blanks. Placing the butt down he leans on the muzzle.

'Well partner, it looks like it's all over for them there critters.' Salinka's smile says it all, she stands and limps towards him, taking the weapon, she makes it safe, a routine procedure drilled into her through training, and leans it carefully against the wall. Placing her arms around his neck she's now grinning full throttle.

'Hmm, not bad, for someone who flaunts a Pink Panther apron.'

TWELVE

The departure lounge at JFK is like a graveyard, it's 4.22 am and Salinka has gone to put her face on, despite my pleas wild horses couldn't keep her here a moment longer, in her words "The history is being made up" and she just has to be part of it. Joe Cainem had been hit in the legs, he's in a pretty bad state but he'll survive, he took some convincing the Russian is friendly but, in the end, I think she won him over. The police weren't interested in the fact she's a KGB agent, nor for that matter what happened at the scene of the shooting, that puzzled me, until one of them, a plain-clothes officer, took me to one side and showed me his credentials, he was a CIA agent. Something's going on back in the USSR. he said he didn't know what, anyhow it seems this KGB agent has been given the all-clear, and I've got the job of seeing she gets out of the country in one piece, and that is exactly what I'm doing now.

I heard a door close behind me and recognised the pitch of her stilettos, I turn and there she is, that tall, slender, green-eyed brunette with a fair complexion as far as the eye can see, she approaches, smiling right at me, her freshly painted lips red like wet cherries. She sat opposite on the low PVC-covered seating and crossed her legs, they're the best legs in the business but I'm too busy nurturing my post-case depression to appreciate them.

'Well Dick, what to say?' I rallied and smiled at the girl who twice saved my life, it would have been twice, except for a technicality, I know what to say though and I'm not too proud to say it.

'I owe you my life, if it wasn't for you, I'd be playing deadman for the Black Sea Swordfish.' She laughed.

'There are no swordfish in the Black Sea.'

'Well, there you are, *Colonel Palchikova*, I'd have been the only one in the team.' She guffawed.

'It is true, but only honouree, because of my degrees, you can call me ma'am.' She grinned and sliding next to me wound an arm around my neck, it's a strange thing, I knew then, instantly, she could kill me. 'If anyone should be grateful it is me, you really saved my life.' I looked into those wild green eyes, of all the women, in all of the places, this one can play it again, till we're the folks who live on the hill, I became aware she's smiling at me. 'What is going on in that head of yours, you look as if you are miles away?'

'I was just thinking, we mustn't forget Cainem's part in all this, he really came up trumps as the unexpected hero. Tell me.' I paused, already starting to regret what it is I'm about to ask, she put her smile on hold, waiting to hear what I had to say.

'Did you love John?' Her smile broadened, she removed her arm.

'John and I were in love, yes, we were to be married in the spring.' Her eyes filled and her smile escaped, she looked for it on the floor, then at me again, her composure was instant, Russian.

'What will you do, do you have a family?'

'But of course, two sisters.' She laughed as if suddenly remembering some schoolgirl prank they'd all been party to back in their pubescent youth.

' 'Will all passengers bound for Moscow via London, please make their way to gate four, thank you.'

We walked arm in arm across the polished concourse remembering as we went small gems of activity that had surfaced over the past few days, and laughed at them together. As we reach the barrier there are a handful of passengers waiting to show their boarding passes, we hung back at the end of the queue.

'Excuse me, if one of you is on this flight you must board now, it's about to leave.' It's the girl at the desk, we drew back from a last passionate kiss and without a word my KGB agent crossed the barrier, she turned and walked backwards for a moment, smiling and waving, then, just as she had arrived, she was gone. I took a long breath before going over to the giant picture windows that allowed me a view of the plane and possibly a last chance to see her, I didn't see her.

Dawn is just beginning to break as I watch the row of lights taxi off to take pole position on a distant runway, almost immediately, they're raging past the terminus like some demented bus in a drag race, then, screaming, they tilt and head off into the lighter eastern skies. I'm staying with the darker western skies, but even as I approach that famous skyline in all its proud glory that is New York, it's beginning to be washed, ever so slowly, but irreversibly, with a new day. It's too easy to let a scene like that control the taps of patriotic fervour, you can almost hear the dawn chorus joining in a rendition of The Stars and

Stripes Forever, I always remember the tramps and down and outs who sleep rough in the parks and subways. Well, I guess that's it, another case bites the dust, it's always a sign when I begin worrying about the winos of this world. As it turns out there will be a couple of enquiries on the answer phone when I get back, one of them is gonna pay real well, I have to take up a night shift surveillance post for a month, but this is the city that never sleeps, so when the insomnia kicks in, I guess that's when I'll be doing my shopping. Things with Helen turned out pretty neat, the key factor being the amnesia brought on by the drugs. There had been a phone call from the chief, Vanessa Broadmain and surprise, surprise, it wasn't Leo Schoeman who got off the train it was Mr. Petroleum himself, Mrs. Broadmain has been charged with aiding and abetting the murder of Red Haywood-my statement was key. That little freeway café came with fifteen acres of prime building land and it's exactly where the pair wanted to start developing their hotel empire. I'd think about Miss Russia from time to time, like when I see a fish tank, or the time Helen had a surprise for me, she wanted to take me out to dinner, guess what, it turned out to be the Spaghetti Boat? A funny thing did happen one night though, it was a couple of months later. Helen and me were making out on the sofa, the TV was on low, when all of a sudden, I see it on the late news, like ants, jubilant crowds are clambering over the Berlin Wall, they're pulling it down block by block. Some new Russian President guy is offering world peace, disarmament, the removal of soviet forces from East Germany and something called glasnost. I didn't know what that was but it sure as hell sounded like that KGB agent and her cronies had hit the jackpot, Helen was talking but I wasn't paying attention.

'Hey Dick, your performance rate has dropped off, I think I'll record that lingerie commercial, you were great through that.' I was miles away on that hot afternoon in my car, the rain pounding to a deafening pitch on the roof. 'Mmmm, yes Dick, yes that's much better.' I was playing the game of love, Russian rules, Salinka's gentle cries of ecstasy replaying in my head. 'Oh yes that's it, that's great.' I was glimpsing Salinka on the TV… Hey, she is too on TV, she's part of that new President's entourage, well I'll be, just look at that, she's standing in the background smiling right into camera right at me, she's waving and saying something, I can read her lips, it's my name, she's saying my name, Salinka.

'Salinka!'

'Oh, Dick yes! Oh God yes…Mmmm…YES!…. Who the Hell's Salinka?'

THIRTEEN

THREE YEARS LATER

The days are beginning to draw in, and the once perpetually shimmering green canopy of Central Park has finally flumped to the ground like a knackered dancer. After a long summer, that now seems like it had followed the Ice Age, the Big Apple spends most of its waking time under a thin veil of grey cloud. One thing is worrying me though, my insomnia's returned, Helen, who's still my girlfriend, says it's brought on due to the total lack of yoga in my lifestyle, what does she know, after two hours masquerading as a lotus while breathing only three cycles a minute, I just *have* to make myself a pot of coffee and spend the rest of the twilight hours watching the early movie on TV, and that really sets me up for any appointments I might have the following day.

'How do you explain your symptoms Mr. Chase?'

'Well, it's simple Doc, every time I drop off, I wake up.' Don't they teach these doctors anything at medical school these days? He can't write and speak at the same time.

'O.K. Mr. Chase, I'll prescribe you some Benn.. o...tog...kop...uoo...lait.' He gave me a patronising glance. 'Funny name isn't it? They should help you relax more easily, the net result being you'll sleep better.'

'Well, if I don't Doc, I sure as hell won't be bored.' The ensuing silence was only punctuated by the doctor scratching for a hidden button beneath his desk and soon the nurse is holding on to the back of my chair ready to drop it into a vat of disinfectant the moment I leave the building. I exchanged some small talk with the girl at reception, picked up my pills from the dispensary and headed for Funtangos coffee house, where I'm already ten minutes overdue for a decaf and hot waffle with Helen. Funtangos is New York City's premier gay coffee bar, a cosmopolitan hive of sexual diversity and racial harmony, its ambient tolerance, inclusivity and just plain good manners are the work of its owners, Ruby, that's not his name, and Errol, that is his name. Their mantra is, *if you don't like the heat, Love, get out of our kitchen.* The venue was Helen's idea, she's as straight as a die with a bent for social welfare, if she hadn't flunked high school, she'd probably have majored in sociology, with me it was the other way around, I socialised with the majorettes and flunked high school. It turns out an old school friend of hers and co-member of the celebrated nineteen seventy-five New Jersey High under sixteen netball team, winners of the coveted Northern States Charity Shield, has turned pro, only now she's netting balls of a different kind, if you get my meaning. It seems her friend is having a spot of bother with her landlord, whose wife is on a permanent headache, and her pimp, who just happens to be the landlord's brother-in-law, I've been called in to slap a few wrists. I spotted Helen sitting in the corner with her nose buried in a book, she's wearing the red dress I bought for her birthday, her hair is cropped short now and gelled tight back, today it's peroxide. I raise my tray in the air and make my way over.

'Hey lady, is this seat taken?' I startled her, Helen was busy building those Far Pa-vilions that materialise in the mind's eye when reading a book of the same title, I sent them crashing to the ground only to re-emerge in the more tangible shape of the hot donut and fresh coffee I'd just slapped on the virgin pages right under her nose.

'Hey, mind my book you dumb ass.' Helen is pleased to see me, I sat down.

'O.K. Baby, where's your girlfriend?' She looks anxious.

'I'm worried Dick, Julie should be here by now.' She scanned her watch. 'You're ten minutes late, what happened, did you fall asleep again at a red light?' She laughed out loud, so I took a bite outta her donut. 'Hey, that's not fair.'

'Life's not fair Honey, today it's a bite outta your donut, tomorrow some cop'll be serving you a parking fine because you've dozed off in the toll jam.' I popped a couple of pills from a plastic bubble strip and put them on my tongue, then sipped my coffee, and sat, eyes closed, savouring the burnt bitter taste of that beaned elixir of life. Helen shakes my arm.

'Dick, this is no time to count sheep, Julie's here.' Her arm shot upwards in a feeble attempt to attract her friend's attention, before they can make eye contact, someone of indeterminate gender butts in.

'You're in trouble when Big Eddie finds you little one.' There's a large mirror behind Helen so I guess I'm looking straight at Julie, I see her turn and run, ruining my diary for the morning, Helen makes to go after her friend, but I hold her arm.

'Hey, wait a minute Baby, we don't want any of these nice Bohemians knowing we're involved, it kills the element of surprise and shuts people up should I need to ask questions.' A gut-wrenching squeal of brakes shatters the mood, there's a two seconds silence before someone screams and a car drives off like it has to be in Seattle in time for lunch.

'Jesus, it's Julie.' Helen tears herself away from the table, the whole coffee house seemed to mobilise itself at the same time, leaving Helen, stuck at the back of the crowd bottlenecked at the door. I swan over, put my arms around her waist and murmur kindly in her ear.

'I'll go see, you wait here.' I square up to the back of the horde. 'Let me through, I'm a doctor.' Crouching beside Julie's motionless body she seems void of any signs of life, her smile has gone, she looks more than her 30 or so years, her head is contorted in a way that would normally be impossible, the zip down the back of her neat woollen dress is no longer a problem, now she could see it in the mirror. The stark reality dawns as a small private ambulance pulls up and soon Julie's body is covered and being placed into the back of it. I stand up amid the humming throng, Helen's at the back looking pensive, hopeful, I close my eyes and shake my head.

As I make my way through the dispersing crowd, I stop and methodically go through all my pockets, I'm not looking for anything special, I'm earwigging a conversation between two people, one voice I recognised as belonging to the Bohemian who is privy to Big Eddie's jobs to-do list.

'I'm seeing Eddie later Dear.'

'What will you say?'

'I don't know, I'll cross that bridge when I get to it, come on, our coffee's getting cold.' He turned and walked right into me. 'Oops, sorry Love, I wouldn't hang around here all solo.' His mouth curled and he gave me a wink. 'Hunky men are a premium around these parts, Dear.' Damn, that was unfortunate, he's bound to remember my face. I didn't join Helen at our table, instead, I did what any hot-blooded heterosexual would do who'd just been pitched, I declined politely with my feet. Around the corner, I pick up a vacant cab, it started to rain and for a moment, from the warm, dry confines of this yellow cocoon, I watch the world get wet. I ask the driver to pull forward a couple of yards, so I can see Helen as she leaves Funtangos, there she is now, I wave frantically as she looks my way and soon, she's sitting breathless and wide-eyed next to me.

'What happened, I thought you were going to floor him?' The question provoked a bellicose attack from the cab driver.

'Where to Buster, I don't have all day?' I told him I wanted the police station, I figured control will let me have the destination of that ambulance and I had a hunch it's what Helen might want, you know, to pay her last respects. I told her that Hermaphroditus over there thinks I'm a rare hunk around these parts, Helen's sadness over her friend only allowed her to nod her head in recognition.

FOURTEEN

The New York City cop shop is a massive chequered block of smooth, grey concrete slabs and black polarised glass, a characterless rectangle standing on its end, its shape must have taxed the architectural brain like a baby decides to do a dump in its diaper. It was built on the site of the original Manhattan General Hospital, Lovett's Hat and Cape Emporium, and Furnival's New Giant Drug Store, how do I know that? It's inscribed on a bronze plaque fixed to the wall right next to the main entrance. We entered and Helen took a seat in the public waiting area, while I made a call to the nerve centre of the whole setup, the automatic coffee dispenser. I handed her the hot substance that had fallen reluctantly into a plastic cup, she took one look at the powder-strewn frothy creation.

'What am I supposed to do with this, dunk my jewellery in it?'

Dipping and diving between blue drill, going about its business, I proceed along the cream-coloured corridors, swapping one nerve centre for another - McDougall's office, I knock and walk in.

'Sure chief, I'll get straight on to it…yep…yep, I got all that, Hi Dick, take a seat, I'll be right there…O.K. chief…right away.' McDougall pressed the hook and began making another call. 'Hold it Dick, just..let…me…punch…this..num..ber…Er…

yes, thanks, it's one seafood special with green olives, pineapple chunks, err, peanut butter garnish and fries...and a Coke…It's the police station, on account, and tell the desk clerk it's for the chief will yer….McDougall……okay, thanks.' He hangs up, slumps, in his chair and mops his brow.

'Doogie, that sounds like an interesting case, why don't you loose the details on me?' He shrugged off my remark with some wisecrack about the chief's inability to prove his parentage, we made some small talk, and before long I'm getting down to my raison -d'etre. I told him about the hit-and-run outside Funtangos, and out of curiosity, I wondered…'What was the destination of the ambulance that attended?'

'Just out of curiosity, eh, it wouldn't have anything to do with a case you might be working on, would it?' I eyeballed my friend with surprise.

'You're a genius, tell you what, if you ever give up the day job, call me, I could do with someone to fetch my pizzas.' Grinning, he picked up the phone and called ambulance control, I already gleaned the gist before he hung up. There's been nothing for forty-second street, no police, no fire department and no ambulance, that's interesting because there was an ambulance. He's right about one thing, the hit and run is tied in with my case, but it was something else he said that put a rat up my nose – no police, the perfect setting for a homicide. I had a hunch, I asked him who gets all the calls for that area? There's the usual bunch and some new names, one sticks out, McDougall thinks he's a strange guy, difficult to get to know, his name is officer Ethan Cooper. 'Cooper? Hmm, thanks ex-partner, I'll let you know if anything develops.'

Tonight, Helen's gonna cook me a steak, she'll be home around 6, so I'm pretty made up over that, for now, she's got ten minutes to get back to work for the afternoon shift. I've arrived back at Funtangos with one of Helen's discarded paperbacks she's taken to leaving in my car door. I ordered coffee, and between sips of that and long blank stares at "Mrs. Dalloway" I settle down to see if I can find out who this Big Eddie geezer is. Somehow, I drop my book on the floor, and no sooner do I reach down to pick it up I find myself surrounded by two pairs of legs. I glance upwards to see if it's a quadrupedal waiter come to top up my coffee, it isn't, but I'm halfway there, it's my Bohemian fancier with a new boyfriend. I notice Bohemian's got a glass eye, he's tall, about six feet, I'd say he pumps iron on a regular basis. The other guy's similar but a smaller model and he doesn't have a glass eye - he's totally blind, stupidly I telegraph my mirth. Bohemian leans on the table creating an atmosphere that smells like a five-acre rose garden has just been stuffed up my nose.

'Something tickling your ass?' I bring my pinkie to the corner of my mouth and stick the nail between two molars.

'I've got a bit of meatloaf stuck between my teeth and it won't budge.' I remove my finger. 'Sit down, the coffees are on me.' They sit down and straight away Bohemian starts to fiddle with a gold bracelet, pulling it around his wrist.

'Tell me, aren't you the *doctor* who attended Julie this morning?' He used the noun with an inflection that said like hell you're a doctor, I have to be careful here, these two are a couple of regular polar bears who've left their fur coats hanging on the backs of their chairs next to their vanity units, I decide honesty is the best policy.

'The name's Chase, Dick Chase, I'm a private detective. I'm looking for a kid, she's sixteen, walked outta high school one morning, and hasn't been seen since, I've been hired by her folks to see if I can find her, I thought someone in this joint might be able to shed some light.' Well, I got my name right anyhow, little Bohemian blurts out.

'He's a Sugar Daddy, maybe we should call the cops.' I wanna demonstrate to the little squirt the strength of glass is directly proportional to its thickness, except Bohemian, sensing my anger, has pulled a gun and is aiming it straight at me.

'You mustn't mind Big Eddie, Dear, he's only jealous.' He leans forward pushing the condiments to one side with the barrel. 'So, you're a gumshoe looking for a runaway.' He smiles at Big Eddie. 'O.K. gumshoe, let's see the photo.' If luck be a lady she must hail from Lesbos, because I'm not getting a look in. So, I've found out who Big Eddie is, great, but I'm in a corner, I've got a gun waiting to tap my beer store and I've left the holiday snaps at home. Slowly I put my hand in my jacket pocket, I don't know why it just seems the right thing to do. My fingertips fall on a sharp flat card, it's shiny on one side and has two pointy corners uppermost, it feels like a photograph, but it can't be, I'm making this whole thing up. Suddenly I hear this strange voice coming from my mouth and it's saying, sure thing, take a look, have you seen this kid? I pull my hand out and to my surprise find myself gripping the butt of a sawn-off shotgun, Big Eddie screams, Bohemian tenses up, and me, I just squeeze both triggers.

FIFTEEN

I woke up with the same bolt that dispatched a wicker basket full of sugar cubes around the surrounding floor, Ruby is onto me like an Exocet missile, ready to give me the kiss of life, I've never been awake so quickly, I hold my hands up.

'Insomnia, it's insomnia.' I'm smiling but my attention is focused on Funtangos' window, it should have displayed a grey, damp New York afternoon full of the hubbub and clamour of daily life, instead, it's an electric light show, set in a jet-black night and full of the hubbub and glamour of nightlife. I look at my watch, geez is that the time, if I don't make my apartment pronto, Helen will be getting the guided tour around Rhynmould Mansions, including the obligatory peer into the doggy litter?

Blinding headlamps contract my pupils as I struggle with my car keys, an off-duty cop on his way home to a hot meal and a hot bed followed by a deep replenishing sleep, I feel wide awake thinking about it. I turn into eighth street east and pull up behind Helen's gold Beetle, my luck's in, she hasn't despaired of me and gone home, strangely I don't feel hungry anymore, I think I'll go straight for the hot bed. As I walk into my apartment there's no sign of Helen anywhere, I'm just thinking, too late, she must be in with Ethel, when I see the note stuck to my fridge door.

Dick, you're late! Ethel wanted to go visit her sister, it's her birthday. I've taken her over in a cab, dogs and all. Goldie won't start, sounds like the lead again, be an Angel and fix it for me. See your 'Big Boy' later, Big Boy.

I found her car keys hanging on the plastic dog's nose in the kitchen, it's a throwback to the previous lessee of the apartment, it came with the dog fleas in the shag pile and the zebra-patterned wallpaper in the spare room, it cost 150 bucks to get the place fumigated and still the wallpaper persists.

For the first time in months, I slept solid all night, I've got a cooked TV and a crick in the neck to prove it. I rise gracefully from my couch and tour my apartment, ending up in the bathroom, that's funny, there's no sign of Helen anywhere, either she didn't return last night or I fell asleep watching the late movie and she went off in a huff. I meet my bathroom mirror and vacantly watch my right-hand stroke my morning shadow, mmm, mental note, a bunch of flowers and some candy is required.
I had a shower and was catching up with today's news, over a bowl of Carob-Coated Corn Clams and a coffee, when the phone rang.

'Dick Chase, private investigator?' Coming from the other end there's this "Hmmmm, hmmmmm" in what sounds like tones of constricted mirth, I know instinctively it's a lady. 'O.K. lady, count to five and start over, from the beginning will yer?'

'Hmmmmm? Hmmmmm!' It's the same again, only this time pitched a little higher, it's a funny thing, I know that tone, now I'm smiling.

'O.K. lady, I'm getting warm, try me once more.'

'**Hmmmmm!**' I've got it, I interrupt.

'Hi there, Aunt Sylvia, how are you, what are you up to these days, how are the old pins?'

'Hmmmmmmmmm......' There's a pause, followed by a bit of scuffling and dropping of a handset, then. 'Dick, Dick, my pins are full of cramp you dumbhead, it's me, Helen, I've been tied up and gagged all night, get your ass the hell over here, I'm scared.' She burst into tears.

While I pump gas on a short stretch of vacant carriageway, through Holland Tunnel, my waste disposal is finishing off the remainder of the Carob-Coated Clams to an empty house. Helen, rents a second-floor apartment in a brownstone building over in Jersey City. As I bound up the 6 or 7 steps that bridge the basement flat and lead to her front door, I'm oblivious to the clicks and whorls of a motor-driven, zoom-lensed Zenit that's shooting me into posterity. Helen, has freed herself and is sitting at her breakfast bar drinking black coffee, almost as black as the mascara that had dried on her cheeks. Momentarily, I hold her in my arms, before pouring myself a coffee and asking what happened. Oblivious to the fact all she's saying is being monitored via a small bug hidden inside the hollow base of her liquidiser, Helen began spilling the events that led me to thinking she was my Aunt Sylvia.

'One of Ethel's dogs caught my tights, I decided to come here and change, I used my key but the door fell open. I saw the frame had been smashed, before I could think, someone grabbed my wrists and pulled me inside.' Nervously Helen bit her lip while she composed herself. 'There were two of them, they had stockings over their heads.'

'Were they white?'

'No, more a battleship grey.' Absent-mindedly I peeled a nicotine patch from my wrist, then, instantly being overcome with a raging desire for a cigarette, I slapped it back on.

'What happened next?'

'They dragged me screaming into the bedroom and pushed me onto the bed, Dick, I thought they were going to rape me.'

'Is that why they were screaming?' Helen smiled between the tears.

'No silly, I was the one doing the screaming.' We made for some more comfortable seating, the place had been systematically turned over, someone wanted to put the frighteners on Helen and they'd succeeded. Her lounge is a long, cool room facing north, the sun doesn't usually creep around here till late afternoon. As we sat in the early gloom, I put an arm around her neck and pulled her towards me, I blew into those familiar curls and watched them play across an orange band buried in her soft locks. I spoke quietly into her ear, unaware all I'm saying is being picked up by a small bug hidden behind a framed jigsaw of the Grand Canyon hanging on the wall behind us.

'Why don't you move in, we've talked about it often enough, just for a couple of weeks, till this whole thing blows over?' Helen feels safe now and snuggles comfortably up against me. She stayed there, unmoving, silent, for a long moment, I can feel the tension draining out as she calmed herself. She spoke, sounding reassured, determined.

'O.K. Dick, but on one condition.'

'What's that Honey?'

'I get to cook.'

'You got it.'

*

The LED on my bedside clock tells me it's 3:30 a.m. Helen's soft breath is lightly playing on my right shoulder while my insomnia is hard at it counting the cars that pass down the street, we've lost count but that doesn't mean a thing. My mind keeps riffling through the various aspects of the case, it looks like it's gonna be another freebie unless Julie had the foresight to direct the executors of her will to pay the gumshoe who finds her killer. I watch twenty-four's or is it twenty-five's ghostly apparition creep across the ceiling, slink down the wall and disappear behind my bookcase. Hmm, maybe her parents will cough up, or there might be a boyfriend. Another apparition appears, that's odd, it stopped on the ceiling and went out, the strange thing is, across the street there's a total no stopping zone. I slide out of bed and go over to the window, with my back to the wall, I crane my neck as far as I can, and peer out. At first there's nothing, just the brief hoot from a boat somewhere out there on the Hudson, then I see it, the orange glow of a cigarette as someone draws in, oddly, it seems to be looking right back at my window, straight at me. I watch the little light glow then dim as the sucker indulges his habit, I'm dressed and on the street before you can count ten, someone is taking an interest in my apartment and I don't remember giving notice to quit. I crouch behind Goldie and look diagonally through her windows. The vehicle is one of those big jeep jobs, that makes a trip to the shopping mall look like a three-week vacation to Zabriskie Point. A passing bus gives me cover to advance and disappear between two buildings opposite, I dash to the far end, turn left, run about fifteen yards and turn left again, down the alley that serves all the fire escapes and garbage chutes, it comes out right in the middle of that big jeep job. I get halfway when I'm jumped on by what feels like the combined muscle of the New York Giants out on a late-night shopping spree, some two-hundred-pound dumbbell, who has a grip like a pneumatic vice, grabs my head and begins a drive to the Buffalo twenty-yard line. To keep the drive alive, two of his teammates make a play for my arms, and just in case I'm not being obliging enough, my legs are scooped up on the run and the whole of me is being rushed forward for a touchdown, or?... Geez, they're gonna ram me into the vehicle. I struggle to free myself but it's no use, Pneumaticman just turns up the pressure, I brace myself as he hits the brakes, leaving the rest of the pack to pile in. I'm dragged inside the big jeep and sat on by the other three, the rear doors slam shut and we head off. Just then I pick up a piece of the luck, it's black beneath this arm, but I sense the flashing blue light of a police vehicle close on our tail. As we veer and screech around every corner it stays with us, after a violent right and a lot of backpedalling down a steep slope, we slam to a halt, the rear doors open and everyone bundles out like I'm carrying the plague.

'Get the hell out you slime ball.'

'Yeah, let's take a look at you, dung brains.' I manage to sit, only to find my head is permanently facing to the left and fixed at a downward slant, the whole of my neck and head feels numb. I pull myself out of the police vehicle, because that's what it is, the blue light was fixed to the roof all the time, I'm standing in the police compound looking down at a floodlit pair of size sixteens that must belong to the waste heap who had hold of my head.

'Let's see your face, ass hole.' Slowly I lean back so I can eyeball the big one.

'Which ass hole do you want me to face first, you brainless bunch of dumb heads, you've just brought in an innocent member of the public?'

SIXTEEN

As I walk back to my apartment dawn is just beginning to break above the skyscrapers, setting their lofty extremities ebony against its wispy blue bits, that even as I walk are slowly increasing in size until they envelop the entire space over the Big Apple, engulf the whole of New York State and by daybreak, saturate the entire western hemisphere. As far as I'm concerned, my little skirmish with the cops is history, they thought I was some vagrant on the lookout for an open door, maybe a scrap of food and the chance of somewhere dry to spend the night. Our current mayor is clamping down on that kind of behaviour, it's called zero tolerance, what puzzles me about this whole intolerance deal is, who's cashing in on the tolerance that's what I wanna know, anyhow the big guy bought me breakfast so what the heck, we all make mistakes. I reached my street with the crisp dawn air numbing my temples from the inside, standing across from my apartment I can see the lights are on, Helen must be wondering where I am. The vehicle that turned out to belong to the police department has gone, but in the gutter, adjacent to a small oil spill, something is calling me, I pick it up, an empty book of matches, I flip it over, Funtangos, well I never.

I enter my apartment with all the show and bravado of a homing pigeon that had just completed a west/east passage across our hallowed State, in the hope of finding his mate, preened and ready for action.

'Geez Dick, where the hell have you been? My new floor manager starts today, I couldn't dry my hair, do you know where the dryer is? Look, don't tell me now Honey, I'm gonna be late for Fred's pep talk.' Helen's mind is spinning, searching for some more programme. 'Ah, I'm gonna be an hour or so late tonight, Baby, I'm going swimming with Diane from personnel, okay, oh, and by the way, your eggs are simmering on low.' She walked a couple of yards down the hall, stopped, and turned around. 'You just keep them simmering till tonight, Babe, and I might turn up the heat – ciao.' That's Helen all over, a regular whirlwind, I'll tell you one thing though, when she makes love it's worth staying in for.

I switch off the electric, the eggs can wait, I pour myself a coffee and pick up the phone, I know McDougall has the morning off, he's looking after his kids while Lucy, his wife, is having a wisdom tooth removed. We started with polite conversation, but I swiftly moved on to some filthy expletives about my experience last night, I wanted him to hear it from me first, McDougall couldn't hold himself together and speak at the same time, I butt in.

'Hey McDougall, it's not funny.'

'Yeah, no, but Dick, you gotta admit,' He's cracking up. 'It was nice of Maloney to stand you breakfast.'

While McDougall explains to one of his kids, he can't make popcorn by putting Rice Krispies in the toaster, my concentration drifted to the year planner, stuck on my freezer, and the word "wings" that had been carefully inserted on my birth date in a few days' time. I knew straight away what it meant, it meant Helen had booked me that flying lesson I've always wanted, it meant, on Friday, instead of the endless grind of pounding the Manhattan sidewalk, in search of the elusive link between a book of used matches, a failed high school netball champion and an unidentified, speeding ambulance, it was gonna be,

'Twoo and three. Come fly with meee, doobee doobeedoo, Fly me to the Moon, yeah.' McDougall cut in.

'Hey Sinatra, do me a favour will yer and put Dick back on the line?' McDougall was unmoved, he's more your all-night fishing type with a flask of warm coffee and a tin of greasy maggots, not me, I've always wanted to fly a plane. Hey, that's it, aerial photography, surveillance, surveillance camera why didn't I think of it before?

I'm now back at Funtangos, only this time I'm across the street in Laskie's Book Mart, in the gents on the mezzanine floor. A recce from the sidewalk, shows a camera on the outside of this wall where I'm now standing on the pan, craning my neck to see out of a frosted louvered glass vent. O.K. now let's have a lookee here, ah ha, yes, it's a Spy-You, great, I know the receptionist already, her name's Hazel, mmm, Hazel with the dark-brown hair, actually she's a redhead but who's talking about her head? We bumped into one another about four years ago, at a fancy-dress party, she went as an "available" married woman, and I went as her husband's private dick. It turned out his suspicions were right, but he didn't tell me he was the sole proprietor of, Pimps are Us, and that he couldn't keep his hands off the merchandise. Hazel felt jilted and let down, so we became lovers and started a little side-line of our own. I climbed down and had a quick Bruce Lee, I didn't put that in my diary, but I did pencil in a sortie to Spy-You's coffee vending machine is pressing. With that aim, I'm now heading for Laskie's main entrance, two plate glass doors, each with a large embossed chromed brass handle in the shape of half a pseudo book, the closed doors make a very nice contemporary mock-up of The Adventures of Huckleberry Finn.

Well, there's a thing, I'm being paged over the in-house Tannoy system, to go to the gift wrap counter where I can take an incoming phone call. The assistant is a real pearl, Pearl Harper, senior supervisor, a blue rinse from Yonkers.

'Hi Pearl, the name's Dick Chase, I believe there's a call for me.' She handed me the phone, with one hand, while at the same time she puffed her bouffant with the other. I announced my presence with the disdain of a vulture that's just gobbled down a corpse's eyeball.

'Mr. Chase, the name's Ted Crawford, I'm with Air Flights East Coast. To tell the truth this is a bit of an awkward situation, we've been in communication with Ms. Helen McCluskie, about a surprise flight for you in a few days' time, she put us in touch with you this morning. I know this has kinda gone and blown the whole element of surprise here but, well, the thing is we've double booked your flight time and we're wondering, if we can bring it forward a week. I can take you up, personally, today, and you could be taking the controls in say, two hours from now.' Suddenly my stomach feels like it's digesting an eyeball, I've heard of Air Flights East Coast, s'funny though, I don't remember telling Helen I was coming here this morning, or maybe I let it slip while we were preening our feathers on the doormat. My schedule's fairly empty, there's no reason I can think of why I can't take up their offer, hell, I'll go for it. I told Ted, my pilot, I'll be straight over just as soon as I pick up my parachute, we both laughed at my joke and he gave me directions for once I reach JFK.

I'm heading for Laskie's main entrance, only this time I'm gonna call a cab, I see a vacant one sitting outside so I put a spurt on. That's when it happens, that stroke of fate that never happens in the same place twice. My arms and legs splay out sideways with the shock. My head is jerked hard to the left as an excruciating pain burns deep into my right cheekbone, jarring the whole side of my face, as I'm struck by lightning. Actually, I'm not struck by lightning, I've just run into Laskie's two plate glass doors that were closed in my path, in my haste I didn't see the oversized pseudo-book handles...hell, I've read Huckleberry Finn already and I didn't like it the first time around.

SEVENTEEN

By the time my cab reached JFK, and pulled up outside area 19, south side, private flights, my face is no more than a dull ache and apart from a tendency for my left knee to tingle, my limp has almost disappeared. As I walk into the compound, a twelve-foot-high wire-fenced parking lot, about the size of a soccer pitch, my adrenalin level is as high as a kite. I'm busy looking for AFFECT, when a small blue jeep draws up beside me, the driver turns out to be my pilot, Ted Crawford. He's got jet black hair, greased straight back into a ponytail, he's well-built with a scar on his left temple. Wearing a brown bomber jacket that looks pre-war, over jeans and a t-shirt that look like they're straight out the box, Crawford offers me some gum and a smile that's reminiscent of Jack Nicholson's Joker.

We're now bumping across the tired, heat-worn grass, heading far away from the main traffic of JFK, to a distant corner where a few small aircraft are glinting in the noonday sun. Once seated in a crate that looks like it's done time crop spraying some Columbian poppy fields, Crawford explains this isn't a flying lesson per se, but more a hands-on flying experience once we get up there, so, he doesn't initiate me into the pros and cons of radio speak or take-off protocol. That explained permission is sought and granted for our advance to runway and before you can say up, up and away, we're heading off to go smack some greenfly.

As I sit in the front left-hand seat awaiting my turn at the wheel, there's nothing but a vacant sky ahead, and there's nothing at 1 o'clock, geez, I hope I didn't say that out loud, I bring a diverting hand up to my mouth and cough. Crawford's hands are gently caressing the controls, he speaks, raising his voice above engine noise.

'We're at five thousand feet, look, the Atlantic.' As I look down, Crawford continues. 'It's 1 o'clock, it'll be your bird in about fifteen minutes.' He smiles and gives me some more gum. As I chew, vacantly, looking down at the flat green-grey ocean, my eyes fall onto a small boat as it ploughs forward, leaving a whiff of white behind it, this turns out to be a surprisingly long and ever-widening V of a wake, that makes me follow it back to its source only to realise it's a ship. As I peer into the void it becomes the take-off platform for a helicopter, just visible, but I lose it as the ocean changes its skin.

I've wanted to fly a plane since my short pants days with Mom reading me those pop-up-book Pan Am Polly adventure stories, when grim, determined Pan Am Polly would fly through rain, sleet and snow, battling on against impossible headwinds only, at the turn of a page, to burst through the clouds. Now, with a port-to-star-board grin, as Polly, who just happened to be a talking Boeing 707 is rewarded for her efforts with a blue sky, a yellow sun, and an endless carpet of snowy white hills. I've done Concorde since then, I've got the small gold lapel badge and silver knife and fork set to prove it. I've experienced the phenomenon of my stomach expanding by three inches as we hit Mac 2 and I down my third glass of champagne.

The first indication I get there's something wrong is the noise of the engine, it's silent like we're running on a rubber band. Then, in the blink of an eye, we're upside down and to top it all some new g-force has me glued to my seat. I try to eyeball Crawford but can't turn my head and I'm unable to speak, my mouth seems to be forced shut. Jesus, this is it, we're plummeting out of control towards the Atlantic. Grasping the hopelessness of our situation, Crawford hits the radio and the full plight of our dilemma becomes crystal.

'Hey Brad, putting that "Mickey", neat, into the gum has worked a treat, Chase is sitting here like a corpse already, he went out like a light.'…'No way, I'll wait till ten thousand feet, as planned.'…'Hell no, that's the best bit, I'll just open the door and tip the wings, he'll drop like a stone and hit the sea like a crate of fish food.'

With all the adrenalin I can muster I manage to right the plane and my hearing's returned. So far so good, but I still can't move a muscle, I'm a sitting duck, a sitting dead duck. As Crawford reaches over the controls, I notice his watch, it's 1:15, I also notice we're at nine thousand feet and climbing, that's not on his watch, that would be one hell of a watch. I make a supreme effort to punch his lights out, but only manage to raise the index finger on my right hand by half an inch. Giving me that Joker smile he tips the plane abruptly and I slump against the door before he rights it again.

'Just practising Chase, next time it'll be for real.' Once more Brad is surfing the airwaves.

'Hey Ted, I've just received our next assignment, and you're gonna love this one, white male, 43, and guess what, he's a cop, his name is McDougall?'

'You hear that Chase, you're in luck, some cop's gonna investigate your demise, personally, from the other side?' Crawford doesn't know it yet but he's a dead man, all I gotta do is get myself out of this predicament, that would be easier if I could move more than just the index finger on my right hand. Why is Doogie on their hit list, he's just a small-time cop with a reputation for securing more traffic convictions than anyone else on the precinct? Crawford reaches over to fiddle with the door, if I go for his wrist, with my teeth, and don't let go, I might be in with a chance, only the slipstream is keeping the door shut, his arm withdraws, nope, my head is still in the headrest. I can't move a muscle, I can mumble a bit though and must be making some sound or other.

'Chase, you're just in time to say goodbye, your flying lesson is about to begin, I'm sorry I won't be around to see your treble somersault with twist and a pike into the ocean, but I've got a dinner date with my gorgeous P.A. she takes care of all my "bullets". Any last requests before I tip out the garbage?'

I seem to be able to mumble a bit clearer now, but what I can't do is entangle my feet in the seat stays to anchor myself in. 'This is it Chase, your flying lesson begins now.' The plane starts to tip and I'm bracing myself, maybe I can hold on by the seat of my pants, I slide over and out through the door, maybe not.

It's done, I'm done, there's no way out of this, I'm dropping like a cartoon character towards an intransigent Atlantic, I try not to look, but no matter what I do I end up confronting my doom. At first the ocean seems to keep its distance, but as the seconds flash by there's no doubt about it, I'm going down. I'm twisting and turning and in that fleeting moment when I don't know which way I'm facing, out the corner of my eye I see something looming close by, I know exactly what it is, it's an Albatross. I spin over again, Geeeez! from right outta nowhere some helicopter has just missed me and now I've lost the bird, I mustn't hit the darn thing I might break a leg. In an instant the damn bird slams right into me. '*Jesus H*' I shouted '*What next.*' Already I can hardly breathe with this crazy g-force grabbing my face, now I'm being crushed to death by a pair of legs gripping me around the waist. Hey, wait just a second, something's just snatched me out the goddamn sky. I struggle to look up, it's not an Albatross after all, and judging by the state-of-the-art gear, including the mirror-visored-helmet, it belongs to a marine or maybe a navy SEAL. He struggles but manages to slip a harness around me and pulls it tight before giving a reassuring thumb, whatever drug Crawford had slipped me it's fast wearing off and I'm able to raise a thumb in return. As I look down, the ocean's coming up a bit too fast for comfort, this must be an attempt to put as much sky as possible between Crawford and me before giving the game away. Without warning my stomach smacks into my pelvis as a parachute deploys and we decelerate big time, the marine's grip has doubled through what I can only guess is a tricky manoeuvre, only when the chute is fully opened and we've slowed down does my saviour relent.

We're getting really close now, it'll soon be over and for the first time, I'm feeling good about the situation. I'm just wondering what my rescuer has in mind for his next trick, when a pack releases from his lower back, it misses me and dangles on a taut wire below us, then, just feet from the sea it bursts into a Day-Glow orange dinghy. Five seconds later and I'm rolling about like a two-year-old, while Superman stands there rigid, balanced, holding a carabiner, I've been released quickly for the user's health and safety. We're both home and dry, and for the second time today, my luck's in, the water's dead calm. My saviour switches on a small device he removed from a pouch in the dinghy, I guess it's a homing beacon, someone's gonna pick us up. Then, standing there, black leather gloved fingers undo the visor straps, the suspense is tangible as my hero pauses for effect before finally throwing off the headgear and speaking in a familiar voice.

'If you only knew how difficult, how impossible that was, you are one hell of a lucky Dick.' She slams a beaming smile right at me and starts laughing as Salinka, or should I say, Colonel Palchikova, sits opposite and throws me a Hershey bar.

EIGHTEEN

So far my day hasn't gone to plan, how could I have known I should have packed my swimming trunks, or that my wisecrack about going to collect my parachute would turn out to be prophetic? If I'd known Salinka was gonna grab me out the sky I'd have worn my best suit. I was gonna speak when a blast from a ship's funnel made us both look out to sea, there, steaming towards us is a pall of exhaust, I guess, is our lift. This agent's sudden appearance made today's events seem manifestly unreal, what was she even doing here and without so much as a postcard? Her intervention must mean the interception of intel, agents mobilised, high-level planning, someone having a hunch, she's got a ton of explaining to do.

'Dick, look, I know I've got a load of explaining to do and you've got a lot of questions you need to throw at me, but first you must listen, we don't have much time. When we're picked up, they'll be expecting a stunt coordinator, from an amateur film company "Time Lapse" based in Colorado, your name's Chick Solomon, I'm your assistant, Power West, I chose the names, what do you think?' I stared hard at Power.

'Chick! How come I get the lousy name?' She's telling me something but I'm not taking it in, I'm confused, I'm still living the nightmare and besides, there's something else on my mind.

'Are you listening to me?' The thought arrived like a juggernaut slamming all its brakes on at once.

'Hold it, I've just remembered, they're after McDougall, he's their next assignment, I heard it over the radio.' The Russian thought for a moment.

'Yes, that was unexpected, look, it's being dealt with, I *have* got back up.' She grabbed my arm 'But for now you're Chick and I'm Power, we mustn't get it wrong.' We didn't get it wrong and judging by their total lack of interest in me they'd never even heard of Chick Solomon, they were all over Power West though.

As I'm now dead, for the time being, we must reach the safe house Salinka has already established. While driving away from Manhattan wharf, I'm thinking about the woman behind the wheel, it's the same woman who once walked into my life, then breezed out, leaving me in turmoil. I'll never forget the night we slept together, well, it's the bits when we were awake, I'll never forget. Amongst the smell of diesel, and erect, traversing cranes, it struck me what an inconsequential action that can be in the wrong hands, I don't know where that came from, maybe it's guilt, after all, Helen was laid up in hospital at the time.

'I'm a little surprised to see you, I take it this is business, not pleasure.'

'Saving you is always a pleasure.' I smile as I study her more closely.

'O.K. what's it all about, or am I gonna find out when you read my eulogy?' She went through the gears like a bat out of hell.

'The last time we were together you saved our lives by killing three men?'

'Yeah, well, there was that, one of them tried to cave your chest in with the muzzle of his Kalashnikov, not to mention fracturing my jaw. I did kill him, and his two stooges, it was them or us as I recall, anyway, you missed.'

'I never miss, one of the stooges, the younger one, was the brother of an oligarch, you have a price tag on your head.' I looked at her, she glimpsed at me while driving, she glimpsed twice.

'That's not all is it, there's something else?' She paused as if preparing herself.

'He killed my two sisters, the oligarch, don't, don't say anything, there are no words, it's all been said. Now he's after me, you, McDougall, and possibly Helen, though that hasn't been confirmed.' After my "flight" today, I had no reason to doubt her, and I have a bad feeling this jerk will stop at nothing to achieve his aim.

'Who is he, does he visit the States, can't we get him first?' She hovered over my words before answering, clear and definite.

'No, I must get him, before he finds me, we have history, and I want to avenge my sisters.'

We reached the hideout, a mobile home parked up with fifty or so others in neat rows down a dusty track off the main highway. As I climb aboard *'The Enterprise'*, that's the name above the door of our slick, silver, eight-wheeled safe-house, I'm about to witness a level of competent ability to put German efficiency on the back foot. Inside I found Helen and McDougall, with some guy I'd never seen before, sitting at a table playing cards while finishing off what looked like a very nice California red. The guy stands up with obvious relief written all over his face, he's about my height, good-looking, with strong hair, he speaks softly, in Russian, his smile is contagious. I glance back at my saviour, she's blushing like a ripe strawberry, he isn't talking about the weather. She let him continue before, laughingly, interrupting in English.

'Lenny, Dick understands Russian.' There's a pregnant pause, Lenny is looking a bit embarrassed, I glance at him, raise my eyebrows, and smile, Salinka broke the silence.

'Dick, I'd like you to meet Lenny Brodsky, he's my husband, Lenny, this is Dick Chase, the private investigator who saved my life.' He came straight to me and spoke in perfect English.

'Then I'm pleased to meet you sir, I've heard a lot about you.' I shook his outstretched hand.

'Take no notice of your wife, I don't have a word of Russian, but I got your subtext.' He went over to her, I guess he wanted to know how her morning had gone. I homed in on Helen, she was all agog as I told her I'd gotten her reminder about my birthday present, coded on the year planner on my freezer. Who else had she told, that's what I wanted to know, she was speechless. I'd had my eye on the last of the wine, but as I was talking, McDougall quaffed it down.

These preliminaries were all too much, considering the threat level and task ahead, Lenny had outlined the story to Helen and McDougall and brought them here. The threat to them was calculated to be so severe the CIA arranged that they can be absent from their employment, that had the undesirable effect of putting the fear of God into Helen. I put her mind at rest by reminding her about my flight this morning and if I can walk away from that, she can walk away from it too, I think that did the trick, Helen straightened me out.

'Chick, number one, that doesn't help, and two, those wings I'd drawn on the calendar, they weren't about a flying lesson for you, they were a reminder to me to get some ladies' things, you know, pantyliners, for the use of, I was running out you dummy.' It looks like my thinking is getting a bit loose, I need a break, someone knew I was desperate to fly though, knowing who that was could be key to this whole operation....

'Chick!!?'

It turns out The Enterprise was quite a find, I don't know how long we'll be holed up here but as temporary accommodation goes, it's in the express elevator. Helen was tired and went to bed, our space is at the far end, it's got a tiny porthole and an emergency exit, so that's good. The rest of us are sat around the table discussing our options, I began, I've got a lot of questions and I need some answers.

'This oligarch who's trying to kill us, who is he?' Salinka did the honours.

'His name is Ivan Kozlov, he made his money, predominantly in vodka, but his portfolio includes military munitions and gold-plated bathroom ware. It is said, if you have a Kozlov shower you become squeaky clean.' She laughed. 'That is what the schoolchildren sing in the playground when skipping the rope. They do not know his celebrity status is because he is corrupt, his wealth is built on dirty money he accumulates by bank-rolling key members of the KGB so they turn a blind eye to his corrupt deals. He was,'…She paused and looked at Lenny, who just folded his arms. 'He was my husband, but that is history, a nightmare I wish to forget, I was a young, naïve KGB agent, my head was turned…. you outline the plan, Lenny.'

'Hold it,' I interrupted, 'I've got a couple more questions. Why is Helen in danger, who were the people behind the ship, and is there any more wine?' Silently Lenny left our space, I asked McDougall to join him for a while, I need to speak to Salinka. She sat there smiling, anticipating my words. 'What you did today, I have enough physics to know that it was damn near impossible.'

'It was, you are right, damn near, but possible, I had one chance, you had one chance, and it worked. Did I tell you I studied aerodynamics at university? I wrote a dissertation called *"Dropping and Catching out of Aeroplanes and Helicopters",* I'll let you have a copy one day, had you been dropped at anything less than 10,000 feet you'd have been fish food.' I reached across the table and took her hand, I disguised my action as gratitude, but I knew it was much more dangerous than that.

'Thanks, thanks a lot, I owe you one.' The others are returning, I withdrew my hand.

'Hey Dick, Lenny tells me you don't know what happened to me today.' McDougall placed out a clean set of wine glasses while Lenny began pouring from a fresh bottle. 'First, I roll up at the station in time for afternoon shift, when Diaz, on the desk, tells me the chief wants me in his office, pronto. Well, I assume it's the donut run see, only this time it's definitely not, just get a load of this. The chief tells me at 2 pm the FBI are gonna storm the building and arrest me and I've gotta go along with it, officially I've been thrown in jail with no chance of parole, my case is waiting for the courts and it's gonna take as long as it takes, if you get my drift.' I can see McDougall's brain working overtime. 'Geez Salinka, just how long is this deal gonna take?' Lenny steps in.

'O.K. everyone, no more questions, the sooner we get moving on this the sooner it'll be over and you'll be able to get back to your wife and kids, Peter, agreed?'

The Enterprise fell silent, I had a feeling they'd better enjoy the peace because the way I feel I'm going into warp drive and that means I'm gonna unleash hell.

NINETEEN

As I lay awake trying to reboot the salient facts in my head, to see if I can find any flaws in our plan, Helen lay fast asleep beside me, totally unaware she's sharing the same tactical headquarters as the Hit Squad, well, that might have been the wine talking, but let's face it, it's better than the Kill Factory, and I just had to point that out.

Earlier.......

'O.K. now listen up, so, you're about to deliver the coup de grace, saving yourself and your team in the process. Unexpectedly the factory hooter goes off for coffee break and before you know it your concentration wanes and it's a bullet in the head, it's not rocket science!' McDougall, broke the polite silence.

'O.K. Dick, we'll go with your suggestion.' They all look at one another and nod in agreement, I heard an echo of myself and decided not to finish my wine.

Still no sign of blissful oblivion, hmmm. We came up with a loose game plan, but we all know it can change at any moment. Kozlov, the corrupt entrepreneur with the stupid name, I hope he's enjoying the view because his days are numbered, has got so much wealth he's unaware his ex-wife still carries a "Slush Funds are Us card" in connection with one of his Swiss bank accounts. It holds about $50,000,000, just to drip-feed his Politburo has-been cronies. The Barren Bulls, as he calls them, are in it up to their red necks, in return he gets immunity from anything and everything. Salinka says he's worth a cool $40 billion, well he might be, but money doesn't buy you everything. He didn't know he'd hired a ship complete with helicopter and a fully functioning crew who thought they were taking part in making the latest blockbuster with, Chick Soloman, directing and starring as *The Man with the Solid Gold Parachute,* and, Power West, as *Janie Bond,* "Power" couldn't get over how the Philippine crew took all that garbage on board so willingly. This case, if I can call it a case, is the real thing though, I'm just your regular private eye, with a fairly average clientele, until I met this KGB agent, I'd never killed three people in one day before. Don't get me wrong, I've had my share of close shaves and hairy moments, I guess it goes with the territory, let's face it, when it's you or them, it's gotta be them. It turns out Kozlov is a regular visitor to the States, his private jet is often over here. According to his ex-wife, his raison d'etre is to exterminate both of us in revenge for the death of his brother, but there is another reason he's here and that diversion might be our salvation. It's the final of The American Baseball Leagues, *All States Challenge*, to win the coveted *Golden Balls Trophy* being held at the Shea stadium. Kozlov, owns the challengers, *The Long Island Liberators,* but he's gonna have to wait for revenge, tomorrow we top my pilot, Crawford. I have been putting in my take on all our planning and no half-baked Ruskie Oilyshark is gonna thwart this little gem, it's one of mine…ZZZzzzzzzzz.

Something woke me, I'm out of bed and silently making my way down the Enterprise, someone had opened and closed a door and for some reason, I found that compelling. It turned out it was Lenny, who'd been out to get some vittles, he slung the newspaper at me.

'What do you think Dick, you've made page two?' I caught the early edition and went straight there.

"PRIVATE EYE WHO WON'T MAKE CORPORAL. Private Eye, Richard Lincoln Chase, known as Dick Chase, turned up at the city morgue late last night after his dead body was discovered on Manhattan beach by a dog walker. The New York City Police Chief, who was Chase's one-time boss, said "Chase was a good friend, a good cop, and a good private investigator, he always did his best, whenever he could".

Did my best, whenever I could! I knew there was a reason I didn't get that promotion, the chief had me down as a sometime underperformer, if he saw me doing my best trying to fly yesterday, he wouldn't have said that. One thing did turn up though, as it happens, Lenny's an excellent cook, his scrambled eggs are to die for. Probably not a good choice of words, given the circumstances, let's just say he's an artist, that makes me feel a whole lot safer.

Just Salinka and me set out to top Crawford, I don't need anyone to hold my hand, but it's nice to be chauffeured through the morning rush hour. I've got a plan, I swapped clothes with McDougall, who's a tad smaller than me, and Lenny insisted I borrow his amazing Buffalo skin jacket. I smartened up my growth to make it look a bit more designer, and I think I look totally believable as Dick's twin brother Ray. This time there's no blue jeep to escort us to that far-flung corner, I spotted AFFECT on the side of a shabby-looking portable concrete garage, so it won't seem odd that we drive ourselves straight there. As we entered the bunker the geek operating the radio switched off and turned toward us.

'What d'you two want can't yer see I'm busy?' I took this low life to be Brad, we haven't met, but I'd recognise officer Dibble's voice anywhere, before I can open my mouth, Power West has stepped right into the frame.

'Hello, I'm Tina Chase, this is my husband, Ray. Ray's a bit upset at the moment he's just found out he's lost his twin brother Dick.' Brad looked dumbstruck, but he recovered nicely by standing up to offer me his condolences and calling me sir.

'I was sorry to read about that in the paper, if there's anything we can do sir, you just let me know.' Tina, my 'wife' is on a roll Chick Solomon only has the best Hollywood 'A-listers' on *his* books.

'The thing is, Mr?'

'Call me Brad, Mrs. Chase.'

'Brad, the thing is, Brad, Dick left a message to say he was going on a flight with your company the day he died, and we were wondering, Ray was wondering, what was his state of mind when he left you? Did he have a good flight? Did he give any clues about where he might be heading next?' My gut tells me Brad is bought, hook, line, and sinker, I have a feeling this whole exercise is gonna be a walk in the park. Brad is eager to help, I figured he thought he was covering his own and Crawford's ass convincingly, he got on the radio.

'Come in Ed.' There's a swishing noise.

'Brad, what now?' Officer Dibble genned up his partner pretty much as we had spilt the beans, I can hear Ed is a different animal – Mrs. Chase and me are gonna have to up our game. I interject purposely to be heard by Ed.

'Brad, tell the pilot not to rush, I just wanna sit here awhile and maybe have a coffee from that machine, like my brother would have.' See what I did there? Ed, replied.......

'I'm heading back now, my ETA in about ten, this new air filter has done the trick, over and out.' Brad, told us to help ourselves to coffee and we sat on an old couch perched along one wall that gave us a panoramic view of the airfield, we're finishing off just as a plane landed. I asked Brad if it was the same plane my brother had flown, he confirmed what I already knew.

'Is it alright if I walk over to meet the pilot? I'd like to see the interior, for sentimental reasons.'

'Mr. Chase, you just do that, I'll tell the pilot to expect you.' As I approached across the coarse dewless grass, Crawford remained seated and looking busy. I tapped on the offside door, the one I'd fallen from only yesterday, he leaned over to open it. I slightly tweaked my voice as a ruse.

'Thanks for letting me do this Ted.' He smiled, he's chewing gum, but this time he doesn't offer me any.

'It's Ed.' I thought I saw a puzzled expression but instantly he looked resigned, he's made his mind up, I'm the genuine article. He spoke, showing little emotion and less concern. 'I read about your twin you look a lot like him.'

'Yes, I know, I hear that…I heard that a lot, we were identical.' I'm not gonna waste any time on this low-life scum, I get in and sit beside him, I'm tempted to flatten his nose as a starter but I fight the urge. 'So, this is the seat my brother piloted his first plane from, how did he do?' I'm studying the controls and wondering what Crawford's gonna come up with.

'He didn't do too badly, I've seen worse.' He picked up a mill board and began filling out what looked like a load of aviation protocol. 'I've gotta fill in this data request, you have a look around, ask any questions yer like, you won't hold me up.' I scan the interior and notice it's a six-seater.

'I'll just squeeze back here and check it out, maybe someday I'll get you to take me and Mrs Chase up for a joyride over the Big Apple.' As I move to sit behind him my gun is quickly in my hands. 'I do have a question.' I've attached the silencer. 'How's your P.A. you know, the one who takes care of your bullets?' Crawford froze. 'I mean, will she take care of these bullets?' Instantly I loose three off into the back of his seat, he made a shallow gurgling sound with some exhalation of air, then collapsed forward, his seatbelt creaked with the dead weight. 'I'll take that as a no, shall I?' His crumpled shape revealed the controls, those dials and gauges, all spectators, the usual front-row voyeurs, waiting to witness me slip into the void. The moment I jumped down from the plane my accomplice exited the office like she'd been waiting for my cue. We met midway, Mrs. Chase is grinning all over her face.

'We won't be hearing from Brad again he had an accident with a fire extinguisher, he fell and smashed his head against it.' Outside the buildings there's no one around, so we calmly head over to my car.

'Geez, that wasn't on the itinerary, what the hell happened there?'

'Dick, the one thing we know about Brad, he was in league with Crawford to kill you and McDougall, trust me, we'll have our work cut out protecting ourselves as we go after Kozlov, we don't want to be watching our backs if Brad decides to get his revenge for his dead partner do we?' I guess Salinka was right.

We knew something was up, a mile off, there's a pall of grey smoke hanging over the trailer park, and as we drew close it became clear, the whole area is strewn with police cars and fire tenders. My driver carried straight on past without batting an eyelid, I rubbernecked the scene to confirm our worst fears, the Enterprise has been blown up, there's no other way to put it, the home has all but disappeared. Salinka is surprisingly calm considering her husband has probably been blown to pieces. I'm silent, thoughtful, worried about Helen and McDougall. My Russian agent appears to be weighing things up before speaking, seemingly at a tangent.

'Dick, do you know the story of the Trojan horse?'

'Yeah, it's the one about a Trojan horse.'

'O.K. what if it's relevant here?' I eyed her with surprise.

'Are you kidding me?' The thing with Greek legend is it's my Achilles' elbow. 'Trojan horse, hmmm, people hiding inside a wooden horse who surface when the coast is clear, don't tell me the Enterprise has a basement?'

'That's right, we hadn't got around to mentioning it but Lenny knew the drill in an emergency, as we speak, they'll be beneath the ground huddled on beanbags, eating Hershey bars and drinking mineral water, waiting for us to give them the thumbs up.' We drove on looking for somewhere to get a bite to eat while we wait for the coast to clear. I didn't say anything but I've got an immediate concern, how three people can disappear into an underground safe room, at the optimum moment, defies belief, did they take turns keeping watch? The first time I saw them together they were all sat around a table playing cards and drinking wine like it was the office Christmas party.

We pulled up at an empty diner, sitting at the far end I took my usual place with my back to the wall, I like to see what's going down. We discussed the menu and my Russian friend went to powder her nose. I sat there feeling strangely lightheaded, as if events had carried me into some postmodern, surreal, utopian western. I closed my eyes and rested them on my palms, it felt like I hadn't slept for days. I got the girl, her husband and Helen have both disappeared, all we have to do now is terminate her ex and we can sail off, arm in arm, into the sunset. No, that's no good, because in that scenario McDougall would probably be dead and where would that leave Lucy and the boys? All that is a pipe dream, what am I thinking? I can't be in love with Salinka again, can I? I am.

The door to the cloakroom opened, and there she is, that tall, slender, green-eyed brunette with a fair complexion as far as the eye can see. She approached smiling right at me her freshly painted lips red like wet cherries, she sat opposite, her voice a sprinkling brook.

'Do you ever get that feeling of déjà vu?'

TWENTY

'Tina?'

Like the Grand Canyon, Salinka is miles away, with her Russian roots, surviving a nation that's known extreme hardship is in her blood, then, losing her sisters so cruelly. I took her finger, a silent gesture of understanding, I thought I could shoulder some of the pain, I wanted to, I let go, anyway, she smiled, she understood.

'Valentina was my sister, Tatiana was my other sister, I thought they sounded too foreign so I plumped for Tina.' Unexpectedly two men walked in and sat inside the entrance, my spy didn't look around, I'd asked her not to, I used the diversion to change the subject.

'How come your English is so…English, the first time we met you had much more of a Russian slant?' She smiled.

'You noticed, well, you will be surprised to know I've lived in England for the past eighteen months, Cambridge to be exact, you will be even more surprised to learn Lenny Brodsky is not my husband's real name, it's Thomas Vaughan. He's an Englishman, an expert in the Russian language, he adopts a pseudonym, that's his sense of humour, he says it makes for a better tutor-student relationship. He's a university lecturer in Russian language and culture, while I've been working as a linguist for a firm of solicitors. If I tell you any more, I'm afraid I'm going to have to kill you.' Salinka is back to her old self, our two friends order coffee, I raise my eyebrows, that had the effect I wanted, she fell silent.

'And we'll have the hot waffles with the fruit and cream, have the nice day.' I spoke under my breath.

'Hmmm, nice accent, shame about the grammar. So how come you married this low life, what's his name, Kozlov?' She fixed me with a look of venomous loathing.

'Don't ask, to begin with I was singled out by a tutor at university, he owed the KGB a favour, I don't know, something like that. Anyway, I was persuaded into joining because of my language skills. Then my services were loaned to Kozlov, I had no say in it, I see now money must have changed hands. He wanted a linguist to scrutinise his crooked, foreign contracts, my abilities were crucial, we had to work closely together.' I notice our two friends are paying us more attention than is good for them. 'I come from a poor family, while Kozlov…his wealth is up there beyond the dreams of avarice, he infatuated me, he was handsome, charming, and I thought I loved him, I did love him, he said he loved me. It was a whirlwind romance and we got married, he lavished every gift on me, the President came to my wedding, can you imagine that?' Her tone darkened. 'His true character surfaced when he began seeing other women, like everything, he thought he owned me, he thought he controlled me, he misjudged me. I told him I wanted a divorce I didn't want to be part of his stable, whatever the benefits. To my surprise he let me go, I soon found out why, he is vindictive, he wanted to punish me, he threw me out, penniless.' Glimpsing our red nemeses, I thought I saw, I did see, a revolver being handled beneath the table. Salinka continued. 'I was so angry my world had collapsed, I applied for an active role in the department, I am a weapons and explosives expert, a trained subversive and I have other skills.'

'Other skills?'

'My sister Tatiana was blind at birth, he shot her mercilessly, I intend to return the favour.' I nod my head.

'How come we end up killing his brother, you must have recognized him?'

'I didn't know it was his brother, that day, with Streckovitch, Kozlov didn't know it either, they'd fallen out and not spoken for years, I'd never met him. After you killed Streckovitch, eventually leaving the way clear for glasnost, I was rewarded, I was allowed to leave the KGB. I got a good position interpreting for a bank, until one day my world fell apart, Kozlov found out his brother had been killed. He paid heavily, only to learn it was me, the wife who divorced him. He went berserk, he murdered my two sisters. That's when the chauffeur warned me and got me out, he risked everything for me…I owe him my life. I came to England and disappeared.'

My intuition just blew a gasket, and I knew we had to make the first move.

'O.K. my trained subversive, let's do some subverting. In your best American, announce to the world we need to get a move on, be creative, you're good at that. Start to walk out, I'll be right behind you, as you reach the two by the door say something in Russian, leave the rest to me. Don't go shooting anyone unless you have to, let me do the talking.

O.K. let's do it.' Salinka stood up and looked at her watch.

'Jesus Bill, look at the time, if we don't make a move we're gonna miss the show, I told you we didn't have time to stop for food.' As she walks out, I'm bringing up the rear, I'm also gobsmacked, I didn't see her place her revolver down the back of her skirt. She halted a yard or so in front of the two, her finger on the trigger. She spoke Russian with an inflection that sounded as sweet as a summer's day in a Moscow park, her beauty had captivated them, they answered in unison. On intuition Salinka dropped like a stone, I still wasn't 100% sure, they might be tourists and I didn't want that on my CV. The moment she disappeared they saw I was armed. From her vantage point the threat was clear, the one on the left suddenly looked totally panic-stricken, my money says she's thrust her weapon into his groin. She spoke in Russian, then, as his revolver clattered to the floor, she spoke to me.

'I told him if he moves one inch, he'll be a dead eunuch.' The other one is studying the barrel of my gun that's aimed right between his eyes. My partner stands up, keeping the eunuch in her sights.

'I hope you two speak English.' There's no reply. 'I'll take that as a yes. This is how it's gonna be, too many people have already died because of that penis-headed dung beetle, Kozlov, so we're gonna get into our car and drive off, you two are gonna sit here and enjoy the coffee, are you getting this loud and clear?' They look at each other but still don't speak. 'I'll take *that* as a yes.' I glance out the window. 'That's a nice Mustang you pulled up in, does it shift?' The younger one spoke, too keenly.

'Like a demon, naught to sixty in 5.3 seconds' Pitifully Salinka shakes her head, she rests her elbow on her hip displaying their pistols hanging from her index finger. She speaks in English.

'Forget about us, the next time we meet you might not be so lucky.' The distant, featureless look of recognition that passed between this agent and the senior one escaped Dick, he is ready with his English lesson.

'By the way it's have *A* nice day, you're welcome.'

As they walk hastily to their car, Salinka is grinning all over her face.

'Penis-headed dung beetle?'

'That's the best I could come up with, I was on full tactical alert.'

'Well, you might have insulted the dung beetle, but it was nice of you to let those two off the hook.'

'I am nice, didn't you know.' This KGB agent took my arm, I think, for a moment, she forgot who I was. It didn't take us long to decide our next move, my new partner has a death wish to go visit the Shea stadium, to give it the once over, the big match is tomorrow so I guess it's now or never. I figured it was my turn at the wheel, we need to disappear quickly and I can lay down rubber like an Old Daytonian. First, I pull up, take out my Colt and wreck the lead Pirellis on the Mustang. I give my partner a satisfied glance.

'Rock, paper, scissors, bullet.'

TWENTY- ONE

As we arrive the stadium is being made ready for the big event, bands practising, cheerleaders leading and strutting their stuff, we have to hope Kozlov and his heavies aren't around, we know we're taking one hell of a risk just being here. We had a quick recce to acquaint ourselves with the backstairs and the fire exits and we had a chance to plot the extent of the red-carpet area, it was roped off but someone had removed the rope and tied it artily around a pillar. I thought I was displaying my minimalist credentials by the understated yet nevertheless subtly ironic use of the reef knot, with stylised abandonment. There are eleven steps up to five viewing galleries all with panoramic views of the ground and all comfortably furnished to watch the game in VIP style. A young girl in one of them is busily polishing the glasses on a heavily laden drinks trolley, she quietly giggled to herself and carried on as if we weren't there. Salinka asked if she knew which room belonged to the Liberators, the girl smiled and stood up a framed notice she'd laid down while she worked, it read, **Welcome to The Long Island Liberators Management Team.**

'Have you lost your tongue?' The girl giggled, shook her head, and carried on with her work. Salinka took a package wrapped in gold paper, with ribbons and a card, from her handbag and carefully placed it on the table. 'This is for the boss of the Liberators will you see it stays right here?' She makes the card prominent, the girl smiles and nods her head. Looking at the young lady while delving into her bag a second time, Salinka places a twenty-dollar bill on the table. 'You've made such a beautiful job of those glasses this is for you.' The girl stared at the bill before picking it up.

'Thank you, miss.' She's the very essence of the beautiful, innocent, fresh-faced all-American school-girl, who has the whole world at her feet.

'So, you do have a voice.' Salinka went over to Dick. 'What next?'

'I think we've seen enough we'd better go we've tempted fate too much already.'

There's a large cleaner's store off the fifth room with a fire exit leading down to a circumventural passage, on the second level, that mimics the one in the basement, four compass-point stairwells connect them. We descended to the ground floor where we found sports shops, souvenir stalls, coffee bars, and exits, we left via an exit turnstile and are heading towards the motor. A military band is pouring out through the main entrance and filing in the same direction, some members have already reached their bus parked on the road in the shadow of the stadium and are embarking enthusiastically. My car is further down and to the right, opposite the stadium, in an outside space of a huge parking lot. As we approached, something drew my attention and I knew we'd been compromised. I'd spotted a handprint in the grime at the bottom of the driver's door, my guess is a bomb's been planted on the underside and the bomber used the door as a hand up, now I'm winging it. I take, Salinka's, arm and reroute towards the bus queue, she's puzzled, but now isn't the time to explain. The band's director occupies the first seat, he's already on to us and is frowning at the only two band members wearing mufti, he speaks assertively with a southern drawl.

'Where d'you think you're heading, this is my band and only I say who gets to go on the bus?' I sense he's a reasonable pragmatist, it's a gift I have, it works in unison with me being a physiognomist, it all comes with the job. Inexplicably, Abraham Lincoln sprang to mind, so I thought I'd run with it.

'Sir, we need yer help, I'm a private investigator, here's ma card. This here young lady is ma client and I'm doing my damnedest to protect her, trouble is the fifth column has got us surrounded, my car's been compromised and I'm asking you sir, if we can hitch a ride on your waggon as far as the exit, then we'll slip out the rear door and disappear?' Now, crucially, a big leopard is standing right behind me, carrying a bass drum and asking if he can get by. A tense situation wouldn't be the same without a bass drum carrying leopard, I squeeze forward obligingly. The band's director looks to the back of the bus and raises his voice.

'Who's in the seat by the rear door, Hanna, Styles, clear out a moment, that seat's reserved for our two guests?' He looks back at me. 'I'll see we stop briefly at the Jets' gate, you two can sneak off then, and good luck.' I thanked him and made with a quick salute, we're now sitting in the seat waiting to go, Salinka is bursting at the seams.

'What was that all about, why are we taking the bus?' I lower my voice.

'It's simple, a bomb's been planted under the motor.' She looked surprised.

'Oh, come on, how could you possibly know that, a bomb, aren't you being a touch melodramatic?' I looked at her, a bit puzzled.

'One word, The Enterprise.' I knew I said it, the moment I opened my mouth.

'That's two words, and anyway how come you know that?'

'It's years of getting it wrong and I'm not prepared to take the risk, are you?' She paused as if getting her head around it.

'O.K. so what do we do now?'

'Well, we've got three options, we can stay on the bus and disappear to fight another day, we can get off the bus and hide till the coast is clear, make the car safe and drive off, or we can hide out there and watch. If they think we've escaped they might retrieve the bomb, in which case I'll use it as target practice and blow them sky high.' Impulsively, Leopard Man, who's sitting in front of us, turns around and butts in.

'I'd go for blowing them sky high, that way you'll cut down on the opposition at the same time.' I look at our leopard-clad strategist, then at Salinka.

'I think he's got a point, those in favour raise your right hand… those against… It's unanimous, we blow the suckers sky high.' The bus stopped and we slid out the rear door to drop behind some shrubbery, a few yards further on there's a closed ice cream parlour in the shape of a giant cone, the door is at the rear, cautiously we slip inside. It turns out to be an excellent vantage point, if the bomb is retrieved and they head our way I'll get the perfect shot, now all we gotta do is wait. Salinka asked how I know it's been rigged, I explained what I'd seen and said it was the fate of The Enterprise that put me on my toes, that made us think of the others.

'They'll be above ground by now, with Tom's ingenuity they've probably found a new safe house, with on-suite and room service.'

'How come an expert in the Russian language and lecturer at Cambridge is involved in a highly toxic case like this.'

'To tell the truth I couldn't keep him away, Thomas Vaughan, was Captain Thomas Vaughan, British Army, Special Forces. That's all I can tell you, he doesn't talk about it.' I pause thoughtfully.

'What's with the gift-wrapped parcel you left on the table?' Salinka is grinning.

'It is a little present, a gift for Ivan Kozlov from the President of our country, well, to tell the truth it's really from me. When the President came to our wedding he gave me his special presidential card, I think it was meant as a souvenir, anyway I kept it until now, when I found I had a use for it.' Simultaneously we froze, two men are hovering around my motor, they're looking about, checking to see if the coast is clear. One of them gets down and starts feeling about underneath, the other one passes him a holdall and in no time they're heading our way. The windows of our cone are covered with stickers so we can't be seen, I've slightly opened one of them already, now all I gotta do is kill the holdall.

'It's like taking candy from a baby.'
Without warning three men burst through the rear door of our cone, they're armed and screaming, they mean business. They shriek long furious sentences

in Russian, strangely, I understand every word they say. I place my gun down on the counter and put my hands above my head. One of them picks up our weapons and speaks in English, he's gloating all over his oratory.

'Dimi, how does the saying go? Ah yes, it is like taking the candy from the baby.'

TWENTY-TWO

There's no possibility of getting out of this situation in a hurry, but there is one thing going for me, I've already been dumped out of a plane at ten thousand feet and survived. One slight reservation I have is the person who saved me is sitting opposite tied to a bench, we're both orally taped, so I guess a round of I Spy is out the question. We'd been sitting stationary in some delivery van for what seemed like hours, then, after what must have been a twenty-minute drive we pull up, we haven't crossed the Hudson but I sense we're pretty close. With a jolt we're off once more, but now it's stop start, stop start, like we're being let into some compound. At length, the rear doors are flung open and we're herded out at gunpoint onto what looks like an airfield, there're a lot of distant lights. It's dark now, cold and wet and I'm feeling thoroughly off-piste, it's not JFK, but some private setup, this must be the place where Kozlov, whatever his stupid name is, keeps his personal kite. It's a sizable hangar with a first floor, we're led up an iron staircase to where I'm about to get a big surprise, sitting, bound to three chairs, are Lenny, McDougall and Helen. On seeing us Helen let out a frightened wail, one of the Russians approaches her and raises his hand, another shouts, the first one stops dead in his tracks. That's good, that's very good, I recognise the placid one, he's one of our friends from the diner. He doesn't make eye contact with us, instead, he studies the other three while we're being firmly tied to our chairs. The five of us are sitting abreast, that's me, Salinka, Lenny,

McDougall and Helen. The placid diner man, from now on I'll refer to him as PD1, looks at his watch and hastily draws the others to him. After what I hope is a quick *résumé* of his house rules, he makes a swift exit. This leaves just three, no, there's a fourth, there's an office at one end and I've just spotted another goon standing inside nosing our predicament. So, there's the one we know has a short fuse and three others of whom nothing is known, one of the unknown approaches.

'I am going to remove the tape, keep the noise to a minimum or Dimi here will sort you out and that, I can assure you, will not be a pleasant experience.' He began to de-gaffer our mouths, I'm the first to speak.

'Are you okay Helen?' The poor girl is bent forward and quietly crying. 'It'll be alright, you'll see, hey, think of me falling out of the sky and how I'm still here.' Lenny is catching up with his wife, so far they've been treated all right, she asked what happened at the Enterprise, his reply is interesting.

'They knew we were down there, in the hole, they came straight to use, they must have had inside information.' I spoke to McDougall.

'Doogie, how you shaping up, have you taken anyone in yet?'

'Yeah, I'm shaping up good, they're all up in front of the judge in the morning, you'll be my chief witness won't yer?' The first unknown returns.

'Limit your conversation to the weather, and don't think you can escape.'

'Hey listen Pal, do me a favour will yer. The girl at the end, Helen, she's got nothing to do with this, she's innocent and doesn't have a clue who you are or what's going on. Can you cut her some slack and let her go?' He looked at me, uninterested, bored.

'You ask too many questions I don't intend to end up in your East River wearing a concrete overcoat.' Instantly I know we're at LaGuardia Airport.

'This boss of yours, when's he due, before the match?' I'm beginning to race his motor.

'He's arriving from Chicago, when the big game is over, he is coming back here for the grand finale, you are all in the losing team, including the women on the end, now that's enough, so shut it.' The conversation is annoying Dimi, who is losing it back in the office, my informant immediately replies with equal force, for some reason I found that interesting. Now they're all in the office, it has windows right along, there's a coffee machine, a wall heater, and a television. They're keeping an eye on us as they no doubt prattle over the state of the potato harvest. I speak to my KGB P.A. who's about to earn herself a pay rise.

'Did you pick anything up yet?'

'A number of rubles were exchanged, as if in a wager, because the idiot Cooper actually came up with something useful, but… I don't have a clue.' Cooper? Funnily enough I do have a clue, but it'll have to be parked up for the time being, she continued. 'Pegasus 2 is giving trouble, that's one of his planes, the bad news is the game is tomorrow, so we're all going to be spending the night tied to these chairs.'

We passed what felt like an eternity listening to McDougall's history in the force, in anecdotal form,

I'm just about to ask Dimi, to blow my brains out when a new nursemaid emerges from the office. This one hasn't spoken to us yet, but as he approached a bell rang, it's the eunuch from the diner. Strangely, he makes a beeline for his adversary, to my surprise, Salinka, speaks quietly and kindly to him.

'Victor, it is you, the civvies suit you, how did things work out with Anastasia?'

'We got married Colonel.'

'You must drop the protocol Victor, okay. Are there any children?'

'We have a little boy, Josef, and one on the way, ma'am.'

'Good, I thought I recognized you at the diner, it's been a long time. I'm pleased things turned out the way they did, you have this private detective Mr. Dick Chase to thank for that.' Dimi approaches, he's being nosey, Victor shuts up.

We endured a lousy, cold night, it was almost a relief to see the dawn beginning to break through the translucent sections of the roof. I was woken by Salinka returning from what must have been a visit to the little girl's room, Victor is trailing her at gunpoint, back to her seat, he tied her in and stood up.

'There will be some food,' He began until Dimi interrupted.

'There will be nothing for you scum.' The one I'd spoken to earlier, who luckily seems to outrank this cretin, interrupts.

'Dimi my friend, we must at least try to be civilised, we do not want these people thinking the

Russians are nothing but a bunch of thugs, do we? They can have a drink, Victor, see to it will you?' Cursing under his breath Dimi retreats to the office and turns on the TV, now we can hear the build-up to the big game, but the volume is too low to make any sense out of it, other than quick bursts of The Washington Post March and Liberty Bell, I've seen it all before, I know exactly what's going on. The Russians are in their cubbyhole watching the event unfold, I ask if anyone has come up with anything, any ideas how we can get out of this mess? Miss Russia calmly drops her bombshell.

'I'm not tied in and I'm sitting on a seven-inch jagged-edged knife, and I know how to use it.' I look at her with disbelief.

'You're kidding me, how did you manage that?

'Well, it was down to you wasn't it, your tactic with the two in the diner payed off.' This revelation is a real boost, I just wish we were on some sort of level pegging, I am her backup goddamn it.

Something concentrates my attention and straight away I'm thinking a drink is off the menu, I know Salinka and Lenny are hearing it too. Planes have been coming and going all the time, but this one's on a mission, first it taxied away, that's the nature of runways, it turned full circle and began heading back, proving the Doppler effect works. It became louder until it stopped, and the hot, whining engines died right beneath our feet. We all know what it means, it had to come, it's been expected, it means that, unequivocally, without any doubt, our nemesis has landed.

TWENTY-THREE

The sign on the door reads The Long Island Liberators Management Team, it's printed on a gold-coloured aluminium strip, with black lettering in Vladimir Script. This is the culmination of the Shea Stadium's public relations office attempt to woo the Russians. PD1 was unimpressed as he entered the correct viewing gallery, he has an aversion to aluminium. A framed sign with the same title but in easy-to-read Times New Roman, standing in the centre of a table laden with drinks and glasses, is enough to confirm he is in the right place. A steward wearing a jacket in the colours of the Liberators, blue with yellow pinstripes, welcomes Mr. Adamov to the Long Island Liberators Management Team gallery, confirming, once and for all, he is not lost.

We can now identify PD1 as Hanrik Adamov, because of the lapel badge he is wearing on his smart Russian-tailored tuxedo, the steward continued with his professional duties by asking Mr. Adamov if he would like a drink.

'No thank you, but tell me, have the women arrived yet, we discussed them yesterday?'

'Yes sir, they are here already, would you like me to have them sent up?'

'No, not yet, Mr. Kozlov is due at ten, I would like to see them here just before then.' The steward nodded while withdrawing, more drinks are required.

PD1, or Adamov, as we shall now refer to him, was the first person to arrive, that was always his plan. He's Kozlov's current overseas security kingpin, it's his job to make sure everything goes smoothly, right down to arranging the "entertainment", if you know what I mean. Adamov is an intellectual, a man of principle, since the end of the cold war it was hoped, by him and other enlightened Russians, there might be advancement towards genuine democracy, there are political parties of course, but try raising your head above the parapet and see what happens. In Russia, fortune favours the murdering oppressor.

Standing by the huge windows Adamov is happy with the view, his only hope is the Liberators are victorious, Kozlov will be unbearable if his team lose. Then there is the problem of the five hostages, Adamov can be violent when required, he is after all a dyed-in-the-wool Russian agent, but it's not him who's getting a rake-off for carrying out this task, he is only following orders. As far as he's concerned Chase and Palchikova did Russia a favour by getting rid of that scum Streckovitch and his cohorts, as for the others they are completely innocent. Adamov tries the seating for comfort.

The steward returns and places a few ashtrays around, the Russian takes the opportunity to request coffee. While he's waiting something catches his eye, it's a small box wrapped in gold paper with ribbons, placed on the table just in front of the glasses, he investigates. It's light, it doesn't rattle and there's a card, *To Conrad Ivan Kozlov - Bring back the cup, signed, Your President.* Adamov manages to slide the ribbons to one end, that enables him to unwrap it just enough to see the box inside, it's covered in smooth light blue velvet. On this exposed side there's a small gold oval crest, embossed with the word Fabergé. He puts it together again, slides the ribbon in place, and with the card prominent, he replaces it back on the table.

'Your coffee sir.' The Russian takes the cup and thanking the steward he stands again in front of the giant windows and begins to drink. The instant the taste, that elixir of life, saturates his taste buds, he is transported back, not to a time when this liquid panacea had bolstered him out of yet another wasted, reckless, vodka-fuelled night, but just for a moment, back to the diner. He is acutely aware Colonel Palchikova was quite capable of killing him, a let-off he won't forget in a hurry. Then he finds himself wondering what is in the box, the obvious thing, he thought, is a diamond-encrusted egg, or maybe a drinking vessel, how the sycophants ingratiate each other. As early as it is the stadium is already a third full, for the entertainment of the burgeoning multitude there's a marching band parading up and down to the strains of that quintessential anthem the Stars and Stripes Forever.

Back at the hanger Dick can hear the Stars and Stripes coming over the TV, but he can be excused for his total lack of any feelings of patriotic fervour, Ivan Kozlov is on the premises. Dick is thinking, under the circumstances Salinka seems surprisingly calm, she must be feeling the pressure. Someone shouted in Russian to turn that TV off, he knew because the TV went off, a couple more weeks of this and he'll have fluent Russian.

Victor surreptitiously checked the captors' knots, then went and stood in the silent, tense office. Dick asked the question.

'Are you untied?'

'No, not now.'

'Well don't try anything, remember, it's the game first, he's saving us for later, something'll come up.' Something is coming up, someone is bounding up the stairs and instantly there he is, Ivan Kozlov, we haven't met but I know it's him, one of the richest men in Russia, tall, handsome, elegantly dressed, my guess is he's too well-dressed to start anything now. Dimi went straight to him, they embraced, that's bad news, Kozlov looked at his watch, that's good news. He strides over to his ex-wife and stands in front of her tapping his left foot, he's impatient to get the deed done but he knows he'll have to wait, he sneers viciously.

'Colonel Palchikova.' He bends down so they are almost head-to-head. 'Or should I say Mrs. Vaughan, and this I suppose is your current husband, I'd watch her if I were you, she doesn't seem to be able to make her mind up.' He stood in front of Lenny and spoke to him at length in Russian. That's odd, he just mentioned Henshaw, he's talking about the game, it must be a man thing, Lenny replied in English, probably to keep us in the loop.

'I don't follow the game, but it said in the paper the other day that Kozlov's Liberators have an eighty percent chance of pulling this one out of the bag, that's if Johnny "The Hammer" Henshaw stays off the high ones.' Lenny's playing for time, so I cut in.

'Hey now, just you hold it right there, the last I heard it's a one hundred percent certainty the Long Island Liberators are gonna win hands down, sure, Henshaw must leave the high ones alone but…' Now it's Kozlov who cuts in.

'Who asked for your opinion *and who the hell are you anyway?*'

'I'm sorry we haven't been introduced.' While I'm telling him who I am Kozlov is glancing at his watch.

'Let me understand you correctly, you are Ray Chase, Dick Chase's twin brother, Chase's body was washed up on the beach two nights ago.' Kozlov holds his palms out to a confused-looking Dimi and the rest of them. He's speaking in Russian and judging by his tone I know exactly what he's saying, he's saying what the hell's going on here, where's Chase he's the one I want to see strung up with piano wire. Kozlov glances again at his watch. He turns back to all of us then instantly he grabs his ex by the throat, they're face-to-face. 'Who the hell is that and you'd better tell me the truth?'

'He's Ray Chase.' Salinka chokes, 'Dick's twin, Dick is in the morgue, he was dumped out of a plane, why not go and see for yourself.' Kozlov releases his grip.

'I heard he got away with that and you had something to do with it.' His ex-scoffed.

'You know I'm good but even I can't fly.' He stares down at her displaying the hard, steely chauvinism of a big-game hunter who after the chase has his prey, in this case the last Russian tigress, unequivocally cornered.

'Are you, *good,* Mrs. Vaughan, really, hmmm, I think not, if you were any good you wouldn't be tied to that chair, would you?' A broad smile crept over his face as he swaggered towards Dimi who's saying something. While he's listening Kozlov looks at Helen, he speaks. 'This one?' Dimi nods his head.

Now I'm really worried, not because of what Helen might say, I'm worried for her safety. He approaches her, grabs her hair and pulls her head back, Helen draws breath. 'Now you listen to me, tell me the truth and I'll personally take you to duty-free, buy you some Chanel No 5 and let you go, lie, and you won't see another day.' She sobs as he pulls her head further back. 'Who is that on the end?' Helen whimpers as he keeps up the pressure.

'It's Ray.' She cries out. 'Ray Chase, I don't know him, Dick was my boyfriend and he's dead.' Tragically she burst into tears 'Dick's dead.' She's crying her little heart out, she's good, she's damn good, Helen deserves an Oscar for that performance. Kozlov turns to his ace team and gives them hell, he's not happy, again he looks at his watch and speaks to Dimi, before turning back to us.

'I've got a game to win, but when I get back you are all going to be strung up and beaten to within an inch of your lives, you'll be begging to be finished off.' Full of themselves Kozlov and Dimi exit the building.

We all praised Helen at once, I didn't think she had it in her but what do I know? We're still here with no real plan and I thought I was good at this game. Salinka has cast off her steel exterior.

'His plane making him so late was a bit of luck, Helen, you were amazing, Ray, that was a good one you pulled out of the bag.' She turns to her husband. 'I didn't know you were so interested in baseball.' The TV came on again and Salinka asked Victor if she can go to the bathroom, I know she's angling to be left untied. All of a sudden a huge prolonged cheer floats from the TV.

Even behind glass in the semi-soundproofed gallery belonging to the Liberators management team, Adamov's attention is drawn outside as a huge prolonged cheer greets the home team - the Long Island Liberators - as they run onto the pitch, twenty-five or so team players, reserves, coaches, and team medics, all basking in the glory of being in one of the USA's greatest baseball teams, a sea of light blue with yellow pinstripes doing a lap of honour before heading for the dugout. Adamov looks at his watch, his boss is late this won't bode well, he doesn't give a damn, he just has to feign due sympathy. As it turns out the three women, standing among the other guests who have been invited into the gallery, are stunning and he knows Kozlov's anger will be tempered once he gets to see their potential. Then, like the precursor to a bad storm, Dimi is standing in the doorway, secretly Adamov despises him, hates him intensely. He knows exactly why he's made a beeline here, it's to sample the eye candy. It means Kozlov won't be far away, probably in the adjoining gallery wishing the opposition well. Dimi, unfazed, approaches, they speak in their mother tongue, the conversation goes something like this.

'Dimi my friend, you are here at last, where is comrade Kozlov?' They compare heights.

'Hanrik, Ivan is next door giving his condolences and eyeing up the opposition.' Dimi nods towards the three women, 'Though why he thinks the potatoes are always better dug from a neighbour's field is a mystery.' Adamov outranks Dimi, but he would never call Kozlov by his first name, Dimi continues. 'First the game, then the afterparty.'

'If our team wins.' Always the air of caution from Adamov.

'Precisely, if we win, but even if we have to forego the canapés, it is back to the hanger to cause such wonderful pain and suffering and then kill off that Colonel and her friends.' Adamov picks up his vodka straight.

'I'll drink to that.' He is covering all possibilities. Kozlov enters and strides over to them.

'Dimi, Hanrik, you have found each other and those I take it are the women.' Kozlov playfully digs Dimi in the ribs, 'I don't fancy your one.'

Another huge roar concentrates everyone's attention and the whole gallery decant over to the windows to see the opposition, the Chicago Devils, enter the ground. Amid the clamour and expectation Kozlov ever looking for a drink, spots the gold-wrapped parcel sitting amongst the glasses and sees it's addressed to him. Although the Chicago Devils are sporting the largest team of cheerleaders the Shea stadium has ever witnessed, Kozlov is fascinated by his gift from the President. He unwraps it and opens the light blue velvet box to reveal a beautiful pair of diamond-encrusted, gold binoculars. Except for him the whole gallery is on its feet witnessing the familiar sight of the Shea stadium doing what it was built for, to entertain the American public with spectacle and spectacular baseball.

The cheerleaders and the band are pulling out all the stops when, unexpectedly, the crowd let out a terrific roar as a single girl streaks naked to the centre of the pitch chased by two cops in a scene reminiscent of a Keystone Cops' caper.

The three women guests, the 'entertainment', all of who know each other, are here to earn some easy money and help themselves to free drinks, not watch a bunch of girls aimlessly flinging their limbs about. So when one of them employs *the code,* by pouting while holding her glass upside down, they all head towards the drinks table. What greets them as they turn around at first doesn't make any sense, a man sitting back in a big comfortable chair, his arms hanging down to the floor with, of all things, a pair of diamond-studded, gold binoculars anchored to his face. Just two seconds was all it took, two seconds for the full horror to dawn, two seconds, the precursor to a scream so traumatic, so shocking no one in that room will ever forget it. If a reminder were needed they only had to read the paper, the result of the post-mortem. Ivan Kozlov, Russian Billionaire, owner of the Long Island Liberators Baseball Team, died instantly from shock when blades, three and a half inches long, were propelled one from each lens from a specially adapted pair of binoculars, into his eyes.

TWENTY-FOUR

The game between the Long Island Liberators and the Chicago Devils had long been anticipated, hoped for, craved by both teams and moreover, the fans. Today's crowd pitch a full house at eighty-two thousand. Both teams boast best pitcher and best catcher, thus the powers that be have decided the game will go on despite the catastrophe. There will be an announcement at close of play, of course the police and medical services are here already, and the press have been informed, the last thing the stadium wants is any hint of a cover-up, with the bad press that might ensue. The three women have long been out of there and are being looked after in the main bar, management is supplying free drinks, so we can expect their recovery to take a little longer than it otherwise might have. Adamov, immediately knelt to cover the surrounding floor with his considerable bulk, he knew first aid would be superfluous and he has no intention of removing the binoculars, that is a job for the medical profession. No, Adamov is no fool, he'd read the card that is now safe in his left hand, he knew this was not at the behest of the President, and any possibility of that accusation being levied had to be quashed. He also has a good idea who was behind it and he wants to protect them. He's one of a handful of people who know all the President's cards are coded and he fears, if this card were to fall into the wrong hands, eventually the deed would be traced directly back to Colonel Palchikova. He spirited the card away before picking up the gold wrapping paper, looking through it he headed over to the table to pour himself a drink, Dimi joined him.

'You have the card, good, we do not want the American police sticking their noses into our affairs, let me see it.' He held out his hand, Adamov, is the senior agent but he knows Dimi thinks himself above protocol, he will have to tread carefully.

'There's no need, the President briefed me before we came away, something like this, though unlikely, might happen and he must be the first to see any evidence, so you see Dimi, on this occasion, my hands are tied.' Dimi, forced a sympathetic smile.

'The pressures of being the eyes and ears of the President must fall heavily on you Hanrik.' Hanrik, retaliated.

'I think not as heavy as it was for you being so friendly with Kozlov.' Dimi stared threateningly at his tiresome counterpart.

'Yes, and he knew I will carry out his wishes to destroy that pestilent female who you are so keen to protect.' Hanrik counselled a word of caution.

'Dimi, my friend, I wouldn't underestimate that female if I were you.' Dimi gritted his teeth.

'She is no threat to me.' With that he turned and walked off, Adamov had no option but to follow.

The news had not yet reached the hanger, Salinka is unaware her precarious plan, that had come to her during a visit to a museum in Paris, had been so effective. Kozlov, dying from shock was a real bonus, obviating the risky business of finishing him off in some private hospital, though she will always regret not being able to convey to him, personally, she hoped he was pleased to see her, before she shot him at point-blank range. As far as Dick is concerned the game is going on as normal, the TV reveals the highs and lows of the match as though nothing out of the ordinary had happened, but then he didn't know the plan and the terrible vengeance it had wrought. He has a chance to ask one question of Salinka, and for her to reply, before their metal is infinitely going to be tested.

'Are you untied?' She nods her head.

'Yes, I am, thanks to your quick thinking and thank God for Victor.' Downstairs an iron door slams open and the sound of heavy footfalls can be heard hurrying across the floor, then, without pause, they're bounding up the stairs. It's Dimi, who doesn't stop at the top but heads straight for his nemesis and lands her a crashing backhand that would floor most men, she remained seated. Dimi stood relishing the fact at last he's been able to do something he's wanted to do for a long time, he raises his hand again, then lowers it.

'I want you conscious so you can see what a mess I'm going to make of that dumb, spineless husband of yours.' With the sudden commotion the TV went off and the others emerged from the office, one of them speaks.

'Shouldn't you wait for Kozlov?' Dimi eyes this pest.

'What have you got to say about that?' Salinka stares back at him, what she'd like to do is head-butt him on the bridge of his nose, that's a speciality of hers, then take the knife she's sitting on and slam it into his guts a couple of times, what she does is torment him.

'I don't know, is he playing centerfield?' Dimi steps up and gives her another backhand, harder this time, pitiless. Still she remains seated, but Dick can't take anymore and to everyone's surprise, except perhaps Victor's, he stands up. While taking a few steps backwards, he goads.

'Dimi, is that short for Dimitry, or are you just Dim?' Dimi isn't fazed, the bloodlust has gone to his head and anyway he's far too self-confident.

'You might pull the wool over their eyes but not over mine.' As Dick is still slowly retreating, Dimi is edging forward placing himself adjacent to Dick's chair, putting the sad, beaten bitch behind him. He speaks again. 'I know exactly who you are, while you were attending that stupid woman of yours, after my men had ransacked her apartment, that gave me the opportunity to look around your dump, you have no twin.'

'If you know that much, then you will know Colonel Palchikova *can* fly, that being the case don't you think you're playing, just a bit, with fire?' Dimi quickly looked at her sitting tied to the chair, blood and mucus hanging from her nose and mouth, her head bowed and trembling. Pathetic, pitiful he thought, he looks back at Chase, but before he speaks, he draws his gun from his shoulder holster.

'She is beyond the point of no return, soon I will have blood coming out of her ears and she will be begging me to end it. No, it is you I am interested in, what have you achieved?' He sneered, 'Nothing, you have escaped being strung up with piano wire and beaten to a pulp, yes, perhaps that is so, but still you will die, you have no answer to me, I'm too good for you.' He threatens over his left shoulder, 'All of you.' He looks back at Chase, the smile comes easy. 'Now I am going to kill you.'

Before he can cock the weapon the brightest of lights like three tiny supernovas exploded in his head, it was done. Too late, another weapon cocks as someone speeds from the office. A third weapon and the assured voice of Victor.

'Vladimir, **stop right there**'.

Dimi heard none of this, the life-draining sensation below his ribs, first on the left, then on the right and then through his back grazing his heart, owns his failing senses. Salinka was fast, silent, and deadly. Dimitry's arm fell, the gun fell, without fuss or remonstration he collapsed to his knees. Slowly he turned his half-closed eyes towards his adversary who is now standing there looking down at him, far from the point of no return. He opened his mouth but nothing came out, instead, she speaks.

'You chose the wrong side Dimitry, he killed my sisters, one of them was blind, you were eager to torture and kill me and these others.' She lowered her face towards his. 'Now do you get it?' Dimi looked at her as if suddenly realising, after all this time, everything he stood for, every threat he'd made, every extortion he'd forced, the hits he'd carried out for Kozlov, all that was wrong, he'd made his life checking other people without once checking himself. In a flash he saw the error of his ways, and just as he got it, he knew it was too late. He suddenly remembered, once, a long time ago, he'd been religious, now he is about to meet his maker, he is going to have to explain himself. Worst of all he is going to die with regrets he has no way of righting, he wonders if that last thought might grant him a small amnesty with God. All this his slayer saw etched in the perplexed, acquiescent face of a dying man. She bent down close to him and rested her hand on his shoulder. Then, ever so quietly, she spoke in their mother tongue. 'Don't worry Dimitry, I forgive you, everything is going to be alright.' Whether he heard those words we'll never know, he crashed forward onto his face, for him the game of life is over. His vanquisher stood there looking down, the blood-stained, jagged-edged knife still in her hand. Carefully she slid the gun, with her foot, to an empty space where she placed the knife on the floor next to it. Then turning towards the office, she raised her hands in the air, immediately Victor stepped up, stood in front of her and faced his crew, now he knows where his loyalties lie. Dick followed suit and raised his hands, for the first time he noticed Adamov standing in the doorway at the top of the stairs, he didn't know how long he'd been there. Was it long enough to have intervened, was he rooting for this woman from the dugout? He guessed he'd chosen the right side, now Adamov advances and takes control.

'All right Victor you've made your point, you can stand down. You two, put your hands down and get in the office.' He spoke to his subordinates. 'You three, untie these and give me ten minutes, come on what are you waiting for?' The three of them are standing in the office, it feels strangely like no-man's-land, the battle is over, but have they won the war? Adamov speaks calmly and in command. 'Colonel Palchikova, you have exceeded your reputation, this is going to be difficult to explain at the Kremlin, although the President always thought that one day, Kozlov might try and use his wealth to secure Dimitry the "top job", though I cannot think where that idea came from.' He gave them a nuanced glance.

'The Colonel is honorary because of my degrees you can call me ma'am.' She laughed. 'I always say that, my name is Salinka, but you already know it.' She offered her hand, that ancient sign of mutual nonaggression, the universal manifestation of peace. Adamov took it, and so, the war is over. Salinka began speaking in Russian, Adamov listened politely before pleasantly interrupting and saying his bit, she interrupted him and so it went on. Dick is guessing they're sharing a moment of mutual appreciation for not killing each other, funny though, he mused, he didn't hear his name mentioned. Adamov took a business card and some folded gold paper from his pocket and handed it to her. As she took it a broad grin surfaced. She looked at him, then in English.

'Why are you giving me this?' She chortled.

'Well for one, we cannot implicate the president no matter what we think of him, and two, it can be traced back to you.' She looked at the card, perhaps remembering her wedding day, to a time when she loved Kozlov. How circumstances have changed she thought, once only good things were in front of her, the best things, things she could only dream of, now she has to kill for her survival, but hopefully that's all over. She looked at Adamov.

'Dick hasn't a clue what happened, will you tell us both?' He filled us in on the day's events in a cold, matter-of-fact way, as though these things happen every day in Russia, I was gobsmacked, it was the last thing I expected. If Salinka had asked me to guess what was in the gift I'd have come up with nothing more sinister than a fake hand grenade crystal paperweight. As Adamov finished Salinka handed him a plastic card, he scrutinised both sides, a look of puzzlement crept across his face.

'It's a bank card.' He handed it back. 'What is it to do with me?' Salinka, you're not gonna do what I think you're gonna do are you? My God you are, she's giving it back to him.

'Hanrik, there's a million dollars here in a slush fund, I have my share, if you act quickly the rest is yours, give some to Victor and your crew, won't you? Once news gets out about Kozlov, I am sure his advocates will close it down, and here, you'll need this password.'

Compared to the last twelve hours we've got quite a party going on here, people are dying to get in. I've spoken to Victor, I told him I couldn't have let a nicer person off the hook, he said that goes for him too. Now he's talking in English to Colonel Palchikova, and he can't stop calling her that, or ma'am. She's enjoying every minute of it but remains completely grounded, in her words "It is honorary" she doesn't have a pretentious bone in her body. Helen and McDougall wander over, they've been talking about events with Lenny or Thomas whatever his name is, I put my arms around Helen.

'Hey Baby, am I proud of you, you're one hell of a tough cookie, you really stood your ground with that base rat Kozlov.'

'Yeah, yeah, I know Honey, I went to some tough summer camps, I'll still need pampering with candy and flowers and taking out to dinner occasionally. Speaking of which Doogie and me have decided, after this the five of us are gonna go uptown for a slap-up meal.' The idea sounded like it had wings and for some reason I couldn't help smiling at my reference. The Russians have loaded Dimi into a body bag and are taking him away. Adamov shakes my hand and gives me the keys to a van.

'Get it back to the van rental by nine in the morning will you old chap.' I look at him hard.

'Yeah well, you can cut out the colloquialisms, I'm American not British, MI6 would probably see you coming a mile off.' Adamov laughed out loud.

'Well perhaps you are right.' He looked across at Salinka who is busily talking to his crew. 'She's some woman, isn't she?'

'Yeah, she is, she's incredible, but I think you already knew it.' For a long moment Adamov is reflective, in a couple of seconds a whole other life had flashed before his mind.

'Yes, I did, anyway.' He raised himself and looked back at me. 'As we say in Russia, I've got potatoes to dig.' He smiled, 'Looking on the bright side, at least now I get to fly in the co-pilot's seat

.

'A word of advice on that one,' I said, as he left the building. 'If he offers you any gum tell him to stick it where the sun don't shine.'

TWENTY-FIVE

The Russians have gone, the threat from Kozlov and Dimi has evaporated. Salinka is relaying her story, Helen has just rushed to the bathroom, the thought of Kozlov sitting there wearing a pair of binoculars held in place by seven inches of cold steel is too much for her to bear. I'm sitting here wondering what might be on the menu later. Who won the All-States Baseball Challenge? Well, that's easy, the Chicago Devils won the game, 4-3. It turns out the van is in the car park just a hundred yards on, so we're now walking five abreast down the middle of a deserted road. It's a funny thing, we're in the same order we were sitting when we were tied to those chairs, someone should write a thesis on the subliminal effects of jeopardy and how it materialises in day-to-day life. I'm just thinking what a smartass I am to come up with that when suddenly something happens that's gonna pull me down to size and destroy my self-esteem, big time. A heavy weapon is cocked behind us and someone hollers.

'*Don't anybody move.*' Without pause. 'Chase, you think I'm dead, I thought you were dead, well here's the thing, you're not the only one with a guardian angel, *don't anyone move.*' It's Crawford, that jerk of a pilot, Jesus this is trouble. 'Did you think I was dumb enough to fall for your "twin brother" routine? I saw you coming a mile off in your flashy jacket, but is it bulletproof?' Before anyone can think, or react, what sounds like a burst of ten bullets in a one-second burn throws Lenny to the ground, immediately Salinka lets out a horrified scream.

'*Dick, No, Dick.*' I gotta hand it to her, faced with the incomprehensible, the utterly heart-wrenching tragedy of it all, she can still think on her feet, I know exactly why she called my name instead of Tom. In that last instant I had, before chance ran out, I saw Crawford's heels disappear as he ran off between two hangers, the closest of which is the one we're passing. There's a rear door and I'm through it already, the far side is the business end where planes come and go. There's a car with its door open and engine running, I'm sprinting towards it. I glance to my right and through a small window I catch someone flash past, we're both about halfway, I've got the advantage Crawford can't know I'm here. Picking up a giant wrench en route I reach my position at the right-hand side of the huge opening. The car's facing right to left, the driver's door is my side so as Crawford gets in I'll have his back, he'll be about three yards away. I saw all this in the second and a half lead I had. I'm gonna sling the wrench, I'm not chancing missing his head, it'll be right in the back between his lungs. There he is now, as he chucks his weapon in, I lob the wrench hard, it turns through the air, it's a heavy blow that's right on target. His face is propelled forward and slams into the roof edge, that little line of gutter that's not going anywhere. I go in, glued to the wrench like the tail of Halley's comet. I grab his collar and that stupid ponytail, yanking him in reverse I do a backward roll, fixing my feet into the small of his back. I push with all my might sending him flying through the air banging my head in the process but that doesn't mean a thing. Crawford lands on his front, on his face, good. I scramble onto his back and bang his head some more into the concrete, again and again. He kicks his legs and struggles but I'm heavy and I'm incandescent with rage. Immediately I have a concern, I quickly look around, there's no one about, good, it's a day off for the big game.

'Crawford, in case you haven't twigged, it's Chase, and you're dead, no honestly.' Squatting heavily on his middle back, I put my right arm around his neck and join hands. I pull his head back as far as it'll go, too far, and some more. Crawford's struggling while I'm pulling and tightening my grip, I'm using all my strength, pulling and tightening. I sense he's running out of steam, but I've got no intention of letting up, I've killed him once already, I'm not falling for that one again. He's motionless but to make sure I pull and tighten really hard, for ten long seconds…. there's no reaction. I drop him, his face smacks into the concrete, he's dead meat. I fetch his weapon, it's covered with his prints so I'm careful not to contaminate it with mine. I take his foot in an oily rag and drag him to a corner, then instantly, he's riddled with bullets, I'm making sure this time. I lay the gun next to him, it's dark in this corner, there's a tarpaulin close by, I cover him over, with a bit of luck he'll be there till he's ripe.

McDougall's movement catches my eye, he heard the shots and is standing in the far-off doorway. Traumatically, worse than a hammer blow, the terrible reality of Lenny's fate smacked me in the mouth. I amble back, I'm feeling useless, ashamed, emotional, strangely emotional. How can I face Salinka, I didn't finish the job, and yet she disposed of Brad, she achieved where I failed? Because of my carelessness her husband has been gunned down in cold blood, right in front of her. Lenny insisted I borrow his jacket, that amazing Buffalo skin jacket he was so proud of. I know before I get there, it's riddled with holes and covered in his blood and it's all my fault. A memory, long since forgotten came flooding back like it was yesterday. I was working with my first partner, officer Paul Carrillo, shot to ribbons on our watch, it was bad luck crossed with a desperate criminal. In those days I was no more than a green rookie, hearing Paul's last words and watching him die really choked me up, that hasn't happened to me since, I thought blubbing was the domain of fresh-faced rookies. As I reached McDougall, I sobbed on his shoulder, he's an old friend, we go back a long way, I figured he'd understand.

TWO MONTHS LATER

When Kozlov and Dimi were alive I didn't think things could get any worse, but two months on and I'm shrouded in a black cloud of despair and despondency. Helen is trying hard to pull me out of it but somehow, I seem to have lost the will to live, well work anyway. There have been a couple of inquiries on the private eye front, I've just had to turn them down due to pressure of work. I spend a lot of my time sitting staring at the TV watching films whether I want to or not, at night I prefer to walk the streets. Helen tells me she wants a quiet evening in watching one of her programmes, so she's arranged for me to have a few drinks with my good friend McDougall, the old team together, what I wouldn't give to be back in those days, Doogie and Chase, we could have been a TV series, I should never have left, whatever made me think I'd be any good as a private eye? As I arrive at Johnny's Bar, our favourite dive, Doogie has already got them in.

'Dick, take your drink, we'll grab the table in the corner.' My friend stands aside to let me have the seat with my back to the wall.

'You take it, these days I'm not so fussy, I don't know why I ever was.'

'Hmmm, this is what I've been hearing. Now you listen to your old partner, I'm not gonna beat about the bush. Helen tells me you've been a bit down lately, I know that incident is weighing heavy on you, but you shouldn't beat yourself up about it. What was it Salinka said? "You mustn't blame yourself you shot the jerk three times and he played it perfectly". She would have been fooled herself is what she said.'

'He played me for a perfect fool is what she meant to say.'

'O.K. right, now listen up, I don't know her as well as you do, but I know her enough to tell, if anything, she's sincere, she tells it as it is, and if she says she would have been fooled, then that's exactly what she means. When you pump three rounds into someone, at close range, you don't expect them to walk away. Are you in contact with her, where is it she's working, Cambridge Shire, England isn't it?'

'Yeah, that's where she is and Helen's in New York City, she's a good kid, look at how she didn't spill the beans with Kozlov, even with the chance of some Chanel No 5, that showed true grit, she must have been frightened out of her skin. And she was very generous over my working relationship with the Russian, she harboured no jealousy over Colonel Palchikova. I think that shows great trust, don't you, don't you think Helen is one in a million?'

'Well, yeah of course I do but in return I think she'd like the old Dick back, I mean by all accounts you're a pretty hard task to live with at the moment. Listen, don't think I don't know what you see in that girl, but us mortals must stick together, you've made your bed with Helen, you must accept it for both your sakes.' I draw a deep breath and slowly let it out, the present looks back at the past, that is only the future waiting to happen, hey, that doesn't make any sense, maybe the old Dick is coming back. We had a couple more beers, I thanked Doogie for pulling me back from the brink and pointing me in the right direction, and we went our separate ways.

By the time I got in Helen had gone to bed, I took a shower and sneaked in next to her. She couldn't feign sleep for more than thirty seconds and pretty soon we're doing our bit to keep the world population from booming to unsustainable levels, Helen's back on the pill.

Over breakfast she filled me in on her plans for the day and why don't we meet up at Funtangos, there's something pressing she wants to talk about. Yes, I think to myself, I'll face my demons head-on, I've got to pull myself together and that's where it all started.

I plan the route for my morning stroll to end up at Funtangos, Helen got there before me and is already tucking in to what looks like coffee and pancakes with all the trimmings. I order a large Americano and sit opposite her, she's got some news and I'm just thinking, well, I've been so caught up with my own problems, pre-turning over a new leaf and all, I'm wondering if she might be waiting for the right moment to tell me we're having a private eye with tiny feet.

'Dick, I've got something to tell you that might come as a big surprise, you remember my old school friend Julie, who was run over and killed outside here, well it turns out she wasn't killed after all. I spoke to her on the phone last night, actually I've been talking to her over the past month, it turns out she set the whole thing up with a couple of colleagues. Things got so bad with that landlord and her pimp, she thought the only answer was to get right away, so the hit and run and the ambulance thing were all fake.' Just for a second she almost had me, I smiled.

'Are you saying your friend faked a pregnancy, I mean a twisted neck?'

'Yes, and Julie says to say she's sorry about that, the woollen dress she was wearing, the one with the zipper, she deliberately put it on back to front and laid her head at a funny slant, plus she's been a swimming champion and can hold her breath for over seven minutes. A pregnancy! What the hell are you talking about?'

Well, hey-ho, it's not junior private eye, but the other thing, I guess I was fooled again, that's just great, that's par for the course. But I'm not gonna let it faze me, I've turned over a new leaf for both our sakes. If Helen and me are gonna get back to some kind of cohabital bliss, I've just gotta grow up and smell the coffee.

'Good for her, she's made a brave, positive decision to turn her life around. I think more people should do the same.'

'Well, I'm glad you see it that way because Julie has asked me to join her in Seattle. She's started her own business and is looking for a partner, I'll be moving there if I decide to take up her offer. Actually Dick, I wanna go, I've always fancied running a beauty parlour, it's a part of the country I'd like to see and Julie and me, well ever since first grade we've been like sisters.' I suppose I should be broken-hearted at Helen's news, but strangely I'm not. I gave her my blessing and wished her all the luck in the world. I said with the hard-line training she's just been through she'll have no trouble dealing with those difficult customers, just make sure she keeps a seven-inch jagged-edged knife in the tray with the rollers. As for me, well, it turns out Lady Luck is finally batting for the heterosexual league, and that means I've suddenly become a free agent, that in turn can only add up to one thing, I've got a date in Cambridge Shire, England.

TWENTY-SIX

My newfound energy finds me worrying about officer Cooper, well, not so much worrying more, keen to see him banged to rights. I had an idea that I'd put to the chief and McDougall, and now the trap is set, the three of us are sitting in a darkened corner in Johnny's bar, waiting for the shark to arrive and begin nosing around the bait. I'd slipped a note under his apartment door offering a substantial reward for information on officer Bygraves, it was signed, Adamov, KGB. Cooper has just walked in and is getting himself a drink. As planned Johnny is pointing to our table and as he approaches, I stand up, keeping my head down, and offer him my seat, I also motion to Johnny who obligingly brings up the lights. Cooper finds himself sitting between the wall and me and opposite the chief and McDougall. Any further description of following events would be superfluous, needless to say we had him bang to rights. The chief read him his rights, something he says he hadn't done for ten years, and in quick time Cooper is being led out by three officers, to their squad car, to spend the first night of many locked up. We made a night of it, the chief reckons he hadn't had a drink with the lads since his prostate took off, me, I'm just geed up over spilling the beans about Helen's plans and my subsequent hopes of joining up with Salinka in Cambridge Shire, England.

By the time I get back to my apartment it's too late to call Salinka's office. I set my alarm for 4 a.m. that'll give me a head start. We haven't been in touch because she said she'd surprise me one day and call me at home, just as soon as she felt ready, in her words, she wanted to "Tie up the past and let it go". That covert agent did once mention the firm she worked for, well, me being a private detective, I don't let information like that go.

My alarm went off, I made coffee and got dialling, it's four in the morning and I'm feeling extraordinarily awake, the continental operator is putting me through now.

'Lush, Husband, and Burke, Solicitors, can I help you?'

'Yes, ma'am, my name's Dick Chase. Will you put me through to Salinka Vaughan please?' The company is on the ball, I gotta answer some security questions.

'Just one more Mr. Chase, incidentally, this is Salinka's question, who won the recent All-States Baseball Challenge?'

'Well, that will be the Chicago Devils, do I get a prize?'

'No prizes, but I can tell you she's not here.'

'O.K. ma'am, can I call her apartment?'

'She's leaving the country she's going back to Russia.'

'Going home, are you sure, she didn't say anything?'

'I'm sorry to say it's true, her flight leaves Heathrow tonight at 9:50. We're all very sad, Mr. Lush says she's a highly intelligent, highly skilled linguist. She lost her husband in a terrible accident, she wouldn't tell us the details only that it was a tragedy and no one was to blame, is all.' The unexpected reminder stunned me.

'Yes, I know, it was a tragic accident. I gotta go ma'am, thanks for your help, you have a nice day now.' I hung up, that last bit, the sudden reminder of my bungle coming out the blue like that. First she risks her neck to get me out of East Berlin then she returns with her intel and her plan to catch me outta the goddamn sky, well in my book we've gotta be together and the only way that's gonna happen is if I pop the question. Time is running out, I managed to get a ticket, everything is booked-up except an Air France flight departing at 2 p.m. arriving at ten past nine at night. I'll be cutting it fine, that will give me, geez, I won't have enough time, yes you will Dick, think positive.

All that now seems a day away as we prepare to land at Heathrow. On the plus side we're on time due to a tailwind. Now let's see, that gives me just forty minutes to get through customs and get to where I'm supposed to be heading. I had an idea, I asked the stewardess if she will let me off the plane first, I have to meet a VIP before they take off, and I've only got a small window, Gabrielle couldn't have been more helpful.

I'm through customs and on my way to terminal two, gate nine, that's where Salinka is due to depart from. Of course, *we* were scheduled to land at terminal one, which is fine and dandy and totally understood, by everyone except me, I barely have ten minutes to go. As I finally reach terminal two, I'm running, I had been running, but now I'm on the home straight I put on a spurt. Some gate ahead of me has just shut, is that gate seven or eight? As I close in I can see it's gate nine. I look at my watch, geez they're early, there are still six minutes to go. I call to the Aeroflot staff member as I pull up.

'There are still six minutes to go.' The young woman takes a look at my watch.

'Your watch says 4:44 sir, you are five hours early.' She smiles and for a brief moment I'm stunned by this young Russian girl with dark shoulder-length hair falling from her suitably liveried pillbox hat, her heavily accented English so pleasantly familiar, it could have been her.

'No, no,' I'm pulling myself together. 'I've just arrived from the States, over there we're five hours behind.' She looked at me, sympathetically.

'I am sorry sir but your watch is five hours and six minutes behind.' She picked up her shoulder bag ready to walk off. I started to speak, soon realising I'm wasting my breath.

'Was there a tall slim brunette?'…I tailed off, 'It doesn't matter, have a nice day.'

Kicking my heels, I walk over to the seating arrangements. My day has caught up with me, I'm feeling tired and deflated, it's been a long one and I've got the blues. I'm sitting alone on a row of seats staring at a wall with two doors separated by a faulty neon sign that intermittently flashes, The City of London by Taxi, but my eyes are out of focus, you know, the feeling you get when the brain can't be bothered. I've flown three thousand miles to see the woman I love, the woman I've loved from the moment I first laid eyes on her in an Italian restaurant by the docks in Manhattan. Three thousand miles partnered by hope and anticipation to arrive six minutes late, my partners have both fled. I watched her leave once before, in the early hours from JFK, I loved her then, but I thought she was an impossible catch, too good to be true, too involved with her country to be worried about some crummy western gumshoe with no prospects. Now, when I think I have a chance, I think my luck might be in, I miss her by six minutes. My blurred peripheral vision perceives some movement or other. I've heard when a person loses one of their senses the brain compensates by sharpening another. Inexplicably I hear a pitch of stilettos I recognise, no, fate plays these tricks. I struggle to throw off this blue funk that has gripped me, to drag my retinas back into focus. And there, walking towards me, I see through the dust and grit in my travel-weary eyes that tall slender green-eyed brunette with a fair complexion as far as the eye can see. I know this trick, I've nodded off, I must be dreaming. She sits opposite me and smiles, I don't want her to speak, I'm afraid if she does, I might wake up.

'I let my flight go.' She is real.

'I was hoping to change someone's plans,' I said 'But I arrived too late.' She smiles.

'You are real then, for a moment I thought I might be dreaming. I changed my mind I'm now heading to America.'

'That's funny, I've just come from there, do you have anyone over there?' She frowns.

'I did, but now I'm not so sure.'

'I hope to settle in Cambridge Shire.' She staunched a little smile.

'Do you know anyone there?'

'I did but now I'm not so sure.' She is beautiful.

'I have a job waiting in Cambridge, I just have to make the phone call.' I stood up and held out my hand, she stood up and took it. 'I'm so glad you came.' She said, we kissed, and kissed, and kissed again, before walking off together arm in arm across the polished concourse.

Five phone booths in a row stand in front of a glass wall looking out at the night sky full of stars. That's where all the cats go when they die, they lounge about up there in heaven, nice and warm and cosy keeping watch over their folks to see that all shall be well.

TWENTY-SEVEN

The Office Christmas Party

It is a truth universally acknowledged in the western hemisphere the gentlemen are always waiting for their ladies, in the eastern hemisphere it's the other way around.

'Dick, are you ready yet? The taxi's due at seven and it's two minutes to. Your shoes, tie, and jacket are down here and you're still prancing about in your underpants.' In the time it took Salinka to say that, I'm dressed and halfway down the stairs already.

'Hey, I'm almost there, you look stunning by the way.'

'Oh, thank you, Darling.' She did a half turn and smiled vivaciously, while I'm finishing off my tie in the mirror.

'No, I'm talking about me.' The taxi driver tooted his horn over Salinka's retort, I took her arm and led her out into the night. 'Come on, shift that cute Russian butt of yours or we're gonna be late.' It's the office Christmas party, I could do with a quiet night in with a good film and a bottle of wine, but my Colonel-in-Chief, she's raring to go. I guess I can't blame her, it's the first time the office gets to meet her new man on the block, and as for her, well, she's all geed up over showing me off.

As we pull up at the hotel there's already a bunch of people standing outside talking, for the time of year, as they say in Manhattan, it's too warm to wear your poodle around your neck. We all shake hands, someone mentions the bar and like a shot it's like the Black Death has returned to the streets of Cambridge Shire.

'It's Cambridgeshire Mr. Chase.'

'What! Did I say that out loud?'

'We've met before, well we've spoken, I'm Shirley, I answered the phone, you remember, when you made that enquiry about Salinka, it was the Chicago Devils who won…the All-States Baseball Challenge.'

'Shirley, it's nice to meet you in the flesh, hey, please, call me Dick.'

'I know what you're thinking Dick, I sounded a lot younger than I look, most people do, I retire in four years. I've been working for the firm for forty-seven years, Mr. Lush was twenty-something, fresh out of university when I started here. I knew old Mr. Lush, he was a bit of a tyrant, but his heart was in the right place, I need a drink, where's the bar?'

'Hey, that's a good idea Shirley, let's do it.'

'Dick, *Dick*, sorry Shirley, he's mine.' My girl grabs my arm and whisks me away. 'I want you to meet some people, come with me.' She takes me to a group who, lucky for them, seem to come already plied with drinks.

'Dick, this is June, she's Mr. Lush's P.A. This is Natalie, P.A. to Mr. Burke. Brian here is a very important member of the team he takes care of filing and looks after the computers. And this is Gloria, she's our main legal boffin, you can ask her any question you like and she'll know the answer. I can't help noticing, everyone in this little knot of folks seems to be looking at me.

'O.K. Gloria, let's see, are you a member of the Bar?'

'A most honourable position, that is my territory I'm afraid, I must declare an interest there.'

'Well in that case I'll have a large white wine on the rocks.' Amid the howls and hoots of laughter, I'm grabbed by the arm and at last we're heading towards the bar.

'Dick, that was very amusing, Gloria will be loving you, you gave her some of her own medicine. We're never quite allowed to forget her exalted position, in the nicest possible way.'

'You're not in any trouble are you, I hope I didn't offend the dame, what's with the wallflower... Brian?'

'That's very perceptive of you, ah, I forgot, you're a private detective. Brian? He's a painfully shy soul, he has no friends outside work, he lives in a converted shed, it's very plush, electricity, toilet, shower, kitchen. It's a home from home except there is no real home he lives at the end of Mr. Lush's garden. He was living on the streets and got badly beaten up one night, Mr. and Mrs. Lush found him, they were on their way home from the theatre, they took him in. Come on, I want you to meet Gerald, he's Mr. Burke, everyone calls him that, but for some reason, we're Gerald and Salinka, don't ask me, I haven't got a clue.'

As we mosey across the room it's easy to see why my girl likes working for this firm, maybe it's the season, being Christmas and all, but the observer can't fail to notice the friendship, the concern and the fun they all seem to be revelling in. Being a private detective can be a solitary business, there's a lot to be said for office camaraderie.

Gerald is younger than Mr. Lush by at least fifteen years. He's about five eight, has boyish looks, and talks like one too. He doesn't have the mature, establishment demeanour you'd expect from a senior partner. While we're talking partners, there is no Husband, he died some years back, that's why on all their letter headings, designed in red, Husband appears in black.

'Gerald, this is Dick Chase.' Dick hales from Cambridge these days. Darling, this is Gerald Burke, he's one of the partners.' I shook Gerald's hand, smiled and made small talk the way you do to an adult faking juvenile. I wanted to ask him how come my girl's allowed to call him Gerald, while everyone else has to settle for Mr. Burke, but I let it pass. I listened and laughed in all the right places. At length I asked him if he was related to Edmund Burke, 1729-1797, British Member of Parliament who pleaded on behalf of the American colonists for independence. And in fact, in 1780, single-handedly led a campaign, here in Great Britain, to see if he could persuade the crown to reduce its influence over there in the Americas. I knew I'd lost Gerald halfway through my little history lesson, he's looking over my shoulder and I can see the cogs whirling.

'What? Yes, yes, absolutely, but if you two will excuse me, I've just remembered I need a word with Brian, my computer keeps playing up - Salinka.' We watched in silence as he negotiated his way across the floor, I have my doubts about him, there's something? Salinka is smiling at me with her knowing expression, I look about the room and soon cotton on to what she was realising, the Christmas party had reached a hiatus, the alcohol is kicking in, everyone is talking and laughing at once. The disco has gone from a pleasant background caress to a full-on tantrum of what will later be known as that eighties sound. I grab my Russian Beauty around the waist and pull her to the centre of the floor, and as if the whole office were suddenly being given what they had waited for all evening, a huge cheer went up as their, unknown to them, ex-KGB agent and me began to dance the night away.

This is my first taste of the English Christmas office party. Whether it's her Russian agent background I don't know, but while this whole gathering seems to be sinking, very slowly, into a sort of controlled, but slightly drunken mob, Salinka hasn't altered from the way she was the moment we walked in, and neither have I, I guess it just goes to show how compatible we are. We're smiling at each other across the room when I notice Gloria is working her way towards me, she has succumbed to the demon drink a little more than I would have expected.

'Dick, *Dick,* so you're a private dick.' She hushed me while looking around, before placing her face close to mine. 'Are you for hire?' she winked 'You know what I mean?' She seemed to stumble, it was probably a ruse, I grabbed her arm just in case.

'Gloria, you know the answer to any question, you should know the answer to that one.' I can see she's too far gone to get it. 'No Gloria, but your secret is safe with me.' She looked at me, half in, half out.

'In the morning.' She's slurring. 'In the morning you'll be sober, while I'll be...I'll be.' She reared up to a height comparable to mine. 'I will still be Ugly.' She held her head swan-like, giving me a knowing glance. 'Churchill....you Americans...Americans' She seemed to lose her thread and walked off.

I look across the room to see my Baby in deep discussion with old Mr. Lush, I go over and join them. They cut short what was business to include me in their conversation, Mr. Lush put his hand on my shoulder.

'Dick Chase, private investigator.' He looks sharply at his interpreter. 'The first one I've ever met, a rare husband indeed, oh.' Mr. Lush looked devastated, I think, in his eyes, he saw his error as a terrible double whammy, Salinka spoke kindly, she understood.

'It's okay Mr. Lush.' She beamed her reassuring smile. 'Tom *was* a very rare husband, and, Dick,' She put her arm through mine. 'Dick is also very rare, so you're right on both counts.' I changed the subject.

'Mr. Lush, I believe congratulations are in order, I read in your annual Christmas letter to staff, this has been a good year, the best ever in fact and your turnover for the fiscal year is heading to double that of last year, that's very good news, Salinka will be able to keep me in the manner to which I've become accustomed.' She took Mr. Lush's arm and adopted a shrewd, hawk-like demeanour.

'As I said, he's a rare breed, do you know he likes to wear an apron when he's working in the kitchen?'

'Does he indeed, well, that evening job you were enquiring about, for him, as our night-time cleaner it's still in the offing?' Old Mr. Lush and his interpreter are turning out to be a couple of comedians, let's hope they don't start singing.

All too soon the party is drawing to a close. The disco has reverted to the slow love songs that are hopefully indicative of things to come in the dark, private bedrooms of all these couples, lovers, or just one-night stands. Unexpectedly, that old perennial, Autumn Leaves, no pun intended, sauntered into our ears, bringing with it a memory that made Salinka stop as we were about to exit the ballroom. She looked at me, lost, bereft of any sense of the present, it was as if this whole evening hadn't happened. She took my arm and we headed once again to the dance floor. She rested her head against mine and we rocked, ever so slowly, as the leaves gently fell around us. My spy spoke, dreamily, of a past that, like the fallen leaves, will never return.

'When I was at university, back in Moscow, just around the corner from the campus, there was a little jazz club called Dixx Place, I know, strange, isn't it? There was a delightfully gorgeous old, black piano player, his name was Wilfred, we all loved him, with his little jazz trio, this was their signature tune.' Salinka can't see but I'm smiling to myself as I hold her close. This enigma, this one-time Russian agent, who had lost two dear sisters in the most tragic and unnecessary way, had devised and pulled off a scheme to get their murderer. While under huge stress, and in pain, she managed to terminate a violent man intent on killing her, me, and others. She saw her husband, Tom, tragically gunned down in circumstances that even now can break me if I think about it. And yet…and yet she had it within her to see that chance in a million that enabled it to happen and to understand and forgive. Salinka is my Russian Beauty, and I have no intention of getting her gunned down.

TWENTY-EIGHT

Three years ago tomorrow, was when I got to meet my first KGB agent, for me the earth moved, for her it was just another day at the office. She was stunningly beautiful, sharp, with bright green eyes and a fondness for short skirts, I guess that's an occupational hazard I'm just gonna have to live with. We struck up a normal relationship, she saved my life, I saved her life, then she saved my life again. There is just one small thing, I was the cause of her husband's death, that was…that was unforgivable, I don't need reminding. She says it was a mistake anyone could have made, only I'm thinking I bet that's one mistake she never made, anyhow, it's an anniversary, I guess that says it all. I should explain we're an item and although she has decided to carry on working, we're very wealthy, no, really wealthy, we're Mr. & Mrs. Midas. She transferred it out of her first husband's slush fund, it's a long story. As we're lovers in every sense of the word, my girl says I can help myself. I've chosen not to work, well, I guess once a private dick always a gumshoe. I've placed business cards in two local newsagents, here, in Cambridge, where we live, love and wine and dine, that's what the Midases do.

To celebrate I've booked tickets for Tchaikovsky's 4th Symphony, I know, I'm all heart. Tchaikovsky is my Russian's favourite Russian, and as luck would have it that piece, as she says, is her theme tune. We gotta go to London, so I've booked us a night at the Hilton, overlooking Bucking Ham Palace, whoops, Buckingham Palace. The performance is on Sunday afternoon, we travel down by train, I've arranged for her to take Monday off. She couldn't believe I've never been to a concert hall before, but as it turns out she has never been to a dog track so, it's like I said, we're level pegging, she looked at me and slowly shook her head, after the concert I got it, we won't be rushing to the dogs any time soon. We found a nice little Italian not far from the hotel, where I find myself sitting opposite a grinning Cheshire cat.

'That was wonderful, a lovely surprise.' She reached across the table and took my hand. 'And we're in an Italian.' Her smile increased. 'We first met in an Italian, of course I'd already made your acquaintance, you were strapped to a trolley at the time, snoring and dribbling like a baby.' She put her hand over her mouth in a bid to hide her glee.

'Yeah, well, I was drugged up to the eyeballs don't forget and anyway, you didn't look your best with that Kalashnikov caressing your breasts, making them bleed.'

'Touché.'

For the first time my girl is short on words, I know she's got the 4th intruding into her thought process. I pour the last of the wine while absorbing her vital gorgeousness. Then, disturbingly, she's miles away, she came to, she sees my concern.

'I'm a little bit worried about work, all of a sudden I'm not translating letters from Albania. The customer is one of Gerald's, it's a new account, usually there's lots of correspondence from him. Another thing, the business finances have been blocked from the computer, and none of us have access, I spoke to Brian, he said it was Mr. Burke who gave the instructions. I asked him if he knew anything about the translation account, he went silent, he does that, he can't deal with too much information at once, anyway, the next day he handed me this printout.' She took a piece of paper from her bag, it shows Burke's foreign letters, one only, being translated by Cheryl Conway of Unicorn Yard, the payment is for £1000, that's a lot for a translation. 'I'm a little bit worried, do you think I'm about to lose my job?'

'No, I don't think so, not based on this. What does old Lush have to say?' Salinka raised a brow and shook her head. 'O.K. I'll look into it, in the meantime just put it out of your mind and try to enjoy the rest of the night. We'll mosey along back to the hotel, room service some champagne, and see if we can raise some noise from that top-of-the-range Hilton bed of ours…It turned out it was like a troop of monkeys at a clambake.

*

It's Tuesday morning and despite my reassurances I can tell Salinka's a bit subdued over Ms. Conway's sudden appearance in her career. I decide to visit our interpreting interloper, I know Unicorn Yard, it has a nice friendly coffee bar, often frequented by art students, the walls are covered with paintings, the subjects are either pop art or unspecified apocalyptic scenes of cities, there was one titled Cambridge the Dying Tears, someone had evidently been sent down. I'm sitting inside already, keeping an ear to the ground, when right on cue, this vivacious woman turns up, as chirpy as anything, peddling a green racer. She orders a skinny latte to go, I bet my eye teeth that's her. The barman nods a wink and communicates with his customer like she's a regular, at last it's…

'Anything to eat Cheryl?' She declines and after some small talk about the weather and the price of a punt these days, she's across the yard and letting herself into her empire. I'm sitting here browsing through a house newspaper while working out which of my professional personas will best suit the situation, hmmm, I think I'll go with the FBI agent, I've got the false ID already, I had it made especially, it's illegal but so was the fixer who arranged it for me. As I enter her tidy ground-floor office, Cheryl, is nowhere to be seen, but a small voice calls for me to take a seat. I'm sitting there detecting when behind her desk in a bookcase I see a line of folders, on the spine of one of them is the name Burke. A zipper goes up, we're changing our attire from perfunctory cycling classic to more comfortable office chic. No sooner had I identified my goal when Ms. Conway makes her appearance.

'Yes, I'm, Cheryl Conway, may I help you?'

'Miss Conway, the name's Chase, Dick Chase, I work for the FBI.' I show her my ID. 'I'm here as part of a worldwide investigation into money laundering.' I glance behind into Unicorn Yard, I want it to look like this information has to be on the qt. 'What I'm about to divulge must be between you, me, and these four walls, is that okay with you Miss Conway?'

'Am I in any trouble?' I grin assuredly.

'No ma'am, you're not in trouble, I'm the one in trouble, would you believe I gotta speak to every bicycle owner in the city, and today you're only number fifteen? Money is being laundered, hidden inside the hollow tubing of bicycles, and being shipped all over the world in their millions, well, I guess you get the picture. I noticed you ride a little French job.' She gave a knowing nod. 'Exactly Miss Conway, at the very least it's come across the channel. Do you mind if I call you Cheryl? What I'd like you to do Cheryl is go and tap your "French Swift", I think that's what you have isn't it? If you will tap it all over with something solid, a steel letter opener like the one you have on your desk, we'll know straight off if it's stuffed with money.' Cheryl picked up the opener and popped out the back, I can hear her complying. It took me 8 seconds and when she returned, I'm standing on the same spot as if I hadn't moved at all. 'Phew, you're in the clear Cheryl, it rang like a bell.' I look at my watch. 'Only about another eight hundred go, remember, mom's the word, we don't want to be giving these criminals a heads up do we?' With the folder neatly placed down the rear of my pants and covered by my jacket I make a beeline outta there before Cheryl notices it's missing.

I'm now back at Midas mansions, my girl and me rent a small semi on the outskirts, we're looking to buy but there's plenty of time to find the right place that suits our taste. Surprisingly the correspondence only amounts to two letters, one in Albanian, at least I guess it's Albanian, the other is in English, that must be the translation, it's only nine words, it says simply "It's tonight, Jerry, and very important bring that P.A." My instincts kick in straight away, I reach for the phone and call the office, Shirley answered, she sounds upset, something's wrong, I didn't ask, she's putting me through, I hear her say it's Mr. Chase for you. I heard the receiver lift, Salinka takes a couple of breaths, I don't rush her.

'Dick, we're too late.' Four words that I knew spelled disaster for Lush Husband and Burke, also, strangely, I fear for Natalie. 'Gerald's done a runner and it looks like Natalie's gone with him, can you get here, Mr. Lush is going to speak to the office?'

'I'll be right there Honey, I've got the translation and I don't think Natalie's gone on vacation.'

As I walk into Lush Husband, Mr Lush is in his office with an ex-KGB agent, it's surreal. It's a modern setup, amongst the oak skirting and some scrolled panelling there's a wall and door completely of glass that has vertical blinds. I don't interrupt, they seem to be having a serious conversation, Mr. Lush is quite animated and looks upset, he sits at his desk and puts his head in his hands. Salinka is leaning on the blotting-pad, talking, looking very assertive, I know that expression, she's probably volunteering to go looking for Burke herself. They emerge from the office, all the staff are upset, Shirley is close to tears. Salinka comes and stands next to me at the back, I put my arm around her waist, she whispers in my ear.

'Come on Honey, let's go.'

'Let's hear what Mr. Lush has to say.'

'You stay, I'll see you at home.' Discreetly she makes her exit while Mr. Lush begins to speak.

'As you all know Mr. Burke has left the country, the police confirmed it was late last night, he wasn't on their radar, and neither was Natalie, who sadly left with him.' There's an audible intake of breath. 'There are two pieces of news, firstly, Mr. Burke has emptied our business accounts, there's nothing left, it's all gone.' Another intake of breath. 'You must all realise, ordinarily, this would mean the end of the business and the loss of all our jobs.' Mr. Lush takes a moment to contain himself before he continues. 'But extraordinarily I can tell you all is not lost.' He looks for an empty chair and slowly lowers himself into it. 'An extraordinary opportunity has just presented itself, quite out of the blue, totally unexpected, we have been given a lifeline, a gift. I have in my office a cheque for half a million pounds, to keep the business afloat.' There's a mumble of shock, a buzz of hope. Mr. Lush stands and looks humbly at everyone. 'For this wonderful gift, this unbelievable and amazingly prodigious gesture, we must all thank Salinka.' In one move the whole office turns around and looks our way, my way, I smile and raise my eyebrows.

'I'll,…I'll let her know.'

TWENTY-NINE

We both agreed the translation was worrying, "And very important, bring that P.A.", posted from Vlore, Albania. Is it prostitution, enslavement, from what I know of that depraved underworld, finding Natalie will be like looking for a needle in a very dangerous haystack? Salinka arrived home after her selfless act of generosity that I thought was typical and didn't surprise me one bit. Having read the line herself, she bet her bottom dollar it's curtains for Natalie.

The next day our "AFA" agent phoned Cheryl Conway and gave her some of her best broken English.

'Ms. Conway, I am Colonel Palchikova of the Albanian Federal Agency, have you seen the papers today?' Cheryl replied, in Albanian, that she had, Colonel Palchikova is stating our theory, straight. Cheryl, now too shocked to translate, has reverted to English, where she feels safe.

'No, I knew nothing of this, I was surprised to read it, and you think... that poor girl.'

'Ms. Conway, I can assure you our best team is on the case, what you must do is return the money to Lush, Husband, and Burke, and I promise, for you, that will be the end of it.'

These were times when there was still a second post, June, Mr. Lush's P.A. handed him his afternoon mail, he opened the only handwritten envelope first, it contained a cheque for £1000. He sat back in his chair, a smile crept over his face as he murmured. 'Salinka.'

*

The advantage of being the in-house philanthropist is you can take an impromptu vacation, no names, no pack drill. And that's how we find Dick and Salinka, mid-air, on their way to Corfu, not only the nearest airport to their destination, Vlore, but Salinka has an old friend, an associate there, who lives in a flat overlooking the sea in Corfu City.

'Lemmy served thirty years in the French foreign legion, don't mess with him, talk about fishing and you might just survive.'

'I guess you were both on the same side.' Salinka is hesitant, reluctant to spill the beans.

'Put it this way, I am here because of him, don't mention I saved his skin, will you? Hey, you could say it's become a bit of a habit.'

The pair are making their way along a sun-drenched, crowded, pedestrian, paved lane, full of shops, selling everything from a whole smoked pancetta, to a silk dress, to a toilet brush. Salinka grabs Dicks arm and pulls up, a couple of yards in front of them stands a big bruiser of a man, Dick immediately thinks best avoid this one. He's holding a cast iron fish pan and seems to be bartering with the stall holder. Salinka raises an eyebrow at Dick, she takes a note from her bag, strolls up and tells the surprised owner she'll pay for it, to help the poor man out. The big bruiser shoots this strange woman a look.

'Salinka, my friend.' Everything stops as this holidaymaker is thrown in the air, caught, hugged, kissed, and observed with wonder. 'Coffee my comrade, you will have a story to tell me about why you're here.' He turns his head, aware he is being studied in a sphinx-like manner by some stranger, immediately Salinka steps in.

'Lemmy, this is my partner, my backup, Dick Chase, he's one of us.

Over coffee with apple strudel, a captivated Lemmy is taking it all in, just a few words from Salinka, and she knows, his keen military brain has grasped it.

'You will have your work cut out my friend, don't let on what you are up to, or your associates will have their throats slit instantly.' He looks hard at the pair of them. 'I'm sorry I cannot accompany you, I have…obligations.' He grins 'But my boat, The Julian, is at your disposal, she is the envy of the fishing club, the fastest boat this side of the island, and who knows where else, she has a dicky port light but, mañana, it'll be mended. The ferry takes seven hours, I can get you there in three, well, three and a half, give or take.' He alters tack. 'Salinka, tell me about my good friend Ivan, I heard you two got hitched, you finally tamed the serial womaniser?'

'You could say that, I killed him.' Lemmy sees his friend has lost none of her bravado.

'Yes, well, news travels fast.' A supporting weapon of a hand gently clasps Salinka's and that face, with its greying, bushy eyebrows knitting together, suddenly takes on the mantle of Kronos. 'I was broken to hear of your sisters.'

So far Dick hasn't managed to get a word in, but he's glad *that* difficult situation resolved itself. Lemmy, turns to him.

'This woman saved my life, did she tell you that, I expect she did? You are in good hands my friend, treat her well, and she might save your life one day.'

'Yeah, well, as a matter of fact…' Salinka steps in.

'We could go on all night saving each other's egos, but…..Natalie!'

Battling the sea breeze and the salt spray, Lemmy informs.

'Those are the lights of Vlore ten minutes will have us pulling in. This is the Ionian Sea, ahead is the Adriatic, once, on these straits, I caught a big blue-fin tuna, it put up one hell of a fight.' Salinka handed the wheel over to Lemmy to get them safely into port. With the boat bobbing against the sea wall Dick makes his way up the ten or so steps to dry land, carrying the small holdall that contains all their gear. Salinka hugs her friend, words are exchanged that only the sea breeze can spill, and she began the climb, purposeful, unrelenting, to save her friend, Natalie.

And so it is, our two brave warriors are standing on the pier at Vlore where the Adriatic Sea shakes hands with the Ionian Sea. The sun had long set and in this dark, this very dark place, standing there the sky seems to be bursting at the seams, so full, they can't see the stars for the milky way. Beneath nature's crowning glory are our two minor miracles, by comparison two tiny insignificant examples of her creativity. It's Dick and Salinka, standing, looking for a taxi to take them to a good hotel, with a bar, some food, and a noisy bed.

THIRTY

Overnight Salinka had transformed herself from the poised, cherry gloss-lipped brunette with the fair complexion, to a cropped, gelled-back, black-haired minx. A black-lipped, alabaster beauty who could walk right into Lush and Husband and the only response she'd get would be, "Yes madam, can I help you?" as for me, I left my razor. We're sitting in some main avenue coffee house, on the comfy seats, looking out the window. I guess we're both hoping to see Gerald, or better still Natalie, walk past, but it's been two coffees and an hour and a half of endless anonymous pedestrian free-for-all. Salinka is sitting there bathed in the early spring sunshine that's pouring in, looking like the lead singer in some Punk band, she's translating a story from the daily newspaper. Two weeks ago, a girl of eighteen Margareta Vittua was found murdered, lying beside the road that runs below the foothills that are the backdrop to our temporary home in Vlore. The young local woman is thought to have been trafficked to Brussels, under the pretence of working in a hotel. It turned out to be nothing but a brothel where she was beaten and forced to work as a sex worker. Somehow, she managed to escape and travel back home, her murder was an example to other trafficked women and girls. Maybe I'm getting old, let me just clarify that, I'm not, but there was a time when a story like that would just have been another sad statistic, now, as I sit here nursing my coffee, listening, understanding, I'm angry, I'm very angry.

Salinka's investigative career is rooted in espionage, whereas domestic violence, homicide, or tracing missing persons is right up my street. O.K. I've found a couple of lost cats in my time, but let's face it, they can't read those notices. The first thing we need to do is find someone who knew Margareta, preferably trace any relatives, I'm guessing Natalie might have been forced down the same route. This is gonna be tricky, we can't just walk into the police station and start asking questions, my rock chick is more in Russian agent mode.

'Dick, what we need is information about this girl, I'll walk into the police station and ask around.' I wasn't about to dampen that insatiable spirit, but she must be cuckoo if she thinks the local police are gonna listen to her, some unknown Punk rocker, a skirt of questionable, taxonomic classification, but we're a team and she's keen to give it a go so what the heck? We arrange to meet back at our seedy hotel in two hours, that's all the time I need, I've got a gigantic idea of my own.

There's a Catholic church not far from our accommodation and I'm now walking up the aisle looking for the confessional. I don't have a clue how it works, I guess I let myself into this box, no appointment required, sit down and wait for divine intervention. Soon enough it begins, and I'm about to experience something that's gonna be a complete anomaly to me, and that is exactly what I'm gonna be to the priest who's just entered the adjoining box. A small dividing curtain slides back and I can see him through an ornamental brass mesh screen as he makes first contact.

'You have sinned my son, do you seek absolution?'

'Well, there's a miracle right there, how do you know to speak English, no, don't answer that, I get it, God moves in mysterious ways? Now I come to think about it, no is the answer to your question that isn't why I'm here.' There's a pause in proceedings.

'Then I am at a loss, what brings you into God's house?'

'Excuse my errant ways Father, I'm just a small-time private investigator with a penchant for sorting out the bad guys, but first I need to know that what I have to say will be in the strictest confidence.'

'You have my word, in the name of the father.'

'O.K. well, I guess if it's good enough for your father, it sure is good enough for me.' I gave him the lowdown on yours truly, I didn't mention, Miss Russia, I figured that would complicate matters. I said I'm investigating the murder of Margareta Vittua, there's a crash like the priest dropped the collection plate on the floor.

'Poor Margareta, she was once a child of this church, a charming, polite, always helpful little girl, her's was a very sad, tragic end. And what are you, another member of the press, wheedling your way in looking for a story to sell and make profit from her tragedy...forgive me Father?' He said that last bit under his breath, now it's my turn to ask for forgiveness...

'Forgive me, I don't wheedle, it's like I said, I'm a private investigator with an interest in seeing her killer receives justice. Can you tell me anything about her, where she lived, why did she go to Brussels? Do you know who killed her? Do you know Natalie Lowe?' At last I seem to have grabbed the priest's attention, he invited me into his office where we can be more comfortable, it was then we really gelled as he offered me a sherry.

Two hours later and two people who just have to be punctual find themselves walking towards one another from opposite directions, both making a beeline for the hotel. We're soon back in our room, a sterile square box devoid of luxury, except for a carpet, a picture of the Grand Canyon hanging on the wall (I thought of Helen) and the bed we're now laying on. We're both immersed in thought and for two whole minutes all you can hear is the faint rumble of traffic permeating the white plastic double-glazing. Eventually my girl moves close to me and puts an arm around my shoulders. She speaks quietly, without emotion, without her usual zest for life.

'This place is one rotten stinking hole if you're a young woman of no means and few resources.' It was like she'd been with me listening to the priest's story…The control some men have over hundreds of women and girls. The no chance authorities have of being able to do anything about it. The victims' families and friends are always known to the gangs and threatened with violence or death, if they speak out. Endless stories, reports, facts, about murders, beatings, of being sold into slavery, trafficked for sex. Promises of better-paid jobs in Brussels, Italy, France, Germany, and England. All these promises will generate joy and raise hopes only to be cruelly dashed because it's all lies. What it really means is prostitution, enslavement, more beatings and possibly death… and he'd never heard of Natalie Lowe. That's when Salinka hits me with the big one, it turns out a certain policeman can arrange a date for her, tonight, at some disco. Someone he knows, a friend, can get her a job in Brussels and introduce her to a Punk band and their manager, who he absolutely knows are looking for a singer, if she goes with him, it will be the beginning of a new life. She looked at me, every bit that young hopeful Punk rocker. 'I can't believe my luck, it's the big break I've been waiting for my chance of rock stardom.'

In the foyer we're separate entities, the danger levels on this job have gone through the roof, Salinka is about to get herself trafficked for the greater good and as if that isn't enough from now on she's on her own, somehow I've got to be invisible. What isn't invisible though, is the visitor's book, open right under my nose, at the page before we'd signed in. There, in failing green Biro are Gerald Burke and Natalie Lowe. When I think about it, it's not so far-fetched Burke and Natalie had been in the same hotel as us. What is amazing is neither of us noticed their entry in the visitor's book until now, right when my attention is needed on Salinka, who's just been whisked out the door by some evil-looking bruiser wearing sunglasses, even though it's pitch-black out there. Their taxi pulled up at a place called Canarsie's Love Disco, a dingy, rundown, converted cinema with half its neon lights out, strangely it reads, " **i Lov Di c** " hmm, I didn't know they cared. As I enter the dive, I immediately spot my girl at the bar with her toxic date, she knows I'm here. I sidle over, not too close, and get myself a drink. The girls behind the bar are only half dressed, that certainly concentrates my attention, Maria here knows how to mix a B52-Kahlua, just the way I like it. I lean back on the bar and begin taking in the sights, now they're dancing and my Punk is putting on a good show, she certainly knows how to shift that butt of hers. Lucky for him the jerk in the sunglasses is managing to keep his hands to himself. I spoke too soon, he just flung his arms around her ass. At the moment I have his back, so Salinka is looking straight at me, she's communicating with her eyes. I know whatever that jerk is thinking she has his measure, she's in total command, in rhythm, they spin around, and I divert my eyes.

There's a girl standing next to me, she's trembling, distressed, frightened, keeping an eye on the dance floor I speak to her.

'Excuse me ma'am, you look like a damsel in distress if ever I saw one, do you wanna talk about it?' She's trying to pull herself together.

'No it's alright, really.' She's lying, I remembered what the priest had to say about the evils of man.

'Hey, lady, I'm not from these parts, I'm an American, on a business trip.' I give her my funny face. 'We sell car tyres, I know, sad isn't it?' She's about twenty, and yet like a little frightened bird. I can see it in her eyes, such sadness and worse, exhaustion, devoid of hope. 'It's okay, I'm a friend,

I'm just visiting these parts, I'm only interested in car tyres.' She looked at me, there's a slight easing of tension.

'Are you on your own, tell me you didn't bring your wife to this place?' I was taken aback I know concern when I hear it.

'No I didn't, would you like to tell me all about it, are you alright, are you safe?' She looked at me, the rims of her eyes filled.

'I'll be dead by the morning, I know it.' She looks so sad. 'Do you know anything about this country? I'm refusing to go to Brussels with a man who says he wants me to work for him in his bar, I know he's lying, but I can't get away from him, he won't leave me alone. I know he will beat me and make me work in a brothel.' While she's talking I'm keeping my eye on Salinka who in a timely manner glances over. I flash her a look, I need a word. She speaks to her stooge, I know she's gonna get a round in. He's confident she's a cinch and lets her go, now I have this gorgeous Punk standing next to me. I speak without looking at her. 'This girl needs my help, it's life or death, you're on your own kid.' She speaks without looking.

'It's Brussels, the Rue d'Aerschot area, the hotel St Legion, don't take all week.' She picks up the drinks and heads back to the tosser in the sunglasses. No sooner has she left when the girl gasps and turns towards the bar, she's shaking like a leaf, I speak quickly to her.

'Listen, go with him and leave everything to me, and try not to worry, I'll sort it, I promise.' I turn and walk off. I see some jerk walk up to her and pull her away. He's a little shit, it's written all over his face, he's probably handy with a knife, guess what I won't be taking any chances? I'm outside getting some fresh air the pair leave together, the girl is more dragged than walking. As soon as they're outside away from the crowd, he stops and forces a kiss on her. Now he's speaking, he's loud, on the verge of shouting, the girl begins to cry, the little shit slaps her hard across the face, that's it Pal I can see we're gonna be best friends. He grabs her wrist and drags her across the road, I turn around to see them disappear up some ill-lit side street. I'm across the road and behind them already, I dive into a darkened doorway. He dashes around the back of a parked car, gets in, leans over and pushes the passenger door wide open, he screams at her to get in, she's petrified, she knows she can't escape, he screams again. By this time I've stepped up and moved the girl to one side. I lean in and grab his outstretched wrist then jump in myself. Taking his upper arm with my other hand, I slam his elbow down hard onto my right thigh, his arm snaps like a twig, he screams with pain. I grab the back of his neck and slam his open mouth hard onto the steering wheel, that shuts him up nicely. Looking around the coast is clear. I think of the priest and divine intervention, I think we're getting some right now.

'Sorry about the arm, listen asshole, did you kill, Margaretta Vittua?' There's sobbing but no reply. 'Don't make me hurt you, if you wanna get outta this alive, you'd better tell me the truth, did you kill, Margaretta Vittua?' I released him just a bit to let him speak.

'Yes, yes, may God forgive me.'

'O.K. now you're earning your freedom, so make it count, what do you know about Gerald Burke and Natalie?' He's moaning but I'm not getting any answers. I force his mouth hard against the steering wheel and for good measure I give his broken arm a tweak. He screams, so I push his mouth harder against the wheel. When I release him, he can't speak fast enough.

'Yes, yes, I knew them, I knew them.'

'Where are they now?'

'Burke is dead, he didn't have the money, there was no money.' The poor jerk's crying, my heart bleeds.

'Did you kill him?'

'No,' I tweaked the arm, 'NO, it wasn't me, it was Burano.'

'What about Natalie, where's she?'

'She was taken to Italy, no, no, it was Brussels, yes Brussels. Now please let me go, before God I am sorry, please God forgive me, please forgive me.' He broke down.

'Why don't you ask him, face to face.' I lined the creep's Adam's apple up with the steering wheel and didn't stop pressing, till it was all over.

THIRTY-ONE

Salinka is Salinka Palchikova, who is Colonel Palchikova, who is an ex-KGB agent. She will tell you the Colonel is honouree because of her degrees, well, that is partly true. What she won't tell you is she has been trained by Russia's elite army specialists, the SPETSNAZ special forces, an ultra-elite unit that delivers highly trained killing machines. Out of the one hundred personnel, mostly men, she spent six gruelling months training with, Palchikova came top of the class. She won't tell you three comrades died during training. She also won't tell you she had to endure a series of humiliating scenarios including one of simulated rape. And what she definitely won't mention is, on one occasion, as part of her training, she *was* raped. That wasn't the highlight, the highlight was when her parachute was tossed out of a helicopter at twenty thousand feet and she was thrown out after it. These thoughts were nowhere in her head as she flew with her minder over the Swiss Alps on their way to Brussels and her new life as a Punk rock singer. Mr. Burano, her new manager, is unable to give her any more information about her musical career. This rock chick thought she had detected a total lack of interest in the Punk band department, let's face it, that was to be expected. She knows better than to labour the subject, that might cause early and unnecessary angst, her prime objective is to locate Natalie, she will cause Burano angst enough when she's good and ready, and at a time of her choosing. She did wonder what the circumstances might be when his real motivation surfaced and Burano forced her into the sex trade. Two things bolster her, one, there's nothing she doesn't know about sex, and the other, she knows she will seriously maim or kill if she needs to. Her mind wandered to her partner, and how he got on helping the girl, he would never have left her unless things were really bad, it's a matter of life or death he said. She smiled to herself as she guessed how he'd dealt with the lowlife degenerates.

As Salinka's plane is landing, Dick's plane is taking off from Tirana airport, and as the flight time is only two hours and forty minutes, we know backup isn't far behind. However, the Colonel doesn't know it, and even with her training, she'd give anything for a heads-up. There is one piece of luck though, thanks to Russian technology, they each carry a short-range personal tracker, it's a small device about the size of a matchbox, it has a range of three hundred feet, that's just short of a hundred yards. So, our heroes are only two hours, forty minutes, and one hundred yards apart, things could be a lot worse.

Dick isn't travelling alone, the girl he'd helped turned out to have no fixed abode, being disowned, through fear, by her family, she speaks excellent English, her name is Angel. She's now sitting looking out the window on her first flight, all her cares have vanished, her spirits are lifted by this kind, heroic, American tyre salesman, Angel is feeling like it's her birthday and Christmas all rolled into one.

'So, Angel, what's your occupation? Are you a dentist, or a brain surgeon?' She smiled at her saviour like she'd just won a million dollars.

'I'm a beauty therapist, I worked in a beauty parlour. I see your nails could do with a good manicure Mr. Chase.' He glances at his fingers.

'Mmm, handling car tyres all day does take its toll, please, call me Dick.

'Mr. Chase, Dick, I saw what you did for me back there, it was amazing, I can never thank you enough, you saved my life.' Angel is giving him a kind of funny look.

'What?' He's curious, she frowns.

'I think you are not a tyre salesman sir.' Looking down the plane he smiles to himself, he thought about his partner, that brave girl who puts her neck on the line without question, now she's doing it again, big time, for her friend Natalie, he turned to face Angel.

'There are two of us, a friend, she's not a friend she's more than that, she's done for me what I did for you, more than once. We're looking for a girl, Natalie Lowe, did you know Natalie?' She didn't. 'Anyway, we think she's was taken in, like you were, only this time it's all moved on a bit too quickly and we have to find her, fast, then figure out how to save her, believe me, you were easy.'

'Where is your friend now?' As Dick looked at Angel, an unexpected and embarrassing burst of pride came over him.

'She's gone ahead, she's penetrated the gang.' He paused. 'She's allowed herself to be trafficked for the greater good.' He looked deep into Angel's eyes,

for some reaction, some sign of response. He's gone too far, that's my trait he thought, Angel is moved.
'Hey, don't you go worrying yourself about my friend, she'll have them for breakfast.'

Salinka's situation is no picnic, it requires all her strengths, her ability as an actor is crucial to her character. Already she's pretty convincing, her performance is measured, timely, not a moment does she waste, always looking, listening, planning. Two promising things are certain one is the sign read from the taxi Rue d'Aerschot, the other is the hotel St Legion. Shaking and crying another disillusioned saddo is manhandled and dumped in a room, this is part of her training. Oh yes, even these despicable creatures of no moral fiber and less brain, have organized training sessions for new interns. "She'll wise up or commit suicide" is their mantra. There's a third option that always makes them laugh over their coffee, "Does a bear shit in the woods, she'll conform?" The room has a chair facing the wall, it has installed a fixed mirror that gives the looker a view into the next room. It contains a bed and a chair, nothing more. The Punk is told she can forget the band, she'd better "watch and learn". Soon, a scantily dressed girl of about eighteen enters, at no time does she look at the mirror, Salinka took from that the girl knew someone will be watching her perform. There's no need to explain the gruesome details of what happened next. A man in his mid-forties entered, he has no idea he's being watched. He removed his clothes and, shall we say, got down to it. I think that's all the description required here.

As for the trafficked girl, the victim, she's acting her little heart out, the observer, with all her worldly experience, is on fire. I said earlier the girl didn't look at the mirror, that wasn't true, she did glance at it, once, at the invisible savior, who saw in the girl's eyes such a look of shame, self-disgust, self-loathing. But more than that, a look of total abandonment, it's as if she had already lost everything, as if she'd given up. That was the moment Salinka knew she had to close this place down, even if it meant killing every one of the soul-destroying suckers who are running the joint.

Dick has it all worked out, but he's got to move fast, although he's seeing the worst of mankind, he's got faith in his roots. He took Angel to the American Embassy in Brussels, he sat her down in the plush, marbled interior entrance hall, hung with paintings of past American presidents and an embossed copy of the Gettysburg Address, then went over to the ubiquitous, multi-talented coffee machine and got his charge a hot chocolate. O.K. Dick, he thought, now for the big one, you *must* get to see a senior commissioner, and fast. He recognised the name Denby... Duke Denby? According to the roll of honour hanging behind the main reception desk, he's third in line to the Ambassador himself...Denby, hmm. Eureka! Duke Denby, that's it, if Dick's not mistaken he was at college with his old boss, the chief of the New York police department, way back when, how does he know that, because Denby was the one-time Mayor of Ohio and as for the chief, he's only the biggest serial name dropper in the business? He's now at the desk asking to speak to him.

'Tell Duke it's a friend of chief Carmichael, NYPD, and while you'll there just mention it's a matter of life or death.' That usually does the trick, he turns and gives his charge a wink.

Dick's one-to-one with Duke Denby was very heartening and rekindled his faith in mankind. He explained Angel's plight, he didn't spare the details, and what he hoped the great American nation, the land of the free, will do for her, he didn't want much.

'Firstly, all of America is asleep just now, and for reasons I can't explain I can't hang around. So mainly, I'm requesting you sir, and your staff to sort it all out, I wrote a list.

1. Confirm who I am with chief Carmichael.

2. Speak to officer Peter McDougall, ask him, on my behalf, to meet Angel at JFK and put her up for a few days.

3. Also, ask him to contact Helen McCluskie in Seattle, and ask her, as a favour to me, to employ Angel.

4. Emphasize I'll pay the airfare, her keep, and her wages until things take off.'

Observing Denby, Dick IDs a look of terminal dizzy confusion that's crying out for more. 'Now, that reminds me sir, in the meantime you'll have to keep Angel safe in your accommodation at the embassy, organise her flight to the States and inform officer McDougall of timings etc.' Denby looked hard at Chase.

'If I do this, and it's a very tall order, I'll have to pull a lot of strings, I think it's only right you explain to me why you're in such a hurry.' I gave him the brief, by the time I'd finished he'd gone from relaxed, laidback man in charge, to intense, serious, job to do, rationalist, who also happens to be very decisive. The next thing I know I'm calling Angel into the office and introducing everyone, she's ecstatic about my plan, I know she's in good hands and hopefully, now, has some sort of future. I'm just leaving the building when someone calls my name, I turn around only to be run into by Angel, who flings her arms around me.

'Thank you, Mr. Chase, Dick, you're my guardian angel.' I smile.

'Well, that's not me, but if you do find one, ask him/her to hang around will you, now, if you'll excuse me ma'am, I've gotta go?'

We know by now the level of training Salinka has endured, it means she knows how to make a plan and we are about to witness her coup de grâce. She's been manhandled into a room with a bed and a chair, nothing more, this time there's no mirror. A man, it isn't Burano but some other creep, pushes her onto the bed, he sneers at her.

'I've always wanted to fuck a Punk.' She couldn't help herself, it just slipped out.

'I've always wanted to shag a greasy shit.' She realised her mistake straight away, he flew at her and smacked her across the face, then, with a gleam in his eye, he put both hands behind his back and pulled out a knife, Salinka turned her head away as he placed the cold, sharp, blade against her cheek. His face is close to her's, she doesn't know what's worse, the threat of the steel, or the all-prevailing reek of garlic.

'You're still serviceable, even with a scar.' He pushed the knife carefully so as not to break the skin, he knew not to damage the merchandise, he replaced the blade.

'Just for that I'll bring you a big fat one.' Was his throwaway line as he left the room and locked her in.

It took half an hour for the fun to begin, a key turns in the lock, the door opens it's the greasy shit grinning all over his face, he stands to one side to allow the punter to enter. The man, shall we be polite, is obese, the greasy shit speaks.

'I'll be back in one hour,' He nods towards the chattel as he leaves. 'This one likes it rough.'
There's no introduction, the man shamelessly begins to remove his clothes.

'So, you like it rough.' He sounds loathsome, vile. 'You're my kind of shag.' He's got white foam in the corners of his mouth. Salinka speaks in nervous, frightened tones.

'I'm only sixteen, they've made me up to look older, I've been trafficked.'

'Good, that's good.' He's excited, eager, it's the green light she was looking for. Standing on the bed she lifts her already short skirt and moves her body provocatively. The man advances and begins to undo his trousers, he's smiling to himself all his dreams have come true at once, he's thinking they'd better have at five hundred dollars a throw. The moment he's in range Salinka strikes, from her elevated position on the bed, mercilessly, she lands him a mean headbutt, it's a speciality of hers that she knows exactly how to perform. The man's nose is seriously splattered across his face, immediately she punches him hard, in the throat, three times in quick succession. As she throws the punches, left right left, she visualises his windpipe collapsing. She turns full circle and slings the hard edge of her right hand against the back of his neck. He drops to his knees, his hands feeling his throat, he's turning blue, will that be enough? The man looks at her without seeing, he's having trouble breathing, he can't breathe. She shoves him hard with her foot, he crashes onto his back, his obesity spread across the floor, he shudders in the throes of mortality, from now on, it's a waiting game.

When the hour is almost up Salinka stands quietly behind the door, the key's in the lock, she braces herself. The greasy shit bowls in hoping to catch some sex act being performed by the Punk, all he sees is the man lying on the floor and the empty bed. Grabbing the top of the door she jumps up and with both feet explodes with everything she's got, a massive kick into his back that knocks him diagonally across the room, slamming his head against the wall. He lands on his side, on top of the fat one. Coolly Salinka closes the door and kneels beside them, already she has the tosser's knife in her hand, she plunges it deep, twice, below his ribs on his left side. She drags the knife out, pushes him onto his back, and powers the blade through his chest, stopping his heart in a beat. Withdrawing it a third time she stabs the fat one in the chest, this time leaving the knife in situ. She rolls the little shit over and places his hands around the handle, it's done, she's done it, they've killed each other. Salinka sits on the bed and shrinks into the corner of the room as if trying to escape through the wall, to escape the horror and the carnage, while she awaits her cue.

With her knees beneath her chin, her arms cradling her shins she starts to sob, she doesn't have long to wait, it's Burano. Rocking back and forth while trembling all over, now she's sobbing and shaking uncontrollably, she's so upset she can hardly speak.

'What's going on, why have these two killed each other, *why*?' She gesticulates loudly while holding her trembling arm out, pointing as she speaks, her curled fingers dripping mucus and tears. She shrills, 'They were stabbing each other.' At this point Salinka storms out of the room and into the passage where two men are blocking her path. She vomits down the wall, she's good, she's damn good. Inquisitively she plunges into the room opposite, where, sitting on the bed, half frightened to death, dressed only in her underwear, Salinka stumbles upon Natalie.

THIRTY-TWO

Dick is sitting in a wine bar across the street sampling a very nice chardonnay while checking out the hotel Saint Legion, and trying to get a handle on how many gang members there are. He had to have a drink to justify his raison d'etre, but the last thing on his mind is whether the grapes came from the wet side of the valley or if the picker had a wooden leg. The hotel is a dilapidated, four-storey terraced job, similar to many of the buildings in this rundown part of Brussels. Most of the houses are private but as luck would have it the St Legion is attached at the hip to the hotel Capitol, a smarter building with its fresh apple green exterior, its name in spacy 3D chromed characters sitting on a plinth, and the flag of Belgium, proudly hanging above the porch. There's no visible sign of activity so Dick decides to move the game up a level. The woman at the desk in the "Capitol" is tall, black, with dreadlocks down to her shoulders, Dick takes up the invitation of her wide beckoning eyes and poised, delicately chained Biro.

'Do you speak English?' is his opening gambit.

'I do speak English or if you prefer, I can manage American.' She introduced a southern drawl, the unexpected humour took Dick by surprise.

'I'd like a room for the night, maybe on the third floor and possibly'. He did a quick calculation. 'Possibly on the east side of this fine establishment.' He noted the receptionist looked a bit thrown. 'My folks were strict feng shuists.' The grinning woman cast an eye down the ledger displayed in front of her, her dreadlocks forming a curtain that hid her face.

She looked up quickly whipping them behind her shoulders in a practiced manner that Dick wasn't sure was supposed to be amusing, but he smiled anyway.

'I've got just the room, you'll have to pay in advance for one night, them's the house rules.' She beckoned again with her eyes, Dick paid up and soon he's standing in the room on the third-floor chewing over his options. He knelt on the bed and leaning against the adjoining wall he tries out his Russian-made tracker in the hope he isn't surrounded by hordes of Russian agents all waiting to get him.

In the meantime confusion reigns next door, all of a sudden the gang have two bodies to dispose of, one of them obese, who they suspect is a member of the British establishment, that is going to be tricky, on both counts. In the confusion a rare moment of compassion, the door to the two girls is closed and locked leaving them alone together. Natalie is sitting looking at this strange female who is suddenly her best friend, whoever she is, Salinka asks the question.

'Are you alright?' Natalie is thrown, no one had taken the slightest interest in her well-being since this whole nightmare began, strangely she felt she knew this person, but she doesn't know any Punk rockers, she can't put her finger on it.

'Are you Stella Kill of Stella Kill and the Pubes?' The rock chick laughs.

'You're not even warm, look more closely, I'll give you a clue, I hope they don't cheap on the coffee in this place?' The tears are flowing before a euphoric Natalie throws her arms around this Punk rocker, Salinka cradles her as they both sit on the bed. Gentle laughter.

'Haha, there, there Nat, it's okay, everything's going to be alright, you'll see, trust me.'

'But how can it be?' Natalie is beside herself. 'We're both prisoners, these men are ruthless murderers, the threats and warnings I've had, one girl killed herself.' With a look of horror she came straight out with it. 'They killed Mr. Burke, right in front me, he'd done nothing, one of them just stabbed him, it was Burano, however you say it, he's still here, he's the one in charge. Salinka disguised her shock, poor Gerald, she smiled as she brushed Natalie's hair out of her face and gently placed her thumbs beneath her eyes to wipe away the tears.

'Listen, Dick and I have come to take you home.' Natalie tries to speak, Salinka places a finger on her lips to stop her. 'You're doing brilliantly well, I'm very proud of you. Now listen to me, most importantly, you don't know who I am, okay, we've never met, I'm probably going to kiss you, if I do, go with it, is that alright, have you got that?' Natalie was saying something but just for the moment her saviour is elsewhere, she's thinking about poor Gerald, he was a casualty, stabbed to death by Burano, she was sorry she couldn't help him, that was bad news, she wondered if Dick knew.

Salinka has no idea he is standing on the other side of the wall trying to contact her, but something made her delve into her waistband, take out the little device and switch it on. Then, the miracle, a tiny flash of feedback awakened a dormant memory. During her military training there was a joke they used to play, when a comrade was on a stealth training mission a tracker might be placed in his pack, already switched on. At the crucial moment when he turned his tracker on, the feedback would give him away, to the delight of everyone as the trainee was hit with a hail of rubber bullets. Salinka knew Dick was close, she hushed Natalie while quickly looking about the room to orientate herself. She knelt on the bed next to the adjoining wall and slapped it twice with the flat of her hand. Again Natalie attempts to speak, Salinka holds her palm up, listening, there it is, Dick's muffled voice calling her name, like the cry of someone trying to wake her from a dream, a nightmare that's all too real, her backup is here, her private eye has landed, she never doubted he would. She switched her tracker to speak, they only had a brief moment before the door opened, it's Burano, looking as if nothing had happened.

'You.' He pointed to Natalie, 'Outside.' Natalie is beside herself. 'Out.' The shit yelled at her. Instantly, Salinka grabbed the girl and kissed her full on the mouth as though she meant it, Burano is transfixed, spellbound by the performance. She whispered in Natalie's ear. 'You're safe now.' Then louder, hotly. 'I hope we see more of each other, Sweetheart.' As the bolstered Nat' turned to leave, Salinka patted her behind. Burano told this new girl to sit on the bed, he stood looking at her as he closed the door on the pair of them.

'What happened between those two?' The killer rock chick is wondering if things get nasty what her plan of action might be, how she'll pitch this jerk out, he stabbed Gerald, she might dispense with the quick kill and terminate the shit hard. She'd already noticed their big mistake, like so many fashion-conscious sheep they favour the knife sheafed along their spine, she's acting again.

'It was all of a sudden, your man just came out with it, he wanted some cash, he asked for more money.'

'Agron always was a greedy bastard, what happened next?'

'I thought the man was going to give him some, he put his hand in his pocket then quickly withdrew it and hit him really hard, your friend was knocked flat, a knife fell from somewhere, the fat man picked it up and began stabbing him, I shut my eyes I didn't want to look. Eventually it went quiet so I did look, and there they were, as you found them.' She's trembling again now.

'You're no good to me like that, business is slow today, get some sleep.' Quickly and carefully Salinka spins her web.

'Will you send that girl in?' Burano looked at her, she knows what's on his mind, she'd planted the seed. 'Please.'

'If I send her in, the pair of you will have to return the favour.' He smiles, as the temptress nods her head.

'Anything, but please, send her in.'

While all this is going on, Dick's had an idea, it's a long shot but if it works it might save a lot of trouble. It involves him removing enough bricks in the adjoining wall to let a person crawl through, it all hangs on the age of the building and how crumbly and porous the wall is, he hears the tracker come into life.

'Is the coast clear, can you talk?'

'Yes, for now, I've found Natalie'

'Hey, that's great news, how is she?'

'Considering everything, she's doing fine.

'That's good, listen I'm gonna try making a hole in the wall, below the bed, where's your bed?'

'It's here, against the wall, I'm kneeling on it.' Dick thought, that's one box ticked.

'I'll let you know in five minutes if it's gonna work.' He pulled his bed away, took out the Swiss army knife Salinka had bought him for Christmas and began to rake. At first it seemed impossible, the plaster's rock hard but it's thin, and as soon as he penetrated it the blade sank into the mortar like it's a chocolate brownie. He'd removed five bricks and the lime mortar in no time. He rapped on the wall, Salinka turned her tracker on.

'How's it going Dick?'

'Yeah, it's going good, I'll carry on, give me another five minutes.' His plan is working better than he imagined, it's a double brick wall, his guess is the building dates back to the late 1800s, that's about the time of the Brussels Conference Act, a collection of anti-slavery measures signed in Brussels, it's a shame the act seems to have expired. Dick reckoned an area of 30 bricks, that's 60 counting the double wall, will be enough to allow an adult to crawl through. Already there's a hole in the plaster, he lays close to it and peers beneath the bed in the adjoining room. The door opens, a woman and a man enter, he sees the woman's shoes rush towards a pair he recognises, the man mumbles a few words and disappears.

'How's it going Dick, now will be good?' Dick pulls at the plaster and soon, apart from the jagged edges, it's done, this time when he speaks it sounds like he's in the same room.

'Pull your bed out and let's get her safe.' The hole, at floor level, is large enough for an adult but is still hidden by the bed. There's no time to waste, Natalie goes through, Dick helps her as she appears in the hotel Capitol, he's ready for Salinka, but she has other plans.

'Give me half an hour, Burano said he'll be back soon and that we should be ready, I'm ready.' He knows there's no changing her mind, he passes her his Swiss army knife. The bed went back, she smiles to herself, only Dick could come up with that one, there's no sign of the hole. It wasn't long before Burano returned, he locked the door and put the key in his pocket, Salinka knew that was a big mistake, he turned and took a couple of steps before he realised.

'Where's she gone?'

'Just after you left one of your men returned and took her away.' A flash of anger raged across his face, that relented into a stupid grin.

'Don't go away, I'll fetch her.' The imminent prospect of making out with two women at once, especially the Punk, who in his twisted, sick little mind Burano thought might be dirty, has calmed his temper. He turned his back on her and put his hand in his pocket, he touched the key and took it in his fingers, a superfluous move, Salinka, already behind him, stuck the blade deep into the right side of his neck, she put her left hand around his mouth and pulled him backwards onto the floor. Dragging the knife out she plunges it again, now into the front of his neck, blood and breath rush out of the first wound, and she knows she's got him a second time in the windpipe. The avenger jumps around and kneels astride him.

'That's for Gerald Burke.' Burano can't speak, he's struggling with his legs but his heels can't get purchase on the flat, taut carpet. 'And Margareta Vittua, remember her and if Natalie hadn't been compliant where would she be now, would you have sent her home, or drowned her, how many girls and women have you trafficked for sex? How many have killed themselves to get away from the likes of you and your gangs, you little shit?' Burano is struggling for breath, she taunts him, she floats her clad breasts in his face while she reaches behind him for his knife. Feeling its blade she raises an eyebrow. 'There's something else, those two jerks, you don't really believe they killed each other do you, I killed them, it was me?' She put her face close to his. 'Does that worry you, because it should?' His eyes widen. 'What happens next? Oh yes, I'm going to slash your throat.' She's motionless for five seconds, to let the thought sink in…then she slashed his throat, it was done.

As Salvador and Deana make their way from the basement to room twelve, on the third floor, they couldn't help recalling how, only an hour ago, their boss kept ribbing them about how he was going to have the two new women who hadn't yet been shagged out of their wits by the whole fare-paying filth of Brussels, the fuckarazzi, as they call them. Burano especially wanted to see what the Punk would do for him, well, he found that out. As Salvador reached the door, he said out loud.

'You've been a long-time boss, have you died of a heart attack?' They both burst out laughing. 'Boss.' They knock again. 'Boss?' Deana tries the door, it's locked, he has a key but the other key is in the lock and half-turned. They look at each other, then simultaneously charge at the door, it flies open. What confronts them is everything they didn't expect, a normal room with the bed neatly made up, there's no sign of either woman, and their boss is laying on the floor with his throat slashed. Gobsmacked they look at one another, they don't know what to do, Burano was the boss, he gave the orders.

THIRTY-THREE

Dick and Salinka are sitting on the sumptuous seating in Duke Denby's office at the American Embassy awaiting his arrival, at present he's in with the No.1. Natalie is sitting on the spare seat next to the receptionist, learning the ropes and having a friendly chat with Estelle. Two marines, fully armed, are at a desk just inside the door, ready for action if required. There are moments when speaking to Estelle, Natalie finds the whole experience of the past week forgotten about, that is exactly what Dick wanted when he first leaned over the desk to arrange this little parley with the receptionist.

To explain what happened the moment Salinka appeared through the wall into the adjoining hotel, with Dick on his hands and knees dragging the bed the remaining two feet back into place, would only serve to slow down the journey of our three warriors back to Cambridge. I say three because I doubt Natalie will ever disclose the full horror of what she went through, but now we know, in embryo, what went on and is still going on today in Albania, Brussels, Italy, France, Germany, Great Britain, the USA, to name but a few, we can be proud of our true warrior Natalie.

Duke Denby returned to his office and was surprised to see this femme fatale Punk rocker parked on his brand new pale green leather seating, but she and Dick stood up as he entered so he thought no more about it. He introduced himself, Dick introduced Salinka... but before anyone could finish there were three strong knocks and two weaker ones on the door, Duke straightened up and commanded.

'Enter marine.' A tall marine entered the office and saluted.

'*Sir,* High Commissioner Willis, *sir.*' He brought his hand down and stepped to one side, the High Commissioner walked in and once again Duke made with the introductions.

'Sir, this is Mr. Dick Chase and this is, er, Salinka, sir.' He realised he hadn't done his homework. The High Commissioner stepped towards this fit, tall female and saluted.

'Colonel Palchikova, Salinka, it's so nice to see you again.' They shook hands warmly. 'You look like you've been in the wars.' She replied, to the surprise of everyone, especially Duke Denby.

'Melvin, how nice to see you again, I think though I should call you sir, that might be more appropriate.'

'I note, Salinka, you are incognito, I see no reason why I too cannot be incognito for one day, now my friend, let us retire to my office where we can talk, and leave these two to get on with the minutiae. Duke, when you've finished here, will you be so good as to have Dick Chase, top American private detective, and that nice young English woman, who is currently sitting in reception, brought into my office. He motioned to the door.

'After you Colonel,' and they left the room.

'Colonel Palchikova, you'll be telling me next she's a Russian spy?' Dick said nothing.

'My God, she darn well is.'

'Retired, she's retired.' He gave Duke a puzzled look. 'Your high commissioner, before he got this gig, was he something in the CIA, around three years ago?'

'Yes, he was in charge of Washington DC with special responsibility for the whole of New York State.'

'That's how he knows I'm the top American detective.' Dick looked at Denby. 'I'm kidding, that's how he's on first-name terms with Salinka, we were involved in a special case. Do you know it was because of that Colonel and me the Berlin Wall came down?' Duke laughed.

'Yeah, Chase, next you'll be telling me the Statue of Liberty is made from green iced Genoa cake.'

Dick outlined the long and short of their whole sordid trip to Denby, who in turn was able to confirm Angel is currently on her way to the United States. Natalie was sent for and introduced to the number 3, and the three of them are now installed in the commissioner's office with Salinka, waiting for the main man to come off the phone. The commissioner replaced the receiver, looked at everyone, and gave them a satisfied smile.

'That was the chief of police, they acted immediately on our information, Duke, will you do the honours?' Duke explained how Dick's earlier visit had flagged up concern and although the embassy couldn't take direct action themselves, they were, from the get-go, observers.

'As soon as your rescue was accomplished, we informed the police who promptly moved in. Over to you Melvin, if I may, as you're incognito today.' The commissioner smiled.

'Thank you, Duke. Well, there was a total of four gang members in there, two of them dead, a missing British MEP was bagged up in the basement ready to be dumped, it seems there had been a financial disagreement with one of the gang members. Fourteen young women and girls are now in a safe house with the Salvation Army.' The commissioner stood up, and with his official hat on, he made a short speech. 'On behalf of the good people of Brussels, the Belgian authorities, all the staff at the embassy, and myself, I want to offer you our greatest esteem, total admiration, and our warmest thanks.'

A taxi was called and as they were leaving the building Estelle came to shake their hands and say a special goodbye to Natalie. The two marines presented arms and as the taxi pulled away the high commissioner turned to his number three.

'Do you know Duke, if it wasn't for Palchikova and Chase, that darn Berlin Wall would still be standing, and that's a goddamn fact.'

Dick, Salinka and Natalie, have been given a night in a top Brussels hotel, they fly home in the morning. Three hours later, all cleaned up and looking more like tourists, they find themselves sitting at a table in the restaurant. Natalie can't get over the fact these two people who she hardly knows had travelled all this way, managed to find her, and then risked their lives to get her safe. And what Salinka had done for her, Natalie covered her mouth with her hand, just thinking about it made her cry, she reached across the table and took Salinka's hand, her lips are trembling.

'Thank you for saving my life, if it hadn't been for you, I would have died.' Salinka smiled at her.

'That's alright, it was my pleasure, just remember, don't cheap on the coffee, or I'll kill you myself.' Natalie pushed her chair back.

'Excuse me I need the bathroom.' Dick looked at his Russian rock chick.

'A missing British MEP and a gang member killed each other over a fare, that's got your name written all over it?' Salinka guffawed.

'Yes, and how they deserved it, tell me about your girl, what happened there?'

'She's on her way to America, her name is Angel, pretty much like your two, he really had it coming to him, and he was the scum who killed Margarette Vittua.'

'Good, did he tell you that himself?'

'Under pressure, he was eating a steering wheel at the time, and I found out it was your friend Burano who killed Gerald.'

'Yes, I know, Nat witnessed the whole thing, does she know I killed him?'

'I think, yes, she's got a pretty good idea.'

'Well, that's all she needs to know, and that's too much.' Natalie's back, they ordered the first course with wine, Dick entertained them with anecdotes about his police career, then the pudding arrived with more wine, and by the time the evening was coming to an end you would have thought Natalie hadn't a care in the world.

It was going to be a cold night in Brussels, only two degrees with a slight breeze and rain expected around midnight, tomorrow is going to be ten degrees, clear and bright from about eight in the morning. That's what it said on a removable card that had been placed in a chrome frame fixed in the lift. They've got a suite between them, Natalie has the adjoining room, she said good night and closed the door, Dick called out.

'We'll be right here we're not going anywhere.'

Everyone is up bright and breezy the next morning. At breakfast Natalie is looking more like her old self, the couple of glasses of wine followed by a good night's sleep had done her a power of good. Getting to the airport, the flight, Salinka's, insistence on getting a taxi straight to Cambridge, it all went smoothly. There was one important conversation they had to have in the taxi, what was their story, more importantly, did people need to know about Natalie's ordeal? It was decided she would be plucked in the nick of time before anything happened, if she needs support Salinka will be on hand, or Dick. About Stella Kill, there were no heroics and certainly no Swiss army knife action. Of course, they'll have to report Mr. Burke's demise, there's no hiding that.

*

Unexpected the three of them breeze into the offices of Lush and Husband, everyone crowded around, Mr. Lush, came out of his office, new coffee is made and a bottle of champagne is brought out from the fridge. Shirley and a few of the others made straight for Salinka, this is their first opportunity to thank her for her massive financial gesture that saved the firm and their jobs, Shirley was particularly tearful. Mr. Lush made a short ad hoc speech welcoming them home with a special greeting for Natalie. When Salinka began to speak the room fell silent, she looked around and smiled at everyone ending with Dick.

'It's wonderful to be back among friends, there is some good news.' She looked at Natalie. 'And some bad news. The good news is we managed to find Natalie before she came to any real harm, Mr. Burke told her it was a sudden business trip on behalf of the firm, she had no reason to doubt him, when in fact Gerald had got himself mixed up with a bunch of crooks whose sole aim was to extort all the money from the firm. The bad news is we were not able to save him, to be clear on that, they killed Mr. Burke.' There's a huge intake of breath. 'We haven't been able to trace any of the money.' Dick interrupted.

'Though I have an idea on that one.' Salinka smiled at him, this is news to her, she moved away from her spot indicating her few words are over.

'This is news, you know something I don't.'

'Yes, I think you're gorgeous.' He gave her a fleeting kiss. 'Let's get Lush into his office and I'll tell you what I know.' The three of them are soon sitting in the office, Mr. Lush, always striving to modernise and be on trend has an announcement to make.

'Before we go any further, please call me David… it's long overdue I know.'

'David, okay David, I've got something interesting. The reason they killed Gerald, though they probably intended to kill him anyway, was because there was no money, he didn't have it with him, if you get Brian to search Burke's computer you might find it there, it's a long shot but worth a try.' Immediately Brian is called and put to the task and within five minutes he'd come up trumps, he found almost all of it sitting dormant in three bank accounts. This meant another impromptu speech by Mr. Lush, who also closed the office and told everyone to take the rest of the day off.

Much later, back at Midas Mansions, before they drifted off to a well-earned sleep, Dick and Salinka spent two wonderful hours making love. A funny phrase if you think about it, they do not need to make love, they are already in love and have been for some time. No, they are enjoying their love, enjoying each other, loving being close, how close though, we'll have to leave to the imagination, for now we are going to leave our two heroes and award them the dignity and privacy they deserve.

*

A month later and everything is pretty much back to normal, the firm is called Lush Husband, Lush is in red and Husband's in black, like Rolls Royce only spelt differently. Natalie is now P.A. to David, June, who was his P.A. is taking some maternity leave.

It's David to all and sundry Shirley says some of the older clients wince at the familiarity, his father will be spinning in his grave. It's three in the afternoon and the boss has a task to perform and I've been invited in for some celebratory tea and cakes. It's taken almost four weeks for Gloria, the firm's legal boffin, to get all the money back from Burke's three bank accounts, him not only being absent but dead to boot made it, according to Gloria, la hurd'l masseef, I think she makes them up.

'And so, my friends, it is with huge gratitude and great pleasure I hand over this cheque for half a million pounds, to our saviour Salinka.' A huge cheer and round of applause ensued, as for me, I'm just geed up to get it back, after all, it is my ticket to an easy life. As I look around the office, I have to admit I'm missing out, there's been no enquiries on my business card enterprise, I'm thinking I need to expand in that department if I'm serious about wanting any work. I've noticed there doesn't seem to be much competition on the private eye front, maybe it's got something to do with Cambridge being all academic and learned. Uh-oh, talking about academic and learned, Gloria's heading my way.

'Gloria, what brings you this side of that table, or have you got an aversion to Japanese copy machines?'

'Don't worry Dick I'm sober, I think one has to be drunk before making advances to you.' Gloria hasn't forgiven my little joke at her expense about her being a member of the Bar.

'Well done on getting my money back, if you ever find yourself short, I'll always be there to buy you coffee.' Gloria gave me a look of distilled envy.

'If there's one thing I'm sure about it's not your money it belongs to Salinka and if she can give that amount, there must be lots more, you can tell me, what's her pedigree?' Looking around the office I move in for a more private tête-à-tête.

'What I'm going to tell you mustn't go any further, Salinka was a Russian agent, married to a billionaire oligarch, he was a womaniser and used to beat her, so she murdered him and stole a nice little wedge for herself.' Silence ensued before Gloria burst out laughing.

'I was completely wrong about you, you do have a sense of humour.' I look at her with my tongue in cheek, and raise an eyebrow.

'Don't forget, mom's the word.'

Four adjacent trees with their leaves just open like little hands reaching out to shake the hand of an advancing summer, look down on Salinka as she tends Tom's grave. The sky is a mass of vacant blue that reminds me of those hot, endless summer days in New York during the sizzling heat wave of 89. Looking around at the neatly kept gardens with their spotless, winding footpaths and automatous grey squirrels that suddenly run off and disappear up the nearest tree, I'm reminded of Central Park. As I look across a tulip-tipped green expanse, and on through the railings, I see a retro ice cream van, and in the queue, eager and excited, there I am, a small boy, standing next to Mom, holding her hand, while our cat Lincoln weaves himself in and out of our legs. For a brief moment my heart stands still as I fight to make my consciousness hold on to the scene, I'm trying to ignore the little voice that's calling me, it gets louder, it's Salinka. The bubble bursts and with it the thought vanishes. I turn into the present to find my girl heading towards me with her beaming smile, her arms outstretched, she gives me a hug, and in that very special moment, that soulmate moment, she bridged the transcendental void to plumb the depths of my mind.

'Dick, I'd love an ice cream.'

'Hey, that's exactly what I was thinking.'

PART TWO

THIRTY-FOUR

'Dick, it's your turn to make coffee, remember, I won at cards last night and it's the loser who gets to make it, it was your idea.' She stretched and rolled over. 'Take your time Yankee, while I lie here and count my winnings.' Like the loser I am I head off to the kitchen, fill the kettle and turn on the radio.

'and that, as they say, is that, Michael, I mean, Michelle, sorry, those gremlins certainly seem to be out in force this morning, mind you, this is local radio.'
'Yes, Seth, they do seem to be affecting you today. Here's someone who we hope really might be getting it wrong, it's Zachary, with the weather.'

I switch it off, it's raining, I can see it through the window, I don't need the running commentary. Back in the bedroom, Salinka sits up and sips her coffee.

'That's just right, I die for coffee, but not today I'm second in command, David is away till Friday, Gloria and me have to sort out the Browne, Trent and Davenport case.'

'Is that still going on, I thought Gloria had it sewn up?'

'So did David, but she screwed up a legal submission.' What are you doing today? I hope you're keeping that brain of yours active, you know how important that is.' As she speaks my girl is smiling all over her beautiful face, ours is a marriage made in heaven, just as long as she remembers who's

God. We're not married, no more than I failed not to use that cliché, it's her by the way, it's Salinka, she's God, Goddess, my Goddess.

'Me? I think I'll go hand out a couple more business cards, I'm gonna give them the benefit of my presence in Unicorn Yard, well, the option anyhow.'

The Yard has a little coffee shop that's situated across the quadrangle from our interpreter friend Cheryl, she rents a couple of ground-floor offices.

It's a little gem of a place that reminds me of a shady square I once knew, off the beaten track in Manhattan. The café is usually frequented by students, art students in particular, it's a place I've been using since late last year. It displays and sells artworks by what looks like a cynical group whose hope of working their pencil in a skilled artisan manner is being taught minimalism is the new zenith. Some mainstream work continues to stagnate, likewise the taste of the super-rich. I see here in the in-house Guardian, a horse's head in a tank of formaldehyde has just been sold for a cool £1.2 million, I can't make up my mind if that's art or just an expensive Mafia calling card.

I pin my business card on their poster board and take a seat by the window. I'm sitting there sampling my second caffeine shot of the day, staring exhilarated across the yard at our interpreter's door, when out she pops, struggling with her bike, the door, and strapping her helmet on all at once. She's in a hurry, no sooner does Cheryl lock up than she's off like a bat out of hell. Now that's what I call timing, some guy, he's in his twenties, has just steamed across the yard and crashed into the locked door. In reflex he kicked it angrily while cursing under his breath, hmm, maybe there's a job here, paid or unpaid, it doesn't matter to me. I decide to follow him, that might give me a clue as to what's going down, and whether our Cheryl is in some kind of trouble, either way the exercise will do me good, and it's like Salinka said, I've gotta keep my brain agile if I don't wanna stagnate. I know straight off he's a drug addict, I recognise the Marijuana users' gait, this jerk needs funds. That's why he made a beeline for Cheryl, he was hoping to get some cash from her, maybe she's a supplier, I'm kidding. My guess is he telegraphed his intentions, or someone gave her a nod, possibly the jerk's girlfriend, a bit of female solidarity.

As he turned left out the yard, I'm out the door in hot pursuit. One good thing, the rain seems to have stopped, although up there it looks like it's just taking a rain check. Immediately he's at the bus stop looking like a firework with the fuse lit. I'm three behind him as we climb aboard the 55, in five stops, we've travelled seven hundred years into the future, into what is now a more modern, suburban landscape. We're in a down-at-heel part of Cambridge, but given the bar is set high for heel opulence in this part of the world, there's no apology offered for that slight. The 55 pulls up, I'm sitting near the exit, the youth gets up like he owns the bus. As he reaches the last seat, opposite me, he grabs a woman's handbag and very quickly makes a run for it. Well, I hate to be the party pooper but I've collared him before he steps off the bus, my face is close to the back of his scrawny neck.

'Listen son, you might be thinking things can't get any worse, put up a struggle with me and you'll see they can, on the other hand, if you let go of this nice lady's handbag, I'm gonna let you make a run for it, what's it gonna be, Punk?' He thought for a moment then let go of the bag, I released him. He ran a few yards, turned and gobbed, then flashed me a couple of vees, as the bus pulled off I tipped my brow, Cheryl will definitely be getting a visit from her friendly FBI agent.

Much later Salinka is intrigued by my story, like me she thought it was drug-related and said I should get involved.

'Cheryl might be in deep poo and require a lifeline.' She threw in. 'Did I mention Natalie's got herself a boyfriend, we're taking them to dinner Saturday week? I want to check him out, make sure he's okay, his name's Joe, he's a junior accountant, I thought Chinese, what do you think?'

'Sounds great to me… do me a favour and turn the radio up will you Honey?'

"…in a ditch on farmland in the area, the farmer reported the find late this afternoon. The pathologist report says the body of this male, in his early twenties, had only been dead a couple of hours. A full autopsy will be carried out in the morning. The police say there was no means of identification on the body. Anyone missing a family

member or friend should get in touch
with them on this number, 012..."

I switched off the radio.

'Well, it might not be the handbag snatcher but if it was and I hadn't foiled his getaway, he might be alive now.'

'If you're that worried, my big soft detective, why not go visit Ms. Conway in the morning and put your mind at rest. Now get the cards out, I'm going to beat you into submission at gin rummy, if I lose, I'm going to have a shower, then I'm getting into bed, and d'you know what I'm going to do then, Yankee, huh, can you guess?... I'm going straight off to sleep.'

It's the next day and I'm sitting in the Unicorn Yard coffee shop, meditating over my morning fix, while I wait for Ms. Conway to show. I lost at cards last night, I don't know how, to be fair I think I must have cheated, boy was it worth it. Gee, just take a look at that, a big sign has been fixed to the wall above Cheryl's office.

EIGHTEENTH CENTURY THREE-STOREY
WAREHOUSE
FOR SALE FREEHOLD
Ripe for conversion into living accommodation
These staggering premises come with the added
benefit of
an office area on the ground floor
VACANT ON POSSESSION
Anyone interested please apply

While I'm reading, Cheryl turns up, it's no coffee today, we're straight in the office. I give her a few minutes to change into her office chic attire, then it's over to the counter.

'My friend Cheryl, can I have her regular to take out?' I've been coming here for over three months now and Romeo, the main man, is still as remote as a punt-pusher's starting handle. 'Make that two and a couple of them there croissants will you Pal.'
Across the yard I back into her office, a bell rings and Cheryl creeps in from the rear and immediately I see she's pleased to see me, or at least, she's pleased I'm not someone else.

'Cheryl, I was passing and thought I'd do a bit of after-sales service.' She gives me a quizzical look.

'What, the FBI doing customer satisfaction now, you only sounded my bike and as I recall, it was your idea?'

'And how are *you* today?' She looks unhappy, something's wrong, the question is, if there's a problem how do I get her to open up?

'Mr. Chase, it's very nice of you to fit me in between sounding bicycles, but I'm very busy this morning.' She's stressed out.

'Cheryl, at least have the coffee, you can find time for that can't you? You'll feel a whole lot better.' We sit looking at each other for a strained minute. 'I came to see you the other day, yesterday morning, before I had a chance to call, I saw you leave the office in a big hurry. Just after you left, would you believe it, a young man in his twenties came steaming across the yard, he was so desperate to see you he nearly broke down your door.' I altered my tone. 'Later that day a young man was found dead in a farmer's field on the outskirts of Cambridge.' I give her my kind, concerned face. 'Is there something you'd like to tell me, it won't go any further than these four walls, I promise?' Cheryl is thinking, I can see she's scared. 'Ma'am, I'm not the police, I'm an FBI agent, I work alone, nobody knows I'm here except you, if you're in any sort of trouble I might be able to help you out, now, what have you got to lose?' As if she'd been bottling it up like a corked wine, Cheryl seemed glad to get it out in the open.

'He was my boyfriend, Josh Clements, we split-up six months ago. Josh was an art student, he was clever, funny and he could draw, I mean really draw, he hated all that minimalist minimal talent shit, as he called it. Anyway, he got into drugs, he was a man of habit, his decline was fast, I tried to help him but he was hooked, I lost him. He began loading onto me for money, I refused but he became pathetic, always crying, at worst he would try to be violent, it wasn't him. He had so-called druggie friends who would always be pushing him.'

'These friends, do they know you're here?'

'Yes, they were with him a couple of times, or they would hang around the coffee shop while Josh came to see me.' I regaled Cheryl with my theory.

'I'm guessing one of them killed him, for whatever reason, a drugs war? For now, they're lying low, but you think they'll turn up here asking for money, is that right?' I can see Cheryl is scared, she needs support, she's in her mid-twenties, trying to build her business, to earn an honest living, I decide there and then I'm gonna help her out.

'Cheryl, you've just got yourself a general dog's body, I'm your new receptionist, from now on I'll deal with whoever walks through that door, what do you say?' She's grateful but nonplussed.

'Mr. Chase, I can't afford you or anyone else and besides, I've been given a month's notice by the landlord, the building's up for sale and they want me out.'

'Cheryl, that's a whole month away and as for my fee you won't owe me a dime, helping you ma'am will be my pleasure. Do you hold the keys for up there?' I'm pointing at the ceiling. 'I'd kinda like to look around, my girlfriend and me, well, we're looking to buy somewhere special and you never know, this might just cook the bacon.' Cheryl's smiling, can you see what I did there, I mentioned the girlfriend in case she might be in need of some female solidarity?

THIRTY-FIVE

While I was with Cheryl, I phoned Salinka and asked her to lunch with me in an hour, at the Unicorn coffee shop, I invited Cheryl, she's just gotta finish off some work. In the meantime I borrowed the keys and while I'm moseying around by myself my mind is thinking about my new role as an American in Cambridge. Slowly I'm getting to know a bit about the place, the river Cam with its elegant, historic bridges, the punts like trays of people sliding gracefully beneath them. The beautiful, elongated splendor of the Gothic spires, with their bells, *the bells the bells,* okay so that's Paris but you get my drift. The universities set in their pristine, green ribboned lawns. I have to admit being surrounded by all this history is a bit humbling. According to Salinka, Tchaikovsky, her favourite Russian, visited Cambridge. That's something we're definitely gonna be looking into, so I'm really looking forward to that. One thing I do know he visited in 1893, I know because that's the PIN on our bank cards, but keep that under your hat. Oh yeah, one other thing, these premises are gold dust.

In the café I breeze through the polite intros, then, eyeballing Salinka, I point to the for-sale sign across the yard and halfway up the building.

'What do you think, Cheryl's given us the keys, we can go take a look?' My Russian is spying me, nonplussed, but with a cute smile.

'So, you do work while I'm at the office then.' I stare at her and let her follow my gaze over to

Cheryl, for the moment I parked any thoughts about our bespoke luxury dream home, to give Cheryl my confident reassured look.

'Forgive me Cheryl, when I said I was on my own, I was being expedient, Salinka here, well, she's my partner, we work together, we're a team, manning your premises and lending you a hand is something we do together. The thousand pounds you handed back, I'm sorry but that was us, it had been stolen from Salinka's firm.' I look at my Russian lover. 'Why don't you do the honours, Colonel Palchikova?' I don't know what Salinka is telling Cheryl, in Albanian, but the girl is sitting there engrossed. As she made with her reply Salinka interrupted.

'You need to speak English, if you will, for Dick.' Cheryl continued.

'I appreciate your help but I'm not sure I want you two stepping into my life again, at the time that money would have come in handy, I was depending on it, running a business like this isn't easy.' There's a difficult pause, Dick steps in with his pleasant, calming, American tones.

'O.K. if we're all finished here, let's give the building the once over, you never know, Cheryl, what might come of it.'

The warehouse is exactly what they wanted, a third of the ground floor for two cars and Dick's play area, plus three vast empty floors with windows on the two long sides. No dividing walls, only 3 ranks of 5 cast iron pillars supporting the ceilings. There are wooden stairs along one wall, and at one end there's an industrial dumbwaiter that, to be honest, has seen better days. As Dick and Salinka looked around, it all fell into place, a large kitchen with utility room on the first floor, the lounge and study on the second. Three bedrooms at the top with the biggest on-suite bathrooms Salinka would let Dick pace out. According to him, you could fit a dog track in the loft. They called the estate agent from Cheryl's office, to realise the whole building came at just over three hundred thousand, a tentative acceptance was given, subject to a meeting.

So began a very busy and exciting period in the lives of the Midas's, such was the lack of interest, by any drug-needy individuals, a sense of security had enveloped the three of them. Dick's need to man the office, though still on the cards, was made less necessary because he was only upstairs with Salinka, or the architect, or someone from city planning, and could be down with Cheryl in quick time if needed. This was the pattern of things for the next ten days, the cash sale went through without a hitch. After contracts were signed, Cheryl was invited to lunch, she knew a change of ownership was on the cards and with it the possibility of losing her livelihood or surely an exorbitant rent hike. She knows monied people are always looking after the pennies, Dick, turned to his associate.

'I think it will be better coming from you.' Salinka looked at Cheryl and with her toes pointing downwards and her hands clasped behind her back, she paced three steps, turned, and paced back, the prelude to some tough talk.

'Ms. Conway, I'll come straight to the point, as of today we are your new landlords. Mr. Chase and I realise these ground floor offices are intrinsic to the running of your business, so we have decided the situation can continue, provided you consent to uphold this new rent agreement I have had drawn up by our legal adviser.' Salinka hands Cheryl an envelope. 'Look at it now, but take it home and study it at your leisure, before you sign.' Cheryl opened it up and began to read, she looks at the pair, she can't contain a huge smile. 'What?' Salinka is grim-faced.

'The rent, it's only a nominal pound a year for ten years.'

'*What?*' The landlady takes the document from Cheryl's hands and looks at it before handing it back. 'Yes, that's right, is there a problem?'

The next day I'm walking into the coffee shop in my usual high spirits, three positives have occurred, we saw the place we wanted, we managed to buy it, and Cheryl's status remains intact, three out of three, that's not bad. On the downside, the builders have gotten underway and already it's a day off for a pre-arranged sabbatical. I'm two hours late this morning because, out of the blue, the front door wouldn't lock and I had to wait for the locksmith to turn up.

'Two coffees please Romeo.' We call him that because of his part-time assistant, her name's Juliet, it's a given. I'm just thinking, what can go wrong next, when I see reflected in the highly polished chrome body of the Gaggia coffee machine, two youths stop and look around, before entering Cheryl's domain. Romeo has made our drinks already, I slap a fiver on the counter and tell him to keep the change. Across the yard I back into the office and announce my presence. 'Coffee's up, how's my favourite interpreter?' Now I turn to face the two young men, quite well dressed for a couple of druggies. There's no sign of Cheryl, I put on my steely, tough man look. 'Can I help you two, or are you just leaving?' There's a stony silence. I stare at them, hard. 'Sayonara, addio.' My tone is chilling, Cheryl steps in from the back.

'Dick, these gentlemen have just arrived from Italy, unless you speak Italian, I'd better deal with it.' In an instant I'm transported to an Italian market where, instead of discussing a bunch of important-looking papers that have just materialised, the three of them might just as well be haggling over the price of aubergines.

*

Saturday night started out to be a real hoot, the House of the Sun Dragon is our Chinese restaurant of choice without actually leaving the country. During our meal I was on a roll, I anecdotallized my misunderstanding over the two Italians and how I nearly adiosed Cheryl's livelihood out the door. Then there was the time, as a New York cop, I single handedly emptied the Madison Square Garden because someone left a suitcase full of panties in the foyer.
Joe, Natalie's new man, turned out to be a real charmer, Salinka took to him straight off, and I have to admit to liking him, he has a pleasant manner I

can see Natalie lapping up. They both have a sort of reticent quality that, judging by their frequent moonstruck glances at one another, is reserved for everyone else.

We're on coffee when a waiter speaks in my ear, there's a phone call for me, that's unexpected. Salinka's eyeing me amid the conversation that's still going on as if nothing's happening, but something is happening, I put the phone down. Tapping my fingers on the counter I'm thinking, what is it in this country, got it? I pick up and dial 999, Salinka's onto that straight away and comes over, I can't speak but she can listen.

'Yes, an ambulance, as fast as you can, it's Unicorn Yard'…. 'No, I'm not there, I'm on my way now.' I look at Salinka, she's about to get a shock, 'It's a woman in her mid-twenties, her name is Cheryl Conway, she's been beaten up.' Now I'm being calm, 'My name is Dick Chase, please get a move on.'…'I'll be there.'… 'No, I'll be straight there.' Salinka's got it.

'I'll pay, you shift the others.'

We're in Joe's car so he's the taxi, luckily, we're only half a city away, I'm feeling bossy.

'When we get there you two stay put, we'll deal with it, is that clear?' No reply necessary.

We're there before the ambulance, the door's open, we go in, I put the lights on, there's no one here. We're up the stairs in a couple of leaps and there, silhouetted against the distant lights of hockey practice is a body tied to a chair, it's Cheryl, she's breathing, thank God.

'Cheryl, can you hear me, it's Dick, help is on the way, keep still?' She moans lightly, they hear the ambulance pulling in. 'I'll go, you stay with her.' The two paramedics are super-efficient and without fuss they're on their knees attending to Cheryl. Her left eyeball is bulging out of place, remarkably no one seems fazed at the sight of it. 'Tell me that's not a problem.' Paul answers, he's the main man.

'It's a luxated globe.' He homed in, 'It looks straightforward.' With what looked like a spoon handle and a small spray he bent over our friend, in ten seconds he'd straightened up, it's fixed, I move away, Salinka came and stood next to me.

'That's a result, thank God for that, have you any idea who phoned?'

'Not a clue, it was a young woman, I'd like to know how she knew where to reach us.' Salinka surmised.

'If they were searching her desk for money, you might have told Cheryl where we were going and she may have made a note of it, why don't you go and see, I'll stay with her?' At the bottom of the stairs I bump into two cops who must have been summoned with the ambulance.

'Excuse me sir, we need to speak to you.'

'Officers, it'll be my pleasure, but can you start with those two out there?' I point to Natalie and Joe. 'They were our lift, they know nothing about this, they may as well go.'

Soon it's me and the cop, his partner's upstairs. In the office I sat at Cheryl's desk, I offer the policeman a seat, he declines like I'd offered him a whiskey.

'O.K. officer, how does it work over here?' I'm diverting.

'How does it work over here sir?' I got him.

'Yeah, I was a New York cop, I know how it works over there.'

'You start by giving me your name sir.' I complied. 'Can you tell me what happened?' I said I can. He asked me what that was. I told him a girl has been beaten up. Did I know why? I told him I can guess. Am I obstructing his investigation? I said I think so. It occurred to me a couple of glasses of wine tied in with my anger might be affecting my temperament, I changed tack. I gave the officer the rundown on our night, fact and theory, the theory being Cheryl had made a note of our pending dining out night, she had, I pointed to the diary.

'Out of the blue I get this phone call, the caller was some young woman I didn't know, she said Cheryl had been seriously beaten up and needed help, we came straight over.'

THIRTY-SIX

As I head towards the hospital in a taxi, I look out at the artificially illuminated Cambridge nightlife, full of ripe and semi-ripe individuals, hoping to pick or be picked. Some hope to be cherished, others just to be enjoyed. Some will be discarded, like our friend, head first into a world that doesn't give a damn. The car radio is quietly reminding me it's a wonderful world, the taxi driver's cursing a green Mini that's doing 30 in a 30 zone and in the corner of my eye I see Isaac Newton holding an apple. As we pull up at a red light, I look again to realise it's a life-size cardboard cut-out, in a bookshop, advertising a new book, The Newton Handbook by Derek Gjertsen.

Salinka has gone with Cheryl in the ambulance, and I guess the police are beginning to make their enquiries, all being well they're planning to speak to her tomorrow. There *was* a note of our meal in Cheryl's desk diary, perhaps she hoped we might invite her, I wish to God we had. I only had a brief word with Salinka before we split, physically, Cheryl's gonna be okay, the eye will be fine, Paul, the senior paramedic said it had luxated during the beating, it's rare but it happens. She'll be going straight into x-ray, they suspect a cracked jaw bone, there's a lot of bruising and a couple of cuts, but it seems, luckily for her, nothing that will cause any permanent damage. She had managed a few words with Salinka, so that's good, hmm, a cracked jawbone, geez that takes one hell of a blow.

The receptionist sent me in the right direction and as I approach Salinka her usual, gleaming, broad smile is nothing more than an ember. We're sat outside Cheryl's room waiting for her to return from x-ray, Salinka begins filling me in.

'The doctor assured me it's all superficial, she'll mend just fine.'

'Good, that's good did she say anything in the ambulance, anything to go on?'

'We'll have to wait till the morning to find out what happened, she seems quite tough but an ordeal like that can knock the stuffing out of one.' That's it, Salinka's English has hit mine right out the park, she's beginning to sound like the Queen of England already. I go and fetch us coffee from the machine, by the time I return, Cheryl's back in her room.

'She's asleep, she's concerned for her business, that's a good sign, I told her not to worry, I'll run it till she's back on her feet, they've given her something to help her sleep. We're going to find these people it's going to be a job for Stella Kill.' I looked at her, hard, she relented. 'O.K. Stella Touch my friend again and you'll be nursing two broken arms and a cauliflower face.'

'Don't you mean a cauliflower ear?' It's Salinka's turn to look hard at me.

'I know what I mean.' I smiled at this one-time KGB agent, sometimes I can't believe my luck.

By the time we finally arrive home it's gone one, Salinka poured a couple of whiskeys and we talked about how we're gonna approach this little problem. Her idea is to adopt her Punk persona, and rub shoulders with the lowest of the low, in an attempt to uncover the trash. As I pointed out, that will leave her acting alone, I came up with the idea of her playing the prostitute to my pimp, that way I can be by her side as we trawl the bars, pubs and parking lots looking for druggies to question, that's the plan. The police are speaking to Cheryl at 2 o'clock on Sunday, Salinka's gonna be there. Later on, if she passes muster, the doctors are letting her come home, for the time being she'll be hanging her hat at Midas Mansions, till the air clears. As I fall asleep, I'm thinking about Cheryl's ex, Josh Clements, the handbag snatcher. Was it him who'd been found dead in a field, I wondered if whoever killed him also beat-up Cheryl? ZZZzzz, in the morning I'll call the New York City police and get my old partner McDougall, fraud squad, to look into it, ZZZZ ZZzzz, it's always handy having a mole, ZZzzzzz….

In the morning I woke with a truth clear and resounding in my head, I don't have a mole, I live in England, the good old days of a hand-up from McDougall are a thing of the past. Later we visit Cheryl, but first we get our skates on, the Unicorn Café opens on Sunday mornings, and Romeo and Juliet's full English is to die for. Over our eggs and bacon, we discuss how we're gonna deal with this case, if recent history's anything to go by we're gonna kill them, hmm, I realise that's out of the question, no, we'll just frighten them to death with a warning. We spend a good half hour looking over our new home, O.K. we're on a mission, but life goes on.

Cheryl is transformed, a night's sleep has worked its magic, she's got a question that's been bugging her.

'How did you know what happened to me, I'm so glad you came, but?' She's almost as confused as we are.

'I had a phone call at the restaurant, a young woman, she referred to you by name, she said you'd been beaten up and needed help, we came straight over.' Cheryl described the events that led to her being attacked, it began with her front doorbell, followed by a forced entry.

'There were three of them to start with, just youths, all male, I might have known them, I'm not sure. They looked out of work, scruffy, the sort of druggies Josh used to hang around with. They thought I had money stashed away in the office, they were certain I had a safe, I've never had a safe.'
First they took her to the bank, this is where Cheryl had been clever, since the Josh days she'd kept a druggie's bank account with little in it, no more than thirty pounds, they made her clean it out. 'Then we went to the office where they found nothing, that's when, Snake, the others called him that, hit me. That's all it took, once he started, another thumped me on the back of the head, a third punched me in the face, then Snake hit me again, it was a free-for-all, I fell to my knees. A woman's voice intervened, she told them to stop, the three were huddled together laughing as she helped me onto a chair, she said that was enough. That's it, that's what happened.' Salinka reassures.

'That's plenty for us to be going on with, there won't be too many people in Cambridge called

Snake, don't stress yourself, we'll get them, they won't be troubling you again, trust me.'

It's now Monday, as expected Cheryl had been interviewed by the police, but the doctor waited till today to give her the all-clear. Dick's upstairs getting ready to make his début as a pimp, he looks in the full-length mirror and speaks to his reflection staring back at him. 'Hmmm, smart but with a touch of the gutter, you'll do just fine.' As he steps onto the landing Cheryl leaves her room, they descend the stairs together. On entering the kitchen Dick does a double take, leaning against the sink tucking into a bag of crisps is Stella Kill looking more dangerously flirtatious and sexually alluring than he remembered her the first-time around. Slowly she eased herself into balance and sauntered towards him, taking his wrists and putting them behind his back, she attempted to bite his lower lip, she spoke in a suggestive voice.

'Mmmm, I fancy you, you gorgeous hunk, I'll do anything for a fix,' She licks his face. 'Anything.'

'Yeah, well, is that a crisp I've got hanging from the corner of my mouth, you can start by licking that off?' Cheryl approached this apparition for a closer look, the Punk stared her out.

'Is that? Are you? I can't believe it's you, do you know who you look like? You look like Stella Kill of Stella Kill, and the…' Salinka, interrupted.

'Yes, I know, the Pubes, someone remind me to get a brazilian, will you?'

Cheryl is given her instructions, help herself to anything she wants, there'll be no callers but just in case, don't answer the door, and don't wait up.

THIRTY-SEVEN

Beauty and the Feast was the brainchild of two New York girls who decided to try their luck at making their fortune in Seattle. They couldn't make up their minds whether to open a continental-type patisserie or go with their original idea of a beauty parlour. It was while discussing the pros and cons of each, Helen, she was once, it now seems a millennium ago, the girlfriend of Dick Chase, it was she who hit upon the idea of doing both and calling it "Beauty and The Feast". It was all going amazingly well for them in this magical, cosmopolitan utopia that is Pike Place Market, in Downtown Seattle. One beautiful late spring day the phone rang, Helen answered with her usual up-tone flourish.

'Beauty and the Feast, how may we help you?'

'Is that Helen, you'll never guess who this is?' She smiles.

'I think, officer Peter McDougall, we were in too close a proximity to death for me to forget your voice in a hurry, how are you and how's that freelance gumshoe Dick, still plaguing that poor Russian agent girl, what was her name, Shirlinkie?'

'You mean Salinka, she's good, they're both good. I've just been contacted by our Brussels Embassy no less, with a message from Dick, he's asked me to contact you. He and Salinka have saved a girl from a fate worse than his cooking, he's asking you, as a favour to him, if you'll employ her. Her name's Angel, she's a beautician who has excellent English, she's from Albania.

'Whoa there, just a goddamn New York minute, is this for real, Dick wants me to set up a strange girl for him, what is he, the father?' McDougall knows the story and knew Helen wouldn't have said that had she had any idea.

'They saved her from being trafficked, being beaten, and possibly death, it was sheer chance and good luck put him in the right place at the right time, all due to Salinka's bravery. They'll pay her wages and accommodation for six months, it'll be a new start for Angel, Dick says the girl needs this break more than anything, what do you say?' Helen knows Dick is a good man and if he's asking this then it's important.

'O.K. McDougall you can tell "Chick" it's a deal, and anyway, he knows I would never refuse an angel?'

Helen, with her business partner and old school friend Julie, were staggered at the full range of skills Angel brought to the business. She's more than a beautician, she's a cosmetologist and a very nice girl to boot. Over a meal and a bottle of wine, Angel held the two spellbound with her story and the role Dick played in getting her safe and free. She described everything, even what she knew of Salinka's, breathtaking acts, the way she allowed herself to be trafficked to save her friend Natalie. As the trauma of the whole experience came pouring back Angel found herself almost unable to speak.

'Mr. Chase stepped in from nowhere and saved my life, what he did for me was amaizing, something I'll never forget, he was my guardian angel.'

For the first time Helen realised it was she who, with no thought for Dick, decided to up sticks and move across America to start a new life in Seattle. It has just hit her how selfish she had been and how Dick might have been hurt. To be fair she isn't fully aware of his true relationship with Salinka, nor that she came with a large fortune, if she had known she might have been less inclined to feel guilty about the situation.

The following days and months were to be the best of times for these three girls, especially Angel, little could they have imagined it was all about to go so dangerously wrong, and their utopia is going to be transformed into a living hell.

Back in Cambridge Dick and Stella, we'll call her Stella in this manifestation, are trawling the early evening streets and getting a feel for their new roles. Stella, like some juvenile delinquent, is blowing bubble gum and letting it pop over her mouth. Dick is practicing his cocky power walk, while secretly hoping they might bump into Gloria, he's dying to hold his hands up and admit this is how they get their money, and if she wanted to earn some extra cash, he'd be glad to take her under his wing. They're at a spot where the river meets a busy thoroughfare and some forty punts are moored up. The pavements are full of youths, some sipping from plastic pints, others are snogging, there's plenty of laughter, a flash of anger between two girls. One geek is hanging off some railings quoting Homer through a cardboard megaphone, just another Cambridge night really. Out of the blue someone, probably for a bet, grabbed Stella around the waist, instantly he's on his knees with one arm up his back, his forehead inches from the ground, she eases off so he can hear her between his helpless protestations.

'Can I help you?'

'I was joking, let me go.'

'You should know better than putting your arm around a complete stranger.'

'I won't do it again I promise.' Stella thought for a moment.

'See that you don't, next time I'll break your arm.' She spots a wine bar just over the road, her mind is ticking over like a well-oiled machine. 'I might have overreacted, get yourself and whoever you're with over to that wine bar, I'll buy you all a drink, don't get your hopes up, it's non-alcoholic, and I'm spoken for.'

The wine bar is busy, but there's a table down the far end and soon six eager people are sitting around it, including the hooker and her pimp, Salinka breaks the ice.

'My name's Stella, and before any of you ask, I'm not Stella Kill, I just look like her.'

'Stella, how did you get me on the ground like that, so fast I mean?'

'Yeah, I wanna do that, how d'ya do it?' Like a bunch of schoolboys on a prank they all join in. Salinka looks at the lads, all of them, no girls. She felt straight off they were untainted by crime, just a bunch of friends out for a laugh. With his golden American tones, Dick makes his presence felt.

'Stella, is a Russian agent, I'm FBI, you've found us on a joint American/Russian drugs elimination exercise.' The lads laugh as one, they don't believe a word, Dick looks at Stella, 'Colonel Palchikova, why don't you give it to them straight.' Stella eyes them, a single brow raised, before speaking at length in Russian. Then she beckons one of them to an open space next to their table and proceeds to show them, still in Russian, how to get him to the floor in an instant. By the time Ricky sat down again they were all convinced. Dick leans forward and lowers his voice.

'Did any of you know Josh Clements?' All of a sudden the party's over, in darker mood the one called Ricky, replies. 'Yeah, he was the older brother of one of our mates, he was trouble, always cadging money off you.' Another lad spoke.

'Yeah, all the time it was like "got any spare dosh"? He's dead ain't he?'

'Yeah.' Another butts in. 'Dead meat.' They all laugh, Stella intervenes.

'Any idea who killed him?' There was no answer, Stella tries again. 'Was it Snake?' At that one of them stood up noisily and left, no one tried to stop him, Dick questioned.

'What's up with him?' They all look at one another, the one called Ricky replied.

'Er, yeah, he's Snake's younger brother.' Those four words seem to be the catalyst that expedited their next move, Ricky speaks again. 'Thanks for the drinks.' He looked at the rest of them. 'Come on, we're going.' They stood up and left the bar, at the door they all burst out laughing. Dick turned to his Russian counterpart, closed one eye and tightened his lips.

'Hmm, I've got a touch of alcohol deficiency syndrome, G and T?' As they sit back and enjoy the bitter quinine aftershock, the ice sings out against the glass. The FBI agent smiles knowingly at his Russian spy.

'What?' she asked laughingly, Dick began…

'164, Isaac Newton,' Stella jumped in.

'Isaac Newton Terrace, East Chesterton, yes, I got that, young Snake couldn't stop playing with his keyring/address tag.' Dick's retort is unadulterated, complacency.

'As usual the Russians come in a good second.'
A grinning Colonel Palchikova speaks in English with heavily accented Russian overtones.

'And tell me, my Yankee comrade, did you get the phone number on the verso?' Dick looks at her, he loves this woman.

'No, I didn't.' Salinka raises one eyebrow and gives him a knowing smile, no comment required.

THIRTY-EIGHT

It was a week before Cheryl felt able to go back to work. Salinka had the two Italian gentlemen's requirements well underway, a job that turned out to be both interesting and lucrative. They had a grandfather who'd lived in Cambridge, pre-first world war, he was a successful businessman who had been in shoes from the age of fourteen. He worked his way to the top and by the time he died, an old man, he owned eleven shops, three of which are in London. Everything was in Italian, Salinka introduced the two to Lush Husband, they were just ordinary lads from the country, Umbria, until now they had never left, and their grandfather, he had never been back. They were keen to know their worth, David Lush, Salinka's boss and owner of the firm estimated, after fees and taxes, the figure to be anywhere between fourteen and sixteen million pounds. Salinka had managed to get the Italians to agree to a translating fee of 0.3% of the final total. That means Cheryl is in line to receive quite a hefty payment.

When the taxi pulled into Unicorn Yard everything stopped, there's a window adorned with flowers and a welcome back frieze, balloons are strung across the front of the premises. Cheryl is made up but can't smile too much because her jaw is still tender. Salinka came out to greet her, Dick clocked her arrival and left the builders to it, and before you can say Romeo, Romeo, where art thou coffee, the three of them are huddled around a table sampling that caffeine fuelled beaned elixir? All things considered, Cheryl is looking amazing.

'You're looking gorgeous Cheryl, almost back to normal, Salinka has got some news that's gonna make your toes curl.'

'Thank you, Dick, sorry I can't smile much, not yet anyway, I'm on the mend though and it's all thanks to my new friends.' Cheryl turned to Salinka, 'So what's this news that's going to perk me up, I could do with a lift?' Dick butts in.

'Now just you wait a minute, let me top up the coffee.'

'No, it must be my turn.' Cheryl stands up, 'I insist.' As she steps off Salinka spills the beans.

'The Italian job, I've negotiated your fee at 0.3% of probably,' Salinka hesitated. 'Sixteen million pounds.'

'Another round of coffees please Romeo.' Dick and Salinka watch Cheryl thinking. She turns to face them. 'So that's.., well that's.., that's...' She mouthed it for privacy. '£48,000.' Salinka, keenly nods her head. Cheryl looks at Romeo. 'Be a star and bring them over to the table for me, I can't trust myself at the moment.' She sat down again, silence ensued while Romeo placed their drinks in front of them. Salinka and Dick are pleased to see Cheryl so made up after what she'd been through, she looks at each of them. 'I've got a business degree but I didn't see that coming.' Salinka commented.

'It's called hard-nosed cheek and experience.' Dick knows there's more to it than that, but he wasn't going to mention radiant good looks and charm.

For the time being Cheryl is staying at Midas Mansions, Snake is still at large but the net is closing. There's been an interesting development regarding the death of Josh Clements, nothing on the radio but in today's paper there's an update. Cheryl spotted the headline and fetched it from the rack, they all read in silence.

The body in the farmer's field turned out to be that of Josh Clements, a failed fresher, an art student. The post-mortem revealed he'd taken a massive amount of pain killers and the police are putting his death down to suicide.

Cheryl let out a long soulful sigh.

'Well, a wasted talent there.' She added. 'I took a detour this morning, to pick up this.' She delved into her bag and took out a small sketchbook. 'It belonged to Josh, I hung on to it, he liked making sketches of people.' Simultaneously Dick and Salinka look at each other like two gold prospectors who'd just panned their first nugget.

*

164 Isaac Newton Terrace is living proof, even in Cambridge, there's hope an uneducated elite can still hold their own when it comes to spewing up on their own doorstep. As Dick and Salinka drew up opposite, for a bit of surveillance, a lad opened the front door and immediately plastered his rig into a flower bed, he looked about, then went back inside. Salinka is leafing through Josh's sketchbook.

'If that was Snake, he's not in this pad, this woman's prominent, she might be Cheryl's saviour.' Dick eyeballed the sketch, a laughing girl of about eighteen, her arm resting on a boyfriend's shoulder, Josh's expert pencil had caught her full black locks with wonderful realism, a caring face, someone not yet on drugs. The lad, an excellent drawing, looking carefree, at ease with the world, someone who still has a brain, Dick noticed a date had been inserted in the bottom left corner.

'This is nearly two years ago, these people aren't affected by drugs yet, this could be our target for tonight, if she's still in Cambridge, we'll find her.' Cheryl is staying in tonight but as we already know it isn't because she's washing her hair. Dick went ahead while Stella gave their guest her instructions.

'How do you think she's doing?' He enquired as they drove off, a little concerned over when Cheryl might be ready to move back to her own place, Stella is more sanguine.

'She's nearly there, she wants her own space too, she's arranged to have some security locks fitted tomorrow, your locksmith left his card on the hall table and Cheryl organised it herself. He's picking her up in the morning and fetching her back when the job's done, she's not going to be intimidated by a bunch of young boys, I sympathised, not when there are so many older ones about.' Stella rested her hand on Dick's knee, while he's trying to work out what had just been said.

'Salinka, I've got a confession.' He paused for art. 'I've been seeing another woman.' She whipped her hand away and spoke without thinking.

'Who is she, who is this woman?' Dick enjoyed the unexpected angst in Salinka's voice, he waited for the moment.

'Her name, her name is Stella Kill, yes!' Dick is laughing so much he nearly had to pull over.

They entered their third dive and there she is, the life model incarnate, personified, stupefied, drunk, that makes things a little difficult. The good thing is she's without male attachment, they're not ready for Snake yet. Surrounding conversation tells them her name is Maxine, she's with a bunch of girls on what seems to be a hen night. But then, as if all the gods were conspiring against them, there's someone else, Gloria is here, not part of the roost, she's on her own, she recognised Dick and came straight over.

'Well, I wasn't expecting to see you here, but now you are perhaps we can get something together.' Gloria hasn't seen Salinka, not that she would have recognised her. Dick's scheming smile, for a brief moment, gave Gloria cause for some hope and excitement, immediately to be dashed.

'Gloria, I'd like you to meet my friend, Stella.' Agent Punk turned around but before she can say anything Dick speaks again. '*Stella,* this is Gloria, an acquaintance of mine.' Gloria looked the woman up and down before reverting to Dick, then she looked back at Stella, and without flinching.

'I suppose you know about Salinka, *Dick's girl-friend.'* Stella smiled.

'Ah yes, the beautiful and delightful Salinka, isn't she just gorgeous?' Stella looked about, then moved closer to Gloria and spoke quietly in her ear. 'It's a ménage à trois.' Agent Punk turned to her backup. 'One game all I think, new balls please.'

A huge scream of laughter from the hens concentrated our duo's attention, Maxine stormed out, quickly followed by Stella who soon realised the reason for the speedy exit was to be sick on the pavement outside. The pub they're in is just thirty yards from the wine bar of the other evening, Stella looked through the crowd at her pimp and pointed in that direction, Dick got it. He turned to see Gloria chatting up an older black man with a bald head and mirrored sunglasses that she is staring into like a budgerigar on heat.

Stella managed to get the drunk Maxine into the wine bar, and as she passed the counter, ordered three black coffees, Dick joined them at the same table of the other evening. Maxine, still the worse for wear, is foggily wondering whose hen party she's at now. Tentatively Stella began a dialogue with this stranger, that she hoped might build into some sort of trust.

'Maxine, I'm Stella, this is Dick, we think we may have a mutual friend.' Maxine is focusing in, the coffee is having an affect already.

'Who's that then?' She asked, with gaining sobriety.

'Our friend is Cheryl.' All of a sudden Maxine is visibly upset, that swiftly turned to vulnerability and self-concern, Stella read the signs. 'Listen to me.'

The girl begins to look about and fidget, the last thing they want is for her to run off. 'Please, listen, it's alright, we think you saved her life, it was Dick you called, we're not the police, Cheryl is fine, and it's all thanks to you. If she was here now, I'm sure she'd be very grateful for what you did.' Maxine is looking scared and tense and still a little drunk, Dick has a go.

'Phoning me when you did was the best thing you could have done.' Her head is clearing, she knows she can't be in any trouble, so she begins to tell them what happened.

'We'd arranged to meet up in Unicorn Yard, for a couple of cans and a smoke, I had no idea it was going to be Cheryl. I hid in the shadows, we just wanted some money that's all. They went in, it was taking too long, I noticed one of them, upstairs, grinning out the window, I got curious and sneaked up. They were beating her up, it was horrible, I made them stop, I found a chair and sat Cheryl down. There was a length of rope so I tied her in, I was afraid she might fall and hurt herself. I looked in her desk diary and saw some friend's dinner date, so I phoned the place.'

'Snake didn't try to stop you?' That was Dick's trick question.

'No, he didn't.' Maxine stopped dead in her tracks. 'I didn't tell you that, that didn't come from me.'

'O.K.' It's Stella. 'But we really need to know the names of the other two, we're only going to speak to them, that's all, you can trust us.' Maxine couldn't bring herself to say anything, Stella felt it was now or never. 'If they try anything like that again it might end badly for all of them, Cheryl nearly lost an eye last time.' That did the trick, Maxine folded.

'I'll tell you their names but you didn't get them from me, promise?' Stella nodded. 'Their names are Jock and Dunlop, remember, you promised.'

'*There you are!*' Four girls had entered the wine bar all talking at once. 'We wondered where you'd got to, who are your friends?' Maxine stood up.

'Just a couple I know.' For some reason Stella stood up too and the hens quietened down, then one of them exclaimed.

'Are you, you're Stella Kill, of Stella Kill and the…' Stella interrupted.

'**Yeah**, I'm Stella Kill, how the fuck are you?'. She walked forward and held out her hand. 'Who's the lucky cow getting hitched?' They were all star-struck, then one of them spoke.

'It's me, I'm getting married on Saturday.' Stella flung her arms around her.

'No shit girl, have a lovely one.' The girl is in shock, she didn't know what to say, then, she just came out with it.

'Where are the Pubes?' Stella looked at her.

'There're on the floor at Hair for Less.' To a girl they screamed with laughter and ran out in fits, their night had been made up, they'd met Stella Kill, it was a dream come true.

THIRTY-NINE

It was wet, and it was cold, and it was dark, and it was 3am in Seattle, and it was not genial, and there was no one afoot. The street, where halfway up on the west side, Beauty and the Feast lay asleep, except for one security light that shone upon an open safe, to show there was no cash on the premises, did not escape the dank bucketing torrents. Thus it was no one saw The Four Horsemen of the Apocalypse sitting there in the wind-swept, pounding rain, silent, resolute, and dry as a bone. Their horses, sturdy, strong, and jet-black, but also, strangely dry. Simultaneously the dark riders coax their steeds on to silently make their deathly way up the street.

An observer, if that were possible to such an obscenity, might reflect on the number of times this catalyst had manifested itself in their lifetime, to cause wanton death and destruction. In years, hundreds, in decades, thousands, and in millennia, well the greed of man proves that one, it's perpetual, and today, today the horses graze in our gardens, prepared, waiting.

At that wretched moment, as the horses pass by, one of them took a fancy to the light and stopped. It turned its head and ominously kicked the ground before taking those six dreadful strides towards the shop window of Beauty and the Feast. Silently it stood, as if being tempted, the other three turn their heads to watch in eerie anticipation. Its left hoof lifts and clicks back onto the ground. Its black head with shiny, silken mane, rising and falling twice, as if in answer to some distant command emitted from the fiery abyss of hell. It raises its head again and snorts loudly, signing the glass with its steamy breath, before turning away and with the others, walked on into the night.

The big day has arrived, at three in the morning Jo Maryanne Goodheart, tossed and turned in her sleep, her subconscious all too aware it's cold, dark and wet out there. Little did she know she was going to wake up to a beautifully calm day, with a clear blue sky and a promising temperature, on this day of all days, the day she was getting married to her childhood sweetheart, Jason Delacroix, she is going to become Mrs. Delacroix.

As Jo Maryanne wakes, her excitement is palpable, immediate, she is starting her day with one of her favourite things, a french breakfast, followed by a manicure performed by her new and good friend, Angel. Then she's having her hair done by another good friend, Helen. After that, at eleven, it's home to mom and sis, to be helped into her wedding dress, all ready for their "big moment at high noon", as Jason and Jo like to call it. Something told Jo she wanted to do this on her own, her sister Connie had wanted to chaperone her, but no, Jo insisted, Connie is going through a similar treatment at her favourite salon, without the breakfast. Since Beauty and the Feast opened, it had fast become a favourite with many of Seattle's young and upwardly mobile, cosmopolitan females. It isn't unisex, not yet anyway, and the food, especially the breakfasts, is a big hit.

Jo had arrived by taxi she was too nervous to drive herself. Crossing the street, the shop was so bright in the reflective glory of the morning sun, she had to hold her hand above her eyes for protection. She pushed the door, a feat she'd done so many times, she knew its weight by heart. On entering the salon, she was taken totally by surprise, instead of the three women she expected to huddle around her, greet her with kisses and take in some of her bridle luck, Jo was confronted by three men, strangers, three carpet fitters, she thought. There was surprise on both sides, then one of the men burst into life, he walked towards the door.

'Those girls, we'll just be half an hour, we'll lock the door behind us they said. You two take that roll of carpet out to the van then come back for the other two, hell Miss it's the wrong colour, we gotta go back to the warehouse and start over.' The two men struggle to put the carpet on their shoulders, a comic scene, like Laurel and Hardy. The mistake, the short one is at the end nearest the door, not on the storyboard, a lady's shoe fell out of the roll and danced a yard across the floor before coming to a halt, pointing directly at Jo, it didn't go unnoticed Jo is staring straight at it. The first creep, still by the door, speaks again. 'That's very unfortunate.' Jo is standing staring at the shoe, of all the options that is probably the best one and certainly the most kind. The next second, she's laying dead on the floor, the scum eyeballs the other two as he locks the door. 'I told you this sixty-dollar silencer was worth every dime, let's get these bitches the hell outta here and tied up in the van before they come round.'

*

Cheryl hadn't asked her friends how they were getting on with finding out who had beaten her up. She knew the police weren't getting anywhere because she'd had a visit and that much they did tell her, but Dick and Salinka knew the time was getting close for some kind of showdown. They decided the next move was to talk to Cheryl and appraise her of what they had found out, over dinner at Midas Mansions, Salinka began to explain.

'So far we know who it was phoned us at the restaurant, the one who saved you, certainly from a worse fate, her name is Maxine.' Cheryl remembered Maxine, she was surprised, she didn't expect her to be involved in anything like this. Dick assured her she wasn't, he relayed the whole story and said they were sure she was telling the truth.

'And we know who the others are, is it okay if I tell you?' Cheryl is keen to know. 'It was Snake, we know, Jock and Dunlop.' Cheryl shook her head.

'No, I've never heard of any of them.'

We already know Dick's an ex-cop, who is now a private investigator, over the years he's acquired a nose for a crooked deal and he's beginning to think this one has all the hallmarks of classic wool pulling. He looks at his partner, an ex-KGB agent, a highly trained, vastly efficient killer, but no detective, she won't have seen it. Dick decides to keep his theory to himself, for the time being, conversation turned to the progress of the warehouse conversion, the Italian job, and that Cheryl thinks she ought to pay some rent, not least because of the fee she's in line to get, Salinka said no.

'We have a saying in Russia, never counter good luck, it has a habit of turning bad.'

A couple of whiskeys and a coffee and the night is over. Cheryl makes her way to her bedroom. Dick climbs in next to Salinka and immediately they're entwined in their intimate, unashamed nakedness, in a king-size bed between crimson sheets and beneath a single throw, these are two hot-blooded beings. He begins to explain his theory they are being fed a line, Salinka is intrigued and wants to know more.

'Well, doesn't it seem odd to you, Cheryl knows Maxine but draws a blank at the other three?' She thinks for a moment.

'It would have made sense had she known them, that's true, what's the deal then?'

'O.K. just suppose Maxine is protecting the real culprits, for whatever reason, and leading us to three innocent people, or three people who don't exist.' Again, Salinka is thinking.

'Well, why would she do that, and it falls down because she only confirmed it was Snake, we got the name from someone else, Cheryl?' Dick smiled.

'Hm, Cheryl, and what if she had been fed a line during the beating.' Without thinking Dick cups Salinka's breasts. 'My poor innocent Russian spy, just because you got a dog into space doesn't mean you have the monopoly on brains, I'm certain the lad who put his arm around your waist knew who you were, the one flashing the address tag, that was to derail us, we've been set up, there is no Snake, Jock, or Dunlop.' Salinka prepares for a full-on attack on Dick's theory.

'O.K. so how come we met Maxine like that?' Now it's Dick's turn.

'Because she put herself about for us to find her, don't you think she was just a bit too compliant, all that way to the wine bar without a fuss?' He has an idea. 'Stella, on Saturday you're going to a wedding, we need some answers.' Before Salinka can say anything, he gives her a tweak and the rest, as they say, is anatomy.

*

Stella didn't go to a wedding on Saturday, but she did attend a wedding reception, it was easy, and this time no one is setting them up. The pub landlord knew which church it was, and the time, it was in the afternoon, the reception is in the hall across the road from the church, he should know, he's running the outside bar. Stella Kill walked in unannounced and amongst the initiated there was mayhem.

Dick stayed in the car and turned on the radio, Hairdo won the 1:30 at Cheltenham, flying saucers have been spotted over Richmond Park and Lord Lucan is seen filling shelves in a supermarket in Redcar.

Stella recognised all the girls from the pub, but there's no sign of Maxine, she began speaking to one of them who is well-chuffed to be seen hobnobbing with this celeb. The conversation is flowing as are the drinks, Stella asked where Maxine is, the girl said they didn't know her that well and she didn't think she'd been invited, Stella laughed out loud.

'You were lucky to find me the other night, what made you look in the wine bar?' The girl said it was Romeo who pointed it out. Stella laughed again. 'We had a fucking ball that night didn't we. Is Romeo here, I need a word with the reptile?' The girl is on cloud nine.

'No, he just bumped into us that night, we only know him through the coffee bar and he knows Maxine, he pointed out where she'd disappeared to.' Being aware of her accidental celebrity, Stella didn't want to steal the bride's moment, she'd made a "Kill" so she got the hell out of there.

FORTY

Dick, is standing in the dark on the second floor of the warehouse looking out the window, the view, a full Moon-swept, part cobbled, part concrete Unicorn Yard, with a single bollard standing dead centre, its shadow casting an uncertain time, a Moondial without calibrations. It's late, and from Dick's vantage point it looks like Romeo is catching up with some paperwork. Salinka is wandering about in the shadows, imagining her huge minimalist decorated lounge. A wide, exuberant six-seater sofa here, a huge Italian marble coffee table in front of it, the grand piano, in that corner, a large Klimt reproduction, on which wall, to be decided? All this, she fancied, being set off against a deep pile, luxuriant crimson carpet, her favourite colour. The layout of this room is the last thing on Dick's mind, he's staring hard at the coffee shop thinking he's had enough of this game, it's time for Romeo to wake up and smell the coffee, that brought a smile to his lips. Salinka came and stood next to him and for a moment they both observe in silence. Dick is the first to speak.

'What do you think he's playing at, I mean, it's not big stuff is it? Whoever beat up Cheryl didn't know what they were doing, lucky for her they were a bunch of amateurs.' Salinka agreed.

'Hm, Romeo knew what he was doing though, he took advantage of the fact that one of us has a set of skills inherited from our forebears who had only managed to get a dog into space.' Dick smiled.

'Well, that's exactly my point.'

Across the yard the phone must have rung because Romeo stopped to answer it, his shoulders relaxed and he began to laugh, then, spookily, Dick can hear Romeo's every word. Salinka held out her little Russian receiver, one of the pair they'd used to great effect in Brussels. 'Woof.' She teased, Dick didn't comment, he was too busy listening in, but he did put his arm around his girl's waist, pulled her towards him, and kissed her soft brown locks.

'Tell your mates you've been fucking lucky this time, I managed to persuade Maxine to lie for you cretins, she wasn't happy about it'…'What?'… 'When Cheryl's two friends realise they can't find the culprits it'll all be done and dusted.'…'Don't try anything stupid like that again, your big brother won't help you out of a fix next time. We'll celebrate, bring the gang tomorrow night after we close, I'll send Juliet home early, come around seven.'…'Don't you worry, 'Snake', ha-ha, it'll be on the house'…'Okay, see you then.'
Dick looked at Salinka.

'Don't tell me, you planted it when we had coffee this morning.' He held out his hand and she placed the bug in his palm. 'Ah yes, it's made of metal, of course, it's magnetic, the first rule when launching a dog into space.' He shifted his gaze in the direction of the Coffee Bar. 'My guess is it's sitting on the underside of that Gaggia coffee machine.' Salinka nods her head, but with a curious frown.

'A magnetic dog?'

'No, no, it's space, space is magnetic, can be.'

Though Dick and Salinka are well matched as human beings, spiritual conduits, and passionate lovers, as far as Salinka's combat training is concerned, she's streets ahead. Dick is old school, and old-school habits die hard, police academy, learning on the beat, taught by a dyed-in-the-wool conformist, a good but static man, and by other law-abiding public servants all of whom went through similar training. All good men and women who put their lives on the line for the peace and security of the people they protect, the populous of New York City, its suburbs, and the whole of New York State. That's not to underestimate Dick, he's as tough as they come, he'd be the first to attend a tricky situation, but he has his own set of rules, it was the rigid adherence to certain, timid protocols as demanded by the law, that eventually determined him to go private, to beat to his own particular beat. Salinka, Colonel Palchikova, and nowadays, occasionally Stella Kill, is a totally different animal. If we could look forward, just a decade or so, into Russia's future, Salinka's motherland, we would see a leadership at the edge of a moral abyss, a downward spiral waiting in the wings as a treacherous new president is quietly positioning himself ready to improve his lot. His macabre mentality, to toy with world peace, a despot ready to support other despots, a desperation to accumulate wealth beyond the dreams of avarice, at any cost. My point, in that explanation, is to highlight the unnecessary training Salinka went through, apparently deemed crucial by a dogmatic ruling elite to give Russia the toughest set of killer soldiers in the world, presumably to protect whoever is the latest self-proclaimed Tsar. A small observation of hope, if I may, this time the four horsemen just passed by, they didn't stop. Salinka is a shining example, indicative of the majority of good, normal, right-thinking Russian people who simply want a fair and just world and not be labelled as the world's premier, pariah State. They want to get on with the West and for the West to like and respect them in return. As they will be ruled by a murdering, narcissistic, megalomaniac, barbarian, the malevolence gene will, at all costs, be attributed away from him, to, well, where would be convenient, ah yes, the West? I digress, as I said, Dick and Salinka are, in most ways, as one, when it comes to matters of their 'trade' she is far more driven and sophisticated, and in this case, very alert to exactly what is required and how it must be executed.

'Dick, I've got a plan and I won't take no for an answer.' Tomorrow night it will be Dick and Cheryl standing, looking out of the 2nd-floor window, waiting for the storm to begin. Salinka's plan is going to involve Natalie, she doesn't know it yet but she's going to be the getaway driver, she is the only one qualified for the job because Natalie knows, first-hand, what Salinka is capable of. She's taking Nat out for their morning coffee break, not to Unicorn Yard, that would never do, but one of the staples in the centre of the city, it's a well-established fact that the majority of Cambridge folk, including the intellectual elite, can't survive without copious cups of coffee, and in Cambridge, there are watering holes aplenty.

Dick, meantime, is at home scanning a free copy of Cambridge Today trying to find the quarter-page ad that he feels is his attempt to even up their workload, when the phone rings. He answers it with his usual throwaway, devil-may-care attitude, when out of the blue he is altered by the voice of a child.

'Well, what can I do for you young sir?'

'Mr. Chase, our cat Matilda has gone missing and it says in our local newsagents that you find missing persons, and my sister and me are wondering if you can find our cat?' Dick thought for a moment.

'Well let me see, first off, I need to know my client's names.' The caller confirmed, in one straight sentence.

'My name is Mikey Little, I'm 10, I live above the greengrocers down Wentworth Street and my sister's name is Anne, she's 6 and a half.'

'Aha, how old is Matilda and when did you last see her?' An increasingly emotional Mikey did his best to answer Dick's questions, right down to the full description. 'Okey dokey Mr. Little, that's all I need to go on, now listen carefully sir, I'll do the best I can, you know Cambridge is a big place, I can't guarantee anything, but I will pull out all the stops and I'll let you know one way or the other, that's a promise.' Dick is smiling to himself as he puts the phone down, he can still remember his childhood cat Lincoln, still there, still strong in his memory, like Mikey, he's emotional. 'Over a cat.'

During coffee Salinka tells Natalie what she wants her to do and Nat is becoming increasingly wide-eyed and gobsmacked.

'Natalie, how come you drive that big Ford Zodiac Executive, it's a funny choice for a single girl?'

'It was my dad's car and his idea, he was right, I'm a better driver for it.'

'Well, all praise to your dad because I'm going to hire a big black limo and I want you to drive it for me, do you think you can handle it?' To chauffeur is going to be the extent of Natalie's input, and after hearing Salinka's plan she wouldn't have had it any other way, except, well, there is just one small embellishment, but more on that later.

FORTY-ONE

The clock is ticking and their course is set, Stella and Natalie are parked up three streets away, awaiting the prearranged time. Dick looks at his watch, it's five to eight, Cheryl has a question.

'Where's Salinka, and why are we standing here in the dark watching four people eating and drinking and having a good time?' Dick is staring out into the blackness.

'Those three, the ones on the right, they're the three who beat you up, Romeo, who you've already met, is the older brother of one of them, he tried to cover their footsteps.' Cheryl is stunned into silence, Dick continued. 'Salinka, or Stella as you also know her, at the very least is going to warn them off, it all depends on their attitude.' Cheryl's confused, she can't understand why it's Salinka, and why she's on her own. 'I know what you're thinking, just knowing her you would never guess.' Cheryl is even more confused now.

'Guess, guess what?' Dick's mind is a maze, a kaleidoscope of Stella's actions, now he fully understands how the trafficker and the British MEP fought each other to the death. Then there was Burano, who learned the hard way what the Punk would do for him. Dimi stabbed three times in quick succession, not to mention some diamond studded binoculars, the list goes on. Dick looks at Cheryl.

'You would never guess that Salinka is an ex-KGB agent, a highly trained, extremely skilled killing machine, keep that to yourself, she'll be here soon.'

As he rounded off his sentence so it began, slowly, with demonic presence, the blinding headlights of a limousine silently crawled into Unicorn Yard, as it did a cat that Dick hadn't noticed high-tailed it out of there. The black limo crept a threatening semicircle around the bollard and pulled up outside the coffee shop, its unexpected, sudden appearance focused the attention of the four inside. The limo's lights went out and to Cheryl's surprise she can hear Salinka's voice coming from Dick's hand.

'Hi guys, it's me, are you ready for some action?' She proceeded to speak in what Dick guessed was Russian, he whips his hand up and Cheryl replies into the little metal box, the pair of them are going at it hammer and sickle. Then, from Stella, English.

'Yankee, did you kill the phone?'

'No, I had three more installed.'

'O.K. thanks for that.'

The conversation continues with Cheryl, until eventually it stops, leaving an eerie silence that gives way to the overwhelming, and exciting tension of anticipation. The driver gets out and slowly walks around to open the door for her passenger. Cheryl is surprised to see the chauffeur is a woman, who like Stella is all punked up and sassy, this little detail was Natalie's idea, it amused Stella greatly, Cheryl informed Dick.

'Stella said she's going to tell them she's my cousin, I told her what happened to me and she's come over from Russia to sort them out.' Cheryl gave Dick a faint smile. 'That's family loyalty for you.'

As if Natalie wasn't enough to salivate their glands, slowly Stella exits the limo like a butterfly emerging from a black cocoon. The four yobs are mesmerised, hypnotised, all eyes, watching their every move. Stella approaches Natalie and kisses her on the lips, this as we know is old territory, it was planned, a diversion, as was the conversation with Cheryl, all to hold up proceedings, to add mystique, to make Stella enticing and to make the yobs gag, it did the trick, their common-sense thinking has gone clean out the window. Stella looks stunning, she's made a special effort just for the occasion, with slow, seductive steps she reached the door, where she stopped and put her head on one side, she didn't have to knock, Romeo opened it as though in a trance. Stella placed an outstretched hand high on the frame and leaned, supported only by her fit, athletic arm, in English, but with a strong Russian accent she speaks.

'A little bird tells me you don't cheap on the coffee in this establishment.' Romeo stands to one side, Stella springs herself to the upright position and strolls in, the viper has entered the guinea pigs' nest, her presence is all compelling, it is she who steals the show, they don't notice Natalie, take a length of wood from the car to perform her other task. The shop door opens inwards and has grab handles on both sides, Nat's job is to slide the wood through the handle so the door can't be opened, that done she sits back in the driver's seat ready to reverse the procedure at Stella's bidding. With the Punk in their midst these four think they've died and gone to heaven, she's put herself between the three and

Romeo, like a sheepdog separates a lamb for the slaughter, she won't waste time, Salinka doesn't waste time.

'What is this, the stag party?' They laugh wildly like an unruly mob all grinning and shaking their heads, accompanied by the slight hum of feet, each fascinated and fantasising she is their woman, while Romeo is thinking, but can't put his finger on it.

'Do I know you, you look familiar?' Salinka hopes he's referring to Stella Kill, she helps jog his memory.

'That is not possible I've just flown in from Russia, there are those who think I look like your English Punk rocker,'

'That's it.' One of the goons gets it. 'Stella Kill, you're Stella Kill.'

'No, I am not,' She speaks in Russian that translates as. "I just told you dumb-arse, people think I look like her." 'No,' She laughed. 'It is as I said, I only look like her, I'm Stella Brodsky, but the interesting thing about me is, I'm Cheryl's cousin, and I've come all this way to teach you four a lesson in manners for beating her up.' There's a stunned silence only punctuated by the Gaggia intermittently hissing like a venomous snake waiting to pounce, Romeo, laughing, ups the ante.

'So, lady, you're gonna teach me a lesson, interesting.' He's grinning all over his face. 'I'm quaking in my boots, how do you think a little Punk kitten like you is gonna do that?' Stella looks at Romeo and plays her ace.

'Well, you greasy little shit, because you're going to help me, like the stupid arsehole you are.'

Romeo is about six feet tall, he's athletic, he has a stroppy demeanour and Stella thinks he's probably smacked a few people in his time. She's calculated he won't take any truck from her, not a woman, not a little Punk kitten, in front of his young brother and his mates, and she's dead right. Without warning he flies at her, fists clenched, someone less experienced would have been in serious trouble, that someone isn't Stella, she snatches his punch, steps to one side, and using Romeo's weight and momentum, in a split-second, his left ear is pressing the floor, his arse is sticking up in the air and his right arm is pointing straight at the ceiling, it's wound up as far as it'll go. Stella tweaks it some more while leaning heavily on it, piling the pressure onto his neck. There's a deep intake of breath from Romeo who slams his left palm flat on the floor and pushes, to try to counter the pressure on his neck. 'What do you think of me so far?' The other three make their play by running for the door, but they can't open it. Stella eyes them with contempt. 'So, the rats are leaving the sinking ship, what about helping this lanky piece of shit, your brother and his friends aren't very loyal, which one of these weak-kneed lady bashers is he?' One of them blurts out.

'Come on, let's rush her, she won't stand a chance.' Is the wrong answer, instantly Stella breaks Romeo's arm, then she puts her foot on his arse and sends him crashing, head first, into a table and chairs, the other three rubberneck his flight. Like lightning, she grabs the nearest one and headbutts him, really hard, it's a speciality of hers, Dick heard the crack through the little receiver, he can almost feel the pain, Stella retreats.

'Aaaah, Jesus, fuck you bitch.' The imbecile put his hand to his nose. 'You've broken my fucking nose.' Stella tells him not to touch it, he screams out loud.

'Too late, you've touched it.' Romeo is rocking to and fro on the floor cradling his arm, Stella looks at him. 'If you're thinking about trying something, the first thing I'll do is break your other arm, the second thing is I'll break your neck.' Good, she's thinking, that's the real threat out of action, nose-job has blood all over the place, his face, his hands, all down his nice Ben Sherman shirt, it's a bad one, he leans forward, now there's blood and mucus connecting with the floor.

'God that hurts, fuck you, you cow, I'm in agony' The ball is rolling, her raison d'etre is out, the moment of dawning realization for the four is relished by the sniggering Gaggia, Stella speaks.

'Is that it, is that all you've got? Nose job, you need to sit down and put your head right back, if you're lucky you won't bleed to death.' Stella braces herself for the finale act. 'Now listen you scum, we can carry on like this, till you've all got broken noses and broken arms, and ruined shirts, or much worse.' She gives them a look of disgust. 'You weak, pathetic cowards, you think you can walk into an innocent girl's life and beat her up, and for what, for fun, for a laugh?' She faces them full-on. 'If anything happens to my cousin, if one of you so much as lays a finger on Cheryl, you'll all suffer the same fate as

Josh Clements, do you understand what I'm saying?'
Sarcastically, one of them ejaculates.

'Josh committed suicide.' Stella gives them a knowing smile.

'Did he, you know that do you, no pangs of doubt I might have killed him? You think about it, because I won't think twice about killing you four, if one of you so much as approaches Cheryl.' Stella jumps backwards onto the counter and swings her legs over, she also glimpsed Natalie, that's Nat's cue to remove the piece of wood, Stella makes herself a latte to go. 'I'm watching you.' She's glancing past the chrome Gaggia, she walks back around the counter, the jerks are huddled by nose-job, who is still bleeding profusely while cursing under his breath. At the door she places her coffee down and takes a couple of steps towards the cowering quartet. 'Before I go, does anybody want to try it on?' There's nothing, not a breath, she picks up her coffee, and with her free hand opens the door, Stella is ready to leave the building. She casts an eye over all of them. 'This is not a joke, I am for real, you'd better believe it, just lay one finger on my cousin and you are all dead, that's a promise.'

The Punk chauffeur is standing by holding the car door open. Stella leaves the coffee shop and like Mafia Royalty, she lowers her head and calmly steps into the back of the black limo, Nat pushes the door closed. At least Romeo has the sense and the broken arm to absorb this surreal scene, and to reflect that this woman means business, from now on he is personally going to protect Cheryl with his life whenever she enters the coffee shop. Natalie makes her way to the driver's seat, she starts the engine that purrs almost silently into life, then, with an explosion of light, they glide off into the night.

FORTY-TWO

The debrief is always an important part of any action, and our four friends are paying this one full respect.

'...and when he said, "my fucking nose hurts" you should have seen the look on his face, I didn't know whether to laugh or cry, and then...then,' Salinka is bursting at the seams, she can hardly hold it together. 'Romeo said, "How's a little Punk kitten gonna do that?"' Laughing, they all scream in unison.

'**A little Punk kitten**?'

'Yeah, I know, that's what he called me, he didn't know that ten seconds later I could have broken his neck, but I broke his arm anyway, so.' They all fell about laughing before Salinka was serious.

'Cheryl, I think we can safely say they won't be bothering you again.' Cheryl wanted to know about Josh and did she really kill him, Salinka stopped her right there.

'No, I was bluffing, I pulled it out of the air, but they didn't know that.'

'And why were you on your own, wasn't it dangerous?' Natalie looked at Cheryl.

'Let me answer that one.' She pleads with her saviours. 'Can I tell her my story, I'd like to?' Salinka eyeballs Dick.

'What's the point of all this training if we can't grab a few headlines.'

Through all this Dick has been supplying champagne, whisky, and coffee for those who want it, and cheese and biscuits. By the time history is retold and all the skeletons are out of the cupboard, Nat is in no fit state to drive home, the sofa is made into a bed and she stays the night. Dick and Salinka talk in each other's arms for a good hour before sleep takes them.

'That was a nice piece of work, I like your style.' Salinka is smiling to herself.

'Thank you, Darling, it was rewarding, especially that lanky tosser Romeo, I grew to thinking he had it coming, you can see why it had to be Stella, solo, can't you, it was the only sure way to protect our anonymity, as we're going to be living just across from the coffee shop?'

'Yeah, I got that, Nat and the limo, was a stroke of genius, and as for Cheryl, I think she's regained all her confidence, by the way, I meant to tell you, I got my first job today, working for Mr. Little and his sister.'

'Sounds interesting.' Salinka speculates. 'Let me guess, brother and sister, hmm, their remaining parent wants to leave their whole inheritance to a cat charity and the siblings want you to prove undue pressure by some local cat-loving charity shop owner?' Dick snuggles up closer.

'Mmm, well, you got the cat bit right.' He proceeded to outline the case, Salinka became alert.

'There was a cat answering that description in the yard tonight, it scampered off just as we arrived.'

'Was there Honey, didn't you call Matilda? Zzzzz...'

'Say that again, Dick...Dick?'...Dick's drifted off.

In the early hours Cheryl woke, pulsating from a beautiful dream, it was she who chauffeured the limo, it was she who, all Punked up and sassy, approached Stella and kissed her fully on the lips. At the bottom of the stairs, in her friend's home, where Salinka, her saviour, lay fast asleep, Cheryl stopped to listen to Natalie's gentle breathing, those carefree, tranquil tones she so wanted to excite. She lost her nerve and returned to her bed, she'd remembered Natalie's bright laughter, the kiss in Brussels was just a ploy, a trap, a trap no matter how tempting, she wasn't going to fall into. Across the hall, Dick turned and listened, someone has gone to the loo.

A new day, Cheryl's moving back to her place, Natalie has just driven off to return the black limo and pick up her Zodiac, Stella has completely disappeared off the face of the earth. Salinka doesn't have to be in the office till eleven, so she and Dick are going to start their day at the conversion, to see how things are progressing before popping into the coffee shop to see if Romeo has surfaced yet.

They're standing in what will be their kitchen, it looks completely different from when they first laid eyes on it, the oak floorboards have been sanded and varnished to a high degree. The fifteen cast iron pillars look as if they've just been forged and polished, a far cry from the multi-coloured, lead-painted, chipped health hazards of the past hundred years. That's the only bit of the old building that will show on this floor, everything else will be contemporary, well, except for an antique refectory table Salinka has got her eye on.

The suspense is killing them, Dick and Salinka want to know what's happening at the coffee shop. As they make their way across the yard, Backup Man reminds Hit Woman not to transgress into her persona's vernacular, she looks at Dick to reply, but her attention is caught beyond him, she indicates.

'Isn't that your cat?' Dick looks in the general direction and to his amazement there's a cat that fits Matilda's description, he ums and errs.

'The problem will be catching her I know about cats that's gonna be difficult.' Salinka quietly approaches the feline, almost there she stops and crouches down, Dick looks on, keeping his distance. Salinka is saying something and to his astonishment, Matilda calmly strolls up and into her arms. 'What do we do now, we've gained a cat and we haven't had coffee yet, and how come, all of a sudden, you're Catwoman?'

'Don't you know females and felines have an affinity, and Juliet is one of us, isn't she Matilda?' For the first time Dick witnesses Salinka go all mushy, as she purrs. 'Yes, Juliet will go all mushy won't she Mattie, trust me, come on, let's try our luck?' Juliet went all mushy, and all amusing.

'Romeo fell downstairs and broke his arm, he'll be in tomorrow, where's Cheryl, he says as she's the only other business in the yard, he's decided, from now on, her coffees are on the house?' Casually Dick relays that Cheryl has taken the day off, her cousin's been over from Moscow and she's seeing her off at the airport. Matilda is quietly sitting on the chair next to them, cleaning her paws, Dick asks Juliet if he can have an empty crisp box. Mattie's head jumps as he punches the first of a dozen holes in it with a lost Biro he found sheltering behind the menu, he looks across the condiments.

'O.K. Catwoman, what are the chances of you getting moggie into her temporary accommodation?

*

Dick is back at Midas Mansions with Matilda, Salinka wants to be part of it when he returns the cat. Tonight, they're going out to dinner, it's Cheryl's treat, there's a nice little Italian she wants to introduce them to, it's her way of saying thanks for saving her from those mindless thugs, memories of the Spaghetti Boat Dick thought, where he first met his Russian Beauty. Matilda is playing with her box, so Dick sinks back in his chair to watch as she jumps in and out in double quick time. Then she stands on her hind legs and peers inside, that makes it snap over and cover her, the box shifts across the floor at a rate of "cat knots" before stopping dead against the sofa. There's nothing for a few seconds before it sets off in another direction. Then, a miracle, the box tips, and Matilda is free, instantly she looks around for the enemy, but there's no one there, so she plonks herself straight down and begins to lick her paws. Dick is smiling to himself, these days he's not much of a cat person, but learning of the affinity between females and felines, especially one female in particular, he's prepared to make an exception.

The greengrocers' is one of a dying breed established as it is in the downstairs front portion of a house along a terraced row, one of many rows still surviving in Cambridge. The garden is two lines of veg stalls leading to an open door, inside the front room are more stalls, and amongst the veg and pot plants, are vases of cut flowers. Dick has the crisp box under his arm, while Salinka goes ahead to be met by the polite seller, a woman, who they guess is Mrs. Little. A lad quietly sweeps the floor for his mother, while a young girl is tidying some dishevelled flowers, both of them working their pocket money, Salinka speaks to the woman.

'They look like they've lost a cat and found a chore.' The woman smiles.

'They have, Matilda's gone missing, hasn't she sweethearts?' The boy carried on sweeping while the girl went to her mother and hid behind her apron. Salinka aims her next sentence at the lad.

'Well, this gentleman is the famous American private detective Mr. Dick Chase.' She might as well have said there's a lorry load of ice cream out the front and you can go help yourselves, Dick gently places the box on the floor and stands back.

'I think this belongs to you.' No sooner had he spoke, the cat, they both hope is Matilda, bounds out, any doubts they had were soon banished from their minds as the two children lit up like a choir of angels singing the chorus, Matilda Returns, from the opera Matilda. Dick looks at Mrs. Little. 'It's Matilda then.'

FORTY-THREE

The harsh reality of life hits home without warning, without reason, and in this case, without any sense at all. The next day when Salinka arrived at the office, she was greeted with the sad news that sometime during the early hours of the morning, Gloria, the firm's legal boffin of ten years, had committed suicide, she'd taken an overdose. This news has affected everyone deeply, much more than the murder of Mr. Burke. Gloria, was in many ways the heart and soul of the office, eminently approachable, always free with her legal advice and special friendship for any member of staff who needed it. She was a mainstay within the firm, an individual who will be very difficult to replace, she can't be replaced. Mr. Lush, David, is finding it particularly difficult, it fell to Salinka, a relative newcomer, to hold it together for the sake of everyone else.

It was to be a difficult morning at Lush Husband, a notice Salinka had placed on the plate-glass entrance simply read, Closed until 2 pm, due to unforeseen circumstances.

Adept at languages as she is, legal issues and the law in general, are out of her league, but thinking on her feet is something Salinka is particularly good at, she leaned into David's office.

'Why don't you call Thompson and Streak, Gloria was quite pally with Muriel Streak, see if they can spare George Short for a couple of weeks, he's your man.' She smiled and left him to it, telephonist Shirley is in need of consolation, the phone hasn't stopped ringing. Shirly replaced the receiver, took a couple of tissues, and dried her eyes, she looked at Salinka.

'Sometimes I think I've been around too long, maybe I should retire.'

'You mustn't do that, it would just about finish the firm off, you're needed here more than ever now.' Shirley divulged.

'Gloria was very envious of you, in a nice way.' Salinka concentrated her eyes.

'Oh, why was that?'

'She told me she found you very alluring, she said you had hidden depths.'

'Well, she wasn't wrong there, Dick was convinced she fancied him, I told him, not as much as he fancied himself, tell me, did she ever mention Stella?'

'No, she didn't, who's Stella?'

'It's a long story - I'll tell you one day.'

A numbed morning passed unbelievably quickly it was already coming up to 2 p.m. It struck all of them, although it went unspoken, Gloria was a person of habit, always taking her lunch between one and two. No matter how much they all wanted it, never again will she stride in cavorting her latest purchase or complaining the Pinot was at room temperature. She was always punctual, never late, and as if a minute's silence had been prearranged, on the hour, they waited, a room full of sad hopefuls, hushed, still, before, unfulfilled, they put on a group brave face and carried on.

By the time Salinka arrived home Dick was already in, and when he asked how her day had been it all came out, she hugged him and slowly told her sad tale, Dick was mortified, not only for Gloria and himself but for Salinka and all the others. They sat in silence their night ruined, no appetite, not yet, that will come. Dick thought about his joke, Gloria being a member of the Bar, and how she fell for it. Salinka remembered her tease about the ménage à trois and how she would probably never say those words in polite company again, that almost tipped Salinka, she stood up.

'Come on, let's remember her at the pub where we bumped into her that night, they do steak and chips and cold Pinot.'

Two weeks on and Dick and Salinka are at the same pub, it was Salinka's idea, the after-service refreshments, a chance to meet and reflect, Gloria would have loved it. This time, with the whole of Lush Husband, a contingent from Thompson and Streak, Muriel Streak read the lesson, and various friends of Gloria's. Strangely there is no family, she came from a long line of being an only child and both her parents are dead. The funeral service was very well attended, eminent members of the Bar, who nobody knew, wore their robes out of respect.

'Hm, a group of celestial beings on a non-uniform day, come to take Gloria up.'

'Dick, you know if you write in your head you'll forget, pass me an order of service will you.'

David Lush gave a glowing yet moving eulogy, a friend read from Horace, "Swiftly they pass the flying years" and told a related story from their past. By reputation, Gloria was notorious for her staggering wit, her seemingly never-ending store of knowledge, hence the assertion she could answer any question, and her willingness to help people, but she could be brusque and very rude if anyone rubbed her up the wrong way. The story from Gloria's past, as told by her friend, was particularly moving and would alter any doubter's opinion.

It was many years ago, on a whim, they decided to take a weekend break in Paris, it was April, and as the friend recalled the weather was typically showery. They both preferred to walk the back streets, those least frequented by tourists, they were strolling along a narrow-cobbled lane when, from out of nowhere, a grey corrugated van slid to a halt in front of them, a young girl was pushed out and the van sped off, the friend continued.

'Until that moment Gloria's French, like my own, had been poor, just enough to get us by, it was pitiful really, considering the school we'd both attended. It turned out this young woman, no more than a girl, was not only pregnant but on the cusp. Without hesitation Gloria dropped to her knees, even in those days she liked to dress well, nothing cheap, she loved silk stockings. On her knees, in the wet, she proceeded to deliver the baby, all the time speaking fluent French, I was useless, I had no idea Gloria could do that, I didn't know.' She halted and bowed her head, her friend is no more, she continued. 'It was the last thing I expected her to do, she carried out a wonderful and caring birth reassuring in fluent

French every step of the way.' The friend recalled with new vigour. 'Gloria removed her expensive Jaeger jacket to wrap the baby in, she handed me the child, then crouched on her haunches and picked the girl up in her arms, she insisted I place the baby on top of its mother, then proceeded to carry both of them to a nursing home she'd remembered passing earlier. The strange thing is she never mentioned it again, we never talked about it, it was as if it never happened. I learned from that moment Gloria possessed great resourcefulness, modesty, and kindness, her French was excellent, she just didn't want to show me up in front of the Parisians.'

Waiting in the wings there's a benevolence in something as powerful as it is calming, an unexpected ally that can bolster the spirit and sustain hope, it is tangible while being ethereal, it is a guiding light, it has been a friend to millions over the dusty centuries, it is a city. For this little knot of people gathered to reminisce and celebrate their friend, it is the city of Cambridge. Here, within its boundaries, everyone's past mingles, where Gloria might still be glimpsed. If you were born "light blue", you might have been one year old say, in a pram, in *that* park, eleven, in *that* library, twenty-one, in *that* bar, thirty, on a Sunday, while being punted beneath a cloudless sky in the arms of the one you love, forty, again, in the good company of congenial friends, in *that* alehouse. If luck is really on your side, on a warm summer's day in late August, you might, at a ripe old age, finally end your days on a favourite bench overlooking the Cam, while delighting at a trailing clutch of ducklings all dipping and diving before suddenly realising, like you, they must move on.

The invitations to the warehouse warming party have been sent out, every RSVP has been returned so catering for twenty-seven is the order of the day. Dick remembered seeing a life-size cardboard cut-out of Sir Isaac Newton, in a bookshop, and with a bit of gentle persuasion the shop owner let him borrow it, after all, as he told Salinka, you can't have a warehouse warming party in Cambridge without a life-size cardboard replica of Sir Isaac Newton. The catering is supplied by Mrs. Little, a facet of their greengrocery business. There's a lot of cold Pinot and an equal amount of room-temperature red, it's all here, Dick and Salinka certainly know how to throw a party.

The day of the party had been sweltering, the best day of the year so far, Salinka had to admit Dick's idea to go for the air conditioning, had, in retrospect, been the right one, it's almost compulsory in the States, whereas in Russia, they're big fans of opening a window. The first people to arrive are Cheryl with her girlfriend Hyacinth, Hyacinth is black, so we're killing two birds with one stone right there, for a bit of fun they volunteered to dress up in little black numbers, with white frilly aprons, to wait on everyone, Dick said that was fine, just so long as they didn't expect free refreshments.

'It's amazing, Salinka.' Natalie is gobsmacked. 'I've never seen a home like it, you must be very pleased, I could easily live in a pad like this.'

'Yes, we are very lucky, it was new on the market, and right under Dick's nose.' Cheryl came up to the pair of them, put her tray of drinks down, and gave them each a hug.

'Hello, Natalie, it's gorgeous isn't it, the boss lady is going to let me stay here when she goes on her holidays?' She retrieved her tray. 'Anyone for champers?'

Dick is talking to Joe, Natalie's boyfriend, he's giving him the grand tour and introducing him to the odd person as they make their way around.

'And they don't come much odder than Shirley.' He said out loud with his usual playful grin, while in his head he knew he would much rather have said that about Gloria. And so, the night went on, David and his wife are overcome with delight, they too have never seen anything like it.

'Salinka, Salinka my dear, I cannot think of a more deserving person, I'm sure you will both be very happy here.' He leaned in close. 'Is that our client, Ms. Conway, Cheryl I believe, I've got some good news, her money will be with her on Monday, would you like to tell her, say it's the full amount, I'm sure she'll be delighted?' And she was, thirty seconds later Hyacinth screamed with delight as Cheryl passed her news on. Mrs. Lush and Shirley grasped hands in a hail of laughter over something only the plush sofa was privy to. Joe and Natalie are standing, arm in arm, admiring the Klimt, of course it's a print, "Forest", it reminds Salinka of Russia. Dick and David are standing talking about things that only men stand and talk about. While Salinka, she is surveying all her realm, her quick mind, in a couple of seconds sampled the whole of her adult life that brought her to this moment. There are some random, unwanted thoughts, episodes she wouldn't consciously think about, like, her sisters paid for all this with their lives. Her first husband, a wealthy oligarch, killed them so Salinka killed him and hijacked quite a lot of his money, that's how all this came about. She'd give it all up in an instant to have them back, even Dick she thought, and immediately felt doubly sad.

'Penny for them.' It's Natalie, who had wandered over seeing what she thought was a wisp of sadness, a glimpse of melancholy, a tinge of regret. 'Penny for them.' Salinka surfaced and instantly it vanished.

'I was just reminiscing, but one cannot alter the past, so.' Her beaming smile battled its way through her regret, while Natalie thought for a moment.

'If you altered the past, you might not have been around to save me.' Immediately Salinka eyeballed her friend.

'Will you do me a favour?' For the first time Natalie sees a vulnerability in this tough woman she didn't expect, she didn't think was possible. 'Ask me no questions, will you be my sister?' Natalie knew, Dick had told her. 'Will you be my sister?' Natalie is delighted.

'I can't think of anyone I'd rather have as a sister, and no questions.' They hugged

There are too many people to paint here, there's a toast for Gloria, nobody mentioned Gerald Burke, can you blame them, he nearly broke the firm.

There's the dumb waiter, that was a huge topic of conversation, as was Sir Isaac Newton. Dick couldn't resist the urge to do his party piece by standing discussing, with Sir Isaac, *his* theory on gravity, twice, for those who missed it the first time. Positive comments about the conversion went on all evening and their friends were knocked out by the deep pile crimson carpet, it's as if they hadn't seen anything like it, and of course they hadn't, not 70 by 40 feet of it anyhow.

Cheryl and Hyacinth insisted on staying to help clear up, a task Dick was all too willing to leave till the morning, but he was outvoted, in reality the two girls are so in love with the place they didn't want to leave, but they ran out of excuses to stay and eventually they had to go. They set off arm in arm, they're going to walk back to Cheryl's little flat. Dick was the first to speak.

'I think that went well everyone was blown away by the place.' He put his arms around Salinka's waist. 'You blow me away kid.' That was the first time Dick had used that expression he had, unknowingly, charmed her, she smiled, what was it she was going to say?

'I'd never have guessed Cheryl batted for the other side, what do you think, Yankee?'

Dick is at a loss, he wanted to come back with a derogatory term for a Russian, but he couldn't think of one, Salinka had planted new thoughts in his head.

'Dick, *Dick*'

Dick can make out Salinka calling but he can't figure out where it's coming from, by this time smoke has filled the room, a room he didn't know, he couldn't recognise, it's the conversion, yes of course it is, it's the top floor, their bedroom, full of acrid, choking smoke.

'Dick, Dick!' Again, he can hear Salinka calling out, then at last the distant reassuring bell of a fire engine.

'Dick, Dick, **DICK** answer the phone will you, it's ringing its head off down there, it was you who said we only needed one handset.' Dick opened his eyes and tuned in.

'The phone's ringing.'

'You're not a detective for nothing, go and see who it is, it might be important.'

Dick is fully awake now and heading down the smoke-free stairs to answer their solitary phone, while Salinka lays there thinking about the man she loves. A strange combination of wit and duty, of passion and justice, she feels very lucky. Tom on the other hand was her husband, who had been mistakenly identified as Dick and shot dead. He was a completely different person altogether, an intellectual, he would never waste his breath on flippancies, not like Dick does. She thought about Cheryl and Hyacinth, and what a nice couple they make, and then... and then she was transported back to her school days, quite unexpectedly, to a scene she hadn't conjured for years. To those salad days when true love first raised its head, to when she was a young teenager, still innocent, still carefree, and how, with her idol Alexandria, they studied the poetry of Sappho together. As Dick crawled back into bed, Salinka, inquisitive, wanted to know what it was all about.

'It's a big problem, that was Peter McDougall, in New York, he was reading through some out-of-State police bulletins and came across something he recognised.' Dick looked at Salinka. 'It's bad news from Seattle, it's Beauty and the Feast, the Seattle police found a dead girl on the premises, there's no sign of Helen, Julie or Angel, forensics say there was a struggle, it looks like whoever did it used chloroform to knock them out and simply drove off with them, no one knows where.' Dick is resigned. 'I'll have to go.' Salinka looks at him.

'We'll have to go, we're a team and besides, who's gonna save your Yankee neck if I'm not there?'

FORTY-FIVE

New York, it's a hot day and it feels to Dick like he hasn't been away. At the desk, in the Manhattan cop shop, is a woman who will faint when she clocks him, just as soon as she's finished with some drunk who's sprawling all over her nice blue check Formica, waiting to be discharged.

'Dick, Dick Chase, is that you, you ol' son of a gun, let me take a good look at you? Well, Dick Chase, as I live and breathe, you're a real hero around these parts, there's not a cop here who doesn't know about Brussels?' Eunice *is* Jamaica, a wonderful, passionate, caring police woman who, for a brief spell was Dick's partner, too many years ago now, while his best friend and actual partner, Peter McDougall, was on his honeymoon. Dick has an idea he's about to make her day.

'Eunice, this is my partner, Salinka Palchikova, I think the chief will let her in.' Eunice's eyes opened wide and for a moment she was speechless. Without hesitating, she came around to the front of the desk and threw her thick black arms around this beautiful, young woman and gave her a tight hug. Salinka looks at Dick with questioning eyes and a wide grin.

'I've heard all about you ma'am, and it's an honour and a privilege to make your acquaintance, you two go right ahead, the chief's in, I'll call and tell him, I'll say royalty are on their way up.' She looked at the pair of them. 'Dick Chase and Miss Palchikova, well I'll be darned, if you two haven't just gone and made my day. Hey, Russell, did you see who just passed through here, well I'll be?'

'Chase boy, sit down, sit down…yes, yes, I'm fine.' The chief voluntarily moved on. 'Now tell me young lady, you must be Salinka,' He stole a glance at the pad sitting on his desk. 'Palchikova, I'm chief Carmichael, but you can call me Ted.' Dick's mouth fell open that's the first time he'd heard that one, Salinka smiled and shook his hand.

'I'm very pleased to meet you Ted, Dick has told me so much about you, I too am a huge fan of seafood pizzas.' For a second time Dick's mouth fell open, and as he looks at Salinka he's relieved to see her face is stoic, before the chief can answer there's a knock at the door.

'Yes, come in, *come in.*' It's Dick's old partner McDougall and much to the chief's chagrin, Salinka has turned all her attention to him. Old friendships renewed they must now get down to business, the chief holds up a hand and immediately phones his opposite number in Seattle, to see if he can shed any light, also, to float the idea that as the three missing females are all friends of theirs, he'd like to send a couple of, the chief looks at everyone and makes a hand motion to express his nose is growing longer. To send a couple of plain clothes officers to investigate, and will he give them assistance if required. This is something Dick and Salinka had to think about, they intend to keep a low profile, they certainly don't want to be seen with the police in tow. Dick concluded that was okay, just as long as it was on their terms, it transpired there is no new information, the three women seem to have disappeared off the face of the earth, Dick and

Salinka can expect assistance if they ask for it, other than that, they're on their own. McDougall insisted they visit the canteen, the moment they walk in there's a loud cheer accompanied by the banging of silverware on the dining tables. Dick raises a hand in recognition, then he points to Salinka with both index finger, tightens his lips and widens his eyes informing all and sundry that it was her doing.

*

Flying is one of Dick's passions, in another life he'd have been an airline pilot, the downfall to that was all those paper airplanes he used to make in class when he should have been studying math. Added to that was the amount of time he devoted to chasing potential young "air hostesses" in his grade, an appetite that formed at about the time a young girl, Sally Freebush, moved in next door and taught him everything he knows.

While Dick is sitting there absorbing every frisson this 707, his favourite plane has to offer, Salinka is sitting back entranced by the antics of Charlie Brown with whom she can't help seeing similarities to Dick. They're about three comfortable and trouble-free hours into their flight to Seattle, when out of the blue the plane tipped violently to the left, then to the right while at the same time plummeting a hundred feet. In the few seconds it took everyone to say their prayers a full recovery is made, but not without instilling the full panic and concern of the ninety or so passengers who have suddenly been decorated with oxygen masks that have dropped from the ceiling and are swinging ominously in their faces.

A hostess scrambles for a particular passenger and immediately he is being ushered into the cockpit. A message came over the Tannoy, everything is under control, there's no need for concern, the masks can be tucked back into their compartments. Dick and Salinka know something's up as they observe two hostesses in worried conversation, Dick decides to go and investigate, that is his stock-in-trade after all, he's soon back and in a whisper, he imparts the news.

'The pilot has had a heart attack, he's in a serious way, there's a doctor in attendance, an interesting upshot, according to the hostess the co-pilot is twelve years old and now that push has come to shove, he's bricking it.' Salinka is curious.

'Bricking it, what is bricking it?'

'It means, my innocent little Muscovite, our twelve-year-old pilot isn't potty trained.'

There's no doubt, since the incident there's a definite underlying uncertainty in the smoothness of the flight, outside Salinka notices an extremely dense cumulus cloud developing all around and five minutes later, rain, rain at 600 miles an hour, rain that must be plaguing the fears of our new, solo pilot, with gut-wrenching monotony as it piles into his screen at the business end. An announcement comes over the Tannoy.

"Will passengers please fasten their seatbelts, we're approaching bad weather and turbulence is expected. Thank you for your co-operation."

Everybody conforms and as a precaution some even scrutinize the advice on what to do in an emergency.

The children continue, blissfully unaware, colouring in Mickey Mouse, or Dumbo, or a brown bear catching his dinner. Dick is studying the airline magazine for a second time, when his attention is drawn by three lightning flashes in quick succession accompanied by some stiff turbulence. He and Salinka had just looked at each other when, frighteningly, there's a breathtaking hit and the plane sways violently with sustained aftershocks, it drops some fifty feet then immediately climbs swiftly, while the lights go out for an agonizing ten seconds. This is worse than anything they have ever experienced, it's enough to concern Salinka.

'You stay here, I think I'd better go see if I can help fly this thing, that's if they let me anywhere near the controls.' Dick takes Salinka's arm.

'Do you mean to tell me you can fly this machine?' She looks at him.

'I never flew commercial but I can handle a MiG-17 in my sleep, and don't forget, we stole the technology from Boeing in the first place.' She touches her forelock and grins reassuringly. 'This is your captain speaking, out…out the way Dick, *Dick* I need to get out.'

He watches his MiG pilot manoeuvre up the aisle in what are quickly worsening conditions, calmly she's negotiating with the two air hostesses, both of whose body language couldn't be more negative, one of them is pointing this passenger in the direction of her seat. Salinka stands firm, folds her arms, and leans against the entrance to the kitchenette, right on cue there's another big lurch as the plane hits more turbulence, one of the hostesses disappears altogether, while the other promptly sits on the lap of the passenger in seat number one. Salinka, the last woman standing, remains upright, leaning against the frame like nothing happened. The hostess who had the unfortunate liaison, sprung up and is looking hard at passenger 46a, she enters the pilot's domain, thirty seconds later she emerges and beckons this passenger in. The next twenty minutes are crucial, but not as crucial as they would have been without the MiG pilot, but that is fate's little secret, perhaps it was Dick's fancy, maybe he was just being partial, but five minutes after Salinka had entered the cockpit the whole flying experience seemed to calm down. It took two hours before preparations for landing were announced, in that time he saw Salinka only once, when she ambled down to ask if he wanted help fastening his seat belt, a grinning Dick fastened himself in. An air hostess swans up the plane checking on her passengers, she stopped at passenger 46b.

'Is that young lady a friend of yours?' She leaned on his courtesy table, 'Only, she's a very good pilot.'

'Yes, she is a friend of mine, she's very good period, tell me, how's your captain?' The hostess froze, her cheeks went white, her eyes said it all, Dick squeezed her wrist. 'You're doing a grand job, some people hold it together by helping fly a plane, while others hold it together for the sake of their charges.

*

The lobster at the hotel Blue Lagoon was something else, harvested from the seabed by a Mermaid, then serenaded all the way to the surface before being handed to a trio of beautiful fisherwomen who gently cosset it all the way to the hotel kitchen, where, instantly, dead in a pan of boiling water, the lobster finds itself floating amidst a host of winged crustaceans in sea heaven. Dick fancies himself as a writer, but sometimes he gets carried away, like that pretentious load of baloney, and has to re-write, it's a work in progress. Returning to reality, he sits back and looks deep into the eyes of the one he loves, he proffers his glass.

'Here's to the pilot who saved the day.' she grins.

'Well, put it another way, this pilot passed out once and came to about five hundred feet from the ground, so luck played a big part that day, as she did today. Our twelve-year-old co-pilot just lacked confidence, but he was confident enough to ask me to dinner tonight.'

'What? I hope you turned him down in favour of me.' Salinka beamed, her tantalizing green eyes sharply piercing her man.

'Of course I did my Yankee Darling, I always prefer my men potty trained.'

FORTY-SIX

'What the hell, a couple of New York cops, undercover cops, whatever that means, they never get out of bed probably, I wish the chief had steered 'em clear, instead we've got a couple of loafers sticking their noses in where they don't belong.'

'Cash, calm down, you'll aggravate your hernia, you've been like a dog who's dug up a wasp's nest ever since we found out this was gonna happen, all we gotta do is let'em in, tell'em what we know, which is diddly squat, and let'em undercover their way outta that.' Cash and Diamond think they're the crème de la crème of the Seattle police department, too high and mighty to be holding hands with a couple of interlopers and besides Cash has other plans. He knows at noon today a boatload of drugs are coming in and both want to be top dog and take all the glory. This little escapade, if it goes on too long, might jeopardise their whole plan and give Lee and Johnson the prize. 'Geeze.'

Cash and Diamond are polls apart. Diamond, of clean cut, fresh-faced demeanour, divorced, is your average all-round nice guy, he's 5.10, always smart with his Elvis quiff, always polite, a decent cop who has gained a lot of respect among the local Seattle community. Cash, on the other hand, never grew out of his juvenile acne, now, at 35, he has a face like a well-used dartboard, women have never taken to him and that has left him feeling bitter, he's also only 5.7, he drinks to drown his sorrows, resulting in a prematurely expanded waistline, none of which helps with his day-to-day relationships. Diamond feels sorry for him so they rub along together. Yeah, Cash has a special relationship with the chief, they've known each other since way back, so a lot of top jobs seem to fall their way, making them a successful partnership.

Light drizzle welcomed Dick and Salinka as they appeared outside their hotel just a couple of blocks from Beauty and The Feast. Their mood is low, the frivolities of last night are over, food, wine and lovemaking, all in their place, are the best things, but now it's all about the serious business of hunting down the abductors of their friends, and more importantly, find them and bring them home before it's too late. A cop car is parked across the street from their destination, the mood Dick's in police officer Cash had better be in a different frame of mind. Cash and Diamond crawl out of their vehicle as our two undercover officers hover outside the crime scene.

'You must be Chase, I'm Diamond, this is Cash.' Cash interrupts.

'Yeah, well, let's get this whole show over shall we, we've got bigger fish to fry.'
Chase didn't give anything away but he could easily have punched his lights out for that, Diamond placed the key in the lock, an act carried out many times by Helen or Julie. As Dick entered the salon it didn't escape him these were possibly the last steps of a carefree, excited young woman who was due to get married that day. The interior of Beauty and the Feast is Helen all over, Dick felt it the moment he entered. Different coloured ribbons and tassels hang on every handle, cheap glitzy chandeliers, Helen

used to dream about glitzy chandeliers, giant flowered wallpaper, gladiolas, all the colours under the sun, embossed with hints of silver and gold. On one wall, he saw it first reflected in a mirror, is that framed jigsaw of the Grand Canyon, it's a funny thing, he remembered straight off the couple of pieces he'd placed himself. Officer Cash brought Dick crashing back down to earth.

'Let's get this show on the road shall we, there ain't nothing to tell you so we might as well call it a day and all go our separate ways right now.' Salinka knows Dick is bursting at the seams, so she steps in.

'And I'm Palchikova, we didn't finish with the introductions.' Once again Cash hits rock bottom with his personal take on glass-ceiling thinking.

'Women in the police force, what's that all about, when there's so much to do in the home, that's where you cuties belong?' Unexpectedly and very quickly Chase grabs Cash by the throat, even more unexpected, when Diamond steps up, Salinka positions herself in his path, she smiles and raises an eyebrow, he falters, partly manners, unlike Cash he has more respect for women, but there's something else, her demeanor, her calm, he sensed she could be trouble but didn't know how or why. The air is toxic, this whole incident is the complete opposite to anything any of them had in mind for that day, Dick holds out his spare hand.

'Give me the keys.'

'We can't allow…..'

'*Give me the goddamn keys.*' Diamond fishes reluctantly in his pockets and hands Salinka the keys, Dick lets go of Cash, while at the same time orientating him towards the street.

'You two get the hell outta my sight.' For a moment nobody moves. '*Now.*'

The two grudgingly pull themselves together and slowly head towards the door, but then, Cash, tough, belligerent Cash, top dog of the Seattle police department, who thinks he can handle anyone and any situation gives these interlopers some passing words of advice, Salinka returns his ball with interest.

'If you want to try me on, I promise you I will break both your arms.' He turns and gives her a cocky inquisitive grin, he's amused, but that falters, now he sees her for what she really is. She's taller than he first realised, pellucidly fit and on the edge, challenging him to take her on, she's willing him, so strongly it's tangible. A strange doubt engulfs him, her cool, calculated demeanour of unqualified hardness, sucking the confidence right out of him. For the first time in his life he's uncertain of the consequences he never was any good at chess, Dick intervenes.

'A young woman was murdered here, on her wedding day, almost certainly by a man, our friends have been forcibly removed to God knows where, again, almost certainly by men, you don't have to be so protective towards men.' Cash finally gets it, he leaves the building without saying another word, Salinka pushes the door closed behind them.

'Jesus, I could have punched that jerk's lights out.' Salinka calmed Dick's venom.

'Yes, well, that wouldn't have done our cause any good would it.' He sat on one of the swivel chairs, and contemplating, slowly he began to turn himself around with his feet, gradually speeding up, Salinka, smiling to herself locked the door, took the keys, and went into a back room, where she unlocked the rear door, by this time Dick has followed her out.

'I thought I'd take a look outside, see if it throws up anything.'

Out the back there's a concrete area and a road that serves all the stores in the vicinity. There's a line of wooden panel dividing walls, separating and containing waste bins. There are endless signs, no parking without a permit, bins emptied on Fridays at 6 a.m. no smoking in the bins area, and one that says don't feed the pigeons or the tramps. Despite that, Dick noticed a cardboard bed with a few sad and meagre belongings, but no sign of its occupant. They spent the best part of the morning on the premises but didn't find anything that might advance their cause. There was one interruption, a young woman from "Drizzles Coffee Bar" across the street stuck her head in to ask who they were and is there any news, she knew nothing.

'No one does, it's a complete mystery, they were loved by everyone, we're all devastated, and poor Jo Marianne, on her wedding day, oh my God.' She whisked a shaking hand to her mouth, Dick frowned and nodded sympathetically, but inside he's still seething over that cop. There's nothing here for them, nothing to give a clue as to what happened, Dick is feeling uncommonly low and Salinka knows it.

'Come on, let's sample some of that Seattle coffee, something'll come up.'

Salinka was right, but it was much later on, at the end of the day. As they wandered back to their hotel, Dick noticed a handful of down and outs settling down for the night, in shop doorways, the stubborn ones who reject any offer of help from the city authorities, in favour of life on the streets. Men and women who have fallen through the cracks, Dick reflected on a couple of occasions it could have been him. At the hotel he took Salinka's arm and to her surprise they kept going, he's got an idea.

'Let's go take another look at the salon, things always look different at night.' They stepped inside. 'Don't put the lights on.' Dick went straight through to the back door and peered out of the window above a small sink where, outside, amongst the bins, a tramp is settling down for the night, on his cardboard bed, with his cardboard covers. Dick eyes his partner, it's something he could do, but it might be better coming from her.

'Go and see if he knows anything, if it's okay for me to show, give me a nod.'

As she approached Salinka noticed a slight shrinking of the covers accompanied by dead silence, she sensed a willing for her to go away, she didn't go away.

'Fella, it's alright, I'm a friend, I just want to ask you some questions.' There's a let-up with the shrinking, some fingers appear and alter the cardboard, just a bit, Salinka can see two coal-black eyes looking at her, she crouched down. 'Fella, I'm a friend, I'm nice, I just want to talk.'

'Wot about?' Is the curt reply.

'I'm a friend of Helen, Julie and Angel, I've come to find them.' An unexpected wail of pain came from beneath the covers, a lament of heart-rendering angst. Slowly the tramp sat up, since it happened, he's had no one to talk to, and he's wanted to so much, he's full of sadness and anger, and now, out of the blue, this woman turns up wanting to speak to him, that hadn't happened since Miss Helen and Miss Angel, and now they're no more.

'My friends have gorn,' He sounds so miserable, 'Thems were good to me.' In that instant Salinka understood everything, they'd befriended him, fed and looked out for him. They've been taken away, and with them, his lifeline, his hope, she took the plunge.

'I have a friend, he's nice too, we are going to find them, can I call him over?' The tramp gave a chin quivering nod, she beckons.

'My name is Salinka and this is Dick.'

'Hello my friend, what's your name?' Dick had heard it all from the back door, he understood, the tramp thought for a moment.

'Don't ave no name, I've forgotten it, John, they calls me John.' Dick continued.

'Well John, it's good of you to speak to us, do you know what happened here that morning?' John looks at them.

'Shan't never forget.' There was a pause, then he came out with it. 'A big white van pulls in ere it wakes me up with its engine roarin' an doors slammin', they didn't see me, people don't, them just walks past.'

'How many were there?' It's Dick.

'Three, there were three o' them devils.'

'Can you describe them, do you remember what they looked like?'

'Oh yes, I remember what them looked like.' John became animated. 'A big geezer was dishing out horders, the other two were doin all the donkey work, carpet fitters, Pah!' John spat. 'One of 'em was tall the other short.' For the first time, John smiled, 'Pie.' Dick responded.

'Yes, you can have as many pies as you can eat.' John is grinning, half toothless.

'Pie, LOS132PIE, that been the licence plate, and,' There's more, Dick can't believe their luck. 'And the big'un in charge.' John, leans forward and raises a hand to his head 'He got scars on his 'ead, just ere, now the airs don't grow.' That was a description made in heaven, John might as well have given them a photograph, Salinka leaned forward and put a hand on his shoulder.

'Thank you, John.' Dick can see the little old fella is made up, but not as much as he's about to be, as Salinka gives him a hundred dollars, in ten-dollar bills.

FORTY-SEVEN

Helen worked out eight people are living in this house, she won't call them a family, that has implications of love and respect, of decency and normality, no, those four attributes don't exist here, in this living hell, only selfishness, arrogance, greed, and cruelty, that's all, and the endless laundry, ironing, mending, and cleaning. Oh yes, the cleaning, everything in the basement area has to be cleaned, spick and span, neat as a pin, a phrase Helen would never use herself but now is all she hears coming from some chargehand, a woman whose name Helen has so far managed to avoid using, she wants to escape, not acclimatise.

The slave, for that is what she is, sleeps down here, eats down here, does everything down here, her only natural light and fresh air comes from a few windows, out of her reach, but can be opened by rotating certain handles that are attached to them by long rods. If she stands, with her back tight against the wall, and looks up, on a clear night, she can see the stars. She knows it's a big house by the size and height of this seven-roomed basement. The smallest room, that she shares with the heating system, is her living accommodation, her bed, a simple sleeping bag on wooden slats suspended on blocks four inches off the ground. Once, when the heating system broke down, she and her bed were bundled, by the charge hand, who didn't say a word, into another room and locked in, the whole day she was there and when she was released the laundry baskets were full, it took her all night to catch up, and she had to catch up. Helen hasn't seen Julie or Angel since that fateful day, she has no idea Jo Marianne had been murdered. The one colourful thought she carries around with her is of Jo getting married, that, she is certain must have happened, somehow, mustn't it? You might think Helen is too compliant, too eager to get on with her jobs, too ready to obey, it isn't eagerness drives her on, and it certainly isn't the non-existent pay packet or the food, she dreads to think what gross ingredients might find their way into the porridge, or the soup, or the fish pie. No, it's the entertainment, she has witnessed a girl being beaten to death for not carrying out her duties, for insubordination, that was enough to keep her going, she got the message. And there's something else, a powerful thought she hangs on to, Helen thinks Dick is somehow going to be her knight in shining armour. It's been three or four months, she's lost count but still Helen holds on to that hope, only in her darkest hours, in her sleeping bag, does she sometimes begin to lose faith. That's when she remembers Salinka finishing off that Russian, with Dick terminating that pilot. She's been told in graphic detail by Angel how Dick saved her, and what happened in Brussels. She thinks her friends are looking for her, otherwise, without that thought, that dream, what hope, she might as well give up.

Julie has no idea Helen is stuck working her guts out in the basement of the same house she cleans from top to bottom, before starting over, it's like painting the Golden Gate Bridge, she certainly has no idea it's Helen who's doing her laundry. All this work is carried out in silence, she's not allowed to speak during the day, only at night, in whispers, to a black man whose name is Harvey, Harvey is a gentleman and he's Julie's strength. They share living accommodation in a partitioned-off section in one of the garages, he has to maintain two greenhouses and look after the grossers' animals, that's what they call them, the grossers, because they're gross, family pets include four dogs and six horses. Harvey is nice, and so is Julie, they each depend on the other for their sanity, on the rare occasion when Julie thinks the worst, Harvey being sent away, or dying, she begins to panic and shake, he knows what she's thinking, they've talked about it, he comforts her by quietly singing lullabies until she calms down. As I said, Julie has no idea where Helen is, no more than she knows the whereabouts of Angel, she would be devastated if she knew what had happened to Jo Marianne. The two friends were both there, watching that beating, cleverly kept apart and concealed from one another, Julie is a survivor, she's been a prostitute, she's tough, she won't be beaten, certainly no pun intended. Helen and Julie have lived and will continue to live, whatever it takes.

Angel could be in deep trouble here, she could, let's face it, be dead, when we think what happened to Margareta Vittua. If we look back to her state of mind approximately eight months earlier, to just before Dick walked into her life, she would have been in trouble, but she has grown since then, she's no longer that frightened girl. For one thing, she has direct experience that miracles do happen, she has first-hand knowledge of Dick and Salinka's determination and courage, she knows, in the past, Salinka allowed herself to be trafficked for the greater good, and who's to say she won't do it again, for her this time? She has no idea Salinka is a highly trained killer, Angel certainly isn't, though she does come with a fine set of qualities, John the tramp will attest to that. Now it's her turn to be amazing, she can't be a guardian angel like Dick was for her, but she can be a rock to a girl named Jessie. Helen and Julie were deemed too old for this game, but don't tell them that, Angel was picked out and sent to another destination, to a different type of servitude, to do that woman's work that's as old as time. After all Dick's efforts, his planning, his sponsorship, still Angel ends up in prostitution, at the moment she's Jessie's rock and transversely, looking after her, caring for Jessie is giving Angel a reason to go on, that, and the hope Dick and Salinka are on their way.

And so it is, our three women have had their liberty, their lives, their very souls snatched away from them, and in a country that welcomes all the world with a huge statue dedicated to liberty, the irony of ironies. It is as difficult to right the wrongs of debauched men, and hunt them to oblivion, as it is for a sparrow to move the mountain, dust by dust.

Dick is listening to McDougall's ringing tone and hoping he's in his office, McDougall is standing just outside listening to his phone ring and trying to get away from jobsworth Bygraves, who wants to know if he should organise the sweepstake this month, as Letterman made such a hash of it last time.

'Jobbie, I'll tell you what, you do it.'

'Yeah, but if I do it, you know what'll happen?' McDougall looks at his phone.

'No, but do it anyway, I've gotta answer the phone.' He looks at it ringing on his desk, then back at Bygraves. 'The phone.' Bygraves does a shoddy about-turn and walks off as pleased as Punch, McDougall is wondering what he's let himself in for as he dives across his office and picks up the receiver. 'NYPD, McDougall speaking.' There's no small talk, not today, it's all still ahead of them, the long journey, the uphill climb, they'd had some luck, LOS132PIE, and a good description, but still there's a lot of work to do. Dick gave McDougall the licence plate number and said he'll call back in a couple of hours. In the meantime, our undercover cops spend another twenty minutes in the Salon, just in case, then it's over to Drizzles for coffee, where Salinka shares her thoughts with Dick.

'Hm, if it's going to be Los Angeles, as we expect, Stella is going to have her work cut out.'

'Hold on a minute, who said Stella's gonna show up again?'

'Come on Dick, you know you like the getup.'

'Yeah, but that's beside the point.' He's deep in thought. 'O.K. you win, but on one condition.' Salinka is gazing past him and out through the window.

'What's that?'

'You wear the getup.'

Her mind is elsewhere, across the street their two Seattle cops are sitting in an unmarked vehicle observing, not them, but some address. A black van has parked behind them, two covertly armed heavies are advancing along each side of the cop's vehicle, probably to coerce them into the back of the van with the minimum of fuss, Salinka sees all this and immediately gets it, she grabs Dick's arm.

'Come, now! *Come,* our two cops are being hijacked by armed men.' No one on this busy high street has a clue what's going down, life in Seattle continues apace, oblivious to the perils of these two cops. Arm in arm our two avengers leave the Coffee shop and head across the street, looking for all the world like any ordinary couple who might be out buying a wedding ring.

They separate, they've got seconds to do this, Dick is hovering while his Amazonian beauty turns to her unsuspecting bruiser, raises an eyebrow and asks if there's anything she can do for him, he's thrown, tantalized, he can't think. Through the goon's jacket Salinka glimpses the shape of a gun pointing at Diamond's back, she grabs it forcing it downwards and away from her, it goes off, shooting the jerk in the leg. The back of her clenched fist flies a lightning semicircle upwards and smacks him violently on the mouth shattering his lips against his teeth, now a tributary to a river of blood, the same hand, mean and merciless chops the bullet wound, hard, the jerk's in trouble. Dick has his man's gun pointing downwards but it doesn't go off, his other arm is around the dummy's neck, he has a knack of pressing the Adam's apple, that instantly spells trouble for the recipient. Diamond, off the hook, comes to Salinka's aid while Cash puts the boot in right where it hurts. The gangster, seized with pain falls to his knees taking Dick, who manages to own the gun, with him, he hands it to Cash. Right on cue a radio message comes over the air-waves.

'Cash, Diamond, a gunshot has been heard in your vicinity, can you attend over?' Salinka eyes the pair.

'Sorry guys you're on your own, Dick's got far bigger fish to fry, while this little cutie, well, I've got the housework to finish off.' Arm in arm, they head for the hotel, leaving Cash and Diamond to sort out their own problems.

FORTY-EIGHT

This time McDougall answers the phone instantly, like he'd been sitting on it, he's got some news that he just knows is gonna blow his friends minds.

'O.K. Dick, it's a hire vehicle belonging to *White Van Line,* that's WVL Los Angeles, I called them up and guess what? LOS132PIE went AWOL and was found two days later burnt out in a disused quarry on the outskirts. I got in touch with forensics, there wasn't much left of the van but they did find something of interest, a silencer. Here's the clincher, the bullet that went through the dead girl also went through the silencer.'

Dick knows there's a WVL New York, and you can bet your bottom dollar there'll be a WVL Seattle. He's right, they're walking into the smart uptown offices right now, so smart there's a brand-new white van sitting plumb in the window, Dick strolls over to the desk while Salinka takes a look at the interior of the vehicle.

'Can I help you sir?' Is the pleasant greeting from the young woman at reception. Dick shows his warrant card, especially arranged for such occasions by the chief, all that O-mega 3 fatty acid, in those seafood pizzas, is finally paying off.

'I'm enquiring about one of your vans, licence plate LOS132PIE, what can you tell me about it?' By this time Dick is joined by his other half. The young woman is very efficient, so is the company, their records are bang up to date.

'That was one of ours, sir, it was never returned and our records show it was destroyed by fire, somewhere iiiiinnn…Los Angeles.' She'd found it.

'Do your records show who was the last person to rent it?' The receptionist returns to her ledger, Dick looks at Salinka, then back at the woman.

'Our records say it was rented by a Mr. G. Washington, it was supposed to be out for the week, but our Los Angeles branch never saw it.'

'A Mr. G. Washington, hmm.' Dick mused. 'Do you think he was related?'

'What was that officer Chase?' For an instant Dick closed his eyes and in that moment he's standing in front of his mom's hall mirror wearing his brand-new uniform for the first time and holding his State coat-of-arms logoed warrant card, his mom's face proudly smiling around his arm, Dick opens his eyes.

'Nothing, it was nothing, how did this, Mr. Washington,' Dick can hardly keep a straight face. 'How did he pay?' The girl returned to her ledger, she ran a delicate finger up and down and side to side.

'He paid by cheque, officer.'

'Do you know which bank, are there any details?' Again, the receptionist returns to her records, she's concentrating.

'Yes, it's all here, it was, ah, no, it's telling me the cheque bounced, it was a forgery.' Dick knows when he's hit a brick wall.

'Thank you ma'am, for your most thorough, diligent, and helpful, err, helpfulness.'

'It was my pleasure sir, and if there's anything else I can help you with, please don't hesitate to ask, you have a nice day now.'

Fifteen minutes was all it took, a roving reporter witnessed the whole thing, two passing strangers, a couple of brave bystanders, heroes in waiting, saved Seattle's top officers, Cash and Diamond, from possible torture and ending up being buried in the foundations of some road bridge, it was these two officers who brought down the notorious Seattle Pacific Drugs Ring, SPIDER, as it was so-called. The press got straight onto the chief for the story, and before you know it a car is sent to pick the pair up, he wants to thank them personally. A squad car stops outside White Van Line, the result of a hunch that paid off. While they book in at the desk, under her breath the young inexperienced female officer makes a curious and unnecessary observation.

'A word of warning to you both, chief Eastwood wears a toupee.' She raises her eyebrows and just manages to conceal a smile.

'Chase, Palchikova, come in, sit down, I've ordered coffee, we don't have anything stronger, it blurs the mind and dulls the intuition, we pride ourselves at being on the ball here at SPD, that's like NYPD only no one has ever bothered to make a TV show about us so it doesn't have the same ring, mind you, after today's little skirmish there could be a contract in the offing.' He laughed, forcing a glimmer of mirth from our two undercover agents. 'What took you to White Van Line, I'm interested to see how team "private eye" works?' Dick told him about John, the tramp, who'd seen it all, how he remembered the licence plate, and that there were three men involved.

'Where're on our way to Los Angeles because that's where the van was found burnt out.' Chief Eastwood, no relation, although he did have his moments when he was a young officer, so he said, thanked them for their due diligence, swift daring action, and....

'Tonight, as a reward, one of Seattle's top brass, a man who was Mayor here two years running, is holding his annual antislavery bash at his home and has invited you along as his special guests, it's his way of showing the city's gratitude and appreciation for your courage.'

Los Angeles is their next port of call, they had intended to take the night Greyhound, it's fifteen hours and they both needed some shuteye, instead, they've altered their plan to catch the early bus.

Tonight it's glam and glitter, unexpectedly they find themselves shopping, Salinka has gone to buy herself something "chic" for the do, while Dick is going to hire himself a tux.

They say there's a first time for everything, only this little gem takes the biscuit, our heroes are about to be announced. Heralded into a large, white ballroom with a marble staircase leading up to a horseshoe balcony. Where family portraits hang out and observe, some in military uniform dating back to the civil war. In a corner, a jazz quartet is gently caressing Cole Porter. On one side there's a large ornate stone fireplace that has above it the family crest, Freedom to Choose-Choose to be Free…it's a pseudo log gas fire. A slick haired, black trousered, white jacketed, master of ceremonies, performs the task.

'Officer Richard Chase and officer Salinka Palchikova of the NYPD.' A hawk-eyed silence followed by some stifled applause and mumbled appreciation, Dick and Salinka, smiling and vaguely nodding, make their way over to a waiter who's circulating with a tray of drinks.

'I bet this isn't your idea for a good night out.' Salinka said, taking a flute of champagne from an ornate silver tray, the waiter nods his head stiffly and continues to circulate. Over Salinka's shoulder Dick can see their host making his way towards them, he's the only one wearing plus fours and riding boots, complete with spurs, his eyes are sharp, like a vulture's, it's these two or nothing, partygoers nod and curtsy in his wake like he's some sort of American royalty, Dick comments under his breath.

'Brace yourself.'

'Chase, Palchikova, Colonel Mackenzie Straith-North, it's good to meet you, I gather you're the heroes who possibly thwarted the kidnap of two of the chief's best men.' Salinka doesn't like him from the get-go.

'There's no possibly about it, we saved their skinny necks.' Straith-North smiled, and in that smile, he told her, you commie Russian trash - you have no place walking on this planet, a rare oversight neither Chase nor Palchikova picked up on. He's an overbearing, larger-than-life character, six foot plus, and full of himself.

'We used to be the Straith-Souths, my great, great, great granddaddy was notoriously involved with the slave trade, it caused the ancestors a great deal of pain, embarrassment, and indignation. So much so my great-grandfather decided to change the family name, we went from South to North, at least now we're heading in the right direction, that's a family joke.' He laughed. 'Yes, well, now we work tirelessly to eradicate modern slavery from across the world, ah, I can see elements of doubt creeping in, but I can assure you, even in our great U.S. of A, it goes on, hence this little annual fundraiser. Now, protocol dictates I have a duty to perform.' He doesn't beat about the bush, he's looking around, 'I just need to thank you on behalf of the whole State.' He raises his voice. 'Ladies and Gentlemen, if I can have your attention, please, *just for one minute…..*
AND THE BAND.'…'Thank you…You wouldn't be blamed for thinking our two special guests are celebrities off the TV, because they are, in fact, directly from the NYPD.' Muffled laughter. 'It is with great pleasure we have with us tonight the two officers who so bravely, and without a thought for their own safety, saved the lives, as I was so vehemently reminded by the young lady, of two of our hardworking police officers.' He humbly looked at Dick, but somehow managed to ignore the Russian female. 'Good people of Seattle, I give you, *our very special guests,* officers Chase and Palchikova.' Applause, adulation, and wolf whistles fill the air, Straith-North turns back to his guests.

'Sorry you didn't manage to get a word in, these affairs do tend to stretch one's time enormously, enjoy your evening.' With that he strode off, Dick turned to Salinka.

'I hope those wolf whistles were for you.'

A strange night unfolded, not what our two heroes expected, or were used to, Dick put it down to west coast superiority complex. It was a night for the hierarchy and the well-to-do, a getting together of the Seattle elite who have a way of rejecting the run-of-the-mill, the hoipolloi, the irks of this world, as they see them, and although Dick and Salinka are good mixers, across all boundaries, this set made them feel like positive outsiders. There are exceptions, there are always exceptions, two women Salinka identified straight away, she had seen them on the street, now, somehow, dressed in a way that appeared completely outside their financial zone, are they call girls, or wives who dabble for their own sexual desires, too bored, too wealthy, two impotent husbands?

'Hello.'

Dick and Salinka turn around, someone is suddenly addressing them from behind. 'Hello, I'm Mary, I'm eleven, it's okay I'm mad, at least that's what everyone thinks, I'm not mad really, I'm eleven, oh, did I just say that? My favourite film is The Railway Children, what's yours, it doesn't matter, it's probably an adult film anyway? What do you think of the champers, it's the cheap stuff, Daddy always gets the cheap stuff out for these occasions? You're the heroes everybody's talking about, I was a hero once, I saved one of our maids, she must have been very homesick she couldn't stop crying, I used to give her sweeties. Anyway, I told daddy he had to let her go, he said he gave her some spending money and her fare home, we didn't see her again.' Salinka smiled.

'It's heroine.'

'Sorry miss?'

'You were a heroine, you're a lady.' A tall thin woman, dressed as a maid, homed in.

'Miss Mary, there you are, it is getting late, and it's school tomorrow, say goodnight to your friends, I'm sorry, I hope Miss Mary wasn't disturbing you with her tales.' The tall maid smiled at them, Dick makes light of it.

'Not at all, Mary has delighted us.' Salinka added.

'She's not a bit mad, surely, it's us, we're the mad ones, aren't we?' For a fleeting moment they saw the maid's smile disappear then return.

'Will you please excuse us?' With the maid leaning down talking to Mary, telling her not to speak to strangers, they walk away, Salinka looks towards the ceiling and comments.

'Are you thinking what I'm thinking?'

'Well, if you're thinking this place stinks and you'd like to dump a ton of horseshit on top of this lot from that balcony up there, then I guess I am.' She marvels at him.

'Do you know that's amazing?'

FORTY-NINE

Dick is in deep thought as they trundle down the freeway, as he sees it they have two options, one is, as Salinka had already pointed out, for him and Stella to trawl the bars and side streets in the hope of coming across their friends, that, or chance bumping into the big bruiser with the scar and the missing hair, hopefully with Tom and Jerry in tow, and show them they've won first prize in the sweepstake, whatever, it all seems a bit hit-and-miss to him, he would have preferred something a little more tangible.

They both slept, on and off, but as the bus pulled into the halfway halt, for their big break, Dick and Salinka find themselves wide awake, the thirty or so passengers all get off and head towards "Terri's Oasis, the home of Ma's Tasty Grilled Chicken Legs." Dick looks at the menu before addressing the hovering waitress.

'Can I have the steak sandwich with all the trimmings?'

'I'll have the same, please.' Salinka spies her backup. 'D'you want a beer?' He nods. 'With two beers, that's it, thanks.' Dick is observing her. 'What?' she enquired cutely, while looking about.

The fat lady with the Chihuahua in her handbag is sitting a couple of tables away, the junior football team are all seated noisily at the back. Three girls, she guessed sisters, including twins, who'd been playing cards most of the journey, are sat in the corner laughing their heads off. There's the tall individual who looks like a down and out has found a bus ticket and is travelling just because he can and for something to do, the whole of America is here in some form or other. Two indigenous Indians are sporting their new-fangled "western" clothes, looking for all the world as if they're trying to fit in, it struck Salinka, it's everyone else who needs to fit in.

'Do I look Russian, is that what you're finding so amusing?'

'No, I was just thinking how completely different this is to the last time we called into one of these places, you know, when we had to deal with your two Russian comrades.' Salinka let out a long thoughtful sigh.

Soon the food is eaten, the beer is drunk, the bathroom has been inspected, and the Chihuahua has christened a bus wheel, everyone climbed on board and inevitably it was as if the stop hadn't happened, it has become the past, the stuff of time travel that will one day be the subject of debate as to whether it can be visited again via some wormhole.

It was nightfall by the time the bus pulled in, a Yellow Cab took them to what the driver assured them was a seedy hotel in a part of the city where he wouldn't walk his dog, it's raining lightly, but it's not cold. As they enter the dingy, dusty foyer, the desk is unattended, a quiet radio plays a feverish crowd enjoying some football match dispersed by two commentators explaining and debating play like a couple of comedians who didn't realise the last joke had already left town. Dick can only wait so long he reached over and turned the radio right up.

'What the fuck' A fat man appears from out the back, followed by a slim young woman, the man is indiscreetly adjusting his fly.

'Can I help you?' He's sweating, he's turning the radio down when he clocks Salinka, his whole demeanor alters. 'Yes, ma'am, and what can I do for you?' He wished.

'We want a room.' It's Dick, the fat man hasn't taken his eyes off the woman.

'Well, that'll be for two hours then, at least.' His inflection wishing it was him, Dick, never wanting to miss a trick, responds.

'Actually, that would be a week, but we'll start with two nights and see if she can keep up.'
The room is a dingy, orange-painted hovel with curiously shaded wall lights, like some big-game hunter had shot and decapitated his prey, there's a Gorilla's head on one wall and a Zebra's head on another. The double bed looks a bit on the small side and strangely high, Salinka gently perched herself on top of it, at least it's soft she thought. Eyeing Dick she threw a suggestion into the heady mix of this sexual enclave.

'Give me half an hour and Stella can be ready.'
Dick is staring out the window, his face is being intermittently lit by the flashing neon he's gazing at across the street, it's a naked couple in blue, copulating, floating in the missionary position on a bed made up of the stark black night, made blacker by the intermittent disappearance of their electric writhing bodies. People are entering and leaving a live sex show, Dick noticed they were mostly single, mostly men, with some couples out for a "starter".

There are women standing in groups, talking, smoking, some girls patrolling solo, all touting for trade, it had stopped raining. He swung around unaffected by the scene, he's seen it all before, he's the consummate professional, he's come to do a job and that job is concentrating his mind, it's all-consuming. He thinks of Angel, how she didn't want this and how he fought hard to keep her from it, he eyes his brave, tough girl, he knows what she's prepared to do, the risks she'll take, a strange occupation, almost amusing, but this is not a joke, and it's not a game.

'O.K.' He approved with absolute certainty, 'Bring on Stella.'

FIFTY

This isn't going to be a walk in the park, and Salinka is in no doubt about it, for one thing she has to be accepted, the new girl on the block, an outsider, potentially waltzing in and stealing their clients, ironically, she doesn't want their punters, but that's not how it looks. These women and girls might be 'pros' when it comes to being practiced in the art of base, sexual allurement, but there's something remarkable about Stella that puts her streets ahead. Salinka is naturally modest, something her mother had instilled into her from an early age, whereas Stella, is a different animal altogether, she's a potent, sexual deviant, a total looker, she's taller than average and pellucidly fit, and she's the only Punk on the block, Dick isn't going to let her out of his sight. Within earshot he stops and peers into a laundrette, empty except for a young couple making out amidst the rumble of tumble dryers pumping hot air into a load of damp, slowly cooking nylon. The man, a young stud, with his back to the windows, sees reflected in a large chromed steel mirror screwed to the end wall, some weirdo peering in, casually he raises a hand and explodes a single stiff finger toward the ceiling, Dick turns his back on them, if the jerk isn't satisfied with that he'll just have to deal with it. Stella makes a beeline for a lone girl standing, traditionally, by a lamp post, the girl speaks to Stella.

'You're in big trouble when my pimp turns up, being beautiful won't save your ass girl, no siree, he'll whip you as soon as look at you.'

'Will he?...Well. Listen Babe,' Stella is branching out into the vernacular. 'I guess if you give me the information I'm looking for, I can get the hell outta here and you'll have saved my skinny ass, what d'ya say?'

'O.K. little miss detective, what have I got that you want?'

'I'm hunting down my sisters, girl, their names are Helen, Julie, and Angel.' The girl, no more than twenty, looked curiously at Stella, but with no sign of recognition.

'That's a lot of sisters can't say them names ring any bells, though, well, one of them might, if I think hard, it all depends.' The girl shrinks like a snail withdrawing into its shell as a rant of disbelief comes from a passing vehicle that quickly screeches to a halt in front of them, a tall, slick-looking waster jumps out and makes straight for Stella.

'What you doin' woman, interferin with my girl when she's sposed to be workin, a, A?' He pushes her, while Dick shifts from leaning to standing.

'I'm looking for work, I need a position, can you help me sir.' Stella knows how to get the best out of this tripe, she can massage their fragile little egos. 'I'm good.' She pleads. 'Will you give me a break, please?' Dick leans back against the wall and melts into the shadows, the pimp is struck by Stella's individuality, though he doesn't know that word, he's thinking more about her cute ass and the money it might bring in for him, he's pleased with his slick business acumen that's going to lead him to say what he's about to say.

'I want a thousand dollars a night, the rest you make, you can keep, that's the deal.' Stella surprises him with her reply as she nods toward the girl.

'A thousand between us and half that if it's rainin.' The pimp smiles.

'What's your name strange girl, and where you from?'

'Stella, my name's Stella, I'm from New York City.' The pimp takes out a thin cigar, lights up and takes a couple of long drags before he spits on the sidewalk.

'Well Stella from New York City.' He stripped her naked with his eyes. 'I've got no doubts over you, I'll tell yer what I'm gonna do, as a special favour just between us.' He nods at the other girl. 'If you can bring that bitch up to five hundred a night, you'll both save yourselves a beating, fall short and I'll whip your asses anyways.' He dropped his cigar and pulverised it into the sidewalk with his foot before getting into his motor and tearing off, it starts to rain again, Stella faces the girl.

'What you said interested me, "One of them might", might what, be known to you, is that what you meant, what's your name anyway?' The girl is perplexed, these are strange times, it's never happened like this before.

'My name's Colleen, I can't help you I must earn some cash or my life won't be worth living.

'Colleen, this is your lucky night, you come with me, you help me out and you'll earn your money, without lifting a finger or opening your legs, I promise. Oh!' Stella stopped short and clicked her fingers, she raises an eyebrow. 'There is one drawback, I've just remembered, we'll have to put up with my pimp.' Stella turned her head and raised her voice. 'Dick, come and meet Colleen.' Dick steps forward out of the shadows, his face, blue then pale, blue then pale, as his white skin reflects the intermittent flash of the neon copulating couple.

'Hi Colleen, I'm Dick, I hope this floozy isn't giving you any trouble.'

The rain decided to take a turn for the worst, there's a bar just fifty yards up the street, so they decide to take shelter in, This American Institution, no, I'm not about to wax lyrical, that's just the name of the bar.

'So how come you work for that jerk, can't you go solo, then surely all you earn will be yours?' It's Stella being curious.

'So you're not one of us then?' Now Colleen's being curious. 'You don't know how it works, I thought you were different, and he's not your pimp, is he.'

'No, you're right, we *are* looking for our friends though, you said you might know one of them, which one?'

'Angel, I know Angel.' Colleen hesitated, then backtracked. 'I was on my own once, before Jason took me over, I had no choice, he turned up one night, as nice as apple pie, saying he was a punter. We went to a secluded spot looking out over the whole of Los Angeles, he beat me up and told me from now on I'm working for him.' Dick wanted to know about Angel.

'It's not that I'm not interested, but you know Angel, where is she now, can you show us?' Colleen looked at the pair of them.

'What's in it for me if I help you?' Stella looked straight at her.

'We'll free you from the pimp.' Colleen tossed her head back.

'That ain't never gonna happen, no way.' Her inflection is sad, nostalgic, remembering a past, pre-him, all gone, Stella leaned forward and spoke with quiet, confident certainty.

'Oh yes it can, you take us to Angel and you won't see that pimp again, and we'll give you five hundred dollars.'

FIFTY-ONE

Colleen figured she has nothing to lose, her life is a pretty sad existence since Jason forced himself into it, so what if these two turn out to be a couple of oddballs, it won't be the first time, she'll just have to grin and bear it, there's nothing new under the sun. Stella can see Colleen is worried, what are these strangers really after? She can't imagine being in her shoes, she's come prepared, smiling at Colleen she takes something from the leather shoulder bag she always carries.

'There's five hundred in this roll there's no need to count it, it's all here, there'll be another five hundred when we find Angel.' Colleen is looking at the roll, her doubt slowly eking away like a balloon that's been pierced just below the knot, she upends it and peers into the verso.

'Get outta here.' She says as she upends it a second time. 'What is this, some kinda joke, this isn't for real, things like this don't happen to me?' Dick does the honours.

'We're real okay, our friends are real too and they've been kidnapped, we're trying to track them down, now, please tell us, what do you know about Angel?' Still Colleen is working it all out in her head.

'And you reckon you can get Jason off my case?' Stella leans back on her chair and folds her arms.

'Don't worry your pretty little head about him.' She leans forward. 'He'll be dealt with, I promise.

Dick and Salinka are now standing opposite a row of rundown stores, but only the dark open doorway between two of them has their attention, Colleen brought them here, she's now back at her lamp post, she's not required for this bit, she'll only be in the way.

The doorway between a closed heel bar and crummy kebab outlet, with its skewered meatloaf slowly turning to the tune of "Love is in the Air" wafting through an open window, is punctuated with men and women entering and leaving. That, according to Colleen, is the brothel where Angel is forced to work. She had been brought here a couple of times by her pimp, some prearranged orgy was requested by a VIP punter and Angel was used, with a couple of other girls, anyway, that's how she knows her, and her friend Jessie.

'I'll go in and take over the desk, give me five minutes, then you come over and we'll take it from there.' Dick can't wait to go, Angel needs him, Salinka knows what's going on in his mind.

'Be prepared if she's not there won't you.' Sensing he'll be disappointed if she isn't.

'She's there.' He turned to her. 'She has to be.' Dick has a look of desperation on his face.

There's some creep sitting at a wide, built-in pine desk, watching a miniature TV, a girl is half lying on a lounger trying to look ravishing, inviting, Dick looks at her and then at the back door willing her to leave, she gets it, important private conversation between pimps.

'I'm taking a pee.' She walks out, the jerk watching the TV, speaks.

'The Bulls have just scored and the Tigers are fighting back, if you're after some ass just wait a minute will yer, it ain't going nowhere?' Dick can't wait.

'Wow, let me see that.' He came around to watch the game, but his concentration is fixed on a small fire extinguisher that's hanging precariously off the wall, the next second the game's over for this jerk, and the crowd roar uproariously. Quickly Dick slumps him onto the floor and under the desk, he opens a couple of draws, in the second one are lengths of rope and some handcuffs, the accoutrements of the trade, Salinka appears as Dick is tying the jerk up, then the girl returns from her pee.

'Where's Johnny disappeared to?' Salinka is on the ball as she distracts her.

'Jason stopped by for him, some punter refusing to cough up with Colleen.'

'It's always happening, those bastards want ya to perform then don't wanna pay up.' The girl slumps back onto her recliner. 'God, it's warm tonight.'
Dick, stands up and instantly the phone rings, he lets it ring twice then answers it with one hand and hangs up with the other.

'Yes,' He feigns conversation, 'Angel, hold on, I'll see.' He looks at the girl. 'Have we got Angel in?'

'Angel, who wants her, she's useless?' Dick looks at the girl, puts his hand over the mouthpiece, and says again.

'Is she here?' The girl takes a deep breath.

'Yeah, she's here, she's in the lounge, with her friend, nervous Jessie, the silly cow, I don't know what she sees in her.' Dick blags a conversation and hangs up, but leaves the phone off the hook, now he's wondering how to do it. Somewhere a male murmur of ejaculation is harmonising with some woman who's faking it, a loo flushes, a distant kettle is answered, a door opens, releasing, for a moment, the source of *Love is in the Air,* the door closes and the football becomes prevalent again, Dick switches it off. Right on cue some punter enters, he's drunk, he leans precariously on the desk.

'Is Angel ready for me?' He looks at his watch and tries to focus. 'I'm ready for her.' Dick sees his chance.

'Stella, follow this asshole to the lounge will you, no doubt Angel is expecting him, she'll take you both to her room, I'll catch you up.' The punter looks at Dick.

'Did you just call me an asshole?'

'Yes, I believe I did, you got a problem with that.' Dick is smiling at him, the punter has got one thing on his mind, he returns Dick's smile and tinged with a drunk's laughter he points at him.

'I like you, I like a man.' He sniggers. 'I like a man with a sense of humour, pity you haven't… pity you haven't…it's a pity you… Oh fuck it.' He said and stumbled off. Stella grabs his sleeve.

'Wait my friend.' She holds an open hand towards Dick. 'Second draw down.' She's grinning, Dick gets it and hands her some rope, Stella gleams at the drunk punter, waiving the rope in front of his face. 'I think I'll join in, I like being tied up.' The drunk, eager, looks at her.

'I like being tied up too.'

'Do you now, come on then, let's do it.'

Angel glances at a small wall clock, she ponders, oh god is it that time already. The door opens, it's her expected regular, expressionless, Angel stands up and heads to the door, another girl remains seated, glued to the TV, Angel speaks to her.

'I'll see you Jess, I won't be far away.' For the first time, she sees this strange woman with her punter, her face is a vivid question, to which Stella responds.

'Our friend here likes to be tied up, so I thought I'll help you, what's your name?'

'I'm Angel.' She speaks quietly, uninterestedly. 'You're new, what's your name?' Stella stands there, she can't help smiling, all Punked up and ready for action, she knows what she looks like, she also knows Angel is aware of her even though they've never met, Salinka is about to get a kick, the rise of a lifetime that will make her day.

'I'm Salinka, but you know me as Stella.' Was all she needed to say, Angel burst into tears, fell to her knees, and buried her face in her hands, her prayers have been answered, her dreams have come true, unperturbed Stella looks at the punter.

'My reputation precedes me, she knows she's in for a good time, look at her, she can't wait.' Stella reaches down and takes Angel's arm. 'Come on gorgeous.' She encourages. 'Show us to your room, I've got some business to attend to.'

Just then it happened, right out the blue, right when you don't need it and least expect it, there are two gunshots in quick succession, Stella swings into action instantly knocking the punter out cold with her 9mm piece, she ties him up and drags him behind the sofa, Angel with her friend Jessie, can only look on in astonishment.

'You two stay here and don't even think about leaving this room.' Stella has calculated it's a 95% certainty she'll be safe just being one of the girls, she's about to find out it's Dick who isn't safe, unknown to her she has 42.7 seconds to intervene before it's too late, before a bullet enters his brain and splatters it all over the underside of that desk. Back in the foyer there're half a dozen girls all cowering and blocking her way, the gunman is standing with his back to the wall in the corridor leading off, trying to avoid a shootout, the allurer, the beautiful temptress, is sitting on the low recliner with her knees drawn up under her chin, whimpering. The wooden desk has two splinter holes, Dick had dropped behind it for safety, but the next shot is going to kill him.

'Go back to your rooms girls.' It's Stella, one of them speaks out.

'Who the hell are you bossing around, sister?' Stella immediately turns on her, forehead buffeting forehead, pushing the girl away.

'Disappear *now*.' She growls, her coarse tones vibrating in the girl's head, there's something about this action that makes the girl flee. There are eleven seconds to go before Dick is a corpse, the gunman drops to his knees and takes aim, he glimpses Stella right behind him, the last prostitute standing, he smiles at her.

'This jerk missed the TV monitor I'll have him this time.' Noticing Stella's long slender legs beneath her short skirt he feels back with his left hand and rubs and pats her calf. 'Then we'll find a room and I'll have you.' And he would have, if Stella hadn't immediately broken his neck.

That isn't the end of it by a long chalk, there's a stampede descending from the third floor, Stella guesses three males, all adults, she grabs the gun, it's automatic, has six rounds and looks and feels serviceable, establishing those facts in the four seconds it took was crucial to deciding her course of action, in the meantime, Dick appeared from behind the desk, Stella points the gun at him and awaits her cue.

'Don't move.' She commands as four men burst onto the scene, her calculation is out by twenty-five percent, Stella places each of the men before one of them disappears behind her, two of the remaining display weapons, they're in alternate order, that complicates matters, the bossman speaks.

'Who the hell are you?' Stella bolsters her aim at Dick and speaks with her strong Russian accent. 'I know exactly who this is, at last I have him.'

'I'm talking to you, you dumb female.' Stella knows time is running out.

'I'm an undercover KGB agent, and this is none other than the Russian defector, Rudolf Nureyev.' The fourth dork has moved back into her field of vision, she calms herself before the storm.

'I'll tell ya what I'm gonna do, I'm gonna kill him for you and save the Russian taxpayer the price of a bullet.' He sneers at the woman as he begins to raise his revolver. 'At least I'm not gonna miss.' Stella, still pointing at Dick speaks to her target.

'Don't worry I never miss.' In an instant she hit the two armed men in the head a third standing close grabs her gun hand forcing it to the ceiling. Stella has her 9mm Makarov in her left hand in her pocket, she shoots him twice. Instantly she has the fourth cretin in her sights - both her sights. 'Tell me my friend are you feeling lucky?' He wasn't, Dick ties him to the chair behind the desk, he looks at Salinka.

'Rudolf Nureyev, isn't he a Russian ballet dancer?'

'That's all I could think of I was under pressure.'

FIFTY-TWO

While Stella's on a roll we'll get all the Los Angeles action out of the way in one killing, she's given another two rolls to Colleen, that's a thousand dollars, and taken up position on the same block, but at the diagonal corner, Colleen has also been given her instructions. It didn't take long before Jason pulled up alongside his women, keen to see how his proteges are doing, he looks around, perplexed and angry.

'Where's New York Stella, I don't remember giving her the night off?' He lit a thin cigar and spat on the sidewalk. '*Well?*' He's loud and threatening. 'Where the hell's my investment?' Colleen is scared, she doesn't want to be hit again, following her instructions, she hands Jason the thousand dollars, he looks at it, that's made him considerably calmer, Salinka knew it would, that was part of her plan.

'What's this?'

'Stella said to give it to you, it's our takings so far.' Jason positively lights up.

'At last, I had a good feeling about that bitch, where is she now, gone for a pee?'
Colleen knows Dick is standing a few doors away and has promised to come down on Jason like a ton of bricks if he tries anything.

'Stella said to say thanks but no thanks, she wants to be solo, she doesn't like the idea of giving her money away, she's on the block somewhere.' Jason is fuming, he grabs Colleen and pushes her against the wall, Dick begins to walk towards them, just a passer-by quietly minding his own business, Jason reluctantly lets her go.

'Did you take anything for yourself last night?' He says, while forcing his hand into her handbag, there's another roll in there. 'Woah, you two did have fun, I'll take this as well I've got a feeling tonight's gonna be crap anyway.'

He couldn't miss Stella, this gorgeous Punk sticking out from the rest of the girls, not quite as tall as an Amazon but a definite Diana in all but birthright, he pulls up in front of his woman's patch, gets out the car and heads over to her, he doesn't walk, he swaggers. Standing next to her with his hands in his pockets he looks for all the world like he owns the joint, he's as nice as pie, Stella knew he would be, she knows exactly how the night's going to play out.

'I knew straight off when I first laid eyes on you, you were a businesswoman, Jason I said to myself, that woman will go far.' He turned towards her. 'I admire that and encourage it in my girls, Colleen, well, she hasn't got what it takes, I do my best to look after her, I nurture her, but you Stella, I knew you were ready to fly the nest before you did.' He kicked his heels. 'I've been thinking, now that we're both freelance, I thought I might put a little business your way, after all you're by far the best-looking girl on the block.' Stella looks at him with a cute smile.

'Only the best on the block?' Jason is full of his own shit.

'Okay, okay, I give in, you're the fittest girl in the west.' He put his face close to hers and spoke seductively. 'I know a secluded spot on the outskirts where,' He pulls a five-hundred-dollar roll from his pocket. 'I always like to help a newcomer out and invest in her future.' Stella grabs his bony arse.

'You're very kind Jason, let's do it.'
Salinka knows little about Los Angeles and even less about the high vantage points and beauty spots that give an awe-inspiring view of this amazing city, day or night. The places where lovers come to dream, to vent their desires, where women and men of the night carry out their private deeds, do their dirty dancing, this is where Colleen learned the harsh truth, where her freedom was snatched away, it's where Jason is going to force another poor defenceless wretch into being his personal property, and this one, he's thinking to himself, certainly knows how to pull in the punters. He loves this part of the job, the control, the fear, the victory that's always his, he doesn't beat up men that would be too risky, the big question on his mind is whether to go for the sex first and thrash the ditch afterwards, he decides on the sex, but what he didn't take into account was Stella. They're stationary, sitting in his car looking out over a vastness of shimmering lights that bedazzle this iconic city, Jason is about to make his wish come true when, right out of the blue, she astounds him.

'How many girls have you trapped in this way, Colleen, we know about, but,' She turns to face him. 'How many other poor wretches?' Jason knows the game's up, that's definitely killed stone dead any thoughts of having sex.

'Well, you're a perceptive little bitch, and I was gonna be all nice to you, but I see I'm gonna have to treat you just like the rest of them sad Honeys. He grabs her around the throat, immediately the car door opens and two hands grab Jason around the throat, they pull him out the motor and drag him, struggling, across the course, grassy wasteland. Dick's timing is perfect, he's now sitting on Jason's back while slightly interfering with his airways, well, don't let's be coy, he's definitely interfering with his airways. A body crouching over its victim, seen from a distance in relief against the night-lit city sky, could be mistaken for Death, perhaps that's how it works, Death adopts a surrogate to carry out the deed, then, when it's done, withdraws, leaving, in this case, a small-time private investigator with a penchant for sorting out the bad guys, who having first retrieved the two five-hundred dollar rolls, stands up and walks away, committing a dead Jason to the ants.

We must go back for a moment to after the shooting at the brothel, there was a squad car in the vicinity and it was mere seconds before an armed loudhailer was calling them onto the street. You can imagine the cop's surprise when Stella, smiling, stepped into the doorway displaying her warrant card and waved them over. They had no authority to deal with this one, so it's a ride to police headquarters. The chief placed their warrant cards on his desk, picked up the phone and called his opposite number in New York City, he talked for five minutes before putting the phone down and studying the pair of them.

'OK, my assistant.' The chief eyeballed Salinka. 'Who you'll be pleased to know is a woman, we do move with the times here on the west coast, Captain

Hilary Hall, is interviewing your Miss Angel as we speak.' He'd just said that when there's a rap on the door. '*Enter*... Hilary, come in.' He held a hand out. 'This is Chase and Palchikova.' He looked at his deputy with his mouth open, wondering what to say next. 'I've just been speaking to chief Carmichael, NYPD, what he had to say about these two was interesting and my guess is what you have to say is going to be equally fascinating.' Captain Hall turned to Salinka, and for a moment took her in, Angel had described in detail the events as they unfolded in Europe, her story as well as Natalie's.

'Let me shake your hand ma'am, it seems you are a rare commodity.' Hilary looks at the chief. 'I think we've got ourselves a couple of heroes here.'

'Yes, chief Carmichael said exactly the same.' He pressed a button on his desk. 'Trudy, come into my office please, pick up our two friends, it's coffee in the canteen while you shorthand a statement, then they're free to go.' He looked at them. 'Your friend Angel is a lucky kid to have met you two, she came to this country to escape this kind of treatment, it makes me sick to the stomach.' He shook their hands. 'I take it there are going to be no more mass shootings this side of Thanksgiving.' Salinka looked assured.

'No more mass shootings.' And there weren't.

This American Institution (the bar) hasn't enjoyed a party like this since the 4th of July celebrations, there's Angel, Jessie, Colleen, Dick, Stella and Salinka, well, Dick can dream, Colleen wants to know what happened to Jason, Stella informs.

'D'you know, we didn't see him, did you see him Dick?'

'Who you talking about, Jason, haven't got a clue?' He raises his brow at Colleen. 'But don't you worry yourself, I don't think you'll be seeing him again.' First things first, there's a financial matter to clear up, Stella speaks to Colleen.

'Come on girl, we need to powder our noses.' In the privacy of the lady's room, Stella gives Colleen a roll of five hundred dollars. 'This is your payment and this is a little parting gift from Jason.' She gives her the other two rolls, Colleen looks at Stella.

'That's fifteen-hundred, that's, wow, that's, that's a lot, I don't know what to say.'

'You went the extra mile, Jason might have punched you on the nose, trust me, I'm a nose specialist, I know the damage it can cause, you deserve it, come here.' She put her arms around her. 'I'm speaking as Salinka now, Stella's my cover, you've got a chance here, to get yourself a job and get off the streets, if you don't take it and sort yourself out, some other tosser, like Jason, will come along and you'll be back where you started, will you promise me you'll try?' Colleen is trembling, she knows it ain't gonna happen.

'I'll try, but what about Jason?' With a look of steel, Salinka flicked a single finger across her neck. It's drinks and steak sandwiches all round, Jessie knows a little bit about this Stella person who's sitting next to her, amid the lively conversation that's going on, she can't help mentioning certain past activities she's heard about.

'Angel told me some pretty weird stuff about you.' Jessie gently poked Stella's arm to see if she's real. 'She always said you'd turn up, it's you and that other guy that's kept her going.' Jessie feels strangely inadequate, useless even, and perhaps, although she will never admit it, envious. 'I wish I was like you and could help people, instead of my sad, wasted existence.' Stella studied her.

'The first thing you need to do is get a proper job, how come prostitution, that guy is Dick by the way?'

'I'm a lazy cow, I didn't use to be, it just happened.'

'Were you one of Jason's?'

'I was but I prefer in house, it's warmer and drier.' She looks sadly at Stella. 'I'm pathetic aren't I.' Stella thought Jessie was worth a chance.

'If I wasn't so focused, so resolute, I'd be dead now, you need to think about yourself, become more determined, shift your arse into gear, get out of bed in the mornings, and get a job girl, it's not too late, anyway, you have a unique gift when it comes to job interviews.' Jessie can't work out what that is.

'What's my gift then?'

'Well, you should have nerves of steel by now, given your profession, you won't be phased by any panel.'

FIFTY-THREE

As we know, Dick's planned intervention was both silent and deadly, there was no mass shooting required, perhaps Jason has at last achieved his ultimate goal, to be his own boss in his very sexy role as a shooting star, punished by God for his sins, destined to shoot around and around some forbidding, giant, nebulous planet, for eternity. There was one small miracle in the early hours of that morning, pieces of the jigsaw fitting together when it was least expected, when an opportunity is spotted and acted upon, hopefully, to help change a life. Second in command, captain Hilary Hall, was particularly impressed by Salinka's actions, she was even more fascinated by her persona that is Stella Kill, and asked her to explain how she even went about being "trafficked for the greater good", to save her friend, while also setting other women and girls free, and to tell once more how she stuck Burano, the gangmaster. Salinka was coming to that bit when, over Hilary's shoulder, a notice caught her eye. Behind a Perspex door in a cabinet on display to the public, is an advertisement for a civilian post in the canteen. The interesting thing is, being a municipal position, the lucky candidate will have job security, prospects, good wages with health insurance, and paid vacations. Stella smiled at Hilary who she guessed had been completely won over.

'Ma'am, will you hear me out for just one minute, I have a favour to ask.
'

Back at the seedy hotel the fat man is excited as Dick enters with Stella and Angel in tow. As this threesome make their way up, he's tuning his TV in already when they make their way down again. Dick looks at the peeved owner of the dive.

'We've decided not to stay after all.' He nods at the two in front of him. 'We need a bigger bed.' As they head towards the street Dick glances over his shoulder. 'And besides, being filmed by the camera in the Gorilla's head is a bit creepy, don't you think…Adios?'

'Hey, just you wait a minute.' It's the would-be film producer. 'What about my money?'

'D'ya know what, you can keep it?'

The fat man sat there, sweat running down his face, his night has just been ruined, the main act has bowed out, he shouts to someone out the back.

'Janice, come here will ya, I want ya to do something for me.

Booked into a smarter hotel the three of them crawl onto their various beds and one by one fall into oblivion. Salinka's thoughts are of Jessie, settling down in her cell for the night as a guest of the LAPD, again that doesn't quite have the same ring as NYPD but it is streets ahead of SPD. The small miracle, the piece of the jigsaw, Jessie is being given a hand-up by captain Hall, that position in the canteen is her's, a second chance to turn her life around, as long as she bucks her ideas up and gets out of bed in the mornings, that is what she's promised Stella she'll do from now on. Angel's thoughts are of hugging Jessie, as they made their goodbyes they vowed to keep in touch, while Dick is contemplating, at least Angel is safe. The last thing Salinka, did, before she fell into a deep sleep was to murmur Dick's name, the last thing Dick heard before he drifted off was Salinka, murmur his name.

It's a sad morning for Angel, sooner or later she had to know about Jo Marianne, there was no way to break the news other than the hard truth, Salinka sat with her for a full half hour before she had cried herself out, her face and eyes red with distress, the knees of her jeans, damp patches where she'd transferred her tears while wiping her palms. Breakfast is a quiet, subdued affair, knives chattering on china, daring to defy the reverential silence, but even though Angel wanted to be sad for her friend, her overwhelming joy and relief at being free is owning her spirits. She is scouring her brain for Helen and Julie, to see if she can remember anything that happened that morning, from the silence, amid the warm flaky croissants, with peanut butter and jelly, and the familiar revitalizing aroma of coffee, Angel began retelling events.

'A well-built, half-bald man came in through the back, he had scars on his head like he'd been scolded with boiling water, there were two other men with him, Helen couldn't remember an appointment to be measured up for new carpets?' Angel is doing her best. 'They paired up with each of us, then pulled rags from their pockets and forced them over our faces, I felt dizzy, I must have passed out and collapsed on the floor.'

'That was chloroform used to knock you out, can you remember any conversation at all?' Angel shook her head.

'No, nothing, all I remember is two of them, a lanky one and a short one, were wearing anti-slavery T-shirts.' Immediately Dick homes in on his partner.

'That could be coincidence.' Salinka is not so dismissive.

'No, I don't think so, one is coincidence, two, that's plain dumb arrogance.' Dick thought for a moment.

'O.K. while we're clutching at straws, the well-built geezer with the scars on his head, what if it's chief Eastwood...I know what you're thinking?'

'You mean like, did you take your tablets this morning?' Dick ignores her.

'What was it the desk officer said, a word of warning, the chief wears a toupee, and how come when he wanted to speak to us, they knew where to look, White Van Line?' Salinka is listening. 'Only Eastwood could have reasoned that one out. And there's something else, what was it Mary said?' The Russian, is searching her brain.

'I'm eleven, I'm mad, I'm not mad, she mentioned her favourite film, do you like the champers, it's the cheap stuff?' Salinka is shaking her head. 'That's the best I can do.'

'She also said - you're the heroes everybody's talking about, I'm a hero, I saved a maid, she wouldn't stop crying, Daddy sent her home, we haven't seen her since.'

'Oh my god, Straith-North is a fourth-generation slave owner.' Salinka reassuringly taps her index finger three times on the table. 'You don't think they're captive inside that house do you?' The idea is as compelling as it is fantastic, they might owe Cash and Diamond a bigger debt than they could possibly imagine, for being their ticket to that fund-raising, gig.

'We need to find a smoking gun to connect Eastwood, we'll have to tread carefully from now on, any hint we're somehow onto them, Helen and Julie will be killed and disposed of instantly, you can bet your bottom dollar that's what happened to Mary's maid friend.'

This time they flew back to Seattle, the three-and-a-half hours of pampered bliss were surreal, their legacy, a freed Angel and five dead men, surely must leave the sixty or so other passengers looking like a bunch of flower arrangers on a day out. The girls drifted off but Dick couldn't rest, he's thinking about the problems that lay ahead, they'd made a lot of assumptions and guesses, great if they were right, but Dick knows things are never straightforward, one thing's for sure if they're wrong they're nowhere near finding Helen and Julie.

Like all puzzles and mazes when you have the start, the key, all the other pieces begin to fall into place.

It doesn't matter who noticed first, but it was apparent to both our Stars, they were being followed by Cash or Diamond or whoever it was drew the short straw. Dick and Salinka revel in the anti-plot, they have nothing to hide, no plans, no clues, and are preparing to return to the east coast, it was Diamond who checked with the travel agent to discover our two friends had just bought tickets to New York, for the following morning. Later that day, undetected, it was Dick who sidestepped into an apartment block and rang the bell of a Miss O'Leary, in the hope of finding a benevolent, kind person who might be only too pleased to help him out.

'Miss O'Leary ma'am, you wouldn't be knowing me, my name is Dick Chase to be sure. I'm just now wondering, do you have a phone I can use, I need to make a very important call, in private, you can listen though, I trust you, you have an honest face, you wouldn't happen to be Irish would'ja?' For some reason Dick finds himself singing in an Irish brogue, he knew he had to get back to his native American vernacular as soon as possible. 'Would'ja let me do that, here, in your lovely apartment, I'd be really grateful?' Miss O'Leary's face lit up with delight.

'It'll be my pleasure young man, won't you come in now, the phone is in the hall, or you can sit in my parlour?' Dick smiles at this sprightly Irish dame.

'Let's be sitting in your parlour.' He's politely looking around. 'I see you've no pets.' Damn it, still the brogue persists, Miss O'Leary is still smiling from the last time.

'No, Sally died last year, she was fourteen.'

'Begorrah, I'm sorry to hear it.' Dick is grief-stricken in Irish.

'Oh now, that's alright, she was beginning to smell a bit anyway, would you like a cup of tea?'

'I'll decline the tea if I may, but can I make that call please?' Dick phoned his old boss, chief Carmichael, it's simple, the chief is going to arrange for Dick and Salinka, once they have boarded the plane to drop down to the luggage hold where they'll hide inside a trailer, to be brought back to the main building. Someone in authority has to organise that little escapade and the chief is their man, Dick furnished him with all the details and the plan is set.

'You have a nice apartment ma'am, I'm just wondering, d'you think you can do me another little favour?' Miss O'Leary thought she'd died and gone to heaven when Angel turned up, and a Catholic angel to boot, this was the perfect pairing for a few days, that and the couple of hundred dollars Dick had to practically force onto her. Angel wasn't to leave the apartment, Miss O'Leary is revelling in the subterfuge and the thought she has a captive opponent for endless games of cards.

FIFTY-FOUR

Dick and Salinka throw themselves up some back stairs from the baggage handling area to the comms suite, the flight staff and ground crew were genned up, the chief had done his stuff. It was Cash who watched the plane take off, Dick and Salinka were spying him via the CCT. They saw him leave the terminal, they watched him file a report on the patrol car radio, no doubt to Eastwood, the two imbeciles from the NYPD have finally returned to the asylum, they watched him drive off. Thus it is we find our magnificent two leaving the building separately, as a precaution they each take a taxi to the same destination, it had been predetermined, it's a nice hotel in the city. While it's Salinka who walks into the *"Seattle Regis"* so named because Elvis Presley once stayed there, it will be Stella Kill who walks out. As Miss Russia arrives Dick is already in their room, she lays on the bed and beckons him over, he drops beside her making the springs creak.

'Got any ideas?' He enquired, Salinka stretches out like a cat dabbling in yoga.

'I take it you're being rhetorical.'

Angel and Rose O'Leary, or almost unbelievably, Angel Rose, that is what her mammy used to call her, way, way, back in the mists of time, in Cork, in the south of Ireland, before little Rose had learnt to say mammy properly, and pitifully before her mammy died so tragically of peritonitis, leaving her and her Daddy alone and broken. That's when he brought her to America, their New Found Land, to start over.

Where she's been ever since, never to return, and never to be called Angel Rose again, until now. Angel is speaking while rearranging her hand.

'Angel Rose, it's your turn.'

'Four sevens, three jacks, and I'm out.' Rose laughs her rhythmic, Emerald Irish laugh. 'Angel,' The name delights her. 'For sure you'll be having to be doing better than that.' A tuneful doorbell sounds. 'You stay here my dear, while I go and see who it is.' In an instant Dick is standing in what Rose O'Leary nostalgically refers to as her parlour, fending off a cup of tea.

'Can we wait just a minute now, for sure there'll be another visitor along shortly?' The doorbell sounds again. 'Shall I be answering that?' Dick can't believe he's dropped into the vernacular again. Miss O'Leary's eyes open wide as Stella appears in her parlour, a total contrast to anyone who has ever stood so brazenly in her apartment before, she wondered what Father Callaghan would make of this apparition, tall, slender, strong, almost, she thought, a heroine out of one of those comic books. Rose O'Leary is an old lady, long gone are those early, vibrant, halcyon days, when *she* was a Wonder Woman, not that she ever was Wonder Woman, that *is* a comic book heroine, no, but Rose had turned heads and broken a few hearts, once, in the drawing office days of her youth. Angel, still surprised to see Dick, is even more surprised when Stella turns up, she makes the introductions.

'Rose, this is Stella, she's a good friend of mine.' Angel looks at Rose. 'I can't begin to tell you how truly amazing this woman is.' Stella smiles as she hears Angel lose control of her emotions, she has also noticed, by the discarded playing cards laying on the table, it was Miss O'Leary who won the game, she sat down and began collecting up the evidence.

'Bit of a card-shark are we?' Stella grins at their Irish host, 'One hand of rummy and the loser makes tea.'

Whether by design or just bad luck, it's Stella who enters the parlour carrying a tray of tea, immediately she is intrigued by the conversation between Dick and the Irish lady.

'So Rose, you worked for the Straith-Norths, when was that?'

'For sure now it's a long time ago, old Straith-North, wasn't he alive then? I cooked for them, there was a long break, then I saw a job advertised as chaperone to their eldest daughter Crystal, she was a delightful child, I took her to school, riding school, and golf lessons.' Rose's face lit up. 'I was driving in those days, after her grandfather died she did a Moonlight flit and hasn't been seen since, the rumours were she was living in Paris.' Rose O'Leary pulled a grotesque face. 'Between you and me and the old oak tree, there's something strange about that family.' Stella is intrigued.

'In what way strange?'

'There was always work available in the big house, sometimes I've got nothing better to do than study the papers, they used to advertise regularly, but now, nothing, it's as if Lady Straith-North, she thinks she's a lady, is doing all that housework herself.' Rose hesitated, there's something on her mind.

'Yes Rose, what are you thinking?' It's Stella being intuitive.

'Oh, it's something Crystal said on my last day. "Daddy will kill me as soon as grandpa dies, I know too much I've got to get away".' Stella is truly oracular today.

'You gave her the money to go.' Miss O'Leary is stunned by this accurate assertion.

'I did.' She looked worried. 'Do you think I did the right thing now?' Dick stepped in.

'You did do the right thing, that's for sure, you dealt her the luck of the Irish.'

While tea is being enjoyed Rose innocently enquires as to what they're all doing here in Seattle "On a day like today" as she put it. Stella did the honours, to everyone's surprise.

'We represent a rival fast-food chain we're trying to establish a foothold on the water-front it's a small plot of land but we feel like it's home already, isn't that right, director of cross-country development?'

'Yes, absolutely and that reminds me.' Dick looks at his watch. 'I've got a meeting with the architect there in half an hour I'll see you two back at the hotel.'

'Oh, Angel, you're not leaving me on my own today are you?' Stella replies.

'You'll see her again our head of personnel has to do something to earn her living.'

Dick had already left when the two women followed suit, their policy of not being recognised together is still being played out. Salinka and Angel are on a mission, it's simple, to see if Angel can recognise chief Eastwood in his toupee. The problem is going to be where to find him, on a hunch they're headed for the mayor's office, it was Dick's idea, he thinks regular meetings between the two men are a good bet, but first it's a trip to the hairdresser and a trendy boutique, for Angel.

'Was it necessary to have all my hair shaved off?' Angel looks in a store window as they pass by, she widens her gait. 'Not bad I suppose I like the mini skirt.' She commented, while taking Stella's arm. 'Doesn't leave much to the imagination, does it?' They both bend at the waist in fits.

In those days the mayor's offices were two floors in the Emerald building, other floors were the arts, publishing, mapping, higher up are several classy apartments, the penthouse, with its beautiful rooftop gardens and helipad is reputed to belong to a wealthy Russian oligarch, Salinka didn't ask.

The world and its mother passed through the foyer that morning but no sign of a toupee-wearing police chief, Stella Kill did sign three autograph books, but the highlight of the exercise was when a group of Japanese school girls wanted to take pictures of Angel, they were fascinated by her shaven head and long white legs, clearly next year's fashion in Tokyo. Time is moving on lunch is calling, the revolving door is a huge slowly turning circular glass menagerie divided in two by a glass wall separating the incomers from the outgoers. On entering Angel caught her foot on the only centimetre of carpet that isn't fastened by a chromed stay, she flies forward and laughing, thumps into the glass wall. The incomers turn their heads toward her, Stella immediately stays away from Angel, who is looking straight at her, surreptitiously Stella throws a frown above her head. Angel gets it, she knows exactly what it means, she's been drilled by an expert, carefree she looks about, the chief is eyeing her, he's thinking, Jesus it's not possible. Angel ignores him, her face giving nothing away, she observes all the incomers with an innocent smile before turning to her front. The menagerie has turned half circle, the clumsy female exits onto the street and casually strolls off. Stella, who is downwind, hails a taxi, she asks the driver to stop in two hundred feet, pick up the girl with the shaven head and take them to the Seattle Regis.

FIFTY-FIVE

'Did you recognise him?' Was Stella's immediate question.

'Yes it was him, I've got no doubts about it.'

'Then he must have recognised you, we must move quickly.' As they vacated the taxi Stella had the temerity to fling a twenty-dollar bill at the driver, she knew that would be more than enough. They plough through the hotel lobby, then in the elevator to the fifth floor and soon they're standing in their room. Dick is already there, he's got some interesting if not sad news to impart but it's Stella who rides roughshod over his attempts to tell it, her news is far more urgent.

'Angel recognised Eastwood and Eastwood saw her.' Dick looked at Angel.

'Are you certain, you must be certain, are you 100% certain, because if we go after the wrong man there will be massive consequences?'

'It was him he looked straight at me we were that close, there was a glass screen between us, for an instant a strange feeling came over me, it felt like if he could he would have reached out and throttled me.' Dick looked sadly at Salinka.

'I've got some news that will put Eastwood right in the frame, the sighting of the white van and the three men, I told Eastwood our source, he was the only one who knew, I went to see if I could find John this morning, I discovered his throat had been slashed while he slept, it was that same night.'

The plan is simple, Angel will walk about town window shopping, taking in the sights, Dick and Salinka will pursue her, he spells it out.

'You will probably be followed and there might even be an attempt to kidnap you, don't worry we'll be watching and if anything happens, we'll step right in.'

'You mean you want to use me as bait?' Angel wasn't born yesterday.

'That's exactly what Dick wants but take no notice I never give him what he wants, only go along with it if you're certain.' Angel didn't hesitate.

'No, it's for Helen and Julie, I'll do it.'

The deed is set, Salinka is a few yards behind Angel, Dick is across the avenue where he can observe without being obvious, the three of them are slowly moving through the afternoon shoppers and stragglers late back from lunch. Pouring out of an art gallery is that contingent of Japanese school girls on their trip of a lifetime, so far the exercise has revealed nothing, only the norm. Then, a piercing moment of excitement as approaching are two fire tenders, to stoke the enthusiasm of little boys and panic their mommies into wondering whether or not they switched off the appliances, as they pass Dick sees a crew member gazing out, running procedure through his head before they arrive, thinking of his wife and child, and then, unwanted, that dreadful nagging thought, will it be my time today? Ten seconds and they'd passed, ten seconds was all it took, Dick looked back across the avenue to realise, amid the bustling crowd, the pair had completely disappeared.

Stella wasn't distracted by the fire engines, she's not casting an eye around to see the hunk at the wheel and whether or not he's got a big ladder, she's wholly committed to the job in hand. She sees two men turn out of a retailers, present themselves either side of Angel, like she's just been caught shoplifting, and march her sharply off down a gap between stores. Stella bursts into a sprint, she's at the gap but it's long and there's a kink, all three are out of sight. She careers on down, past the bend where instantly she finds herself in limbo, out of sync, it's a towel in the face soaked in chloroform, not even Colonel Palchikova has the answer to that one.

Risking life and limb to combat the moving lines of traffic that have built up behind the fire engines, Dick dashes between vehicles to get across the avenue. Now what, Jesus what superb timing what elegant trajectory, twenty Japanese school girls vacate a store all at once to saturate him with laughter and hormones, Dick swims his way through but where's he going, in what direction? He looks about him his stress level at critical, then, right in front of him, a passage between stores. He careers down it on a hunch, just past the kink he stops dead in his tracks, there's a tang he recognises. Discarded on the ground behind him is a small container, out of the drugs cabinet, out of place. Bending down to pick it up his guess is confirmed, he brings it slowly towards his face, a superfluous action, he already knows it's chloroform.

Helen and Julie have already witnessed the brutal, senseless slaughter of a young woman, they had no idea who she was, all they had been told is that she'd been noncompliant, and this is what happens for non-compliance. It was the same maid who Mary had tried to help, the homesick girl who couldn't stop crying, her Daddy said he'd given her the fare and let her go, he cured her homesickness, he did that alright, she's now dead and Mary had seen it all. She'd been searching for her Daddy in the old stable block, to kiss him goodnight, the stables, a period square set of stalls with a yard at its heart…. its heart, there is no heart here. Unknown to innocent little Mary she had walked into the ritual beating to death of her maid friend, she'd crept into one of the stalls from the rear and stumbled across the terrible scene, her friend lashed to a post, being beaten and whipped. She saw in the tragic dimness the slow distortion of that bright, friendly face, punched by violent fists, and the voice, that quiet, sobbing voice, "I'm sorry, help me, please stop," and most painful of all, the faint, pitiful cry, "*Mary*". Mary was traumatised, looking across through the gloom she could see other faces peering out, Helen was one, an empty stall then Julie, Mary doesn't know these people, there was another, a black man, Harvey, he was nice, he looked after her ponies. Then opposite, doing nothing about it is the chief of police with, horror of horrors, her Daddy. Mary's young brain is having trouble dealing with all this, only at the end did her Daddy see her, it was when the poor maid could stand no more, well, that was a time ago, she'd been tied to a stake. As Straith-North leaned forward to see the rope cut, and witness her being brutally kicked to death, that's when he saw Mary's little face staring at him, she backed away, horrified, she had just learnt the true meaning of evil. She ran like the wind back to the safety and comfort of the big house, she ran up the stairs, missing a step and banging her shin. She ran, she ran, she ran back to her bedroom where she slammed the door and locked it. Numb and frightened Mary fell into the arms of Lucy Winkle-Pot and Benjamin Woolhead and a hundred and one other good and loyal friends who showed her nothing but kindness and love.

Dick doesn't waste time, he's already standing in the parking lot at the end of the passage, in front of him is a limo-sized space, it's been hot today the tarmac is springy and he can see action has just taken place, an effort to push people, who must be stupefied, into a vehicle. He looks up, on the far side he sees the long white roof of a limo majestically hunting down the exit, Dick can go as the crow flies and is there with time to spare. Onward cruises the great white shark in search of the open sea of milling traffic, it draws up simmering in drive, waiting to turn left. As limos go it's nothing out of the ordinary, diamond white with black tinted windows. There are two small things of interest, one of them is the licence plate, it's red on a yellow background with a dark blue border, it reads "*Straith-North Seattle*". The other thing of interest is Dick's little Russian receiver that he had surreptitiously activated, and there, in his hand, the uncertain, mono-pitch tapping of Salinka's *S O S*. Dick raises an open hand to his mouth and shouts across the parking lot.

'Hey, Gloria, you stay there, I'll come to you.' With that, he ran off.

FIFTY-SIX

'Prostitute, turn out.'

'How many more times I'm not a prostitute, I've never been a prostitute.' Helen inveighs under her breath, the penalties for insubordination are high, there's a loud banging on her door.

'Prostitute, shift your ass your presence is demanded, I won't tell you again, I'll have you...' Helen opens her door. 'Horsewhipped.' Hickman, she of that name Helen refuses to utter, is almost screaming, she's the charge hand, a horrible stocky woman with a penchant for grey skirts below the knee and brown shoes, her deep brow systematically rises and falls like a little monkey as she speaks, Helen amuses herself imagining the woman has a pixie in her knickers who rhythmically pricks her genitalia with a pin.

'Follow me we've laid on some entertainment and it's not the Lucy Show.' This is rare indeed, a trip out for Helen, to be in the outside world is heaven, she's almost excited, then, slowly, horror creeps over her as she realises it's the stable block, another noncompliant to be made an example of. Helen and Julie are just two stalls apart, both gagged and tied to chairs, neither of them knows the other is there, they're not even aware they are slaves in the same house, the last time they had to watch a punishment they had to wait nearly two hours, so it's a long time with their thoughts and fears, with some hope and prayers, there is always hope and prayers.

Stella is back to normal on the edge and ready for action, the only problem, Angel and she are laying on the ground trussed up like a couple of turkeys ready for slaughter, the one good thing is she got Dick's message, that made her smile inwardly because even under these circumstances it made her happy, saved by Gloria, what a glorious thought.

Let's be clear I think we know Dick is on his way.

There are two men one tall the other short, Stella is thinking they must be Eastwood's stooges, the two so-called carpet fitters. The tall one immediately throws a problem into the mix.

'We'll do the shorn bitch first.' Both the girls are hogtied so there isn't a lot Stella can do, she makes something up.

'I've already done that bitch she's useless, why don't you do me first I'll be more rewarding, I've got a low pain threshold?' The two sidle over to her and look down, the tall one lifts her jaw with his foot then lets it drop.

'D'you know what, no it's the shorn one first, I'll fix the rope you drag her out when I call, and don't slack I'm keen to get on with it?'

'What about the Colonel?'

'North said he'll be along, he's got some business to attend to we can start without him, we're to wait for him before we do the Punk.' With that he took a coil of rope from a hook and stepped outside.

Opportunity has been waiting for a faint tap on the rear door, the short one goes to see who the hell it is, the hell it's Dick, surprise, surprise, he heard the conversation and knows time is at a premium. He grabs the short ass around the neck to stifle his rabbit, and drags him to the ground, Dick whispers in his ear.

'Listen asshole, if you wanna go on living you really need to cooperate, was it you and that ape out there, with Eastwood, who attacked the three girls in their salon - *Beauty and the Feast,* think about it, it's your life on the line here?' The short one is frantically nodding his head.

'Yes sir, it was us.'

'O.K. right so far, what's your name, and keep it down?'

'Bingo sir, I'm Bingo.' He whispered, saving his life.

'Well, *Bingo,* how's this for luck, the chief's report has you down as shooting the girl?' Dick yanks Bingo's neck. 'Remember, it's your life at stake here.'

'He's lying, it wasn't me, it was him, he did it, yeah, it was the chief, he shot the girl.'

'Then you've got nothing to worry about, that's exactly what we thought happened.' Dick reaches around to grab the back of the little shit's head, and with his other hand fastened firmly on Bingo's chin, *Bingo!* with one giant wrench Dick snaps the imbecile's neck......

There's a shout from outside.

'O.K. you can drag her out.' Dick had untied Stella and the call interrupted their kiss, he looks at his partner.

'Go do your stuff Baby, I'll untie Angel and bring her up to speed, as she leaves, Dick grasps her fingers. 'You've got an audience, Helen and Julie are out there in the shadows.' Meanwhile the lanky streak of piss is losing it.

'Hurry up and bring the bitch out, I'm ready already.' As Stella ambles out from the dark confines of the stall, she finds herself weighing up if she can snap a stake that's protruding centre. 'What's goin' on, where's Bingo? *Bingo, I said the shorn one.'* Dick is holding Bingo up, hidden, just inside the door, he lets him drop into the dust, Dick stays in the shadows, the pair look at him, it's Stella who speaks.

'He looks dead to me, quite dead.' She's decided she can't snap the stake.

Helen is spellbound, she knows exactly who this is, and finds herself in the front row, riveted, excited, freeeee! Julie hasn't a clue what's going on, sometimes it's better that way, no expectation, no hope, means she won't be disappointed.' The jerk makes a beeline for Stella, well, that's answered her first question anyhow, slowly she backs away letting him grab her arm, she trips him up, he lets go to break his fall, Stella spins in the air and kicks him in the head.

'Sorry about that, I don't know what came over me, I wasn't thinking.' Violently he comes at her again, she drops like a stone and rolls towards him, once more he has to break his fall, now she kicks sawdust and dirt into his eyes, he can't see. In a mad moment of extreme self-belief, Stella, charges towards the stake, she takes off and smacks into it with both feet, the old, brittle length snaps, providing a pointed weapon, that is exactly what she hoped.

If only he *had* been a carpet fitter, in some quiet backwater, on a break, enjoying the customer's coffee and cake, while fitting 10sq meters of "Sage-green Lammie-Wool Tough-Tech", instead of fighting a killer. The clueless, lanky, piece of shit thinks she's disorientated, he tries a third time, Stella grabs the stake with two hands and whips a semi-circle in front of her, she catches him on the chin, there's a lot of blood, he puts his hands to it and looks down at his fingers.

'You little minx.' He looks up at her. 'You fucking bitch.' There's a saying, not only in Russia but the world over. "Actions speak louder than words", while this lanky piece of trash is studying his blood-stained hands, Stella had launched the stake at him, as he looks up to mouth his obscenities, it slammed into his guts, she runs forward, grabs the stake, and keeps running, he trips backwards falling flat, her momentum lets her vault over him, forcing the stake further in. She rips it out and amid his gurgling protestations swings it down on his neck like a mad axe woman, Stella is bringing it down for the fifth time as Dick trots over to put his hand on her shoulder.

'Hey, he's done, you're done, he's finished.' She stops and drops the stake, Dick hasn't seen her lose it like that before.

FIFTY-SEVEN

The little monkey in her below-the-knee grey number has quietly let herself out the back door, this is a bit more than insubordination, the Colonel needs to be informed. The captors are untied, Helen, Julie, and a man called Harvey who Julie is very emotional about bringing with them. Helen is emotional too, and their combined euphoria at seeing each other has all but frozen them to the spot, all very touching but not a recipe for staying alive, Stella says a few choice words that seem to concentrate minds.

'For God's sake you two get a grip, we can't save you if you're a dead weight.'

The entertainment was not what was expected in this quaint, neglected, 19th-century stable block, missing its equine inquisitors, their large soulful eyes seeking a friendly word and a pat. The stake, symbolic of much May Day frivolity, with children happily dancing a weaving pattern around it, lay broken in the dust. The two dead bodies, the so-called carpet fitters, lay beaten, dead, displaying a master class in role reversal.

Dick is planning to leave in style, he's got his eye on the sleek white limo, but before the group has a chance to make their escape, a door bursts open, dressed in what looks like his full hunting attire, is Colonel Straith-North. This in itself isn't a problem for Dick or Stella, but the added complication of the short-stock submachinegun makes his appearance somewhat tricky.

'Congratulations, you've just signed your own death certificates.' Instinctively Stella plays for time, she's a master of the long game.

'What did the tall one mean when he said the Colonel and the chief are lovers, who was he referring to, what chief, or was it chef?' Dick is looking at Stella, what the hell is she talking about? Straith-North has fallen for it, he eyes the dead men.

'Hah, two-a-dime thugs, I wouldn't put it past them to be a pair of fudge packers.' This is a game Stella relishes.

'Now I come to think of it, it was definitely the chief, why would he tell me that?' Again Straith-North is letting himself be strung along.

'You have your little fantasy, either way you end up dead.' He laughed and frowned at the same time. 'Anyway, the chief's far too ugly.' Dick gets it.

'Oscar Wild.'

'What?' North glares at him, he's beginning to lose it.

'He's far too ugly, Oscar Wild, I saw the film.'

'Enough of this baloney.' Straith-North is brought to the end of his tether. The weapon cocks, not by itself, that was always step two in North's plan. Stella takes a step to the left. 'You stay where you are, one should always aim to shoot in a tight group.' He likes the sound of his own voice, and begins to wax lyrical over his family's farmstead. 'There's a fissure just east of ninety-acre-rift, this year it's corn, that should help keep the country in cornflakes. Family records show the fissure appeared in the summer of 1860 and it has never closed.' He smirks at them. 'My great grandpa called it a gift from the devil, it comes in handy for getting rid of any unwanted vermin.' While Straith-North is working on his aim, Dick is wondering if his crowing has clouded this dandy's brain enough to let him get away with the old, what's that behind you routine, when out of the corner of his eye he observes someone *is* behind him, Stella's time-wasting is about to pay off. 'Enough stalling.' North bursts out as he raised his weapon. 'Your fissure awaits.'

'*Daddy, my daddy.*' Straith-North's head spins around, he steps backwards and sideways to give him sight of both elements of the equation.

'Mary, what are you doing here, go, now, go back to the house?' Mary doesn't go, she stands firm, Straith-North has a dilemma on his hands.

'You killed my maid friend.' Mary is very upset and physically shaking. 'You lied to me, you didn't send her home, *you had her beaten to death,* y*ou horrid man, I hate you.*' Her little voice is screaming in the way a child's does who insists on being heard, Straith-North knows not to take his eye off the ball.

'No I didn't, of course I didn't, where's Miss Hickman, go to her and she'll take you back to the house?' Hickman is listening but too scared to show herself, she has history. Straith-North is running out of ideas. '*Hickman.*' He shouts. **'Hickman where are you, darned woman?'** During the pregnant silence that followed Straith-North has made up his mind, he'll kill the vermin now, get them out the way, Mary can be calmed and bought later, there's a white pony she's been craving, yes, that will do the trick nicely. The intervening time made him forget he'd already cocked the weapon, he reasserts his aim and meaningfully draws back the bolt and lets it go once more.

'Daddy, my daddy.' Mary runs towards him and unbelievably she pulls a handgun from the folds in her skirt, this time North does not turn, Mary scrunches her face, points the gun and pulls the trigger, she hits him in the back, now she has his attention. He turns in her direction and points the machinegun straight at her, Dick flies forward, grabs the weapon and forces it into the air, it goes off firing a burst into the rafters.

'*You had my friend beaten to death.*' Mary's voice is breaking down, without a second thought she steps up and dispassionately fires again, this time at his head, Lucky for Dick Mary's a good shot.

Instantly, she looks over to the far side, she runs across the stable yard, kicks a door open and fires a shot into one of the stalls, at first there's faint, traumatised breathing, then a crash into what sounds like a stack of empty pails, as Hickman drops to the floor.

Hickman, not her real name, has a secret, it's simple, she was born and brought up in Germany, the daughter of a farm worker, she wasn't educated. Her mother died when she was seven and she had to work long, hard days in the dairy, doing her mother's work. Until one day, at just turned seventeen, she'd had enough and walked out, she never looked back, she never saw her father again. Hickman knew the facts of life and used them to great advantage. One night in the late summer of 43, the war was raging, it was everyone else's concern except hers. She was taking a stroll after supper as she often did, when a convoy of German military personnel passed by. Her eye was caught by its commander, Hickman blushed, it was false, everything about her was false.

The night was spent, or better still, enjoyed, in his quarters and from that moment on her life was to change for ever. Through his military connections, this army commander arranged for his 'lover' to join the "*aufseherinnen*" to become a female guard in a Nazi concentration camp. After her training, she was sent to Dachau, near Munich in Bavaria. I said Hickman was not her real name, her name was in fact, Eichmann, no relation, just one of those strange coincidences. It gave her celebrity status, plus the fact, between the higher-ranking officers, she made sure she was always available. Then there was the day job, she became known as the "*swine in grey*" a heartless, cruel piece of work, who pleasured herself by causing pain and grief to the old and infirm, the weak, she relished having power, particularly over weaker women. The camp commandant knew the game was up, the US 7th Army was on its way to liberate the camp. Hickman was a favourite of his, was it not she who made those long nights away from home, away from his wife, so much more pleasurable? And so it was, Hickman's favours began to pay off, she got a transport to Munich, then a bus to Rosenheim, where she spent the rest of the war keeping house for an ageing doctor and his wife. Until one day, when his surgery was late opening, the doctor and his spouse were found dead, they'd been poisoned. Their woman who did, did being the operative word, who nobody in the area knew, had disappeared with the family silver. Ingenuity and free love find her in the USA, Philadelphia, for many years. Then, running away again, she ended up in Seattle, by this time much older but still carrying those traits of the swine in grey. Eventually she finds peace at the hands of one she had tormented.

An angry, confused, distraught little girl walks back, she throws the gun down in disgust and looks at all of them, her bottom lip is quivering, she doesn't speak. Helen approaches Mary and kneels in front of the child, she places her hands on the girl's shoulders.

'Was it you who put the sweeties in the laundry?' Mary nods her head and grins.

FIFTY-EIGHT

Dick and Stella look at each other, a multitude of cars pulling up on loose gravel, doors slamming, an overture of scrambled footfalls, a chorus of at least thirty automatic weapons all being cocked at random, the piercing screech of a loud hailer as it feeds back on someone standing too close. By the third vehicle Dick had grabbed the situation, he also grabbed Angel's and Mary's arms and whisked them to the stalls where he's looking for something, he sees what he wants and hustles them inside.

'Angel, listen, this is important, it's your turn to be the hero....'

'Heroine.' It's Mary, Dick is thrown.

'What?'

'It's heroine, she's a lady.' Dick smiles.

'You're right, but we haven't got time for pedantries.' Mary's thinking about that one. 'Quickly, bury yourself in the straw, you too Mary.' Dick is covering them as he speaks. 'When the coast is clear you need to take Mary to Miss O'Leary's, follow the drive to the highway, turn right and thumb a lift, someone will pick you up, here's fifty dollars, it's all I have. When you get there, call Seattle's top attorney, O'Leary will help you, she's a shrewd cookie, explain that Mary's life is in danger and she needs to be in a safe place. The chief of New York City police will confirm it's the deal, say it's from Dick Chase, can you remember all that?' Mary is curious

.

'Who's Miss O'Leary?' Dick hears the screech of a loud hailer feeding back, he puts a finger to his lips and gives Mary, a wink.

'You'll like her, she's a wizard at cards.' He pushes the age-old wooden slatted gate shut. 'Remember, it's Miss O'Leary - a top attorney - get Mary safe.'

Dick is just in time, as he joins the others, so it begins.

'This is the Seattle police.' Feedback. *'We have you surrounded, you can't escape.'* Feedback. *'Come out one at a time, with your hands in the air.'* M*ore feedback. Dick goes first, his hands wide open and high in the air, to emphasize his lack of threat, he stands motionless on the threshold before slowly walking out. It's turned cold, and it's rained, the wet gravel glistens in the reflective glare of the headlamps that are whitewashing the stables and almost blinding him. It looks like the whole of the Seattle police force has turned up, all decked out in riot gear and heavily armed. Dick thinks this is good, too many witnesses to gun them down in cold blood, Eastwood can't try anything he'll have to wait his chance. Helen appeared next, followed by Julie, then Harvey, and last of all Stella. A swarm of about fifteen unarmed officers swoop in and separate them, they're each handcuffed and hustled into five separate vehicles, Dick is desperately trying to keep track of everyone. Cash is in front driving Helen, Dick is next, his driver is a woman, that's good, he always prefers to be chauffeured by the opposite sex. Stella is in the car behind him with Diamond, Julie is behind them, Harvey is last. Soon the convoy is

powering its way towards the city, down a drive lined with red maples that are chucking rain at them mercilessly in a squall that's just built up, on the highway it comes on to rain again, the wipers are going ten to the dozen, Dick starts a conversation.

'So, where are you taking me in such a hurry, do we have a dinner date, I don't remember asking you out, I think I would have noticed if I had, I'm Dick by the way, what's your name?'

'I'm Cassie, but you can call me officer Lawson, and this isn't dinner, this is what you call an arrest.'

'An arrest, I bet you don't normally do that on a first date, outta curiosity, how come you're on your own, where's the arresting officer, aren't you flouting police protocol?' Officer Lawson takes her time answering that one.

'Yes, but it's the chief's orders, so I guess it's alright.'

'Your chief is a bit of a law unto himself isn't he, a real maverick, seems to me he can do exactly what the hell he wants?'

'Yeah, his favourite hobby is homicide, now hush-up, I've gotta turn off somewhere here, I need to concentrate.' Dick is thinking, police officer Cassie doesn't know how near she is to the truth, he's also working out just what happened back there. Straith-North must have called the chief and told him there's trouble, judging by the rapid response team, the chief was expecting something to happen.
The indicators flash, closely followed by some stomach-grabbing inertia.

'What's going down Cassie, I mean Officer Lawson?'

'My instructions are to take the Boeing factory-workers route, it avoids the snarl-up at peak times.' Dick is already peering out the window.

'What's peak about midnight?'

'I don't know, I'm just following orders.' Dick notices the vehicles ahead of them didn't take this route, he looks behind, Stella's vehicle turned off, but that's all, the rest remained on the highway, something about this detour sucks, Dick smells a rat, he knows the KGB won't be taking it lying down.

'O.K. Diamond, so why have we pulled off, what's so special about us that we get to go first class all of a sudden, don't you find it a bit stage one accomplished?'

'It's the chief's instructions, he knows what he's doing.'

'Right, O.K. that's it, you might want to die here tonight but I don't, you listen to me and listen good.' Salinka knows it's time to spill the beans on their case history. 'Three men raided Beauty and the Feast, it was witnessed by a tramp called John, he remembered the licence plate of a white hire van, one of the men had serious head scars, leaving him almost bald, does that ring any bells? Dick shared this information with Eastwood before he'd twigged, the result, that night our friendly tramp had his throat slashed. There are two dead men in those stables, aside from North, one of them admitted the whole thing to Dick, he also said it was the chief who shot Jo Maryanne, are you keeping up? For the record, we killed them, they were going to beat me and Angel to death. Mary, that's Straith-North's eleven-year-old daughter, accidentally witnessed the beating to death of a non-compliant maid, her daddy and your chief had front-row seats. In case you're wondering, Straith-North is a slave owner, it's in his blood. Lastly, we traced that white van, it had been torched in Los Angeles, a silencer was found in the burnt-out shell, forensics say the bullet that went through the silencer also killed Jo Maryanne.' Like he'd suddenly woke from a long sleep and needs to tell someone about his bad dream, officer Diamond slams the pedal to the metal.

'A week before the Beauty and the Feast shooting, the chief asked me to pick up a silencer for him, also,' Diamond glanced at Stella. 'He came to the police force from the military, he's an explosives expert.' Diamond is now on a mission, he's roaring past Lawson and Chase, all blue lights and sirens, including an illuminated stop sign flashing in the rear window, in a cloud of brake dust and damp heat, all their wheels lock as both vehicles slide two yards to a halt. Salinka, still handcuffed, and Diamond jump out, they're both yelling, officer Lawson and Dick don't hang about. A bit further on there's a lorry park and a weighbridge, there are half a dozen long-haul lorries parked up for the night, a single concrete building stands by the bridge, it has a steel door and a window, it isn't long before they're all inside. Diamond goes over to the window, while Officer Lawson, breathlessly, wants to know what the hell this is all about, Diamond puts her in the picture.

'These are the two who saved Cash and me, probably keeping me from being buried alive in some concrete foundations, Palchikova has just outlined their case history. Listen Cass, remember the homicide and the disappearance of the three women from that salon, well, you're not gonna believe this, the chief's in it up to his neck and I'm part of the evidence that can put him away.' Diamond looks at Stella. 'Come to think of it, it was the chief who sent Cash and me on that surveillance job, the day you two stepped in, he set the whole thing up, he was angling to get me out of the way then. Officer Lawson looks at Dick.

'You can call me Cassie, here, let me remove those cuffs.' Two powerful explosions, accompanied by two huge fireballs that rocket skywards, shake the concrete building and fracture the glass, the occupants can feel the heat from where they are. Seconds later it comes on to rain again, only this time it's not rain, it's what's left of the vehicles falling onto the roof, Stella speaks to her gawping officer.

'Hey, Diamond, do me a favour and remove these cuffs will you?'

FIFTY-NINE

Angel waits for the coast to clear and then another five minutes before she and Mary make their move.

'Mary, how far is it to the main highway?'

'It only takes five minutes in the car, but it takes forever to walk'…Mary has an idea. 'Can you ride a horse?'

'I've never ridden a horse.' Mary frowns before she has an even better idea.

'I know, you can ride two up with me on Strawberry, I've got nine rosettes, three red ones, four blue ones, and three yellow ones, that makes.' Mary is counting on her fingers. 'That makes ten.' She sounds very proud of herself. Angel isn't sure about this but recognises expedience is the better part of valour, and anyhow, Mary has Strawberry out from an adjacent stable block in double quick time so she must know what she's doing, pretty soon the three of them are trotting off towards *South Gates.* When they arrive, Strawberry is spoken to by Mary and gently patted on the hindquarters, the pony happily trots off back to where she came from. Angel is impressed but still there's a long way to go and the big question is, will they get a lift before it comes on to rain again?

Eastwood's plan didn't work out, he watched the disaster unfold in front of his eyes, not for the first time has one of his plans backfired. Back in Nam, his job was to protect a contingent of B Company from a roaming pack of suicidal Viet Cong gorillas who had been terrorising their front line. B Company was out on patrol when the message came over the radio, at all costs he must blow the bridge on the eastern flank, to stop the Cong getting across the ravine. To this day Eastwood doesn't know what went wrong, he'd set the charges okay, it was a simple vibration/heat trigger, a double whammy, it should have been fool proof, it didn't detonate, as a consequence the whole group was lost, sixteen good men and true, their average age was nineteen. If he'd only had the foresight, on this night, to rig the building, a stupid mistake, unbelievable he cursed. Eastwood has a plan B, it's trickier and depends on a certain set of circumstances falling into place, he has to get Chase and the Russian first, they are his biggest threat. He'll always be in that idiot Carmichael's debt, his keenness to spread the word about Chase, his prodigy, and the Russian. Their heroics in Albania and Brussels, forewarned is forearmed, clearly a gifted pair, but Eastwood is confident he won't fail a second time.

Dick persuaded Diamond that his place is with Cassie, she's divorced and has two teenage children waiting for her to come off shift, she knows they worry about her and no matter what time she reaches home there's always, goodnight mom, wafting out from their bedrooms. It's a family joke, for that moment, as they each settle down, they become the Waltons. Diamond needs to stay with her till the morning, while Dick and Stella deal with Eastwood. Two lorry drivers, whose sleep had been destroyed by the explosions, are eager to help out, Salinka wanted the target split, so that was good. Foster

Gates driving his sixteen-wheeler, Missy Mammoth, dropped Dick and Stella half a mile from police headquarters, leaving them to walk the rest. Seattle by night isn't a patch on the Emerald City as it is during the day, it's far less disrupted by traffic. It had stopped raining and the sky is clear and would be full of stars if it wasn't for the light pollution. They enter police headquarters, at the desk it's the same officer they met the last time they were here.

'You won't get the chief for at least a week, he flew out tonight on a short vacation, who shall I say is calling, oops, take no notice of me, that's force of habit, can I take a message or help you with anything else?' Dick answers.

'No thanks, is the canteen open, we could murder a coffee?' Yes, is the reply and soon they're in the elevator, just the two of them, Salinka has run out of ideas.

'What'll we do now Eastwood has given us the slip?'

'We look through his office, you never know he might have incriminated himself.' That's a good idea only the elevator doesn't stop and Dick and Salinka find themselves on the roof, they step out, it's a sight that would tempt anyone. The night is now clear and a few yards ahead of them is a view to take their breath away, standing by the parapet, Salinka is thinking out loud.

'Funny how this reminds me of Sleepless in Seattle.' Dick smiles at his girl, he's dying to put her straight.

'Yeah, that is funny, because it was New York, that's the view this reminds you of, it was from the Empire State Building.'

'Oh yes, so it was.' She places her arm around him. 'Tell me, *you* haven't got any pushy children waiting in the wings, have you?' He gave her a curious glance.

'What's going on in that tiny brain of yours, this isn't leading up to something is it, it's not a leap year?' She tossed her head and laughed.

'No, I'm waiting for you.'

There were five shots in all, a small calibre automatic pistol made in Russia, Eastwood didn't know it was the weapon of choice for the KGB during the cold war, if you were an American spy this is what you feared most, Colonel Palchikova still uses one, and now, ironically, it had been used to stop her in her tracks. She heard nothing, Dick heard all five shots, each one a reminder of his utter stupidity, his total loss of concentration, of how he'd taken his eye off the ball. As he lay on the hard, unyielding concrete, staring at Stella, he knew she was dead, for a brief moment he's elated it's not Salinka, immediately the thought shattered against the hard, cruel face of reality, he went blank for a full thirty seconds, a single shot had hit her in the head. All the luck is with Dick tonight, two had missed but two more had gone clean through him, neither hit a vital organ, it should have been him not Salinka, or both of them, that would have been kindest.

Somewhere in a dark silent office far below them, a phone rings.

> "Chief Eastwood here, I'm out of the office, leave a message and I'll get back."
> 'Eastie, it's Paul Floyd, Whitlow Attorneys, we've been approached by a Miss O'Leary, guess what, she's housing your two fugitives. Contact me, you know where.'

Back on the roof, mixed with the trauma of deep shock, Dick's pain is excruciating, but it's nothing his extreme, his total anger can't cope with, oddly, playing in his head is Salinka's voice the moment Tom was gunned down, as clear as if it was yesterday, *Dick, No Dick.* He knew he had to ignore what had happened and carry on, for the greater good, like she had done, like she always did. All he wants to do is pick her up in his arms and hold her tight, he dare not move, that moment will come soon enough, for now, he can only lay there, listening to approaching footsteps.

SIXTY

Someone stopped at their feet, *their feet,* she who is now dead, the possibility of them sharing anything has become very limited, in truth it has ended. The creature moved to stand at their heads, there it is again, *their, their, their* laughter, *their* dreams, *their* hopes, all gone. Dick had been shallow breathing but now he's holding his breath, in truth he's bursting for air, he's looking at Salinka with a dead man's stare, he dare not blink. It's then he noticed, within the shiny reflective centre of her earring, the animal put his gun away and let his hand fall to his side, almost, not quite, within reach, as tiny as this reflection is, Dick knows it's Eastwood.

'Two can play at that game you pair of imbeciles, getting off the flight, then you fell for the elevator malfunction, Jesus that's pre-school stuff, and I thought you were good at this.' He looks about, there's no possibility of interruptions, too high up, the sound of shots lost on the cool night air, he reaches down to examine Salinka's wounds, to see what damage he'd caused, and in that single act of self-indulgent gratification, he signed his own death warrant. Dick grabs Eastwood's wrist and jerks him quickly off balance, as his body hit the ground, his head followed suit, bouncing hard on the concrete, Dick is immediately on top of him, but he completely underestimated the sheer agony of his own wounds, sharp intake of breath, 'Jesus Christ.' The gun had dropped out, tempting, but no, he decides not to shoot him, that would be too easy, he quickly kicks the weapon to slide it away across the wet surface, all is pain. Still holding onto Eastwood's arm he winds it up as far as it'll go, pushing it to the brink. A revelation, he realises he's adopted a little trick he'd picked up from Stella the night she broke Romeo's arm in the coffee shop.

'You can say goodbye to this, you won't be needing it where you're going.' Using his rage, his uncompromising fury, and the weight of his whole body he snapped the socket, immediately Eastwood hollers in agony. Now Dick grabs the back of his collar with both hands lifts his head off the ground and repeatedly bangs his face into the concrete. 'This is for Jo Maryanne.' Blindly Eastwood is scrabbling about with his good arm for something with which to retaliate, he finds a brick laying there, Dick is onto it, he grabs Eastwood's wrist and forces the brick repeatedly into the side of his head until it's dropped, Chase slings it away. Looking around he notices for the first time the building has a well, from that moment he knows exactly what he's going to do, it's at least ten stories down to the pigeon shit. He came to his senses, Eastwood will have had a full magazine so there'll be three rounds left, possibly five, it's laying at the foot of the parapet just along from a twenty-cent telescope. He moves quickly, but still Eastwood, like some Frankenstein figure, is up on his feet pursuing him. Gun in hand, Dick swings around and fires a bullet into each leg, Eastwood drops to his knees, Chase places the gun down and begins to drag the groaning slimeball by his ankle towards the well, his pain is excruciating but if he can just make one last effort. He pulls Eastwood almost to the standing position where he falls over

Dick's shoulder and tries to struggle Chase to the ground, somehow he manages to stay upright and hoist Eastwood against the parapet.

The untimely interruption, strangely incongruous, four black horsemen appear standing on a distant horizon looking at him, they have totally suspended Dick's life as he knew it, he doesn't realise their significance, the showdown, just for a few seconds, seemed to Dick to last an eternity. The horses kick the ground and swish their tails in eager anticipation, waiting, waiting. "Not tonight my harbingers" they are silently commanded, the horse's heads rise and fall in a huff, as they turn away, disappointed, back over the horizon. Now Dick finds himself falling, a feeling he's known before but can't pinpoint, it's like he's dropping out of the sky. Then, bizarrely, a huge bird gently takes him in her talons, at least he has an overriding feeling it's a she. This great she-bird gently places him on the ground and caresses him with her beak, slowly the pain returns, increasing, unbearable, as he regains consciousness.

Dick looks up from where he finds himself lying on the hard, wet concrete at another dark figure silhouetted against the night sky, this one is for real, still holding the iron bar that had so efficiently knocked him to the floor and almost killed him. Conversation is being had and Dick realises it's Cash, all the time he's been one of Eastwood's lackeys.

'That'll keep him quiet.' Cash slings the iron bar out of reach. 'Chief, you look like you've been in the wars.'

'Jesus Christ, you took your time, that birdbrain has destroyed my arm and shot me up, another minute and I'd have been dead meat, Christ I'm in agony, what have you found out?' Cash is tentative.'

'Not a lot, but we've had a lucky break, it's like they all disappeared off the face of the earth. I called into your office on the way here and found Floyd has left a message, he's got their whereabouts, they're with a little old lady, you couldn't make it up, we can deal with them in the morning.'

Something unexpected gives Cash a warm glow, he's about to make an arrest, first step, some tactical acquiescence, he raises his hands, he knows the pressure of a gun at his neck. As cocky and self-assured as ever he begins his usual calm, winning dialogue.

'I don't know who you are, but we both know you're not gonna pull that trigger on a US law enforcement officer.' Against the odds, and flying in the face of all probability, it's Stella Kill.

'You're right Cash, you know I should be at home now, cleaning up after my man.'

'Well, that's what I say, look I'll tell you what I'm gonna do, I'll turn around right now, you're gonna hand me the gun, and we'll say no more about it.'

'Cash, I was being ironic.' He loses his nerve as his blood runs cold. 'Are you going to face me, or am I coming round there, if I shoot you in the back it fucks up my paperwork?' Cash is psyching himself up to turn and grab the gun, Stella knows it. 'Go on, do it, I'm only a woman after all.' Cash, confident, unstoppable, moves, and she shoots him dead. Stella looks at Dick. 'Don't you say a word Yankee, I'm on a roll.' Eastwood is very slowly getting up, Stella knows that one, she shoots him in the knee, he sits down again sharply his face a picture of agony and for the first-time defeat, he looks at her.

'Make it quick.' Stella is thinking about that for a moment.

'It's more than you deserve, you need to be reminded of something first, her name was Jo Maryanne, it was her wedding day.' Stella casually points the gun, but then she applies the break, she's laying on the agony, before she puts a bullet, the last bullet, clean between his eyes.

SIXTY-ONE

The world revolves, time evolves, Advil dissolves and Dick is taking two in a glass of water as prescribed by Samantha, his sixteen-year-old doctor, well, she isn't but you know what I mean. Dick is laying there thinking, good for her, a stable, sensible career, certainly saving lives, far safer than being a private detective or a member of the special forces, American, Russian, or freelance. Salinka is in the operating theatre for the second time. Dick's been told not to worry, it's only minor cosmetic.

'What are you smiling at Mr. Chase, have those Advils hit the spot already?'

'No Doc, I'm just geed-up to be here and that Salinka's gonna be O.K.' He wanted to tell her the whole story but he knew he couldn't do that, such things only happen in fiction, and this is for real, she'd never believe him. Samantha sat on the edge of his bed and placed a thermometer in his mouth, she put a hand on his wrist feeling for his pulse.

'Well, that's tricky, there's nothing here.' She smiles at him. 'Your girlfriend is lucky to be alive, the titanium plate embedded in her cranium is the smallest Doctor Trumann has ever seen, an inch either way and she would have died.' She removes the thermometer. 'You're cooked, you've got a couple of visitors down the hall, I'll send them in.'

From a distance is the best place to observe Helen and Julie enter Dick's room, to see their pain is bad enough, to hear it will be unbearable. At first, it's hugs and laughter, then some wide-eyed listening as they learn of Stella's role, that's followed by questions and answers, looks of belief, of disbelief, and more laughter. Then, the subject, it had to come sooner or later, there's no way to say it other than come straight out with it. All at once the two girls fall into each other's arms and collapse to their knees, as they learn of the fate of Jo Maryanne. Dick lay quiet while his friends sobbed their hearts out, Helen's sadness didn't end there, she felt unnecessarily ashamed and guilty.

'I feel so bad, leaving you the way I did, especially after what you did for us.' Again she is teary eyed, Dick understands, he never did mention he had the hots for Salinka all along, or that she came gold-plated.

'Say no more about it, everything has turned out just dandy, we've got a real nice pad in Cambridge, you'd love it, what are you two gonna do now? I mean, hopefully, with Angel as well?'

'Yeah, where is Angel, anyway?'

'She's with Miss O'Leary, it's a long story, I'll tell you about it later.'

'We were talking about reopening Beauty and the Feast, but I'm not sure.'

'Sounds like a plan, you said it was Jo's favourite place, why not re-open it in her memory.' There's a knock, the door opens.

'Hi guys.' The tall, imposing figure of Salinka enters the room, Helen and Julie stand up, it was a strange compulsion, a mixture of good manners and respect for this special woman. Dick and Salinka's eye contact is palpable, a sparrow could land on it, both their hands reach out and touch. 'Well Yankee,

I told you I needed to watch your back.' She lightly touched her bandaged head. 'I never thought this old thing was going to be watching my back though.'

'Salinka, there's someone here dying to meet you, Helen you know and Julie.' Salinka turns to face the pair.

'Hello Helen we meet again, Julie I believe I may have lost it the first time we met, sorry about that.'

'From where I was ma'am, all trussed up, you didn't lose it, you saved it.'

They lounge in Dicks room listening to each other's stories, telling it how it was, of panic and fear, the funny ones were Dick's and Salinka's, but Helen had them all falling apart with a certain tale about a pixie with a pin, Dick is looking at Salinka's bandages.

'So, what's with the metal plate then? You didn't mention it before.'

'To tell the truth I hardly ever think about it these days, when I joined the military, it happened in the first month. We were being taken to some ranges in tracked vehicles when a trackpad from one of them became detached, it flew through the air and hit me on the head, it was a lucky shot. I was airlifted back to base, after being made stable I was flown to Paris, at the time they were the best in the world, when it happened, it was a big nuisance in my life, but now, without it.' She squeezed Dick's hand. 'Without it, I would have died, and so would you Yankee, think about it.'

The last ten days haven't been a holiday and they're both keen to go home, but there is the little matter of the law to abide by, and what better news could they receive other than Captain Hilary Hall, is to be Seattle's new chief of police, someone they know, someone who admires Salinka, or Stella as she had first been introduced, a friend who will get the job done with the minimum of fuss. A major concern is Mary, who we mustn't forget shot dead her father. Angel and Mary got a lift to Miss O'Leary's almost as soon as they reached the road, a husband and wife were traveling home late night from a trip south. They live just a couple of blocks away so were able to drop them at their destination. Of course, Angel had to knock Miss O'Leary up but the wise, kind-hearted Irish lass from Cork was all agog to hear their story, and though Mary has no recollection of it, she had been cuddled by Miss O'Leary, just after she was born, so it's happiness all round.

Captain Hall interviewed the pair in Dick's room, most important was to get Mary's story down, a young girl not yet in her teens, she had been in denial over her Daddy's involvement in the death of her maid friend, she just knew he would kill them. She loved him but she had to stop him, the family name is everything, a seed he'd planted in her head from an early age, Dick and Salinka painted clearly what Mary had witnessed, and the role she played in saving the lives of five people. Diamond was shocked to learn of the death of his partner, but there is a caveat to that, he knew Cash was close to the chief in a way he couldn't fathom, there were clandestine activities he wasn't party to that had been swept under the carpet. Though at times he had to admit to a certain jealousy, now, with all this out in the open he wouldn't have had it any other way, Eastwood's major role shocked everyone.

The Straith-North name and family reputation are about to get a knock from which they will never recover, his other daughter was contacted in Paris and is on her way back to give evidence, and to see her little sister, who she misses so much, Mary knows she has a sister but can't remember her at all. There's one other thing, as macabre as it is, it must be mentioned here, the fissure, police gangs working for six days will recover thirty-three bodies in different states of decomposition. A most recent one is that of Mary's maid friend, she was eighteen, her name was Alice Vernon, she came from Grants Pass, Oregon. Two women who shall remain nameless were prostitutes. Police records show that both Eastwood and Cash had known them, too frequently to be anything other than sport, who possibly got over-familiar.

Dick had wandered down to Salinka's room, for the moment his heart is sleeping, she's well away. A nurse is just checking in, Dick sat on a nearby chair, she smiled at him and spoke softly.

'Your friend is Russian?' Dick, with a certain trepidation replied.

'Yes, she is.'

'My mother is Russian.' Dick simply smiles and raises his eyebrows, as the nurse is about to leave, when she's at the door, he turns to her.

'What made you ask?'

'She spoke Russian in her dream, she said папа мой папа.' Dick is intrigued.

'What does it mean?' The nurse smiled.

'It means, Daddy, my Daddy, yes, it does, that's exactly it.' Smiling, she left the room.

Dick sat there taking his girl in, beautiful, even in sleep, it wasn't long before she woke, she came straight out with it he didn't have to ask, it was a bittersweet moment for her.

'I've been dreaming about my sister Tatiana, the blind one, did I mention she was born blind? It was Mary who made me think of it, I'd forgotten all about it. She mentioned her favourite film, The Railway Children, it was Tatiana's favourite too. When she was young, she loved the meeting on the platform, and whenever she sensed our father enter the room, she would say those words, Daddy my Daddy.' Salinka smiles. 'She was a very happy girl despite her blindness, I suppose that's what becomes of being blind from birth.' She pulls herself up straight. 'Dick, I want to go home, can you fix it for us?'

SIXTY-TWO

The long-awaited announcement came over the intercom.

'Will passengers please fasten their seat belts, Heathrow is awaiting our arrival at 1:10 p.m. GMT, or thereabouts. All that remains is for me to get this thing down safely, unlike last time, I'm kidding. On behalf of the crew and myself, we hope you enjoyed your flight with us today, and we look forward to you flying with us again soon.'

Hand in hand Dick and Salinka walk across the polished concourse, simultaneously they glance at one another. This is where it all began two travellers in search of each other, neither knew what the other was thinking, and yet the connection was made, one might almost say, providential. For two hardened, professional killers you wouldn't believe they could be so excited as their taxi pulls up outside Lush Husband, in Cambridge, but they are only human after all. They enter and stand in silence, Shirley looks up, she's old enough and wise enough not to lose it, she leans back in her chair, clasps her hands and smiles, then, spotting Natalie at the copy machine…

'This one's for you Natalie.' A puzzled Natalie looks up and immediately goes ape, she dashes over and hugs each of them, she whispers in Salinka's ear.

'Welcome home sister.' Shirley brings David's, that's Mr. Lush's, attention to the table and it isn't long before all work has stopped and conversation is rife. Try as he might Dick can't hide his limp, as for Salinka, she is not trying to disguise her injury, she has shaved the other side of her head to match her wound and is wearing a baseball cap at a jaunty angle to cover the scar, it's fairly obvious to everyone their heroes are damaged and this brings much distress and concern to all. David sits them down and asks Mandy, the new girl in the office, if she wouldn't mind making some fresh coffee, Brian wants to know…

'How many of the bastards did you kill?' (Tourettes). The answer to that is not for their ears but *we* can review it here, not including Straith-North, who was killed by his daughter, there were nine altogether, Dick disposed of two, while Stella Kill, well, her total is seven, all brought to a well-deserved end. No doubt there are do-gooders out there who think that men who murder, kidnap and beat up women and force them to work the streets, for their own financial greed, require nothing more than a good pampering in prison and should be rewarded with computers, phones, televisions, conjugal visits, that isn't Salinka's way, no, to her, any scum who is guilty of those heinous acts against women, needs to be put down. Dick and Salinka take turns to highlight what they'd been up to, they assured everyone that the other side came off worse, how much worse, Salinka is clear on that, as she ambles over to Brian and quietly informs him.

'Zero out of nine can tell the tale.' He doesn't look up, he just raises a thumb and nods his head.

Two days off and they're back to normal, Cheryl is delighted to have them home, she has grown fond of the pair of them, especially Salinka who, in Cheryl's head, is her secret lover, but no more about that. There's some unexpected and great news for our duo, Romeo decided to give up the coffee shop, Cheryl, using her windfall from the Italian job, with the help of Hyacinth took it on, it was a no-brainer, now it's run by Hyacinth and still employing Juliet, so it's good news all round, Dick is already thinking he might offer to do the odd stint behind the bar. Unknown to Cheryl and Hyacinth their new landlords are Salinka and Dick, what is now the coffee shop was once a store that is part of the original warehouse complex.

*

Dick can't believe it's been a full two months since they arrived home, he has been busy during that time and something he's been planning is about to reach its culmination, tonight he's taking his girl out to dinner, a very special dinner, Salinka is calling from their palatial bed chamber.

'Dick, what do you think, the blue dress, or the black? I think the black, where did you say you're taking me?' Salinka is trying it on again, Dick is surprised she hasn't given up by now.

'O.K. you win.' He raised his voice to waft it up to her. 'They're doing a late-night punt and chips, I thought we'd give it a go.' Dick is grinning all over his face while slouching on their sofa finishing off a very agreeable single malt. Salinka comes floating down the wide ash bannistered stairs that are covered in the same thick pile crimson carpet that is the highlight of this beautifully long and spacious lounge. He's not the only one with a surprise this night, Salinka looks a million dollars in the new figure-hugging creation she bought specially for the occasion, it's silver and gold, covered in tiny shimmering blue, yellow and white stars, it has see-through trace gold sleeves sprinkled with the same effervescent stars, Dick is knocked out, but he doesn't show it, not yet, he looks at his beautiful woman.

'Aren't we a bit over the top for punt and chips?' He said, followed by. 'You look stunning by the way.'

Salinka is curious as they pull up, not as she expected, at their favourite Chinese restaurant, The House of the Sun Dragon, but at one of the colleges, Downing.

'Why here Dick, who do you know in academia?' Salinka is intrigued, and slightly relieved it isn't punt and chips. Dick is having to bluff his way, the truth is he hasn't thought this through.

'It's someone I met in the bookshop, just a conversation we had about Isaac Newton.'

'Since when have you been interested in Isaac Newton?' Salinka's face is bathed in wonder.

'Since I found out his wife is American and bakes apple pie like I've never tasted it before, apparently.' Salinka saw her chance.

'Well, I know for a fact Isaac Newton never married, and I read all his baking was carried out by a Swedish cook named Hanna.' Dick is walking on, silently chortling to himself at his girl's reply.

'Touché…O.K. you win, his wife is my cousin.' Dick has come up with a compromise. 'I knew she was here but it's taken me the last month to track her down.' He's bluffing.

Their host as introduced by Dick is professor Arnold Trevelyan, Dick is telling the truth. 'This is Salinka Palchikova.' He can't be blamed for his faux pas, but this trip into the heart of academia has galvanised Salinka into forgoing her proud Russian heritage for the more accurate nomenclature, she smiles.

'Actually, my name is Salinka Vaughan, my late husband was a master of Russian studies at King's.' Arnold Trevelyan is taken aback.

'I knew your husband, Tom Vaughan, we battled it out together many a time on the squash court, he always beat me, I was so sorry to hear of the accident.' Salinka inclines her head, concerned for Dick, who has wandered off to take a closer look at a painting, she remains stoic.

'In Russia we have a saying, *when you lose a loved one, they will send you a replacement.*' She draws herself up. 'Now, when am I going to meet Dick's cousin, I need to see if there are any skeletons in the cupboard?' Dick spins around and speaks immediately to their host.

'Arnold, yes, where is *my cousin?*'

The dinner over conversation is in full swing, fatiguingly, every cousin-related anecdote that Dick and Silvia Trevelyan can come up with has been exhausted, their host takes centre floor.

'Now Salinka, I must tell you, the chair you are sitting on has a very interesting history, it's 300 years old, it dates back further than the foundation of this college, I can tell you, with total assurance, Peter once sat in it.' Salinka guffawed.

'Don't tell me, Peter the Great?' She's in full flight on this wonderful evening.

'No, it was Pyotr Tchaikovsky.' Stunned silence, Arnold continues. 'Dick has been doing his homework, in 1893 Tchaikovsky stayed at Downing college and we know for sure he sat in that very chair, in this room, indeed, it is known as the Peter chair after him.' Salinka threw her hand over her mouth, this is a seminal moment for her. Silvia is looking at her husband, she stands up.

'Arnold, come, let us leave these two in private, and do you not have a task to perform?' He went over to an old gramophone, switched it on and placed the stylist on a prearranged track, very quietly, it's the hauntingly subtle charm of the second movement of Tchaikovsky's fourth symphony. Still Salinka is speechless, Dick wanders over to her.

'Wow, to think this chair is three hundred years old.' He gets on his knees for a better look. 'Gee, it's all carved and all, it looks like African mahogany.' Salinka places her hand on the back of his neck.

'You remembered, thank you Darling, and the music, you've made my life.'

'Mm, that's good,' He mused, still on his knees, he took something from his pocket and palmed it on the table, then, looking up at his Russian Beauty, his knowing eyes bright and set with expectation, he removed his hand to reveal…to reveal a diamond engagement ring. With it, he spoke the words Salinka hoped, one day, in his own good time, she would hear.

'Will you, Salinka Ivanna Alyssa Palchikova, do me the honour of becoming my wife?' Dick gave her his big bright American smile, 'Well, I am a private detective.'

SIXTY-THREE

The question was superfluous but the joy of asking and the acceptance is the stuff of dreams. While the euphoria and delight of this special moment is being sealed with a snog, elsewhere another matter is being considered, where do an American and a Russian, in Cambridge, get married? That is the question the academics Arnold and Sylvia Trevelyan, sitting in their scholastic, book-festooned study, gin & tonics in hand are contemplating. They came up with an answer, but caution and due consideration have to be paid. As Salinka's husband had been a master at King's, there is every possibility they might be able to be married in King's College Chapel. Salinka will jump at the chance provided the Chaplain is au fait with the idea, to which Arnold Trevelyan smiles and nods a wink towards his wife.

The preparations were immense, Dick had set himself a task that seemed impossible, but it was possible. With the help of certain friends and acquaintances, he slowly began to put it together. All will be revealed on the day, they had plenty of time, the chapel wasn't available for three months, that will put the wedding at the beginning of October, Salinka's favourite month.

*

Before the pair can believe it the day is upon them, it fell in the midst of an Indian summer the like of which Cambridge hadn't witnessed since the late sixties, two weeks of cloudless blue skies gilded the happy event. McDougall has flown over from the States with his wife and boys to be Dick's best man. Salinka has asked her boss and friend, David Lush, to give her away, both her parents had died some years previously. McDougall's sons are going to be pageboys, Natalie is going to be maid of honour, with Cheryl and Hyacinth as bridesmaids. King's college chapel is a famous and prominent house, arrangements have to be correct and proper, standing at the entrance, David is speaking to the bride.

'My dear girl I am honoured to be doing this for you, thank you for asking me, Janice and I, well, we never did have children, this is indeed, a rare and wonderful gift you have given me.'

'It is me who should be grateful, I was a stroppy daughter by all accounts, you would have had your work cut out.' Salinka glanced behind her, two smart looking pageboys in their white suits with her train in hand. Three bridesmaids each of them looking fabulous dressed as Punks. Not Salinka, not on this day, she is looking dazzling in her wedding gown of the palest cream, almost white, contrasted by a train of deep crimson silk that has tiny golden hammers and sickles sown on haphazardly. Her bouquet is of dark velvety crimson gladiolas, her favourite colour, she looks stunning, all they have to do is walk in for the wedding march to begin. As they step inside out of the hot, balming sun into the cool, airy, oaken expanse of this beautiful chapel, it's not what Salinka imagined, in fact it's the last thing she expected, or could have guessed in her wildest dreams. Unknown to her, filling a third of the rear seats is the Cambridge Symphonia, who astound everyone, by sounding the prelude, triumphant, melodic, chords of Tchaikovsky's fourth symphony, a fanfare fit for Dick's Russian Beauty bride, elated and smiling and only just holding it together, she speaks to David.

'What do we do in the pauses?' He raises his voice, there's a tear in his eye.

'We just keep going.' As they make their way up the aisle, with the fanfare a tremendous precursor to her wedding day, Salinka delights in the thought, the kick Dick must be deriving right now. There's another big surprise, she had no idea. It's Angel smiling and laughing with Julie and Helen, both beaming at her, an amazed Salinka blows each of them a kiss, this is completely unexpected, Helen points across the aisle. The bride looks over, and there in her full-dress uniform is captain Hilary Hall arrived from Seattle with, standing next to her in his finery, chief Carmichael from New York. They both stand straight to salute this stunned, and beautiful bride. Still Tchaikovsky's masterpiece is weaving its magic, Carmichael points across the aisle. Salinka's eyes follow, and there is Duke Denby the number three Brussels commissioner with, the main man, commissioner Melvin Willis, both wearing their number ones, both straighten up and salute. This is too much as she beams all over her face. But then, on the same side, simultaneously slamming their forearms across their chests are Hanrik and Victor, flown in from Russia. Who worries about protocol on their wedding day, as this ex-KGB agent lightly returns the salute.

That's all of Dick's surprises for now, he can't believe it all went so well. As the bride approached, the music quietened down, Dick had long since turned to see his girl advancing up the aisle, to enjoy her delight as the special guest list revealed itself.

Now she concentrates on him, and as she does, someone, between you and me it's Brian, begins to clap. This started a trickle that grew and grew until the whole chapel is filled to the rafters with applause, unprecedented on an occasion such as this. Salinka's reputation has preceded her and this group of friends are not going to let an opportunity like this pass them by.

As she draws close to her 'Backup' they join hands and in that instant they both felt a small but certain static charge pass between them, neither flinch, they both know, at that moment, everything is right, all shall be well. Salinka grins, her sharp green eyes quickly giving way to euphoria, as for Dick he's just geed up to be there.

At long last, as the chaplain begins to deliver God's ancient ceremony, they approach the end game, now it's their turn to be helped, to be set on the right path at the start of their married life together, perchance to walk dreamily, arm in arm, along the banks of the Cam, on hot balmy summer days, or in the picturesque, pure, crisp whiteness of winter, for better for worse, till death do us part.

THE END

APPENDIX

Dear reader, if you read the appendix now, it is a plot spoiler.

For the eyes of Professor Glazunov, only.

Yes Sir, another chance to practice your English. How tiresome was this intake.
As promised, my dissertation, the section you liked so much:
Dropping and catching out of airplanes and helicopters.

Thank you for all of your amazing help and patience over the past two years. If the student may offer advice to her tutor, do not try the enclosed yourself'.

Salinka Palchikova.
Moscow, December 1981   XXX

For you Dick as promised
a copy of my dissertation
with all my love
Salinka
X X X

Dropping and catching out of Airplanes and Helicopters

By S.I.A. Palchikova

1. As you initially fall, calculate on 32ft per second – increasing second by second. To achieve this, you drop: 32ft the first second = 21.81 mph at the end of the 1st second, 64ft the next = 43.64 mph at the end of the 2nd second, 128ft the next = 87.27 mph at the end of the 3rd second.

2.The 'clothed human terminal velocity' being 120 mph = 176ft/sec if there was **NO DRAG**, you would reach more than this in 4th second. But 'you' are going to stop accelerating before that – and I can only give you an estimate as to when – all I can say is that it will be 'more than 3 and less than 4 seconds'.

3.At the 'end of the 3rd second' you have only a further (120 – 87) 33mph to accelerate, so **I GUESS** – as the acceleration will slow as you get near the figure, that it will probably take about 'half of the 4th second'.

   4.**NOTE** this will apply to both the 'dropper' and the 'catcher'. So, if you take 3.5 seconds as the 'acceleration time', in that period you will drop 226ft (1st 3 seconds worth) plus 'a fourth second; at about the 'mid Speed' (between 87 and 120 mph) – so say about 103 mph = which is 151ft.

5.**THUS** … at the end of the 4th second you will be doing 120 mph **AND** will have fallen:32 + 64 + 128 + 151 = 375ft.

6. **NOW** (although this is not going to be strictly true because 'the drag is going to be less the thinner the air the higher you go'), this means that the correct moments for the 'catcher' to drop out will be when the 'dropper' is 375ft above him/her.

7. Worth a word hereabouts is that this should be a pretty accurate figure because whatever the **SIZE** of the human, their density is much the same – with a big person having much the same 'drag per body of pound' as a small one, therefore much the same 'falling speed', (i.e.: Babies would not fall more slowly).

8. Now – I suggest you work on a 10,000ft 'faller drop height' and a 7,000ft 'catcher drop height'.

9. Next: note from 8 above that the exact moment the 'catcher has to get out' is when the faller is 375ft above him/her. Why? … So, they both arrive at a point 375ft below the 'catcher's' plane (or helicopter!).

10. So – where are we?   (1) We know the dropper's plane is flying at 10,000 ft and the catcher's helicopter is 3000ft lower at 7000ft. The "meeting point" has to be 375ft below the helicopter (or – therefore - 6,625ft above the water).

11. This means the 'dropper' has to fall 3,375ft to be at the correct height to meet the 'catcher'. He will drop 375ft in his first 4 seconds of fall – and therefore has 3,000ft to go. At 120 mph,

this will take him 17.04 seconds plus the first 4 = 21.04 seconds in all – in 'freefall' - before they meet.

12. The 'catcher' has to also get to 6,625ft above the water at the exact same moment – therefore – subtract one from the other – and you are left with 17.04 seconds.

13. So...the 'catcher' must have a stopwatch and get out at exactly 17 seconds after seeing the 'dropper' come out. **BUT** he must also watch and try to estimate when the 'dropper' is as close as he can estimate to being 375ft above him. Not easy!!

14. However, assume they do meet...at 120 mph or 176ft per second downwards. They have 6,625ft to splashdown = just 37 seconds before (fish soup)

15. So, I suggest you allow 10 seconds to correct any 'mutual height error as the meet' = 6,625ft – 1760ft = 4,865ft to go.

16. Then allow a further full 10 seconds to 'attach one to the other' - which has to be done 'strongly' as the parachute opening will suffer both a considerable if brief 'G' deceleration = 4,865ft – a further 1,760ft = 3,105ft to go.

17. Then allow the parachute – what? - 5 seconds to unfurl and open fully = a further 860ft = 3,105ft – 860ft = 2,246ft before being fully opened and reducing their 'fall speed'.

18. **THEN** – only then - will the rate of descent reduce. A parachute with one person aboard normally comes down at about 20ft per second = about 13.63 mph – try jumping off a 12ft wall

– about that speed.

19. **BUT** – with **TWO** on a single chute I'd add a bit and suggest 30ft per second = about 20 mph 'dropping speed'. How long, therefore from 2,256ft to splash down? = 75.2 seconds – or about '1 and a quarter minutes'.

20. So – for the 'dropper' how long does **HIS/HER** anguish last?

21. 4 seconds to fall 375ft to reach 120 mph.

22. 2, to fall 3000ft to be 375ft below the helicopter where they meet.

23. 10 seconds to get together.

24. 10 seconds to attach together.

25. 5 seconds for the parachute to open fully.

26. 75.02 seconds being really grateful someone was there to meet him at 6,675ft.

27. 1= 41 seconds in free-fall

2.+ 5 seconds of 'Will it open?'

3.+ 75 seconds of 'thank God it opened'.

28. Now – where will the 7,000ft high helicopter be relative to the 10,000ft airplane?

29. Answer:

1 = Exactly behind it all the while. 2 = The ejecting pilot and assistant should be in fairly 'level / straight flight' while they eject 'dropper'. To align the helicopter with the 'dropper' if he/she comes out during a turn would be very difficult.

30. Now – the airplane is travelling at – let's say – 120 mph at the moment of 'drop'. This is 176ft forward per second. When the 'faller' comes out he will also have this 'forward speed'. He has to drop 3,376 ft in 21.04 seconds – during which he will travel <u>forward</u> at 176ft per second =

3,703 ft. This is – 'in theory', but he will actually drop behind the aircraft as he falls. I do not have the slightest idea how to calculate this but suggest a good guess would drop about 1/3 of that = 1,234ft astern of the aircraft as he falls for 21 seconds = so the helicopter should follow the aircraft about '400 carefully judged yards behind it'.

31. Now – in the perfect world – the 'dropper' must– if he/she had a choice, 'fall past' **VERY** close to the helicopter's rotor. In fact, because the 'catcher' will also have 120 mph 'forward speed' as he/she drops, the 'dropper' should ideally pass just behind the helicopter's rotors just after the 'catcher' has gone overboard!

32. So, you will have to factor in – the helicopter pilot has to watch the dropper all the way down. He has to correct his heading so the 'dropper' passes very close astern, but he must be aware that if the 'dropper' passes <u>anywhere</u> but close behind 'it just ain't gonna work!' - and he must be prepared to take evasive action. So – in practical terms – this can only be an urgent turn left or right – but he could not in the few seconds available significantly accelerate or decelerate his 'chopper' out of the way!!

S.I.A. Palchikova.

Acknowledgements

First, I must send a huge thank-you to Downing College, Cambridge, who, without their permission, have featured in my books, the appearance is crucial to my fictional story. The connection, so charmed me, and more so, in the next volume, I am now the proud owner of a Downing College scarf.

I owe a huge bow to Terry Hylton. Who said to me, out of the blue. "Would you like me to put your book on Kindle?" Terry, this technophobe owes you, incidentally, your coffee is to die for.

Crucial, I think, to any writer, are readers, especially ones who, without favour or hesitation, tell it how it is, I applaud all of mine with bells on:
Laraissa, Camilla, Debbie, Jan, Priscilla, Susan, Jenny, Mary and Laurie. All extraordinary readers with the greatest acumen. Let's hope, at least, we get a meal out of it.

To my very own planet of granite, that beats a rock, hands down, Bhajan Kaur, who I am privileged to say is my wife. Among a myriad of other things, without you Darling, I would have starved to death.   *I Love You*

There are three Chicago girls, twins and a big sister, Jannie and I met them on the Euro Express while on our way to Paris. Without that fateful meeting this book, and its follow up would not exist, and that's the goddamn truth. It has been an honour, a privilege and my greatest pleasure to give them a cameo role in my book.

Last, but by no means least, I thank my
Guardian Angel.

Coming Soon

The End Game

Printed in Great Britain
by Amazon